W9-CPD-910

THE SUBSTITUTION ORDER

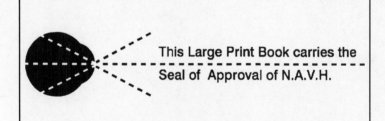

This Large Print Book carries the
Seal of Approval of N.A.V.H.

THE SUBSTITUTION ORDER

MARTIN CLARK

THORNDIKE PRESS
A part of Gale, a Cengage Company

Farmington Hills, Mich • San Francisco • New York • Waterville, Maine
Meriden, Conn • Mason, Ohio • Chicago

LIBRARY OF CONGRESS CIP DATA ON FILE.
CATALOGUING IN PUBLICATION FOR THIS BOOK
IS AVAILABLE FROM THE LIBRARY OF CONGRESS

ISBN-13: 978-1-4328-6742-3 (hardcover alk. paper)

Published in 2019 by arrangement with Alfred A. Knopf, an imprint of The Knopf Doubleday Publishing Group, a division of Penguin Random House, LLC

Printed in Mexico
1 2 3 4 5 6 7 23 22 21 20 19

This book is dedicated to
DEANA H. CLARK AND STACEY WOLFE,
feminis fortibus quae me servaverunt.

The cards were on the table when the law came bustin' in.

There is no bad and there is no good
No lesson for the weary

CHAPTER ONE

For years, I was an excellent lawyer, as honest and effective as you could ever want, and I'm a decent enough person, and despite my mistakes, which — I concede — were hellacious, I deserve better than this misery.

It's the middle of June, hot and stagnant, especially behind the counter here in the restaurant, a Subway knockoff called SUBstitution, and the heat will soon become worse because Luther, the owner, insists that we switch on the old oven at noon and then again at six, as if we *were* really baking fresh bread. Twice daily, when the big lunch and dinner crowds are waiting in line, I cover my hand with a mitt and slowly slide the store-bought decoys out of the oven, a sham show that allows a two-hundred-degree belch to escape and loiter and clot the air. Sometimes, to entertain myself, I quick-drop the lukewarm silver tray, pull off the mitt and shake and blow on my fingers. The few minutes of fake-bake dries and hardens the prop rolls, but I'm able to stash them in the refrigerator and use them over and over for weeks, until the first greenish-gray mold spots appear.

Today, the first customer through the door is a Sutphin girl from the apartments down the street. She's wearing flannel pajama bottoms, the fabric pilled and grimy. Her hair's a mess, straight, dirty and brown. She's hardscrabble bony, pasty white, braless under a T-shirt and covered in tats, none of them worth a damn, amateur ink that some dolt applied with a safety pin and a cigarette lighter. This is exactly how she looked when she went to bed on a floor mattress last night, exactly how she'll look the entire day, exactly how she'll look tomorrow.

She's brought along a kid, and the poor little toddler is shoeless, and, of course, why bother with any kind of shirt or shorts when a disposable diaper will do just fine. A scrawny boyfriend is also with her. He's high and slit-eyed at eleven in the morning, and he's mumbling dopey slang and jibber-jabber into an iPhone. His tennis shoes are new and untied and at least a size too large. His half-ass Afro is uneven, way out of whack on one side. A gauze bandage is taped across his wrist. He flops into the booth closest to the door, the phone against his ear. I'd speculate that the child is his, given the lad's beautifully blended skin and their matching eyes and mouths.

"Good morning and welcome to SUBstitution." *Kevin M* is felt-tipped on my white plastic name tag. My khakis are dotted with faint mustard stains, but the pants are laundered and ironed and presentable.

The Sutphin girl looks at the wall menu behind me. "I want a twelve-inch steak-and-cheese with double meat. Regular bread. Toasted."

I nod at the kid. "And for the young man?"

"He'll be okay," she says dismissively. "I'll pinch him off some of mine." She glances down at the child. "He's done had cereal and a Little Debbie."

I shake the meat from four cardboard tubs onto a sub roll, add cheese slices and put the sandwich in a toaster oven. I smile at the boy, and bless his heart, he grins big back at me.

"What would you like on it?" I ask his mama.

"Tomatoes and extra, extra, *extra* mayonnaise."

I hover the squirt bottle filled with Lowes generic mayo over the length of the sand-

11

wich, strangling the plastic with both hands so the dressing coils onto the cheese dense and thick.

"More! *Extra* means you can't see no yellow under it."

"New rule for me," I say. "Guess I need to read our manual again."

I hear Blaine come in behind me through the rear entrance. He's been working at the restaurant since he was a junior in high school, and he's twenty now, smart as hell and a pleasure to have around. When I check over my shoulder, he's leaning against the wall next to the oven. He's a sizable man, over six feet tall and a weight lifter. "Hey," he says to the girl, "we're not the food bank. It's already *Deepwater Horizon* on your sandwich. Leave Lawyer Kevin alone."

"Screw you, Blaine," she snaps. "I'm reportin' you."

"To who?" Blaine snorts. "God forbid Luther demote me to *assistant* assistant manager."

I slapdash squirt another line of mayo, step sideways and land the tray and food beside the register. "Anything else? A drink? Chips or cookies?" Unlike Subway, we keep the sodas behind the counter so people can't steal them.

"Mountain Dew Code Red," she announces.

We're in Stuart, Virginia — the county seat, though only fourteen hundred people live here — so we have plenty in the cooler, the large size, twenty ounces. Luther hauls it to the restaurant from a Sam's Club in Greensboro. I set the red bottle on the tray. "Okay — your twelve-inch, double-meat sandwich with complimentary extra mayo and the large Code Red will be eleven dollars and fifty-six cents."

She dips into the T-shirt's breast pocket and hands me a credit card, but as soon as I take it, I notice it's an EBT card. "We don't accept food stamps," I tell her.

"Why?"

"Because we don't. It's not allowed. I'm pretty certain you know as much."

"There's nearly twenty left on it," the girl claims. "I could sell it to you for what I owe, then you can pay Luther and keep the rest."

"Which would be illegal," I inform her.

"Drop the legal juju on her, Lord Mansfield." Blaine is smiling. He waves and wiggles his fingers at her as if casting a spell. "Behold the majesty of the law, citizens."

"Either of you have any money?" I pull the tray away from her.

"We could pay next month, after the

third," she offers.

"No," I inform her. "Are you seriously trying to use this welfare card? *Really?*"

"So you ain't goin' to give me my sandwich?" she demands. The child has heard this tone of voice before and understands nothing good is coming. He starts to cry — not a bawl or an outburst, just steady tears with his miniature arms flat against his rib cage and his eyes fixed on his mother.

I frown at her. "I'll gladly sell you the food if you can pay for it. Simple as that."

The boy reaches up for his mom, who ignores him. "Kiss my ass, *Kevin.* Least I ain't no loser fixin' sandwiches for Luther Foley." She makes a splashy, oh-snap gesture with her index finger, air-writes an angry *S* to emphasize the insult. "You ain't even from here," she idiotically adds.

"Adiós," I say. "See you again when you have twelve dollars cash to your name."

"Kiss my ass," she repeats. She snatches her son's hand. "Shut up, LaDarius. Quit cryin'."

"In your case, Malik," Blaine says, addressing the spindly boyfriend in the booth, "you'll need to show up with an extra fifty, right? You're already runnin' a tab, aren't you?"

"Whatcha talkin' bout, bro?" Malik re-

14

plies. "You trippin', Blaine."

Weary as I am, I feel sorry for the sobbing child. I'd planned to slip him a cookie or an apple, but his pissed-off mother is fussing and glowering and dragging him out the door by the wrist. Malik hesitates at the exit and half-turns toward us. "Later, bitches," he says, the words clipped and high-pitched.

The sandwich is wasted, a loss. I jot a few lines explaining the incident in the spiral-bound notebook we keep in the junk drawer, and Blaine and I flip a quarter to see who gets to take the steak-and-cheese home. I win the coin toss and begin scraping away the mayo with a plastic spoon and a paper towel. "Malik's into you for fifty bucks?" I ask Blaine. "Viper account?"

"Yeah," Blaine answers. "He's a worthless piece of shit. Trifling. So is she. I went to high school with both of 'em. Every fuckin' week my eight-fifty-an-hour check is docked for taxes so I can subsidize their blunts and flavored vodka and meth jones and protect their right to never hold an honest job."

Blaine's one of three kids. His employed parents can't afford college expenses, despite the significant scholarships a nearly perfect SAT earned him, so he's living at home and saving thousands by attending Patrick Henry Community College. He'll transfer to Virginia Tech as a junior and cut his education bill in half. A genius with computers and math, he's self-deprecating about his schooling, refers to himself as a "super-senior" and jokes about mastering the "fourteenth grade."

"I thought you were a better business-man," I tell him. "In your trade, credit's a poor idea." Blaine sells pot, and heck, more power to him. Truth be told, I've done what I could to help with legal precautions, sat him down in a corner booth and gave him quality advice several months ago: Never sell dope to the out-of-town "biker" with a long beard and Harley do-rag who's intro-duced to you by some marginal friend. He's an undercover cop, and the friend bringing him around is being squeezed by the police. Never sell more than a half-ounce and risk a felony conviction. Never keep the goods on you or in your car or your house. Always wear gloves; you don't need your prints on any baggies. And, finally, understand that pot sales can't be a career choice in a rural community — sooner or later, word will reach the sheriff's department.

"True enough," Blaine answers. "Lesson learned. Not a debt I can really enforce, huh? You'd think, though, the shitheel wouldn't just swagger in here."

The door alert tones, a two-beat, electronic ding and dong, and I check to see who's there. A stranger is standing on the frayed entrance mat, a chubby fellow with nicely groomed, chemically white hair. Albino Platinum Ice would have to be the color on the Clairol box. He's wearing a lumpy black suit and a dull necktie. There's a red carnation pinned to his lapel, so I wonder if he's been to a funeral. He scans the restaurant, looks at every booth, then settles on me. He smiles. I lay my hand on the .38 under the counter, the pistol right below the cash register.

"Morning," he says cheerfully. He dips his head slightly, ratchets the smile tighter so it's all lips and no teeth.

"Good morning," I reply. "Welcome to SUBstitution."

"You're Mr. Kevin Moore?" he asks, still chipper.

"Yep. I am."

"Any chance I could have a minute or two with you?"

"No offense, sir, but whatever you're selling, I'm in no position to buy it." I say this nicely, with no barb. I appreciate that the guy's just doing his job. I don't want to waste his time.

"Understood. No worries. I'm not a sales-man."

"Oh, okay." I've finished scraping mayo off the steak-and-cheese and close the roll. "You from probation?" I ask. I'm tending to the sandwich, my eyes lowered.

"No sir. My news is actually very positive."

"I'll hold the fort," Blaine offers, then shrugs. "Who knows? Not a salesman, not a probation officer. Me, I'd want to see what's behind the curtain."

I focus on the lapel flower, and — bingo — it hits me: He's a preacher or tract-pusher wanting a donation, or to post a flyer for some revival or gospel singing or youth rally. Luther's all for hanging the flyers, but he has a zero-tolerance policy when it comes to charity dollars. "Thanks," I say to Blaine.

"How about a quick turkey-and-cheese to go, six-inch, plain, no dressings, no toppings, wheat bread, and I'll meet you over there," the man says, gesturing toward a booth.

He stands and waits while I make his sandwich, wrap it in clear plastic and fit it in a white bag, and then I follow him to the table underneath the stereo speakers. We have to play 104 FM, a dreadful contemporary-country station that loops mostly lift-kit odes and three-chord tales of how we small-towners live to blow our stunted paychecks on liquor drinks at the local roadhouse. I sit so I'm facing the entrance, and he jams in across from me, has to swivel and butt-hop a couple times because he's heavy through the middle. His belt buckle scrapes the Formica. I hear change bounce in his pocket.

"I'm Caleb," he says.

"Nice to meet you." I push his sandwich bag toward him. The order is so basic I assume he's just being polite, same as buying a pack of gum when you take a leak at the filling station.

"Likewise." He props his elbows on the table and joins his hands together. "Thanks for seeing me. I'll try not to take too much of your time or keep you from your job."

"Fine," I say noncommittally.

"I'm here on business. A chance for you to perhaps put everything behind you. Not that there's anything wrong with working here. I'm certainly not demeaning you or your job." His speech is crisp, assured. His hands stay locked in front of his face while he talks.

"Business? Me?"

He adjusts the red flower on his jacket,

then clasps his hands again. "You deserve better than this. It's time for you to get back on track. Move home to Roanoke. You've paid enough dues. Half of 2016's gone already. You've served more than a fair punishment."

"No kidding," I answer, the words coming almost automatically, on their own.

"I'd like to include you in a business project. A chance for some solid cash and, more important, perhaps, an opportunity to see your law license reinstated."

"Who exactly are you? You seem to know a lot about me and my circumstances. What kind of business?"

"Am I correct that you'd like to earn more than your current restaurant wages? How much could that possibly be?"

I stiffen across my shoulders. "I make what I make. I also have a second job."

"A shame," he says sympathetically. "Forty hours should be enough."

Instead of responding, I pull a paper napkin from the holder and fold it in half.

"My team and I invest in distressed situations. We make your negative situation positive."

"What's your last name, Caleb?" I ask. "Where're you from?" I fold the napkin again and tuck it into my shirt pocket.

He drops his hands. He smiles, but it's stern, mostly a scold. "Today, right now, my last name is *Opportunity.* I'm from elsewhere."

"So listen, Caleb Opportunity, I'm on probation, with a felony conviction waiting for me if I screw up. I'm already feeling a con or scam. Or some kind of test from the state, though this seems too sophisticated for the apparatchiks in Richmond. They'd still be having meetings and filing memos on the color of your flower and which billing code to use with the florist."

"The loss of your attorney's income would have to be a real blow. I want to correct that."

"Well," I tell him, "I'm planning to play by the rules for a year, keep my nose clean and hope for the best."

"Let me give you an overview. You can just listen. No crime or probation violation there." I start to speak, but he waves an open hand in my direction. "My partners and I search for various professionals who have complications. You fit the bill. We also strive to discover people who've recovered from their problems and are once again reliable citizens. We do not want to partner with junkies, flakes or layabouts."

"A speaking gig?" I ask sarcastically. "Self-help, motivation kind of deal? Bringing my inspirational story and unique brand of encouragement to hotel conference rooms throughout the South?"

"Self-help for sure," he says.

The door chimes, and we both watch a lady head to the counter, where Blaine greets her. It's difficult to hear their conversation from our corner, especially with the radio noise.

"I'm not interested," I tell him and slide to my left, ready to stand. "Good luck, sir."

"Do you recall a client from a while ago, a Miss Melanie Culp?"

I stop where I am, still sitting, but at the end of the bench, my trunk twisted away from Caleb, my palm flat on the table's edge, ready to push off. "I couldn't say," I answer.

"She visited you for legal advice at your Roanoke office during, uh . . . your troubles."

"If she did, that would be confidential." I do remember her. I have a remarkable memory. A routine appointment about a real-estate purchase on the parkway. "I won't be discussing any of my legal business with you. It would be unethical."

He nods at me. "Understood. That kind of judgment and professionalism is why we want you on our team. I wouldn't expect you to break a client's confidence."

"I'm already on the SUBstitution team. I'm the manager here, king of the condiments and cold cuts. And I'm also a member of the commonwealth's probation team. I can't imagine me signing up for any other teams." I stand but stay close to the table. "Sorry. If you're from the state bar or the justice system, I hope you'll report that I'm walking the straight and narrow. And if you're a real hustler, you need to hit the bricks."

Caleb doesn't seem upset or rattled. "It's not so simple." He sounds calm, amicable. "We've already invested in you and this project. We have limited resources, and we'd hate to see this come to naught."

"What the hell is it that you want?"

"Well, as much as it pains Miss Culp to press the issue, you committed malpractice when you handled her case. Because of your negligence, she lost millions of dollars."

"Bullshit." I glare at Caleb. "Are you a lawyer floating some bogus claim? Because —"

"Oh, no," he interrupts, leaning toward me. "But we can and *will* make this a profitable situation for us all. We're allies, not adversaries."

"If I've truly wronged a client, I want to address it and make it right. But I haven't."

"Miss Culp scheduled an appointment with you in July of 2015," Caleb notes. "The morning of the thirtieth." His voice stays measured, his features and posture relaxed. "I'm sure there's a file in your former office. She has a receipt signed by your secretary proving her payment to you on that day. One hundred dollars for a basic consultation. A very fair charge."

"So what?"

"She had an option contract to buy 173 acres in Meadows of Dan, adjacent to the Blue Ridge Parkway. Also near the much-celebrated, five-star Primland resort."

"Okay." I'm still standing. I'm tapping my foot.

"You were to evaluate the option, contact the seller and execute the deal. Those were her clear instructions to you."

"You're making up crap as you go." I raise my voice. "I can't get into the specifics with you, but that never happened." I sit again, balanced on the edge of the bench seat. "Are you this lady's relative? Husband, maybe? Brother?"

"Despite her precise instructions," he continues, "you, because of personal distractions, failed to timely exercise the option, and she lost her opportunity to purchase this valuable piece of land. It was soon sold to another buyer for millions of dollars."

Caleb sounds so confident that I run through Melanie Culp's visit in my mind: She was a scheduled appointment, she asked me to review an option to buy a piece of property, I read the document while she waited and told her it was legal and valid. I'd done cocaine — a lot — the night before but was steady enough to interpret a basic three-page option. End of story. There was absolutely no mention of closing the deal or notifying the seller. "Untrue," I say forcefully. "At least the part about my being instructed to contact the seller and set a closing."

"Miss Culp had an option to buy the land for $975,000. You didn't do your job, Mr. Moore. You let the purchase deadline pass. Thereafter, the local owner, a Mr. Eugene Harris, sold to a company named MAB Incorporated, for the same $975,000. A few months later, MAB was approached by a development company, FirstRate LLC, which bought the tract for six million. In sum, your negligence cost Miss Culp five million dollars and change."

"And let me guess, Caleb, you want me to admit my error and not contest the claim when she sues me."

"Exactly," he says, fiddling with the flower for a second. "Exactly, my friend."

"Let's do the math. No doubt you control both companies, this MAB and FirstRate, though your ownership's hidden behind layers of perfectly legal and impenetrable paperwork. *You* are MAB and FirstRate."

"Correct," he notes.

"You've got a $975,000 investment in the land. You — or your FirstRate LLC — actually still have the land, so your $975,000 is safely parked. The six-million-dollar sale to FirstRate is, in reality, nothing but an illusion, your taking money from your First-Rate pocket and transferring it to your MAB pocket so it appears the land's marketplace value is six million. Certainly First-Rate would've offered the aggrieved Miss Culp the same six million — and there you go, see what Kevin's negligence caused her to lose? Had I done my job and closed the deal for her, *she* would've received the six million from FirstRate. If I roll over now, she's due a big, fat, round-number check for roughly five million — the six million minus her original option price of $975,000. A number that just coincidentally happens to be the limit of my — and most lawyers' — liability policy. She'll no doubt forgive

26

the other twenty-five thousand in the interest of a quick settlement."

"Yes. Simple and foolproof, isn't it?"

"And the two front companies involved, your MAB and FirstRate, are owned by a series of other LLCs and corporations, so figuring out what's what and who's who would be next to impossible even after a tour of Caribbean holding companies and a slog through ten different courthouses in ten different states. You assume we'll never tie them to you or to her or to anybody else."

"We don't do all the multiple-shell-companies razzmatazz, which tends to make courts and insurance investigators suspicious. We generally use only a single holding company, preferably offshore — the key is to make sure there's no overlap or connection between the companies in the transaction, no common people or owners, and also to have other deals, bona fide deals, on the books. There's money to be made in traditional transactions, and we do that as well. Hell, we pay taxes."

"Good for you."

"Better yet, Kevin, we're not greedy. Pigs get fat, hogs get slaughtered. While five million's nice money, it's not so off-the-charts that the insurance company will employ its finest-tooth comb to inspect the case. Three or four smaller projects a year is the prudent choice. You stick a bank or burn the government or involve more than ten mil, the other side becomes very determined. No big flashy bombs for us, no direct hacks of cash, and as an added precaution, we attempt to engineer our projects in sleepier burgs like Roanoke, Virginia."

"Well, you can sue me until the cows come home, but I'm not going to lie. *Not* going to help you. *Not* going to defraud my malpractice carrier."

Caleb tugs at his tie knot. He adjusts his sleeve so that a silver cuff link is more visible. "We don't need you to lie, my friend. It's accurate that Miss Culp visited with you and asked you to review a purchase option. It's also accurate that during the time she consulted you, you were plagued by personal problems and not at your professional best. An 'I don't recall' answer will ring the bell for us on the money question, especially given her certainty about what she asked you to do." He monkeys with the cuff link. "Not any serious dishonesty there. Just kinda how you spin your version."

"Here's my spin, and it's the damn truth: She never told me to exercise the option or contact the seller or anything close to that. I didn't do anything wrong. We're finished,

Caleb. Count me out." I point at the flower. "If I'm being recorded, let me say this emphatically: Hell no."

"Well, the bad news is that we're thoroughly invested already, and I can guarantee the wronged Miss Culp will sue you. The worst case we have is her word against yours. She was clean and sober during the time of your meeting. You were not. Cocaine and booze and other temptations led the state bar to suspend your license. The train, Kevin, is coming. You want to ride on it or have it run over you? Make money or make things worse?"

"How could you possibly have known about my circumstances last July?" I ask. "My arrest wasn't in the paper until August, and the bar didn't act until December."

"We monitor the information received by hundreds of state regulatory agencies and governing boards — doctors, lawyers, nurses, dentists, architects, pharmacists and realtors, virtually every group with a disciplinary board. We learn about addictions and failings long before the general public. In the right hands, it's valuable data."

"How is it that you *monitor* confidential information?"

"It's a walk in the park. Who cares about these obscure, under-funded departments run by bureaucrats and paper-pushers, as the politicians are so fond of saying? And, even better, these very same elected hacks and sin piñatas are in charge of our government. Politicians are eager to be bought, and they can often supplement our efforts. Here in Virginia, your former governor took a Rolex and dirty cash from a patent-medicine grifter and helped him peddle his snake oil. State capitols are high-end bordellos where greedy legislators pimp out favors and dry-hump the public every chance they get."

"How, exactly, did you discover *my* situation? Or is that proprietary information?"

"Most of our efforts take place in the ether. There's no effective online security at state regulatory agencies — why bother? We have the best computer artists on the planet — and I include myself in this category — though most of what we accomplish is child's play. Your Judge David Carson contacted the state bar via e-mail on July sixth to alert them about a potential problem and asked them to look into your erratic behavior. He mentioned the very strong possibility of drugs and alcohol. We know this thanks to our unique version of the Dyre Trojan, which we used to gain access to —"

"So," I interrupt, "artist or not, you're still a common thief. You steal information as well as money. From my experience, thieves aren't trustworthy partners."

Caleb doesn't react to the insult. "My colleague, Miss Culp, confirmed you looked like death warmed over when she met with you, so we knew you were in fact struggling with substance abuse, as the judge had predicted. That's everything we needed for this project to take shape — a single easily hacked e-mail and an in-person confirmation of your addiction. Our position became a complete winner when you were later arrested for drug possession and disbarred — we don't always luck into that kind of bonus."

He's so blithe and cocksure that it grates on me. "Fuck you and your bonus."

He ignores the profanity, doesn't flinch or miss a beat or apologize. "Once we obtain sad tales about a lawyer or doctor or realtor or dentist or whomever, then my group meets to see if we can put together a scenario that will earn us some money. Obviously, we can make only so many plays and invest in so many situations, which returns us to my earlier point. There's significant front-end prep for us here. We're not of a mind to simply punt and waste all the effort

31

and resources burned so far. Not to mention the millions in the honeypot. I truly wish you'd volunteer to help us and *yourself.* There's absolutely no victim, no one's harmed. A deserving man will be rescued — I haven't even gotten around to your benefits yet. We don't expect you to help us for free."

"Or I could report this to the state police. You're pretty bold to show up here and give me all your schemes and illegal blueprints." I glare at him the whole time I'm talking.

"I wouldn't do that, Kevin," he says pleasantly. "What precisely do you plan to reveal? A one-armed man told you about a fantastical syndicate that exploits the state and various professionals? Keyser Soze paid you a visit? You heard a crime report from a white-headed stranger? Maybe they'll issue a warrant for Ric Flair."

"I could start by alerting the state bar. Make them aware you're hacking them with this Trojan virus." I notice his eyebrows are much darker, a different blanched color, and the few stray hairs at the tail end of his brows are solid black. The hair whorls below his shirt cuffs are also black.

"The Dyre Trojan is old news, my friend. They won't find a trace of it. We pride ourselves on innovation. And we never linger anywhere for too long."

"Maybe they'll discover something else, then," I say. "Whatever mischief you have in place now."

"The overwhelmed, underpaid state IT nine-to-fiver whose expertise is hooking the yellow cable to the yellow-rimmed port might indeed bust us. Might just happen. I'll take my chances. But to save you some time, we'd never be reckless enough to continue a hack at an agency involved in a current project. We don't nap in the patch after we pick the strawberries." He pauses to locate the lady and check out the parking lot. "Not being rude, but you're damaged goods. Once the justice system grabs hold of you — for dope, especially — you're inferior forever. The wound leaves a scar. The fine people at the Rotary Club will never fully trust you again. You're suspect and marginal from the instant your name appears in the local court news. We're not worried about you tattling on us to the teacher — who'll believe you?"

It's not easy, but I tamp down my irritation and keep a civil tone. "No offense to you or your Robin Hood plans, but I can't do it. You signed me up involuntarily. I didn't come looking for any of this. I'm not your guy."

Caleb smiles. "Would you at least think about it, please? We'll discreetly put a quarter million in your pocket and contact a friend in Richmond who can help get your law license restored. He's a heavyweight. You can return to practicing law, what you really want. Quit the hoagies and hairnets. We both know that even if you complete your probation and your felony charge is dismissed, there's no guarantee when — or if — you'll get your license back. The only *victim*'s an insurance company, which makes a living beating people out of what they're owed and rolling the dice on risk."

"Honest risk," I interject. "Real risk. Not fraud. And we don't have to wear hairnets."

"Think about it?" he suggests softly. "Sleep on it? The other option isn't appealing, let me promise you. We'd have to compromise you, of course, and I hate that. You seem like a quality man. You were a star. A headliner. When the big shots needed the best, they called Kevin Moore. You're charismatic. Movie-star handsome. 'The Courtroom's Clooney,' according to the puff piece in the *Times-Dispatch,* correct? Look around this dive. This is wrong. Crazy. Heartbreaking. Unnecessary."

"Sorry. No can do."

Caleb sighs and flips his hands around.

34

"Jeez, I'm trying to *help* you. This is good fortune, and you're pissing on it." He sounds exasperated. "Let me at least give you a number if you change your mind. It's active for the next two days; the phone will be burned after that. We might even be able to sweeten the offer to three hundred thousand and arrange for a Virginia congressman to join our other friend in persuading the state bar. The collaborative deadline passes if we don't hear from you in those two days, and darn, sorry to have to do it, but then we become adversaries. Unfortunately for you, both plan A and plan B are guaranteed winners for us. This path is just much, much easier for us both. You have something to write with?"

"You can tell me. I have an excellent memory."

"303-228-7109." He recites the numbers deliberately.

"Listen," I say, making an effort to come off as humble and plaintive as possible. "The truth is, I've been through hell. I've learned a lesson. I'm tired. I'm broke. My wife's gone. I'm living in exile in Patrick County, Virginia. I'm working in a sandwich shop for one of my former clients." I stop. I look him square in the face. "Could you simply leave me alone? Let me be? I want

35

to keep my head above water for the foreseeable future, stay clean and sober, get free and clear of the court system and my felony and start all over again. Your suing me or jerking me around is a setback I didn't invite and don't need."

"We're the antidote," he declares. "Take the medicine, and we'll cure you." He grabs the sandwich bag and starts to squirm out of the booth. "Sleep on it, friend," he says as he's rising. "It's coming no matter how you decide. No need to be a martyr for an insurance company and a justice system that made an over-the-top example of your harmless stumble so it could prove to the peckerwoods and low-rent criminals and editorial writers that it's fair across the board. We both know you got hammered. Slapped in the public stocks. Mistreated. A white-collar trophy for the state."

"Damn," I mutter as he walks off. I study his side of the table. He didn't touch anything or leave anything behind. I crane my neck to see if I can spot a bleached hair. No luck. When I rush to the front window, I discover he's climbing into a blue sedan parked across the street behind an empty building, but I can't read the license plate as he pulls away. Probably a rental anyhow. The country music is gassing me from the ceiling, blather about a pickup truck and the high school football field. "Blaine," I say, prompting him to stop wiping the toaster oven and swivel in my direction, "you need to check the security DVD. Right now, please. I want the footage of the guy who was just in here. And save it."

"Roger that, Lord Mansfield," he replies. "I'll take care of it." A few moments later, he pops his head from the kitchen and announces that the system was somehow powered off and hasn't recorded a single frame since the Sutphin squad left the store. Even though Luther's security cameras are cut-rate junk, designed to thwart crackheads, clumsy sneak thieves and embezzling employees, I take a long breath and bite my lower lip because I'm realizing Caleb Opportunity might indeed be trouble for me. Then it hits me that he sauntered out and never paid for the sandwich.

Evidently, the common bastard who dumpstered the puppies assumed they were all dead and tossed them in one by one.

A week after starting at SUBstitution, as I was walking toward the rear entrance and searching through my keys, ready to unlock the restaurant on a Monday morning, I heard a racket in the dumpster, occasional yips and yowls tinged with metallic reverb from the high walls and partial top, and the noise was so peculiar that at first I didn't connect it to a dog. I took a stepladder from the maintenance shed, positioned it by the dumpster, climbed the rungs and peeked inside the container. I saw four dead puppies, two covered with blood, two mysteriously clean on the side facing me, the carcasses roughly in a circle. They were typical country mixed breeds, mostly hound, with streaks of blue heeler or Australian shepherd or boxer or Lab or chow chow somewhere in their history.

I was spooked because the dogs were definitely dead, but the odd wails continued. I looked straight down, and a bloody puppy was clawing in the corner closest to me, futilely struggling to climb the slick wall and escape. The dumpster was filthy, three weeks into a monthly collection, bags of garbage and rotting meat sautéing in slimy brown rainwater. Even during the winter, the stench was fierce.

I returned to the shed, found a garden hose, tied it around a light pole and dropped the free end into the container. I removed my coat and shirt, rolled my pants to my knees, discarded my shoes and socks and planned to rappel into the green box and carefully land on an island of garbage near the pup. I was standing there on the ladder — barefoot, wearing only a T-shirt despite the forty-degree morning — when Blaine was delivered to work by his pal Nate Rucker.

"I think you need a carbon monoxide source if you're tryin' to leave this cruel world behind," Blaine quipped.

"In a fully enclosed area," Nate added. A black version of Blaine, he's a clever, industrious kid who loves comic books and writes Byzantine computer code for sport. Unlike Blaine, though, he's small, wiry and feisty, and for some reason his friends call him Big Money.

"There's a stranded puppy in here," I told them. The dog heard me and whined louder.

"Holy canine calamity, Batman," Blaine said.

Blaine held the hose so it wouldn't slip loose from the pole, and I slid and skittered into the receptacle and collected the puppy, and it immediately writhed and wiggled and smeared my T-shirt with blood and dark, smelly water. I reached up and transferred the baby cur to Nate, who was waiting at the top of the ladder.

The dog was white and occasionally brown, and he was fouled with blood and putrid trash water, mostly on his hindquarters. There was a gouge in the tender skin on his belly — the path of a small-caliber bullet, I learned from the veterinarian. He collapsed as soon as Nate set him on the ground, trembled and folded his legs into his trunk, then lay there panting and slow-bleeding and watching us with bright blue eyes. The dog's eyes were luminous blue, shimmering gems, unlike anything I'd ever seen in an animal. I drove him directly to the vet clinic, where he received a thorough cleaning, several shots, stitches and two nights in the kennel. Three hundred dollars later — money well spent — I picked him up, and we made him a home in the maintenance shed.

"Mandela," Nate said, when we all kicked around a name. "Great man, unfairly imprisoned, unfairly wounded, a survivor when his brothers and sisters were killed or oppressed."

"He's basically white," Blaine complained. "And Mandela's too difficult for a dog to learn. How about Mitnick after the genius himself? He went to prison."

"I like Nelson," I said. "I don't even know who Mitnick is. I was thinking Sinatra, but Nelson's a great dog name."

"So Nelson it is," Blaine agreed.

Now seven or eight months old, Nelson's smart as a whip, and he's vaccinated, collared, tagged and neutered, and I've trained him to do tricks and avoid the highway, parking lot and front of the store, and when I leave the night after Caleb's visit, he's waiting at the rear door, smiling, tail in high gear, and because I've taught him well, he doesn't jump on me or go nuts. I sit down with him on the warm asphalt and feed him the steak-and-cheese. The moment I'm settled into a permanent address, I'll take him with me, give him a proper yard and a deluxe doghouse.

We buried his siblings not far from the shed, put them to rest in a single grave along with four slices of Luther's roast beef and four pennies, all on heads. "Killin' baby dogs is just messed up," Blaine said. "Who does that?"

CHAPTER TWO

I didn't inherit my woes.

My parents were prosperous, hard-working people who knew *how* to drink. They fancied a good highball or stiff toddy, and almost every Friday evening in the early 1980s — I was an elementary school boy — my dad would come home from his job and, still wearing his coat and tie, sip Ancient Age bourbon while my sweet mom fixed herself a martini. She'd bartender the whole shebang, mix gin and vermouth and noisy ice in a silver shaker, then pour the clear liquors into a stork of a glass, always with a precise flair, gradually raising the canister's height as the alcohol arced out from underneath a shiny metal lid.

During the winter, they'd unwind on the sofa in front of the fireplace, and summer cocktails were usually for the porch, the two of them relaxing in painted wicker chairs, their feet sharing an ottoman. They always stacked the same three records on the stereo: First came Herb Alpert and the Tijuana Brass, then the 5th Dimension and finally Three Dog Night, an amplified bump on the speakers when an LP ended, a vinyl-to-vinyl click when the next record fell down the spindle and nested against its kin. To me, Friday evening and its spirits seemed unfailingly happy and carefree.

My father, Jerry Moore, was a Virginia Tech graduate who ran the Halmode plant in Roanoke during a decade when the region had scads of huge, humming textile factories and employees bragged that you could quit your job in the morning and be hired again elsewhere by lunch. He could spot a fly-speck mistake on a balance sheet, he understood people and their quirks, and better yet, he was a genius mechanic and tinkerer.

Every workday he'd arrive at 6:00 a.m., dressed in his coat and tie and a white shirt pressed sharp by my mom, but he kept a pair of gray-striped coveralls hanging on a peg behind his office door and a toolbox in his closet. Occasionally he'd zip on the coveralls and truck out into the plant to repair a balky machine that no one else could solve or temporarily rig a broken part until the replacement arrived. With bonuses

— and this was in Roanoke, Virginia — he made more than a hundred thousand dollars a year.

My mom, Sarah Beth Rodgers Moore, married him a month after she finished college at Radford in 1971. She stayed at home tending to me until I enrolled in kindergarten in the fall of 1978, then took a three-mornings-a-week job at the city library, where she presided over the kids' reading circle, ordered the adult fiction titles and argued with the fossilized director until he finally allowed her to buy single copies of *Fear of Flying, Semi-Tough* and *Looking for Mr. Goodbar.* My father was a success in business, but my mother handled the family finances — she bought stocks, studied investments, paid the bills and shopped all the banks and credit unions for the best CD rates. Jerry's pay went straight into their joint account, and he told anyone who'd listen: "Sarah Beth is the brains of the family."

Same as a lot of other people who'd worked at the Halmode plant — which was chock-full of toxic asbestos — my father died of lung cancer, in 2011, only sixty-three years old, his last weeks spent tethered to an oxygen tank and slumped over a clattering walker. He urged my mother to mourn for a year in black, then wear red for the rest of her life, but she never so much as glanced at another man or even took a bus-tour vacation with the other widow ladies, and her heart eroded and weakened, and a stent and pacemaker didn't really revive her or stay her grieving, and she died in her sleep three years later.

They both saw me graduate from law school and make a place for myself in the courtroom, and thank heavens, they were dead before I was briefly snagged by dope and drinking and embarrassed myself right smack-dab in the middle of my hometown, the intemperate son of two remarkable souls. My parents could hold their liquor, never had a problem taming the bottle, and growing up in the Moore household alcohol seemed a manageable, friendly, Friday-evening mainstay. No, I didn't get my lush gene from Jerry and Sarah Beth. The summer of 2015 was all my own doing.

On June 29, several days after Caleb Opportunity's unfortunate visit, I receive a call at SUBstitution from the probation office's secretary, a pleasantly efficient lady named Lynn. She informs me I'm required to report for a random drug screen.

"I'll walk up the street and have Ron do

it," I tell her. "No problem."

"Well," she says, "it has to be done here, in Martinsville."

"Why?" I ask. "It's a forty-five-minute drive down there, and I'm at work. Ron's office is three minutes away on foot." Ron Weiss is my probation officer. He's a retired army sergeant, wry, fair and professional, a local guy who came home to Patrick County after his time in the military ended and signed up for a second career.

"It's not Ron. It's a supervisor from Richmond, a muckety-muck with a brief-case. Sorry."

"Richmond? For *me*? Ron tested me, let me think . . . around two weeks ago."

"Yeah, I've never seen this fellow before." She sounds frustrated. "I hate havin' to bother you."

"It's not your fault. I'll be there before five."

I apologize to Blaine and explain it's either go to the meeting or go to jail. He amiably tells me it's a slow time for sandwiches, three-thirty on a Wednesday afternoon, and anyway, the high school girl, Izzy, will soon be arriving for her shift. As I'm leaving, I pet Nelson and toss his tennis ball, then I drive my 2014 Ford Focus the thirty miles to Martinsville with the air-conditioning off and the windows rolled down, saving gas. I watch the fuel gauge the entire trip. I hadn't planned on filling the tank until I got paid on the first of July. It's hot but not too bad, and there's an interesting man on NPR talking about treasure hunting.

I'm puzzled about the summons to Martinsville. I'm guessing the state has decided to check behind Ron and make sure I'm receiving no favoritism since I'm a lawyer and part of the court system. It's also possible that my sentencing judge, a semi-retired, eighty-year-old prick named Tyler Morris, pushed this button in hopes of catching me with hot piss. I'm clean; I haven't used drugs or alcohol in 307 days, every one of them marked off on the pages of a pocket calendar.

The Richmond PO is waiting for me in an office at the end of the hall. The office belongs to the assistant chief, but she's not there.

"Are you Kevin Moore?" he asks.

"Yes sir, I am."

"Eddie Flanagan. Nice to meet you." He's thin and dressed in a short-sleeve shirt and a wide tie that hits too far down on his pleated trousers. His head is shaved, but he's not menacing or intimidating. He's close to bald anyway — his pate shiny and slick, a dark stubble pattern visible on the sides — so the razor cut is the best he can do.

"Same here."

"Appreciate you cooperating with us." He's leaning against a desk stacked high with files.

"It is what it is," I say. "I'm missing work, so if I only have to give you a sample, I'm ready for the cup."

"Couple preliminaries." He's looking at the floor, and his words are difficult to hear. He seems uneasy, kicks at the carpet with the toe of his shoe. "Have you used any illegal drugs, including prescription drugs not given to you by a health-care professional, in the last six months?" He finally peeks up at me near the end of the question.

"Absolutely not."

"Are you still employed? File states you're working at a restaurant."

"Correct," I answer. "I'm the manager. Fifty to sixty hours a week. I have a second job as the caretaker for a small farm — I'm not paid anything, but I receive free rent. And I've already paid my court costs in full."

He stands straighter. "You mind if I search your vehicle before I test you?"

"There's a new wrinkle. Mr. Weiss has never done that before."

"You and Mr. Weiss know each other. You were a lawyer, and the two of you had a significant professional relationship before he started supervisin' you." He almost mumbles many of the words, and I have to strain to understand him. I step closer, cocking my ear toward him. "Me, I'd never have let him handle your case."

"That's completely and verifiably untrue. I'd met Mr. Weiss once in my life prior to his becoming my PO. One time, for ten minutes, in 2009, to discuss a client's probation violation. I practiced in Roanoke; he's from Patrick County. His office is in Stuart. More to the point, everyone knows Ron's the best there is. Honest and by-the-book."

"So can I search? It's in the order Judge Morris signed, a condition of your probation. He gave us permission. I'd just rather you agree here and now, so I don't have to fight it in court with some softie judge later on."

"You've got a court order. It's your call."

"Wait here," he instructs me. "I'll be back soon. The green Ford Focus, right?"

I sit in a lopsided, metal-frame chair and kill time skimming the brochures scattered on a small table beside me, information about venereal disease, GED programs, drug treatment, SNAP benefits and anger-management classes. I'm half-assed reading about an outpatient methadone clinic, and when I glance at the box of gloves and pack of test strips on the desk, it flashes through my mind that I'm being hoodooed, and hoodooed bad. I blurt "Oh, shit" and hustle to the office door and start for the parking lot, but Flanagan is already back inside and walking toward me, his rubber-soled black shoes squeaking on the tile. He strides directly to me and stops. He's wearing latex gloves. He shows me a gun, a .38.

"This yours?" he asks.

"No," I practically shout. "Hell no."

"How about these?" He opens his other hand, and he's palming several makeshift baggies, knotted pieces of plastic wrap with white-powder potbellies. He's facing me, but he's looking off to the side, and there's no conviction in his tone, the words dull, forced.

"You know the answer, since you brought them along with you. I can promise you I didn't drive right up to the probation office with a pistol and dope in my car."

Another officer, Kelly Napier, turns a corner and heads in our direction. Flanagan closes the baggies into a loose fist, but the gun is still apparent, held down by his hip.

"Hey, Kevin," she says as she approaches me and Flanagan. "Everything okay here?"

"Perfect," Flanagan says firmly. "Under control."

"A perfect setup," I reply. "Mr. Flanagan is claiming he searched my car and found the gun he's holding, along with a bunch of dope."

"I'd be surprised if that's true," Kelly says. She's stopped walking. "From all I've seen and heard, Mr. Moore has been an excellent probationer."

"Exactly why I'm here," Flanagan answers, inflating his voice. "To make certain there's no local slack where your friend Mr. Moore is concerned. That's the whole issue."

Kelly glares at him. "Why would there be any 'local slack'? Because he's an attorney? We've actually drug-tested Kevin more than we would any other probationer. He's certainly not our 'friend.' And Ron Weiss is the gold standard — ask the judges or the commonwealth's attorneys. That's why our chief assigned him the case." She frowns. "You parachuted in today, yes? From Richmond, I hear? To tell us how to do our jobs *and* suggest we're being dishonest. When was the last time you actually worked a case in the field?"

"I worked the field for sixteen years," he

answers calmly. "Because I was excellent at my job, I was promoted, and now I'm your boss. Understand?"

"So, Boss Flanagan," I interrupt, "why don't you let Mrs. Napier watch my urine test. I'd like someone other than you to be present. An honest witness."

He smiles, then chuckles. "You want *another* test?" he asks.

"I haven't been tested yet. Not today. Not by you. Not here."

"Come on," he says. He crooks his index finger and beckons Kelly, and we return to the office at the end of the hall. After we all walk in, he veers left, very formally, almost a military turn, takes several steps, puts the gun on a small table and opens the door to the bathroom.

There's a cup of piss, a test strip and balled, discarded blue gloves on the counter. "Not mine, you son of a bitch. Kelly, this is a plant. That's not my urine. He never tested me."

"Check the temp, ma'am," he instructs Kelly. "It should still be warm."

Kelly lifts the cup, encircles it with both hands. "It's warm, Kevin. Seems about right."

"I want it sent to the lab," I demand. "Let Kelly package it and send it to the state lab."

I pause. "And a second sample to the local hospital." I look directly at Flanagan. I can feel my neck filling with blood, coloring red. "The damn gun is a plant. The dope is a plant. The test is a plant. Hell, teenagers and crackheads know how to microwave their buddy's urine before they pour it out in here and try to claim it as their own. This is total bullshit."

Flanagan sets the dope beside the gun. "I think we can agree, Officer Napier, that just about every crybaby probationer who flunks a urine test screams 'bullshit' and argues it's a false positive from 'cold medicine,' or that he's only 'been around' people who were using and must have inhaled the dope secondhand, or that someone slipped the meth into his tea at a family barbecue. You and I both realize Mr. Moore's protests are the typical criminal's nonsense, and I can promise you his story is as far-fetched as all the others you've heard over the years. Why in the world would I come down here from Richmond and stage a huge production to punish an innocent man? A total stranger? In a shake-rag, nothing case?"

"Kelly," I say, slowly regaining my composure, "please don't send the entire specimen." I take a breath. "Mr. Flanagan can't fake my DNA."

"We don't have a process for requesting a DNA sample," Kelly says. "Or an account for drug testing at the hospital."

"Then just keep enough to test later," I urge her. "Seal it, mark it for chain of custody, secure it, keep it safe."

Flanagan shrugs. He's dropping the dope packages into a large, clear baggie. "Don't know why you'd do that. Mr. Moore is positive for meth. End of story."

"How convenient," I say, "that you brought along an evidence bag for the dope you just happened to find."

"I brought along all the items I might need to do my job correctly." He nods at Kelly. "Thank you for your help, ma'am. You're free to leave. I'll finish up with Mr. Moore."

Kelly studies me. She's uncertain, thinking, debating, and it causes crinkles at the corners of her eyes, causes her lips to bunch. She focuses on Flanagan. "I'll send it to the state lab. That's the procedure if there's any dispute. I'll keep some as well. Everybody's protected that way."

"Well," Flanagan says, "if we're going to jump through all those hoops, just give it to me, and I'll drop it off at the lab in Richmond. It's my case, so I'll do it."

"It's a Martinsville case," Kelly declares.

54

"I'll turn half over to *our* courier in the morning." She takes the cup of urine and leaves without saying anything else, pulls the office door closed behind her.

"Let me answer your questions," I say to Flanagan. I'm clearheaded, the blood rush past me, the alarm and panic gone. "You're screwing over an innocent man in a nothing case because someone, probably a chubby hustler with white hair and a boutonniere, has a string on you, and he wants you to lean on me to tell a lie so he can make some very serious money. Am I getting warm, Eddie?"

He scans the room, actually twists to search behind him. He mouths an "I'm sorry" so quietly that it's not even a whisper. "Last chance for you," he murmurs. "Okay?" He gazes at the floor, then raises up and shakes his head, sighs. "Not sure about any of that, sir," he says in his normal voice, "don't know what you're referrin' to, but here's what I *can* tell you, a message you need to hear. If opportunity comes your way, you need to take advantage of it. Opportunity is key for probationers like you. Opportunity. I can't stress it enough."

"You've stressed it plenty already. I understand the message, and the threat's been nicely delivered."

"No threat, Mr. Moore. Like you said, this ain't no big case, and my goal is to work with you, keep it off your record and make sure we give you the tools to stay clean and sober. Short term, I plan to sit on this, treat it as a minor violation, and see how well you do. Offer you *opportunity*. Otherwise, I'll be forced to file a violation. You're facing a felony conviction, which would pretty much end your lawyering days and carries ten years. On top of that, there's these potential new cases from today. This much dope, already packaged for distribution, along with the gun and your admissions to me — you'd be facin' a whole peck of trouble. A serious penitentiary trip, I'd predict. Don't want that to happen, but it could."

"My *admissions* to you? You shitty dishonest motherfucker. Kelly Napier heard me deny this no more than three minutes ago."

"She's not here now." He licks his lips. "You know the drill. You know how the system works: It's automatic — judge always believes the PO. And why wouldn't he?"

"I have a clean record, and my guidelines for the real case recommend no time. It's a frigging minor possession charge. Worst that happens, even with Judge Morris, I might catch six or nine months." I point at him.

"As for this put-up job, the gun isn't mine, the dope isn't mine, and even if they were, good luck proving a distribution case. No chance in hell."

"You want to gamble on all that, Mr. Moore? I sure wouldn't. Supposin' things miraculously break in your favor, you'll still wind up with the original felony and a permanent job squirting secret sauce onto buns. You'll be disbarred forever. Listen to what I'm tellin' you. Nobody's trying to cause you grief. Just pick the smart option."

"You should be really proud of yourself, Eddie," I say. I take a step toward him. "You're a fucking lying weasel." I move closer, until we're almost touching. "Better yet, you're a powerless fucking lying weasel right now, because your crooked masters need my help. All you can do is hold this and threaten me with it." I'm a tick taller than six feet, and Eddie's around five-nine. I grab his tie at the knot and yank it up. He sucks a breath, sort of a backward cough, and meets my eyes for the first time. "You need to understand: If you go through with this bullshit and screw me over, I'll never let it rest. I will come after you till the day I die. Swear to god I will."

He pushes me, the heels of his hands against my chest, but his arms are tucked and pinned between us, and the shove hardly budges me. "You can ride the train," he says, "or the train can run over you. Let go of my tie."

I drop the tie, but he stays close to me, doesn't separate. Our chests are almost touching. "This is disgusting," I say. "Sad. Limp. I'm still not going to lie. Tell Caleb Opportunity he can go fuck himself."

Flanagan takes a couple of steps away so that he doesn't have to look up at such a steep angle. His hands are fisted at his waist. "Listen, Kevin, you seem like a nice enough guy," he says, and he sounds sincere. "I don't wish you any more punishment than you've already had, but trust me, you're totally misreadin' how this'll play out. It can go nuclear."

"I'll take my chances, Eddie." I consider punching the corrupt motherfucker, or kneeing him in the balls, or slapping him upside his skinned head, but I don't do anything, and he's stock-still as I walk off and slam the office door shut, doesn't speak or try to stop me.

I leave the probation office and drive to the Patrick County Sheriff's Department in Stuart, park in a visitor's space and hurry for the entrance. I pass an inmate, a trustee, pouring oil into a push mower, and he spreads a hit-and-miss smile, as many blanks as teeth, and jokes that people usually run *from* the cops, not *toward* them. "Slow down, brother," he advises me. "You're as twitchy as a scalded rabbit."

The sheriff, Don Smith, is standing next to the front desk, reading a half-sheet of paper and quizzing the receptionist about the particulars of a phone complaint. By all accounts, he's a thoughtful, trustworthy man who runs a disciplined office. He's wearing tan fatigue pants and a brown polo shirt. A yellow badge and *Sheriff* are embroidered across one side of the chest, and *Patrick County* is stitched on the other side. He notices me and lowers the paper. "Afternoon."

"Sorry to bother you, Sheriff, but I need to do a little business with you if you have a second. My name is Kevin Moore, and I work at SUBstitution."

"Sure. Let me finish this." He drops the paper into a file folder, instructs the receptionist to check with a road deputy about the complaint, waits for me to clear the metal detector and buzzes me through the security door.

I trail him to his office, and he takes a seat behind his desk. I stop beside a chair but don't sit. "Appreciate your seeing me," I say.

"No problem." His college degree is framed and hung behind him, along with scores of other awards and certificates.

"I want to, ah . . . to make a report and give you some information so there's no question about it later on. And I need some help."

"I'll do what I can."

"This is going to sound crazy and strange, but I'm being set up by some well-connected, big-time operators who want to involve me in an insurance scam."

"Say what?" He uses his index finger to push his glasses higher on his nose. "Not sure I follow you."

"About an hour ago, I supposedly went to the probation office with a gun and a stash of dope in my car and then pissed dirty for meth. I did go to the office, but all the rest — the gun, the drugs, the failed screen — isn't true."

"So wait, you failed a drug test with Ron? You're on probation? Am I understanding you? And he found a firearm and drugs in your vehicle?" Smith opens a desk drawer and takes out a form. "Let's slow down for a minute. In fairness to both of us, I need to go over your *Miranda* rights. Might not even be necessary, but better safe than sorry."

He reads me the warnings, and I sign a waiver. "Not Ron," I continue. "No, some stranger from Richmond named Flanagan. He tricked in a urine sample, then planted a gun and dope baggies." I finally sit, but I'm antsy, so I don't use much of the chair, mostly crouch on the cushioned edge.

Smith traces his jawline with his thumb. "Okay. I think I'm with you now. A little while ago you failed a drug test, and a PO named Flanagan found a gun and dope in your car?"

"During a search only he witnessed."

"You're concerned about being violated?"

"Among other things," I say. "Obviously, there could be new charges too."

"Tell me again: Why's this happening to you? A man you don't know is going to gigantic trouble to make you appear guilty, right? Because of *insurance*?" He's trying not to sound skeptical.

"Yes."

"There's no shame in relapsing, Kevin." He makes it a point to use my familiar name, really emphasizes it. "Happens to the best of us. You and I both know owning up to it is your smartest choice. If you were truly positive for meth, of course."

"I've been clean and sober for months, Sheriff." Every word is loud, frustrated. "Months." I lean forward. I tell him about the white-haired visitor and the insurance scam, how they're trying to persuade me to take a dive so they can make five million dollars.

"Wow," he says when I finish. "That's a helluva story. So you have no useful ID on this character?"

"Nope. And I'm guessing that a record check isn't going to turn up either *Caleb* or *Opportunity.*" I settle into the chair, relax my legs, pull in a long breath, exhale. "I'm also betting he's not a bleached blond."

"He didn't touch anything there in the booth?" Smith asks.

"No. This definitely wasn't his first rodeo."

"Zero DNA options?"

"Zero," I say, almost before he finishes the question.

"The security video's empty?"

"Zilch." I hear a lawnmower and see the inmate make his first trip by the window, cutting a patch of grass. "I realize Luther's security system isn't much more advanced than a string tied to a camera lever, but it's still pretty noteworthy that this guy was able to shut it down. That's a professional touch."

"No big deal," the sheriff replies. "Basically, Luther has a slightly enhanced DVD unit. You could buy a universal remote controller and kill the power from the sidewalk. Or slip in the back door and hit the off button when everyone's busy at the counter making sandwiches."

"Well, I was impressed," I say. "I'd be grateful if you'd make a report of my version of events, so this doesn't sound like some seat-of-the-pants, Hail Mary fairy tale if I wind up in court. I'm going to the emergency room right now and take another test, which I promise you will be clean as clean can be. I'd also appreciate it if you'd talk to Kelly Napier tomorrow and confirm that she sent my urine sample to the lab for a DNA analysis."

"I will. I'll call and remind her." He nods at me. "If it isn't your piss, that'll be incredibly important."

"Of course, I'm thinking they'll never move on the charges. My theory is they just want to threaten me for a while. Try to gain leverage. Impress me with their long reach."

"Possibly," Smith says. "So you were a lawyer over in Roanoke? Kevin . . . Moore. Kevin Moore. Yeah, okay. Didn't you represent the cop who shot the county supervisor's drunk kid at a concert? I think I read where you got him off."

"I did. Represent him, I mean. And he was found not guilty."

"But you're here now, working for Luther at his sandwich place?"

"I hope only temporarily."

"I'm sure it will be." He takes a paper clip from his desk and begins bending it straight. "And you're on probation for . . . ?"

"An under-advisement possession case. I had a brief drug problem. Almost a year ago."

"Gotcha," he answers. "Congrats on staying clean and sober." He's polite, but his expression lets on that he doesn't believe me. He thinks I'm a junkie peddling typical junkie lies.

"Would you also have your folks see what they can track down on this Culp woman? Maybe assign an investigator to interview her? See if she has a criminal record? I have her address and phone number in the file."

"All smart ideas," he agrees. "But — no offense — let me get the clean independent drug test before I engage a hundred percent on this. Before I contact Kelly or start interviewing people." He looks at the floor, then watches the inmate and his push mower pass by the window again. "It's not that I don't believe you, Kevin, though you have to admit this is a pretty bizarre excuse." He makes eye contact with me again. "I'm just askin' that you give me a little verifiable twig to grab hold to before I investigate. Fair?"

"Very fair. Thank you for hearing me out. I'll go over to the hospital right now."

The lady at the emergency room's admissions desk is young, pleasant and petite, and she speaks to me through an open rectangle in a plexiglass divider. "How can I help you, sir?" she asks.

"I need to see about taking a drug test."

"For you? Or for somebody else?"

"For me," I tell her.

"Do you have papers from a doctor's office? Did your doctor send you over, or are you just wantin' it for yourself?" She ducks slightly when she speaks so the plexiglass doesn't block our conversation. Her laminated badge reads *Piper Turner.*

"It's personal. For me. It's not connected to a doctor."

"So there aren't any orders?" she asks.

"No."

"Well, I'm sorry, but we can't do the test unless it's part of your health-care treatment and your doctor's orderin' it."

"Can't I just pay you and have the hospital

take a urine sample and analyze it for drugs?"

"Afraid not. Sorry." The *sorry* is soft and sympathetic. "You could call your doctor, and he can order it, and then we'd do it fast. Who's your doctor?"

"Dr. Simonds," I say. "In Roanoke."

"You want me to look up his number?"

"Okay, if that's what it takes."

She phones the physician's office and discovers he's left for the day. "It's after five," she notes. "Most places, especially the plants, they just send people to LabCorp over in Mount Airy. They'll do it for you, and it's cheaper than a hospital. You might want to try them. Or the urgent cares will almost always test you. There's a couple in Martinsville."

"Jeez." I stoop so that I'm face-to-face with her. "Do you think you could call and check for me before I leave? I'd appreciate it. I don't want to waste the time and gas unless I can actually get tested today."

"Sure," she says, and smiles. Her hair's gathered and pinned and braided tight around her head. "I wish we could help, but our management claims we lose money on 'em."

"Thanks for checking." I quit bending so I'm not crowding her opening.

"Well, I know LabCorp's closed by now. I'll try the urgent care." She finds the number on her computer, calls, and I can tell from her questions and her expression that it's not welcome news. "Sorry," she says as she's clicking off. "Seven in the morning to five in the evening for tests. Both places. But you can go first thing tomorrow, either there or to Mount Airy."

"Thanks again for trying."

"No problem."

"Can you make a record confirming that I came here and did everything possible to take a test?"

"I will," she says. "I log in all contacts."

"But please explain that I asked you for a test, and we checked every possibility. My name is Kevin Moore."

"Yes sir. I'll write it down, and you can count on me if you ever need anybody to be a witness about this." She prints her name on a yellow Post-it and slips the note through the opening. "Similar kinda BS happened to my brother. He lost his lineman job because he got a false positive from the company, and he wasn't able to locate a private screen soon enough to satisfy 'em."

I now live near Meadows of Dan, on the mountain, or "up top," as it's known in

Patrick County, and my cell phone is useless from the Kreager Woodworking plant until I hit Vesta, a high plateau in the Blue Ridge chain, so I call my pal and lawyer, Ward Armstrong, from the hospital parking lot to let him know about Caleb Opportunity and the rigged drug test. Ward's a Duke grad, a lawyer's lawyer who's politely persistent in court and an alchemist with the Virginia code — he can often turn rank guilt into reasonable doubt by mixing in a statute's semicolon or stray Latin phrase or confusing legislative history.

"Man, that's a tough sell," he announces when I finish. "A mystery man with an invisible network of powerful operatives and a probation officer on the take. Lord, Kevin. Sounds pretty crackpot, a bad variation of the two-dudes defense and the classic probation-officer-with-a-grudge complaint."

"I'm aware of how unlikely it appears," I answer. "Caleb and company are counting on everybody's skepticism. But I'll pass a drug test first thing in the morning, and the piss isn't mine. Blaine saw the man who's running the scam come into the restaurant, and he checked the security disc immediately and can testify that it was voodooed. This lady who claims I neglected her option to buy the land is a real person, someone

68

we can find, and these various corporations might give us a clue as to who's running the show if we dig deep enough into their ownership."

"As for the drug test, we both realize coke or meth lasts in your urine for only three days or so. Lots of water or a masking agent will eliminate it even more quickly. Shame you weren't able to get tested today."

"It's not like I didn't try, Ward."

"Well, I suppose my time — which I won't charge you for, yet — would best be spent in the deed room and online, investigating the corporations involved in the land sale." He hesitates. Several static pops come and go. "So, Kevin," he finally says, "you sure you're clean? Sure you're okay? I'm more worried about you and your health than some rinky-dink probation violation. You need any help?"

"I've been living like a monk, and I'm telling you the truth. Why's it so hard to believe that not every con man's a moron with copy-machine hundreds or an Irish Traveler with a driveway-paving scheme? There're people who do fraud well."

"Okay. I'll nose around. But I hope this extremely novel defense isn't a mistake." He emphasizes the part about extremely novel, bites down on every syllable. "I have your promise that you aren't using again, right?"

"Damn, Ward. Yes. I promise."

"I don't have to remind you it would've been helpful if you'd reported this Caleb operator *before* the accusations of hot piss, dope and a gun."

"Well, not being a psychic, I didn't see this coming. Who the hell could've? And who would I have told? Blaine can confirm the basic facts. This is totally out of the blue. I assumed they were bluffing, or if something did happen, they'd slash my car tires or screw with my bank account or goon-squad me. For what it's worth, I *was* planning to mention it to my PO at our next scheduled visit."

Ward grunts. "It makes no sense for such brilliant, omnipotent bad guys to use their massive powers to pull down relative peanuts. As you explain it, these mystery geniuses could hack the Treasury Department and swipe billions, yet they utilize their amazing criminal skills to make a few million in a long-fuse insurance scam."

"Repeat that nice and slow and think about it, Ward." I pause for effect. "Yeah, it's only five million dollars. Far more than most people make in a *lifetime*. Now multiply that by four or five scams a year. It's smart as hell, especially in today's world, where anything under Madoff money seems passé. Seems to me they're patient and deep in the weeds and creative and understand that several smaller paydays spend the same as a neon-lit, made-for-TV, twenty-five-million-dollar scam and also attract far less attention. Remember the Johnny Cash song? He stole his hot rod one piece at a time, instead of trying to drive a shiny new car right off the factory floor."

"Send me the test as soon as it's done. Let's hope 'Folsom Prison Blues' isn't the Johnny Cash tune in your future."

CHAPTER THREE

Melvin Harrell is far and away the richest man in Patrick County, and I'd guess he's close to being the richest person in Virginia. A mechanical genius who holds several patents, Melvin started Micrometrics in his daddy's old Meadows of Dan auto-repair shop, and the tiny tool-and-die company grew into a multibillion-dollar international business with thousands of employees and Big Board stock shares. He's a punishing, take-no-prisoners CEO, yet he hands out quiet checks to local families suffering through a tough patch and shows up to bus tables and wash dishes at the fire department's pancake fund-raisers, a hometown boy who made it big. He pilots his own Citation jet, hasn't lost a checkers game since 2008 and, every year, teams with his high school chemistry teacher, Mr. Rigney, to win the mountaintop Rook tournament.

Back at the beginning of December 2015,

a few days after *The Roanoke Times* carried the notice of my suspension from practicing law, Melvin called to check on me. We've been friends for decades, we're somehow removed cousins, and I've done a fair amount of routine legal work for him over the years. Never a guy for chitchat, he said a quick hello and went directly to my sad, embarrassing fall. "This true, the news I'm hearing about you and cocaine?"

"It's true, Melvin. Sorry to disappoint you. It's behind me now, but I had a few dumbass months — June, July and August — that cost me like hell."

"So you're not using the drugs anymore?"

"Correct," I answered.

"You can't practice law? Not even with supervision? Not even basic paperwork that we could otherwise order off a computer?"

"Nope," I said.

"How long are you benched?" he asked.

"At least twelve months, while my case is under advisement. Then we'll see. The revocation is indefinite, but if I comply with probation and the charge is dismissed, I'll have a solid chance of getting reinstated, so I'm probably looking at a year and a half, maybe two."

"How're you fixed for money?" Melvin asked. Despite his raising on the mountain, he speaks very precisely, no drawl or soggy vowels. "You okay?"

"I hope so. After settling with Ava, I have around fifty thousand in the bank, and I'm planning to trade my truck for a more economical ride."

"Can't make it too long on those dollars."

"Yeah," I answered. "I'll need a job."

"So you're up against a family problem too?"

"Ava and I are separated. Signed the papers. I'm sleeping at my office. But I'm still optimistic we can reconcile. I haven't quit on my marriage, Melvin. Not yet."

"Keep me in the loop. If things become tight and you need some wiggle room, call me." He ended the conversation there, clicked off, no niceties or a goodbye.

I was never naïve about how difficult finding work would be, but I soon discovered that a pending felony charge disqualified me from virtually every tolerable job on the planet, from substitute teacher to Walmart cashier. "I'm not *convicted* of anything," I stressed, and friends and strangers alike sighed and summoned a pained face and closed their eyes for an instant and sighed some more before tossing me a sympathetic "Sorry, wish I could." I was so radioactive that simply delivering dry-cleaning or gofering morning sweet rolls for my lawyer friends might've caused them trouble with the bar, not to mention their liability carriers. I took to telling people the *F* beside my name didn't stand for "felony" but for "fast-fucking-food," which, along with construction work, was the only job option available to me.

I chose air-conditioning over digging ditches and offloading wheelbarrows of concrete in wicked heat, and I chose SUB-stitution because I wouldn't have to wear a uniform or suffer deep-fryers and grease tsunamis, and because my client, Luther Foley, was happy to hire me, pay a reasonable salary and put me in charge of his restaurant in Stuart, starting in the middle of January. There was the added benefit of moving to a rural community miles distant from Roanoke, where I'd be a stranger and the humiliation of making mediocre sandwiches at age forty-two would be ordinary, vanilla humiliation, not a horror show of whispers, giggles, smirks, tisks and clucks from acquaintances or my wife's girlfriends.

At the start of 2016, Ava and I were still separated, and I was headed for Stuart, so Melvin, who lives in Florida, arranged for me to watch over the Harrell homeplace on the mountain. Instead of my paying rent, we agreed I'd feed the horses, chickens — descendants from his grandparents' time — guinea fowl and two rambunctious, mousing cats who patrol the barn. I also promised to mow the yard and ten-acre pasture, fix the fences, do rudimentary maintenance and repairs and, most important, stay there with clamor and fanfare to keep "the dope fiends," as Melvin referred to them, from burglarizing his house. A former dope fiend myself, I mentioned the irony to him, and he replied that he assumed I had the dope fiend's playbook and would be more effective because of it.

I return to the homeplace after leaving the Stuart hospital, a thirty-minute drive. I make dinner, a skillet-fried hamburger steak, leftover green beans, and cucumbers and tomatoes from the farmers' market. I grab a fork and a paper towel section that tears off unevenly, and I eat sitting on the front porch, the plate in my lap. I take a glass of well water and crushed ice from the fancy stainless-steel fridge and set it on the gray porch boards beside me, but I'm not very thirsty, and it's still almost full when I finish the meal.

At seven o'clock, I hear the first pond frog of the night, only a piece of a croak, early to the party, about a quarter crank of vibrating

76

glee, and the king rooster, Nikola Tesla, looks up from pecking the grass and peers at me, sets and resets his head, cracks his beak and flares his cape but doesn't crow. I try to separate myself from the dreadful day and my predicament, try to relax. I close my eyes and listen to the porch fan's blades cut wisps in the air. Soon, I'm drowsy and replaying a long cast to a Bitterroot trout, a scene from Montana, the last proper vacation for Ava and me, and the phone rings, and I'm jarred back into a shitstorm of drug tests and probation violations, my few minutes of relief over.

Melvin's phone is a clunky, avocado-green 1980s plug-in model with a push-button face. I answer on the third ring, but the cord is tangled and kinked and the base tips off the table, so I have to bend over and lower it back down as I'm saying hello.

"Kevin?" It's my wife. Ava.

"Yeah, hello. Good to hear your voice." I sit on the sofa.

"Did I wake you?" she asks. "You sound groggy."

"No. I was on the porch eating supper. I'm glad you called."

"Well," she says, "you probably won't be too glad in a few seconds." She stops. I can hear her take a full breath. "I met with Mrs.

Belongia to file the divorce. I wanted to tell you so you won't be blindsided. I'm sorry. But this can't be any kind of surprise."

I don't answer her, don't speak, and there's nothing but brittle silence in our connection, an empty, hollow tie between us.

"Kevin?" she finally says.

"Yeah."

"I'm sorry. I am. But we tried, and I've given it close to a year. I'll always care for you. I just can't be married to a man I don't trust. I can't second-guess and keep looking over my shoulder for the rest of my life." Her voice breaks midway through the sentence. "I've tried to forget it. Clean the slate. It's impossible. I want to, but I can't."

"You're sure?"

"Yeah," she replies, "I'm sure."

"I realize that at some point my pressing so much starts to seem like begging and only makes my chances worse. Nobody wants to be married to a groveler. But I'll do anything to put us right again. I love you. How about another month?"

"It won't help either of us. And I feel like white trash, dating while I'm still married to you."

"Then you could not date for a month."

Ava teaches history at Cave Spring High

78

School. She's been keeping company with the assistant principal, a flamboyant prick named Brian Saunders who drives a red, waxed-to-the-gills, entry-level BMW with a vanity plate that reads TEACH U.

"Of all the people in the world, you pick Brian Saunders. I can't help but think part of your seeing him is some kind of payback. A poke in my eye."

"It's great, Kevin, you can live in such an egocentric world. Why wouldn't I structure my private life around your reactions?"

"It's just a strange choice. Maybe that's a better way to phrase it. You're beautiful and smart, and far better than that fool." I lower my voice and soften my tone.

"Brian's handsome and fun and energetic. I'm not in the market for anything serious." She pauses, but I can sense she's not at the end. "I was beautiful and smart when you were addled on cocaine and laid up in a trailer with a woman whose stage name is Merlot."

"Eighteen amazing years on one side of the ledger, one night in the bad column. I never should've told you. If I'd lied, we'd still be together."

"Well, you *did* lie for long enough. About several things. We've already plowed this field a hundred times." She sounds weary, defeated. "Before we get farther off track or I change my mind, I wanted you to know I'm still willing to split our money fifty-fifty. You don't have to basically give me everything. I appreciate it, but you don't have to. The money won't convince me to reconcile with you."

I signed a separation agreement that gave her all but fifty thousand dollars of our two hundred thousand in savings and also transferred my interest in an IRA worth another $250,000 to her. I deeded her our free-and-clear house and land, tax-valued at half a million. Doesn't seem like much to show, but we lived pretty ritzy, and smaller-town general practitioners don't earn moon-shot money. Teachers damn sure don't. I kept my Ford F-150 but soon traded it for the Focus and fifteen grand in cash. "You deserve it. It's the right thing for me to do," I say.

"Honestly, the whole Kevin-on-the-cross production has become really tedious. The deli-style martyrdom, the itsy-bitsy Shriner's car, the sharecropper arrangement with Melvin. Giving away your worldly possessions like you're entering a monastery or something."

"Fuck you, Ava," I nearly shout. "What *should* I be doing? There're so many terrific possibilities, right? I'm lucky I have friends and clients to help me, or otherwise I'd be even more screwed. You think I *enjoy* SUBstitution? I'm not seeing these wonderful options I pissed away just to punish myself or impress —"

"You could —" she interrupts.

I talk over her. "I could *what*? Work for minimum wage in a larger city with a higher cost of living? I'm going to pay my dues like a man and get my law license returned. This disaster will be behind me in a year or so."

"You could've withdrawn a hundred thousand, lived on the mountain for free at your cousin Melvin's, kept a low profile and informed people you were taking a break, then resurface and open your office again. You could've easily survived on the money and not had to sling baloney and cheese. I told you when we signed the papers that I'd be fair. I told you more than once that I was willing to split everything down the middle, except the house."

"And I've told you more than once that I need to appear humbled and productive to my sentencing judge and the state bar. Contrite. Sitting on my ass in a relative's vacation home for months on end isn't going to score points with the people I need to impress. I *have* to work somewhere. I

81

have to be Mr. Remorse."

"It's your decision, Kevin. Your choice."

I mix a snarl and laugh together. "I'm the only husband in history who's being vilified for offering *too much* in a divorce settlement. Shit. I wanted to do right by you and have a clear conscience. I accomplished that. No matter what, at least I've set things square in terms of money. Paid my fine, so to speak. Done all I humanly can do."

"It just seems so . . . pitiful. Overwrought. But for what it's worth, I hope this does the trick and you can start practicing law again. I want you to make it."

"I've done great legal work for hundreds of people, and I always charged a fair price. I have tons of goodwill in the bank. In the end, that's what will matter. People forget and forgive. They embrace a comeback story. Nothing I did ever hurt a single client. Judge Weckstein even said, 'I'd rather have Kevin Moore high than any other lawyer sober.' "

"There's a catchy slogan for the reopening banner. Plus, this current plan assumes you don't go on another bender."

"And unless you're busy spreading the news, very few people know where I am or where I'm working. That's intentional and a big part of why I left Roanoke."

82

"I've never been vindictive with you, Kevin. I don't say anything about you or your circumstances, not even to my close friends. Not even to my mom. I'm not looking to humiliate you or make matters worse."

"You've been very reasonable, all and all. You truly have, and I appreciate it. My idiotic mistakes caused this. I'm just frustrated; I want to save our marriage." I wind and unwind the phone cord around my finger. "If you don't want the money, Ava, then return it. Whatever. I was trying to be fair. I'm not worried about it. I'll earn more."

"Well, thanks. Thank you. Partially, it's just that I don't want to seem like a harpy by accepting it, the bitch who wiped out her dope-sick husband. And I don't mean to give you any false hope — the money won't convince me to stay. It's a terrible investment for you."

"I understand."

She sniffs. "I'm hurt and miserable and sick about this too." She's briefly silent. "You're a good man, Kevin. I'll probably sell the house. It's too much for one person."

"I suppose," I agree.

"I've got to go," she says abruptly. "Sorry."

She pauses. "I can't believe this happened to us. I'm sorry. The papers are on the way. The police will be bringing them, maybe today."

"Okay."

"Once we're divorced, you'll be off my insurance. There's no need to send me your half of the payment. I dropped you from the policy as of July sixteenth. Mrs. Belongia said we do this in her office, with some affidavits, and it can be final before August if you don't fight it."

"Thanks for the tutorial," I snap, can't help myself. I slam down the receiver with both hands, so hard that the bell in the phone's guts jangles, and the sound lingers for several seconds, a feeble, tinny ringing.

An hour later, I'm thinking about calling Ava to clear the air, to apologize and end the conversation — and our marriage, for god's sake — on better terms, when I notice car lights in the driveway. A Dodge Charger with giant police-badge decals on the doors pulls in broadside to the porch. A county deputy steps out, leaves the headlights shining, the engine running and the door swung open. It's quiet except for the frogs and bugs, and as he walks toward me, I can hear the gravel crunch underneath his shoes.

He's Darrell Pruitt, he informs me, from the sheriff's department, and he has papers to serve. He ducks his head and avoids eye contact as he hands me the four stapled sheets. "Sorry, sir," he says. He starts for his cruiser, stops and turns completely around. "Hang in there."

I sit on the top porch step and read the heading — COMPLAINT FOR DIVORCE — but I don't bother with the numbered paragraphs or even flip to the second page. I'm heartbroken and bewildered, sick at how eighteen flesh-and-blood years — rings and vows and sex and arguments and encouragements and wonderfully ordinary routines — are put to rest by a stock computer template with our names and dates inserted into the blanks, my marriage and my joys reduced to a couple of code sections and legal mumbo jumbo, nothing special, another green cardboard file among thousands in the clerk's office.

I shake my head, rub my eyes and peer down the gravel drive but can't see much since now it's thoroughly dark. "What a shitty fucking day," I mutter, and the words don't even make it to the bottom step before they vanish, swallowed up, as if they never happened.

■ ■ ■ ■

That night, I go to bed at eleven, but I don't rest well. I skim sleep's surface but never drop too deep and fully disconnect from the sounds of the air-conditioning and the house's occasional creaks and muted pops, the declarations of attic beams and rough-sawn joists that've suffered cold and heat and everything in between since the mid-1800s. I give up around five-thirty and decide to cook an early breakfast. According to the Internet, LabCorp opens at 8:00 a.m., and I can cut across Squirrel Spur and be there in forty minutes, then back at SUBstitution in plenty of time to prep for the day.

I switch on the gas burner and break the first of two fresh chicken eggs against the edge of the pan, and — weird as hell — my vision shimmers, like the herky-jerks in a jammed projector film, and I close my eyes and hard-blink and it stops — well, almost stops — and I decide I need to visit the eye doctor and have my contacts adjusted. Part of the egg, a yellow dribble, has wound up on the counter, and I wipe it away with a dish towel, and there's an oddly solid tube underneath the towel, and I'm thinking it's somehow a penlight, that's how it feels, but when I lift the towel, I see that I've been gripping my own finger, and my left hand is numb and most of my forearm is also, and my eye goes haywire again, and now I'm nauseated and my mind's squishy and misfiring. Son of a bitch, I'm having a stroke. No doubt — I understand exactly what's happening to me.

I'm able to twist the knob and stop the burner, but my brain's suffocating, and it's as if I'm evaporating, coming apart in millions of tiny particles, and I have two thoughts: I'm probably supposed to take an aspirin, and I will've lived longer than my law-school friend Woodrow, killed by cancer three years ago. I see the phone in the den and need to call 911, but I'm losing myself, flickering down to black, and even if I make it to the phone, three digits seem like an impossibility because I'm certain my hands won't work. The final thought I have is: *Where's the aspirin?* That's the end of it, the last I recall.

I come to . . . still in the kitchen, lying on the floor, my face against Melvin's expensive new tile, and I raise up and notice the blood dripping from the tip of my nose, and there's a man crouching next to me, but he's oddly wavy, as if I'm slightly underwater in a clear swimming pool and viewing him through a few inches of liquid filter.

"Wake up, sir," he's saying. His hand is on my shoulder. "What happened? You a diabetic? Seizures?"

"Throke," I slur, and when I hear the word so mangled, even though it was perfect in my mind, I despair. It's hard to be certain, since I'm seeing everything through a translucent film, but I think the man is Jacob Shelor, the farmer who runs his cattle on the lower part of the Harrell homeplace. "Thros," I say, even worse. "Whum I bleething?" I want to know why I'm bleeding. My guess is my brain has exploded and I'm hemorrhaging, and the blood is draining from my nose, maybe my eyes.

"Okay," Shelor says. "A stroke. Take it easy. You're Moore, I think. We met at the café a while ago. I was movin' my tractor down to tedder hay and seen you through the window fallin' like a sack of taters. Let's get you to the hospital. How 'bout I just take you myself? I'm in the rescue squad anyhow. Time is brain, that's what they teach us. Me drivin' ain't protocol, I ain't really supposed to, but it might be a spell before we can get a transport here."

"Go," I say, and it's clear and loud. As he helps me from the floor, I ask again: "Whum

I bleething?"

"You fell on your face, and your eye's done gashed open real bad."

I'm standing, my legs at least capable of that much. My mind is more stable than it was, though it seems to have mutinied from my tongue and arms and, damn, my legs as well, because it's difficult to walk, my left leg nearly dead weight. Shelor wraps his arm around me and guides me through the door toward his truck, an old dually towing a farm tractor. He loads me into the passenger side, clicks the shoulder harness and belt around me and says, "Sorry to take the extra time, but I can make it faster without the trailer." He shuts the door to the cab, and I lose track of him. Blood is dropping from my face. I use my right hand to reach across and grip my left thigh. I pull my legs together so the blood won't land on the truck's seat or floor and cause a stain.

Shelor is soon climbing in behind the wheel, and we kick up gravel as he accelerates toward Stuart and the hospital. He speaks into a walkie-talkie and says, very calmly, with tiny stops between the words, that he's en route from Meadows of Dan to the Stuart ER with a stroke patient. He instructs me to stay awake, asks me some basic questions, tells me not to worry about the blood and rips through the serpentine curves that lead down the mountain. We pass a car on a double-solid near Trot Valley. My brain begins to collapse again, and my face feels as if it's cleaving along a division that begins in the center of my forehead, slices through my nose and ends at my chin.

A small hospital team is waiting at the ER door, and they help me from the truck and slide me into a wheelchair and rush me inside. A doc tells me his name — Dr. Blair — and asks me to wiggle my toes and smile and stretch my arm and hand toward the ceiling like I'm Superman, but my hand just hangs off my wrist, limp and ineffective no matter how hard I send the signal for it to straighten. A nurse punctures me to draw blood. Dr. Blair keeps asking when this started, when I had the first symptoms, and I can't pin down time or grab on to how long ago I was at home, and Jacob Shelor speaks up: "I seen him fall at five-forty-five, and we come straight here. We're only thirty to forty-five minutes away from the event."

"That sound correct?" Dr. Blair asks. He's very close to me, his face crowding mine.

"Makin' eggths," I answer, and now I can remember not sleeping and cooking in the kitchen around five-thirty. "Fith-thirthy," I tell him. "Yeath."

He nods. "Your problems started at five-thirty this morning," he confirms.

"Yeath."

"Sir, you're having a stroke. Your name is Mr. Moore?"

"Kevin," I reply, and it sounds normal. "Morth. Moore."

"Okay, Kevin, we're going to do a quick CT scan to see what's happening in your brain. Do we have your permission to do that?"

"Yeath."

Now I'm on a gurney, and a man and woman are rolling me to another room, where men in loose blue clothes are already waiting, and they count to three and tug and lift and I wind up on another table, then a blue man reminds me not to move and orders me to hold my breath.

Dr. Blair reappears, and he leans close to me again. "Can you hear me okay, Mr. Moore?"

"Yeath."

"So here's where we are. As I said, you're having a stroke. From the scan, and from speaking with a neurologist through our video system, we're pretty sure it's from a clot. But we can't be positive, Mr. Moore, can't be a hundred percent. This hospital

91

doesn't have an MRI machine. If it's a clot, and only a clot, a tPA dose is the correct treatment. A clot-buster. It'll do you a world of good. However, if we're wrong and your brain's bleeding, the tPA infusion will make your situation worse and might . . . might . . . be fatal. Do you understand?"

"All oth nothin'," I mumble.

"Yes sir," Dr. Blair confirms. "All or nothing. Of course, we can package you and transport you to Forsyth, but best-case scenario, we're talking two hours minimum before they can fix the problem surgically. There'll be damage done during that time period. How much, I can't predict."

The moment comes to me lucid and vivid, my thoughts suddenly honed, the sterile surroundings injected with overbaked color, Dr. Blair's voice stark and penetrating. What the hell, the choice seems easy: I don't want to wake up and not recall who I am, or spend my life trapped in a wheelchair battling urinary tract infections, or get forever locked into the soupy, broken head I'm experiencing now. I also catch a rush of self-pity laced with anger — I have no one to help me or take care of me, no wife, no kids and no money for pricey rehab, so the decision isn't difficult: "Bustha. Now."

"You want the tPA dose?" the doc asks.

"Fo thure me." The garbled answer pisses me off. "Fo thure me." The second try is no better. "Shit," I blurt, and it's completely understandable.

Dr. Blair stitches the cut above my eye, and they ask Shelor again if he's positive about the time I fell, and a nurse quizzes me about my weight. "Un-eithy-fize," I say, and she repeats my answer while matching the numbers with her fingers.

I feel an IV needle pierce my arm, and Dr. Blair informs me they've started the tPA dose. I'm flat on my narrow mattress, gambling, betwixt and between, aware of my own breaths, waiting to see if my brain is going to explode. No one is talking. It's *so* quiet. I grip the gurney with my good hand in case the medicine doesn't fix me and the rupture is painful. Close my eyes. Clench my teeth. Soon I'm walled off and siphoned away until all that's left is a meager voice threading through my skull, everything perfectly neutral and infinitely black. I'm not scared, not regretful, not anxious. I realize I've stopped swallowing. My legs are ghosts. I wonder: Maybe so very much *nothing* is the transition to dying, the first hint of what's to come.

I'm not sure how long I lie there before Dr. Blair grips my hand. "The ambulance is ready to take you to Forsyth," he says. "They'll do an MRI and handle the big issues. We've called ahead and sent your scans. How're you feeling?"

I open my eyes and struggle through the blurs to connect with the room, the people. I can see his nametag. His first name is Mott. "Same," I answer. "Same, Mosh."

"Jenny here will ride with you and make sure there're no issues with the tPA dose. You'll need the entire bolus in your system. Should take about another twenty minutes."

"Thankth," I say.

They push me outside — I notice a big lime-green moth stuck to a light — and load me into a square ambulance, Jenny following beside me and managing the IV line. Before the driver shuts the rear doors, Dr. Blair peeks in and asks again how I feel.

"Same."

He steps closer. "Wiggle your toes. Left foot."

I try.

"Nice," he exclaims. "Now we're talking. It's working, Mr. Moore. I think we hit the jackpot."

I relax my hold on the gurney and lick my lips, which remain partially numb, like they're coming off a shot at the dentist's office. The lighting is subdued, barely shadows

94

on the fronts of all the white cabinets and drawers in the compartment. I'm still wearing a pair of ratty house pants and a Davidson College T-shirt, both bloody. By the time we arrive at the hospital in Winston-Salem, I can move my fingers and feel sensation in my left foot. I'm convinced I could walk on my own if the nurses and attendants would allow it. My speech is better, far fewer slurs. I'm not going to die, it seems, and the stocky Hispanic orderly who pushes my gurney through automatic glass doors tells me, "The tPA, it is a miracle drug."

Evidently, tPA is a miracle medicine, but it isn't a miracle *cure.* I spend hours being scanned and poked and examined — something else every few minutes — and I'm exhausted, and worse, totally alone and forsaken and uncertain why my head exploded and whether it will happen again, but I'm assuming that stress played a major role in my almost dying. The bustle is ceaseless — there're orders for more tests and medicine and procedures and blood draws. I quickly become conditioned to despise the powdery, perfume-gone-to-seed smell of the purple nitrile gloves and the shrill alarm on the IV unit that blares if the bag is empty or the tubing kinks.

While much of the feeling has returned to my left side, my foot and ankle still aren't sound, and my mouth sensation isn't restored to where it ought to be. I'm buttoned up in my own head, can't sense that anything is missing or lost, but speaking is an enervating effort, very mechanical. I have to select and pull down every single word, like an old jukebox carousel rotating to each 45 before dropping it under the needle. My mind frays and boils if I have to talk or listen for too long, but at least I can communicate.

I'm also scared. It's so bad that I can't keep any spit in my mouth.

I finally see a neurologist, Dr. Wallace, late in the afternoon, and initially I think my brain's on tilt again, because I simply can't understand three-quarters of what he's telling me. He's cryptic and obscure and occasionally speaks through a baffle of floating hands. Strangely, some words are lost to an affected, sporadic European accent. Thank heavens a nurse is with him and also a young resident, and I'm certain they've seen this show before — the bug-eyed, confused patient — and from the resident's translation, I learn that a tear in my right neck artery, the carotid, caused a clot to bomb my brain.

"A carotid *disezeon*," Dr. Wallace emphasizes, pointing at his own neck.

The resident explains that there's some minor damage to my brain, but the serious danger is past, and the clots are gone, dissolved by the tPA infusion and the blood thinner now dripping into me. With most patients, the tear usually resolves on its own.

Dr. Wallace nods slightly, sagely. "Six months."

"In six months you should be good as new," the resident clarifies. "Your carotid dissection will probably have healed by then."

"Why did this happen?" I address the resident. "Stress?"

"Strokes have various etiologies," Dr. Wallace replies, "from nothing to everything, stem to stern. Once I treated an *aztronomay* — repetitive *moshan,* constantly tracking the stars, and there's your CAD."

"Stress isn't a primary causation factor," the resident tells me. "Trauma can cause the tear, and heavy torques or twists are contributors and — as Dr. Wallace mentioned — repetitive motion can be a factor, but at least forty percent are completely spontaneous. They just happen — no plaque, no family history. A fluke. Auto accidents and whiplash are often involved, but

I see from your admission records that most of the obvious possibilities have been ruled out in your case."

"Mysterious," Wallace says, tenting his fingers beneath his chin. "And genetics — we can't forget FMD. It's possible we might never know, Mr. Moore."

"Can it happen again? Will it?"

"A good question," Wallace declares. "We didn't see *this* thrombus migrating from its pseudoaneurysm. But we hope not. We want you *hellzy.*" There's considerably more oracular gibberish added to that, but only "conservative treatment" and "stay on blood thinners" have any value for my ears.

I kindly ask, and I'm told I can't stand to piss, but the moment they leave and the door shuts, fuck that rule. I want to see how much my left leg has recovered, so I swim through the tangle of wires and IV lines and put my feet on the floor and ease off the edge of the bed and stretch for the urine jug, and my foot and ankle aren't worth a damn. I spot myself in a mirror, and the area around my eye is swollen and discolored — blacks, blues, violets and crimsons — and blood has oozed outside a stitch hole and dried brownish red. The corner of my mouth is melted down toward my chin. I piss in the curved plastic bottle, and thank goodness that much goes well.

Almost as soon as I return to my bed, a young, perky woman — Amy — with a clipboard and a painted giraffe dangling from her necklace arrives to inquire about my "support system" and "care network."

"Do you have somewhere to go once you're discharged?" she asks.

"Yes," I say.

"Do you have a caretaker? A person or persons to assist you with your medical needs and daily routines?"

"Well, uh . . ." I stop. "Not really."

"Are you married?"

"Separated," I answer. "So no." I consider whether I should phone Ava, or perhaps ask Giraffe Amy to contact her for me, but I don't see any gain there, no benefit for the remaining few hours of my marriage. I'm damaged goods, so who'd want to volunteer for that chore, and even if Ava did come to visit and tote my bedpan for a while, I'd simply be more of a millstone, a pity project at best. "Soon divorced," I add, and a tear drips from my swollen eye, stinging as it leaves. "Damn. Sorry."

"No need to apologize, Mr. Moore. This has to be hard for you, under any circumstances." She sounds sincere. She waits a beat before asking the next question. "Are you afraid to return to your residence?"

"What?"

"It's a standard question. We ask everyone."

"I'll be fine." I wipe the tear and brush my bruised and damaged eye, and it hurts like the dickens. "I'm not afraid. I live by myself." I point at her. "Oh. Oh! I need a drug test. Very important."

"A drug test? Were you using some kind of drugs? Is that an issue? The doctors have to know if there are any drugs in your system."

"No, I'm clean. No drugs." I sigh. I don't want to mention that I'm on probation and trying to fend off a felony conviction. "For workth. Work. Really need to get it done today. Was heading to the lab when I got sickth. Sick, I mean."

"I'll tell the nurse or your CNA," she assures me.

"Please don't forget."

"I won't." She glances at her paperwork. "Is there someone who can drive you home and stay with you? A friend or relative?"

I think for a moment. My brain hurts. The words are becoming more difficult to locate and pronounce. "Yeah, my friend Dan. Minivan Dan."

"Sorry? Mr. Vandam?"

"My best friend, Danth." I close my eyes. "Can we please take a break? So tired."

"Oh, sure. You get some rest. I apologize."

My rest lasts fifteen minutes, until the "insurance specialist," another zippy lady with a clipboard, wakes me to discuss "payment arrangements," and when I explain there's an insurance card in my wallet and invite her to take it out, the specialist declares that she's already checked and my coverage ends today, June 30, at 11:59 p.m.

I stammer, "No. No. No. July. July thithteen. Sixteen." I press the disaster around my eye with my thumb, provoking as much pain as possible. There's a tiny chance this isn't actually happening, and the hurt will jar me awake. The pain needles across my head toward my temple, but I remain there in the same room, hospitalized and hogtied.

"I'm sorry, sir," I hear her reply, "but it was canceled a few days ago, effective today."

CHAPTER FOUR

I met Dan Duggan the first day of my freshman year at Davidson College. A redheaded Irish Catholic with a soft spot for JFK, Dan was raised in Boston, and despite our several differences, we became fast friends. We finished college and both decided on law school at the University of Virginia, where we shared a small apartment until we graduated, bought Chek cola by the case, cooked pots of mushy, bland spaghetti nearly every week, and hoarded our quarters for the coin slide that operated the washer and dryer in the complex's damp basement. In three years, we had only one knock-down, drag-out quarrel, a row we settled a few hours later and laughed about when he gave the best-man toast at my wedding.

We left Charlottesville in May of 1998, and the very next month Dan discovered a world-beating career: He married money. His wife, Nancy, was the only heir to her father's mammoth Atlanta-based roofing company, and she was a natural at running the whole kit and caboodle, from managing accounts receivable to bidding shopping-center projects, even better than her daddy, no small accomplishment. She was rolling in cash by the age of thirty, rich enough that her name occasionally appeared on magazine lists ranking the South's wealthiest people. As a bonus, she was a beautiful, engaging lady who — for whatever reason — adored Dan.

Immediately after graduating from law school, Dan became convinced there was a wide and untapped "sporty" minivan market, that the real buyers for these rolling, black-walled playpens were young men eager for a hopped-up version of the full-size vehicle. "This minivan is to the regular van as the MG or Porsche is to the Cadillac," he'd inform anyone who'd listen. So my best friend, a man with two degrees and a Phi Beta Kappa key, supported by a stake from his wife, opened a custom minivan business, dropping monster engines and Jerico transmissions into Dodge Caravans, adding performance suspensions and low-profile tires to Voyagers, and tricking out fenders and sliding doors with audacious paint schemes: dragons, flames, sunsets, cheetahs, lightning bolts and buxom vampires.

Mini Thunder was no moneymaker, and that's being charitable, but Dan never tossed in the towel, and for years discussed his business model with a stilted smile and a gentleman's grace, claiming he was a pioneer in the market and was poised for when the sport minivan finally broke through — just a matter of timing, he'd remark and grin, and you never knew if he was joshing or if he still really believed in the wacky idea.

He was, however, a success as Nicholson Industrial Roofing's informal legal counsel. He reviewed thousands of contracts — nothing sneaked by him — became a self-taught expert on workers' compensation law, and learned how to comply with convoluted immigration rules so the company could keep crews of Mexicans stretching roof membrane all across the country. He joked that he was "indeed in-house counsel," since he worked from his and Nancy's Ansley Park mansion and took care of their daughter, Zoe, from diapers and doctors' appointments to homework and school shuttles.

Dan picks me up from the hospital in Winston-Salem — after my five-night stay

104

— and I fill him in on my various problems: a divorce, a fake failed drug test, no health insurance, the Caleb Opportunity complication and a bum left leg and ankle that cause me to hobble noticeably.

"An accumulation of unwelcome shit there," Dan says, glancing at me and shifting with an elaborate chrome stick as we pull away from a stoplight. "But the insurance assholes can't terminate you so quickly. Not under the law as I understand it."

"There's boilerplate in the policy stating that cancellations are effective the day the company actually receives the written notice, which they evidently got on June thirtieth. Of course, you can also include a specific termination date in the notice to them, and Ava picked the sixteenth and had already paid the premium, so I'm entitled to coverage until then."

"Yep," Dan confirms. "Pretty basic."

"But according to some 1-800 claims flunky with a script, they were done with me on June thirtieth at midnight. We both understand their position's pure horseshit, but I'll have to push back and sue and wait a couple years while they file pointless discovery and ask for continuances. Typical insurance-company bluster and dishonesty, in the hope I'm some old, dying guy who won't know any better."

"Amen, Kevin. Nancy and I have to deal with them every day." Dan accelerates and the vehicle's stubby nose rises. We cross two lanes of traffic and dive-bomb onto an exit, the van sticking tight to the pavement through the ramp's curve. "At least you have your clean test," he says. "From a hospital, no less."

"Unfortunately, it happened four days after the probation-office screen. Cocaine and meth disappear from your system in seventy-two hours, so it's not exactly a home run. I feel lucky to have gotten it done at all. Talk about trying to turn a damn battleship on a dime — the hospital bureaucracy and Dr. Magic Eight Ball Wallace were a difficult combination. God only knows what'll show up in the records because I requested it. I might've made my situation worse."

"Yeah, man, you need an occasional declarative sentence from your physician. I didn't have a stroke, and that jackass is incomprehensible. Spending a quarter for a Zoltar fortune would've been a better medical investment."

"No shit."

"So, I've got at least a week to straighten you out," Dan says. "I'll set up a command post at your house and have you healthy in no time." We're beside a small red car on the divided highway, and the driver, probably a high-schooler, blows the horn and shows us a thumbs-up. "Truth, brother," Dan exclaims, and nods sharply.

It's July 5, the middle of the morning, when we arrive at the homeplace, Minivan Dan babying the custom T&C on the gravel driveway, frowning, his forehead cut with worry wrinkles. "Damn, Kevin," he says when we finally park out front, "this is spectacular. What a beautiful place. You've landed well."

"It is nice," I agree. "Also, it's ten degrees cooler here in the summer. I won't roast for the next two months."

Dan opens my door and grips my elbow to steady me, and I gimp up the stairs to the porch, stagger into the den and spill onto the sofa. I'm tired and dizzy, my eye and face aching. Dan tells me to get some rest, and I pull a blanket over me and fall asleep while he's still talking, something about feeding the horses and whether it's safe to go inside the fence with them . . .

Next thing I know, Dan is shaking me, and it takes a moment to lock into my surroundings — I'm not at my house in Roanoke, not in the hospital room — and he's very animated, and he's telling me to wake up, wake up, his tone urgent, and I notice a burning smell and wonder if the house is on fire.

"You okay, Kevin? Come on. Sorry. There's a cop coming, and we don't want him in here." The ancient oscillating fan is set to high, and Dan's waving a hand back and forth as he speaks. "Let's meet him outside."

The room smells like pot, or something close to it, but only a hint, weak and diluted. Dan helps me stand, and I hobble to the door with him, shut it behind us and wait on the porch. It's Darrell Pruitt again. "Hello, Officer," I greet him. I ease toward the steps, and Dan does the same.

"Evening, Mr. Moore. Sorry to be botherin' you again. I came by yesterday, but you weren't here. I saw Jacob Shelor at the café, and he told me you'd had a health issue. Hope that's behind you."

"I had a stroke," I say. I shift my weight onto my right leg. "The hospital discharged me a few hours ago. This is my friend, Dan. He's a lawyer in Atlanta. He'll be here taking care of me for a while."

"Nice to meet you," Dan says to Pruitt. "Beautiful county you folks have." He sounds normal and composed, though his Boston accent still dominates every syllable.

" 'Preciate it," Pruitt replies, then looks at the papers in his hand. "I got some more court stuff for you, sir. I'm sorry to be bringin' it so close to your stroke. Hope you understand I'm only doin' my job."

"Not your fault," I say.

"No worries," Dan remarks.

I reach down, and Pruitt, who's standing on the bottom step, hands me a show-cause summons for violation of probation. He waits for me to study the details before speaking again. I'm surprised as hell but keep my lawyer's nonchalant expression. "And this," he adds, "is a civil suit, from Patrick County. The circuit court here. You have twenty-one days to respond."

"Okay," I say. I fold the papers in half. Melanie Culp's civil claim is thick and won't completely close at the spine. I try to flatten the pages by running my thumb and index finger up and down the crease, pressing the gap together, and I keep doing it until I realize that the needless repetition makes me appear nervous and guilty.

"Make no mistake," Dan announces, "we'll be vigorously contesting both." He sounds corny and silly, stands a little too erect, forms the words too deep in his throat.

"Well, you gentlemen have a good day," Pruitt says quietly. He turns and walks to his car, never checks over his shoulder or acknowledges us again before driving away.

I flip through the papers. "An even five million, that's what she's suing me for. Unbelievable."

"Wow."

Dan grips my biceps, and I tell him — not because I'm angry or being pissy — that I need to walk on my own, need to start taking care of myself, and he opens the front door and I wobble through, return to the den and frantic fan.

"Lord, Minivan," I say, laughing, "were you getting high? Seriously?"

"Well, yeah, sorry."

"That's a new talent in your game. Didn't realize you'd become a stoner, or is this some kind of lifestyle accommodation for the miniature-van racket? You and Scooby hittin' the bong and cruising in the tiny Mystery Machine, digging the eight-track?"

"As you know better than anybody, Kevin, I live a healthy and very temperate life, especially for an Irishman. I haven't been drunk in years. Years. A Guinness or two and a shot of Powers Gold is a swell party for me. I go to the gym nearly every day. Run a nine-minute mile."

"And what, sneak a joint in your basement when Nancy's asleep? Make sure you cue the Pink Floyd just right, so the music starts after the lion roars the third time?"

"I tried it about two years ago when we were skiing in Colorado, okay? I've smoked maybe three times in the last nine months, including today. When exactly would I have the chance to fucking do it, what with a third-grader in dance and soccer and an average of fifteen new contracts to review every day? Don't be such a scold. Pot's legal in many places. The people have spoken. It's a treat and rare reward and probably better for me than a beer."

"Jeez," I tell him, "you don't have to have a hissy fit about it. I couldn't care less." I can't help but laugh again. "And I'm not the guy to lecture anybody about drugs, now am I?" I'm seated on the sofa. I lace my fingers and rest my hands in my lap. "I advise being careful, though. I mean, hell, I went straight to the bottom in four months. Crazy. The party life doesn't suit some people."

"I think I have it well under control. I took three draws. But I do apologize for the scare and alarm and for smoking around you. I realize I don't need to tempt you or trigger anything. Sorry. I stood next to the window. You were asleep, crashed. I took the edge off and turned up the dial on my colors a notch or two. Didn't expect the cop, not out here in the middle of nowhere. As you can plainly see, I'm fine."

"I barely noticed anything, and it wasn't exactly a pot smell."

"Vaporizer," Dan says. "You heat the pot and smoke the vapor. Better for your lungs and far less smell. Hardly any, in fact."

"Oh," I say. "And believe me, I'm not tempted. Don't you worry. I made it nearly forty-two years without booze and coke, and I have nothing but vile recollections from my collapse. Listen: Three trips to AA cured my ass. Fellowship-hall coffee in foam cups and stratocumulus cigarette smoke and hoarse old broads who look like wizened Rod Stewarts telling tales about shoplifting vodka and passing out naked in a gas-station toilet — that glimpse into the future sobered me right up, times ten. Forever."

Dan takes a seat in a leather recliner. "So, while you were sleeping for three hours, I called your insurer and told them I was you and dropped the law-degree hammer on them and mentioned punitive damages and bad faith, and the entry-level flunky transferred me to a supervisor, but of course I went straight into voicemail, and we're waiting for a return call that'll never come. I will ride herd on this. I will *hound* these assholes. I have the supervisor's name from her voicemail."

"Thanks," I say. "I'm not sure I have the stamina or the clarity to deal with all this myself right now."

"That's why I'm here. Your concierge." Dan smiles. "I'll give Mr. Opportunity's suit a read too."

"Okay. I'm in your debt, my friend. Thanks again."

"I window-shopped some Obama plans for you," he adds. "I can't commit until I know exactly what you're earning these days. There's also the COBRA option if we can ever cut through the red tape, though it'll cost you out the wazoo. Thousands a month, I'm guessing."

"Most of the Obama plans have such high fucking deductibles that they're worthless."

"Assuming you make under thirty thousand dollars or thereabouts, we can get you a gold policy with a two-thousand deductible for three hundred and change a month. And we can start it right away, even with your stroke."

"We'll give it a try, then. I have to do

something."

"Oh, yeah, your sandwich boss, Luther, called the day you almost died and left a message and said he was sorry to hear about your stroke, to take as long as you needed and let him know if he could be helpful. He called back three days later to announce he couldn't hold your job *forever.*" Minivan grins. "Where'd Cousin Melvin find that doozy of an answering machine? You might want to alert him that today's version is smaller than a suitcase and doesn't require a cassette tape."

"Before I forget: I need you to drive to Stuart and check on my dog, Nelson, who lives behind the restaurant. There's cash in my wallet. Buy a bag of the puppy Pedigree dry and leave it there, and some of those soft Milk-Bones. Make sure he's okay and isn't starving. I had a nurse phone my buddy Blaine — he works with me and is very reliable — but I'd feel better if you'd drive down and see for yourself. I worry about the rascal." I put a pillow behind my head and swing my feet onto the sofa. "And if your pot stash is running low, I know somebody who can safely hook you up." I'm relaxed when I say it, looking at the ceiling, trying to keep a straight face.

"I'll be fine, thanks just the same, smart-ass."

"Melvin's a savant," I explain. "He can fix anything. The phone and answering machine and 1960s black-and-white TV in the guestroom are his way of showing off. A hobby. Pretty cool, if you ask me."

Dan makes me breakfast the next morning, early, and he's grouchy because the roosters "were screaming like banshees" and woke him at the first sliver of dawn. I sit beside him at the desk, and we use both Melvin's state-of-the-art computer and Dan's expensive laptop to apply for health insurance through the government's site, but no matter how we do it, or which computer we try, once we've navigated several Byzantine screens and typed in my answers and hit enter, every frigging time the information disappears, and we're returned to the blank first page. Again and again, same failure. Dan calls the number on the screen, and after thirty minutes on hold, there's still no live body on the government's end. "I'll keep at it," he promises.

"I'll dig my creaky, temperamental laptop out of the closet," I say, "and see if the site works any better on it. Worth a shot — Melvin's machine is newer and light-years faster, so I've been freeriding on it, but you never know."

After he scatters scratch for the chickens, Dan receives an e-mail from one of Nicholson Roofing's lawyers, and we learn that the companies involved in the Caleb Opportunity scam are in fact actual businesses. MAB is registered in California but entirely held by a Belizean corporation. FirstRate is from Delaware and controlled by a Cayman Islands LLC. The deed from MAB to First-Rate is signed by MAB's president, a George Brown.

"Probably a bogus name," Dan says. "Since they're only swapping land between themselves, there's no need to be concerned. Just pick a name that's common as dirt and will yield hundreds of search results, sign it and don't worry."

I shake my head. "I'm not sure we have the time or resources to get to the bottom of all these companies."

"And even if we could," Dan answers, absently tapping a yellow pencil across his palm, "where does that leave us? We'd somehow have to connect a bunch of different companies in different states — hell, different *countries* — to illegal deals that on their face won't appear odd or irregular. The possibilities are endless and almost

116

impossible for us to unearth: They extort a doctor or senator in New Jersey to buy a worthless piece of land for a million bucks; they sell stock in one of their many corporations to an alcoholic South Carolina dentist for hundreds of thousands; the corporations or LLCs sue compromised lawyers or accountants for fake malpractice. Legit transactions are sprinkled in along the way. How and where do we begin?"

The sewn-up wound above my eye starts itching, but I can't touch it. "And if we comb through that haystack and luck into something, we'd have to link the companies to people and discover their real names. Hell, there could be hundreds of corporations spread all over the world. Here in Virginia, you can basically create a corporation or LLC online."

"Well," Dan says, "if we force them to go to trial, somebody will have to appear in person, maybe Caleb or one of his partners. Or at least someone who'll give us a tiny clue."

"The *plaintiff,* Minivan, is this Melanie Culp woman, not Caleb or any of the crooked companies. The best we could do would be to put a microscope on her."

"Good news is that it's not your money," Dan says. "It could be worse. Shit, if you lose the case, you lose the case."

I sigh. My face is tingling, and I rub and press my cheekbone with my index finger. "If I lose the case, I'll never be able to afford malpractice insurance again, and these fuckers will've gotten fat by feasting on my carcass."

Dan saws his thumb across his chin. He hasn't shaved in a couple of days, and his red stubble is peppered with gray. "I'm sure you weighed the option of rolling with it, shaping the truth, taking the three hundred thousand and their help with your law license?"

"I'm so far down these days that I might throw in with them if I felt positive I wouldn't get burned. But with my luck as of late, I'd be the clown who gets caught and does serious time in a federal pen. As Professor Bergin used to remind us: The gunpowder in conscience is the fear of failure and the possibility of punishment." I see a guinea flutter across the den window, a black-and-white smear heading for the roof. "It's too late now, anyway. Plus, they're such swindlers that they probably never would've paid me or helped with the state bar."

"Of course," Dan says, "it would definitely be a boost to your probation-violation chances if we could expose the grift and the reason they've trumped up the case. Catching a felony and maybe even new charges and packing for a few years at Jumpsuit City *are* in fact your problems."

"No shit," I mumble. "I really misread the whole fake drug test and dope plant. I figured they'd just threaten me with it. Twist my arm. I assumed they'd avoid court and publicity like the plague. I never saw Flanagan filing a violation. But now their leverage is gone."

"Their leverage might be gone, but I'd say their long-term position's improved. Think about it, Kevin: How difficult will it be to convince your insurer that you were screwed up on dope and dropped the ball on a land deal when months later — guess what? — you're screwed up on dope and dropped the ball on your probation conditions? Hell, if this goes to trial, they might even be able to talk a judge into allowing the failed screen and drug possession into evidence as part of this woman's malpractice claim. Of course, we both realize that a felony conviction — or, damn, *convictions* — is fair game if you testify. So it seems like a win-win for the swindlers. They had it wired either way."

"Doesn't make much difference, though. I wasn't about to jump in bed with them, so this was coming regardless — not as if I ever could've prevented it."

Dan grins, kind of cockeyed. "This is when, as the camera begins drawing away from the shot, the beleaguered sap in the frame manages to locate a speck of solace, smile and say ruefully: 'Well, at least I still have my health.'"

I laugh, and it's deep and genuine, the first time in weeks I've been happily distracted. "Kiss my ass, Dan."

Around three in the afternoon, I hear a vehicle meandering up the gravel drive, and I quickly check to make sure Minivan Dan is still on the sofa sending laptop e-mails and not vaporizing more marijuana. He also hears the car and glances up from the computer's screen. "Probably the home-health-care folks," he says. "Either them or your friend Officer Pruitt returning with a search warrant."

"Home health care?" I repeat. "How —"

"Your discharge orders recommended physical therapy and a nurse for a few days." He shuts his computer, sets it on a coffee table. "I wasn't inclined to debate the topic with you. I'm covering the cost until your insurance kicks in. As it will. If it doesn't, you can reimburse me."

"I can't let you pay my expenses like I'm some frigging charity case. I've got over sixty K in the bank." I hear a car door slam, then another. "Shit. I don't need any of this. I'll be fine."

Dan raises his eyebrows, mocking me. "Yeah, you don't need any of this — especially if you want to gimp around like Chester or Tiny Tim for the rest of your life and argue to a jury with half your mouth melted into a permanent frown. That idiotic response is *exactly* why I took this particular bull by the horns, Kevin."

"Christ. I don't feel like dealing with any more strangers."

"Keep that positive attitude, my man."

The RN is a lady named Lilly Heath. She's dressed differently from my other nurses and CNAs at the hospital. She's wearing yoga pants with an arrow theme decorating the legs, leather flats with gold buckles and a casual white blouse. She's carrying a jumbo Louis Vuitton purse and wearing a necklace with a cluster of emeralds and diamonds that appear to be the real McCoy. Along with the high-dollar purse, she's brought an old-fashioned black leather doctor's satchel.

She shakes my hand, addresses me as "sir," and compliments Melvin's house and the remarkable vistas of the pond and Blue Ridge Mountains. "We might have to pay you to let us keep coming out here," she says. "It's gorgeous." The physical therapist is a slender blonde, much younger, maybe twenty-five, with wire-rimmed glasses and a small silver nose ring. "I'm Bess Reed," she tells me. "We're here to get you better. We'll be your recovery team."

Nurse Lilly informs me that she has to check the angiogram site on my groin. "Hate to leap right in so personally before we have the opportunity to chat a bit, but I need to have a look. It's been, what, over twenty-four hours since your discharge?" She has long, styled brunette hair, immaculate skin and quick blue eyes that put me in mind of Nelson. I debate whether the vivid blue is a contrivance, a pair of colored contacts.

"Uh, yeah," I reply, rattled. "Opportunity?" I repeat. "What would that involve?" I shoot Dan a glance, but he doesn't appear to register my concern.

Lilly scrunches her face. She touches her ear. "Well, I'm not sure. A few more minutes of conversation and introduction." She clears her throat. Gazes down at her black bag. "I certainly don't want you to feel uncomfortable."

"Okay," I say. "Thanks."

"I didn't mean to upset you. You seem sort of anxious. We're here to help with your aftercare."

"I'm fine. No problem."

She has me recline on the sofa, drapes a blanket over me and directs me to lower my pants. She lifts the blanket, leans in, angles her head and matter-of-factly feels and inspects the puncture above my femoral artery where the doc started a trip that took him all the way to a view of the nasty tear in my neck. "Perfect," she says. She checks my pulse and then my blood pressure.

"Where're you from?" I ask as she tugs apart the Velcro on the blood-pressure cuff.

"Long ways from here originally," she answers, "but I'm a local now. I live a hop, skip and jump over the line in Carroll County."

"You been here long?" I ask.

"Several months now." She gives me breathing directions and listens to my heart and lungs with a stethoscope. "How about you, Kevin?" she asks. She folds the stethoscope's rubber lengths in half and drops it into her doctor's bag.

"Roanoke. I'm only visiting here for the summer. This is Melvin Harrell's property."

"You picked an amazing spot."

123

Lilly makes notes and does paperwork while Bess has me use my bum ankle to push against her rigid hands, then we stand in front of a mirror and I repeat the word *lovely* at least fifty times, exercising the droopy corner of my mouth, forcing my damaged lips to arc up.

"Will this go away?" I ask. "Heal? The doctors at Forsyth were optimistic."

"As best we could understand," Dan says it deadpan, with no suggestion he's making fun of Dr. Wallace.

"I feel positive of it," Bess says. She sounds confident. Sincere. "You should be walking and talking normal in no time." She points at me. "Keep practicing your words in the mirror. As much as you can. Focus on making the weak side match the other side."

"You might not believe it," Lilly adds, "but trust me on this. You're a lucky guy. Darn lucky. Lots of patients aren't so fortunate. Most, to tell you the truth. This is a hiccup, so count your blessings. Not every stroke victim gets this kind of second chance. We'll work with you and have you back to where you were."

"What the heck?" Dan says as soon as the door shuts and the two women are out of earshot. "I can't tell if you're flirting with her, or you're embarrassed about her seeing your tiny unit, or you're brain damaged and struggling to make it through routine courtesies."

"There's something suspicious about that whole performance," I reply. "Especially the nurse with the whopper purse and big-time jewelry. The salon hair."

"So evidently she's rich as well as beautiful," Dan answers. "And close to our age, though she's wearing the years much better than we are. Things might be rebounding a little for you, brother. I say that with all due respect to my wife, who's more beautiful than any nurse, and my girl child, whose beauty's celestial."

"Her conversation, the deflections and word drops, the clues, the phrasing — they were a first cousin to Caleb *Opportunity*'s pitch. She even said *opportunity.*"

Dan doesn't answer. He walks to his laptop and begins typing dramatically, the Phantom of the Opera or Dr. Phibes on the keys.

"What're you doing?"

"Googling *stroke* and *paranoia,*" he answers.

"Fuck you, Minivan. 'We'll work with you and have you back to where you were.' What's that about?"

"Fixing your limp and your boogeyman's snarl? That'd be my bet." Dan peers at me over the top of his computer. "You're making no sense. They're done with you. Caleb's offer was the front end of this. They're finished. They followed through with the threat. They aren't back to make the same threat again. He told you as much. You have X number of days to comply or we'll screw you. They screwed you and sued you."

"It feels strange. Seriously. Too many echoes and coincidences. I could still make this a lot easier for them."

"Yeah, and come to think of it, darn, that girl with her, that sketchy Bess Reed, referred to you three as a 'team.' "

We both turn at the same time because there's a knock on the door, and when Dan opens it, Bess is standing there. She's holding a floating Mylar balloon, a small stuffed toy elephant and three white carnations in a skinny vase.

"Lilly wanted you to have these," Bess informs us. "They're from her, not the company. She's so sweet like that. Always brings her patients a little gift or card or pick-me-up." She transfers the presents to Dan. "See you guys on Friday," she says enthusiastically. "We can't be here in the morning."

126

"We'll remember you," Dan says once she's gone again, reading the stitched inscription on the elephant's plush side.

"Carnations," I add.

"Wrong color, Kevin."

"Still carnations."

"You're being a doofus," Dan tells me. "I mean, I get it — if I'd been tagged by such a weird, random, fantastical stretch, I'd be a little paranoid too. But trust your best buddy on this. She's a therapist, the other lady's a nurse, and they have no KGB ties."

"We'll see. It can't hurt to be careful."

Chapter Five

I begged them not to tell me the specifics of my brain damage, but Dr. Wallace and his colleagues were bursting to detail the particular tissues and blood supplies obliterated by the stroke, peacock-proud of their MRIs and micromedicine, so they circled my bed and intoned about emboli and destruction as if they were shamans determined to bring me to heel with their mystical power, this magical ability to see so clearly inside my skull. Wallace gave me the news before I was discharged, and for once I was pleased I couldn't make sense of his report, but a lanky assistant in a white coat helpfully piped up and clarified that the permanent injury, though minor, lies in my "personality locus."

I soon discover that odd, unexpected things make me melancholy. On July 7, I'm eating canned pears and a grilled cheese for lunch, and I somehow get sucked into a kids' animated movie on TV and cry and cry when misfit Arlo finds his family, though I'm not certain it's *all* due to my stroke, because Minivan Dan becomes teary too, despite having watched *The Good Dinosaur* a zillion times with his daughter. "Ain't this some shit," he says as the credits roll on the screen. "From badass lawyers and men-about-town to giant blubberers. Who woulda thunk it back in the days when we ruled the kingdom?"

Later, around dusk, while Dan is Skyping with Zoe and Nancy, the phone rings and I answer, concerned it might be Melvin calling.

"Are you okay?" Ava asks as soon as I say hello.

"Yeah."

"A lady from the insurance company keeps calling here wanting to talk with you, and I just received a bunch of mail from Forsyth Hospital. Then a claim rep phoned and pestered me at school to confirm I'd canceled your insurance."

"I had a small issue," I tell her. I'm tense and nervous, and talking is difficult. I have to locate every word in my brain and match it to my thought and then bolt them together. "No worries. I'm fine."

"What happened?"

"A tiny little baby stroke," I lie. "I'll be good as new in a few days."

"A stroke? Oh my god, Kevin." She almost whispers my name. "I'm so sorry."

"No big deal."

"You sound funny," she says. "Different."

"Probable just Melvin's 1980s phone. Probably, I mean."

"I hope the divorce and everything didn't have a role. I swear I tried —"

"A tear in my carotid artery. In my neck. Stress and the divorce didn't cause that." It's becoming slightly easier to speak. "A fluke, basically."

"Well, I'm sorry. I'd never wish hardship on you. How terrible." She hesitates. "Can I do anything to help? Not, you know, as your wife, but I'd be happy to do what I can. I feel awful for you."

"I promise I'm okay. But thanks. Thank you. Dan's here for a couple days, so I'm covered."

"He's such a sweetheart. Tell him I said hello. I miss seeing him."

"Will do."

"Kevin," she says.

"What?"

"You're clean, aren't you? This isn't from drugs?"

"No. God, no, Ava."

130

"Good," she says, but there's a grain of skepticism in her tone. "I can tell you that it seems something's rotten in Denmark with the insurance company. The claims jerk kept trying to trick me into *confirming* I dropped you from the policy on the first of the month. Tried to sneak it in very casually, then became snippy when I told him it was the sixteenth. They took the money from my check for that pay period. I have a copy of my letter to prove the date, if that's ever an issue."

"I'm grateful." I squeeze my eyes shut. Breathe through my mouth and fill my lungs. Open my eyes. Let the air go. "Thanks. Appreciate the call. See you around, I guess."

Not long afterward, Dan and I are watching a Red Sox game, and we have another surprise visitor, like the goofy Mystery Date board game, where you open the cardboard door and cross your fingers, and this go-round we've drawn a preacher from a church down the road, and we don't realize he's on the porch until he pokes his head into the house and shouts, "Anybody home?" His name is Floyd Grimes, and he's come by, he cheerfully informs us, as part of his pastoral duty to visit the sick.

"Thanks," I tell him. He's slipped over

the threshold and into the den but hasn't taken a seat, and I intend to keep him standing and have him swiftly gone. "We're pretty much okay here," I assure him. "My friend Dan and I."

Dan's not familiar with the remote's volume control, and he stabs a couple of ineffective buttons and shakes the device at the screen before finally just killing the power. He tosses the remote on the recliner and cuts Preacher Grimes off near the kitchen counter. "Dan Duggan," he says, and they shake hands.

"I heard from Melvin you was ailin'," Grimes says to me. "You're Mr. Moore, I reckon?" He's wearing a dark suit and white shirt open at the collar. A gold cross is pinned to the suit coat's lapel. "Sorry to be meetin' you under these conditions." He's carrying a Bible, and he switches it to his right hand and waves at me with his left.

"I appreciate your making the effort," I assure him, "but I'm tired and not really ready for a long visit. Maybe another day."

"I understand," Grimes says. "Don't mean to be no bother to you." He's pushing sixty but has a full head of side-parted silver hair that funnels into woolly sideburns. "Melvin's always been kind to take care of us at the church if we was ever in need, so I

132

wanted to do everything I could when he called me and told me about you. Y'all are cousins, I understand?"

"Yeah, distant cousins."

"Which church are you from?" Dan asks, and I want to slap him.

"New Temple of the True Gospel and Harvest," Grimes replies. "We split from Vesta First Baptist about a year ago."

"Jewish?" Dan quizzes him.

"What do you mean?"

"With *temple* in the title, I assume you're Jewish," Dan says. Every single fucking syllable reeks of Yankee.

"Dan." I sharpen my voice. "Not now. I'm exhausted. I'm certain Reverend Grimes has other business to attend to. We'll see him later, and I'll let Melvin know that he stopped by."

"Uh, no," Grimes answers. His tone remains agreeable, but he bucks up across his chest and shoulders. "We're Christian. We believe in the shed blood of our Lord and Savior, Jesus Christ." He raises the Bible slightly and holds it with both hands. "Are you churched, Mr. Duggan?"

"Churched?"

"I mean a member of a church or congregation."

"Biggest, baddest, high-rollingest, richest

133

church on the planet — Saint Peter's. I was raised Catholic. As you know, it's not only a church, it's also a *country.*"

"Thanks again, Preacher," I say, the instant Dan shuts up. "Appreciate the visit."

"You mind if I pray over you before I leave?" Grimes asks. "Ask the Lord for heal-in'?"

"Sure," I say. "Okay, if you want to. Whatever."

"It seems God Almighty has already revealed a generous blessin' of protection on you. It's a miracle the Shelor boy was drivin' by when you was struck down. A miracle he seen you through the window. A miracle he's in the rescue squad and knowed what to do."

Dan folds his arms across his chest. "Me, I'd argue that this charitable God Almighty revealed a generous blessing of dynamite to blow up my best friend's irreplaceable, one-and-only brain. According to Matthew, chapter ten, verse twenty-nine, which you'll discover in the book you've been brandish-ing at us for the last few minutes: 'Are not two sparrows sold for a penny? Yet not one of them will fall to the ground apart from the will of your Father.' " He's looking at the ceiling the entire time he's speaking, not at me or the preacher. "My reading of that, as a well-trained altar boy," he adds, finally locking onto Grimes, "would be that some god authored this and then, I suppose, made Kevin Moore into a parlor game and rescued him at the last second for sport or to prove a point."

I keep quiet. I've certainly wondered about my stroke, and an hour-long ambulance ride over crooked rural roads — after a clot tried to maul my brain — damn sure focused me on the alpha-and-omega riddles, set me to thinking about the nuts and bolts of perishing, but no matter how thoroughly I pick apart my circumstances, none of it makes a lick of sense. I'm not religious, but even if I were, there's no discoverable relief in steeples and stained glass or the notion of a beneficent Lord chessboarding me and millions of other pawns from square to square. Still, I'm anxious to hear Floyd Grimes's response. Hopeful. I believe in backwoods wise men, and maybe this guy, this hillbilly preacher, is the genuine article. Maybe he has my answer. I turn toward him.

"My faith tells me that sometimes our lovin' Father has to discipline us, jerk a knot in your tail, just like any other parent would do. Return us to the righteous path. Grab our attention so we'll follow His word."

Dan drops his hands from his chest and

settles them on his hips. "My loving Irish daddy would've given me a warning first. Maybe no TV for a weekend. Or grounded me. A lecture. Cut my allowance. He didn't go capital right from the start."

"Not for us to always understand His will," the preacher says quietly. He's calm and civil. "Maybe them lesser warnings wasn't heard."

Dan leans against the kitchen counter, and we don't bow our heads or close our eyes as Grimes kneels beside me, rests his flat hand on my shoulder and prays for grace and healing mercies.

"Nice to meet you both," he says amiably as he's leaving. "I drive a truck as well as pastorin' our congregation, and I'll be on the road tomorrow, but I'll stay in touch."

He invites us to his church, and despite our resistance and obvious heathen bent, and despite my soon making it apparent I'd never be attending his — or any other — religious service, he goes on to visit me regularly until the fall, bringing cakes, pies, church-lady casseroles and a quart of Brunswick stew, and he has the good sense to never wear out his welcome, often remaining on the porch, his Sunday duds replaced by jeans and brogans, and I grow to tolerate his arrivals and can't help but appreciate his steady kindness. On his last July day at the homeplace, Dan grudgingly relents too, and tells the preacher to call if he ever has a tractor-trailer emergency in Atlanta. "Not his fault he can't solve shit that Pharaoh and Sophocles and Julius Caesar and even L. Ron Hubbard got completely wrong," Dan noted as Grimes drove away that afternoon.

When Lilly returns for her second visit on Friday, July 8, I'm mired on the couch enduring the same bleak Non-24-Sleep-Disorder TV commercial for the third time in an hour. She's driving a white Range Rover, and Minivan and I spy on her through the den window. She's carrying her doctor's bag and is dressed in nurse's garb, a smock and loose drawstring pants. She's also wearing sunglasses, and she removes them right below the steps and rakes her hair behind her ear on one side. She's alone; Bess doesn't come until later.

"Maybe I'll see about having an angiogram myself," Dan cracks.

She's as polite and agreeable as she was when we first met. She inspects my groin incision, checks my vitals, goes through the stroke protocol of pushes and pulls and touches and questions, and tells me I'm doing much better already. She draws a vial of blood for Dr. Wallace. Since my insurer is still stonewalling me, I do the rough math, try to figure the cost of the test.

"Thanks for the gift," I say. "That's very kind. The flowers and the elephant."

"The carnations," Dan interjects, smirking at me.

"My pleasure," she answers. "I hope they cheered you up."

"Do you, I mean . . . pick them on an individual basis or sort of give everybody the same?" I try to sound natural, but the question is so awkward and ham-fisted that Dan laughs.

She glances at him before she answers but doesn't seem perturbed or put off, probably chalks up the inelegance to my stroke.

"I always try to give a gift that's appropriate," she says. "For instance, I have lions for boy children and stuffed Disney Elsas for the girls."

"Kevin's a huge dinosaur fan," Minivan offers.

"And you buy these yourself?" I ask, ignoring him.

"I do," she replies. "No chance they're in the budget at Advocate Nursing. I'm lucky to wrangle mileage reimbursement from them."

"Well, thanks again. It did lift my spirits."

The next morning she presents me with a purple *T. rex.* The following day, she brings me a stuffed Elsa. Day five, she warns me about my haphazard diet, suggests I completely avoid sugar and stocks the fridge with Tupperware tubs full of fresh apple and pear slices. She scolds me for not drinking enough water. I learn that she has a nursing degree, a BSN from the University of Michigan, and that she's actually a licensed physician's assistant. She explains more about the tear in my neck and the pseudo-aneurysm and seems concerned when I tell her that my next MRI exam is scheduled for January. "We ought to revisit your appointments," she declares. "You need to be scanned and checked at two months max."

"Dr. Wallace and the docs at Forsyth told me it would heal on its own. Take the Plavix and go easy with my activities, and I'll be good as new."

"You have a nearly seventy percent blockage," she reminds me. "Most dissections do heal by themselves. Some don't. You want to sit on your hands and wait and see, possibly let that blockage grow larger or throw another clot?"

I take her measure sitting there on the sofa, her expression earnest and worried. "Makes sense to check," I agree.

She slides to the edge of the cushion. She rocks toward me and gestures at me with a pen. "I'm serious," she says emphatically. "I'll call your doctor today myself. You can't wait six months with a time bomb in your neck, for goodness' sake. Sometimes you just have to wonder how these neurologists made it through freshman biology, much less med school." She shakes her head.

I tell Dan as she's driving away that I'm pretty positive she's not in cahoots with Caleb and his gang of fraudsters, and hell, if she *is* a plant or a spy, by now I don't care one whit. "No surprise that I'm already infatuated with her. I'm forty-three years old, and I've been separated from my wife for nearly a year. I've had zero sex and zero dates during that forlorn exile. The nurse visits are about all I have going for me."

"The skilled operatives, the pros, they befriend you in order to blind you." He grins. "I'm sure, my man, that your adversaries feel the need to devote their best agent and high-level resources to your situation, given how well you've been fending them off and keeping the advantage."

"She's a delight and a godsend. Anyhow, I

don't think they'd repeatedly send in a real person with a real name and a real history and allow us to trace her to them."

"Pleased to hear you're still marginally analytical, not simply bamboozled by her looks and obvious charms."

"And like you said, what do they have to gain? Why would they go to the trouble? I was scrambled and not myself when I met her. It's still not easy to process things correctly. I can't always trust my own mind — it's weird."

"I've yet to see a ring, but a lot of doctors and nurses don't wear jewelry because it interferes with the job. Of course, she seems too classy and ethical to hop into a romance with a patient, especially a cipher like you who has such thin possibilities and a hitch in his stride."

Before Lilly's last couple of visits, I shave and shower early, and I begin dressing in chinos and leather flip-flops instead of pajama bottoms and hospital socks with the nonslip soles. I empty the dishwasher, sweep the floors, replace a dead lightbulb, organize my pile of mail and hospital papers, and tidy the den so I'll seem less like a sad sack.

On her final scheduled day, I ask Lilly if she might consider treating me for another week.

"I'm not sure that's medically indicated," she explains. She's seated on the sofa, filling in a form. I'm across from her in a large, comfortable leather chair. I make it a point not to slump. I'm clean-shaven and my hair's still damp from the shower. "Your incision has healed perfectly." She sounds pleased telling me this and looks up from the paper and smiles at me. "You're stable. Your ankle's improving and your gait is better. You have no speech or mental deficits. You've been a very determined patient. No one could've been more positive and committed. I'm proud of you. But there's not much more I have to offer. I'd be wasting your time."

I look at her, but she's focused again on the form in her lap. "Well, the truth is I'd just like to have a daily check. It's psychological as well as medical. I'll be here by myself. Dan's leaving in the morning. It's a little scary once you've been walloped with no warning — I don't mind admitting that I'm uneasy about being left alone for days at a time."

"I don't blame you, and it's perfectly normal to be concerned that it might happen again. But there's no chance your insurance company would pay us."

"Hell, it's not as if they're paying now

anyway. I'd pay you out of my pocket."

"I'd hate to see you get stuck with my full price for what would be essentially aide or CNA duties. Why don't I see about lining up an aide to visit with you and help with light housekeeping and your personal care?"

"I suppose," I answer. "I suppose. Yeah." I cross my legs. I roll my wristwatch in a circle. "I'd kind of hoped to continue with you if I could. I'm progressing well, and your care has been a real boost for me, and I wanted to keep on that track. No reason to change horses in midstream." I start to clarify the horse reference, but she speaks before I can round up the words and ship them to my tongue.

"How, Kevin, are you doing with your addiction?"

"My addiction?"

"Drug use will compromise your recovery." Her tone is gentle. There's no condescension.

"August is a year clean," I say. My voice isn't strong and fizzles on the last syllables.

"Well, your hospital records indicate you asked about a drug test."

"To prove I was drug-free. I wouldn't be pleading for a test if I knew I'd fail it."

"Yeah," she answers. "The record entry's

kind of unclear as to what that was all about."

"No surprise there," I tell her. "My request was handed off through three people and finally landed with a doc who prides himself on being opaque."

She nods. "I'll see about another week. I'm sorry, but it's one hundred and thirty-five a visit. Paid to the company, not me."

"Best money I'll spend this year," I declare. "I'll write you a check."

"Well, wait," she says. "I feel awful about accepting the pay and not doing the work. Let me see if I can schedule you at a lower tier. I'd have the company charge you for personal-aide care, and I'd simply do it myself and take those wages."

"I appreciate it, but I'm happy to pay full freight."

For the first time since I've met her, she allows me a tiny personal glimpse: "No need. As you've probably guessed by now, I'm not in this gig for the paycheck."

In terms of my romantic prospects, if anything, I lose ground with Lilly during her extra week. She's unfailingly pleasant, and always upbeat, but she's also very formal, almost cool. She continues to bring me sliced fruit, she walks with me to the

144

double oak and she introduces me to rudimentary yoga, teaches me the tree pose, a
modified Warrior One and basic restorative
stretches that don't involve my neck. She
diffuses essential oils while we go through
the routines and does her best to school me
in breathing properly, reminds me when I
skimp on deep chest inhalations.

She always checks my pulse, temperature
and blood pressure, but my groin incision is
healed enough that she doesn't need to
monitor it. Usually her visits last around
forty-five minutes. She persistently ignores
my conversational prods to talk about
herself and her backstory, though she does
lower her guard once, on the morning I
receive a notice in the mailbox that Ava's
lawyer is submitting my divorce decree to
the court for the judge to sign.

"How are you, Kevin?" she asks as soon
as she pops into the den.

"Not so terrific," I reply. "My final divorce
papers are headed to the judge. Won't be
long now."

"Sorry. Welcome to the club." She smiles
halfheartedly. "Your first?"

"Yep. Eighteen awesome years. A beautiful wife. All my fault."

"I brought you a better yoga mat, by the
way. Should be more comfortable."

"Thanks."

Her last day, I'd planned to walk with her to the Range Rover and broach the possibility of our seeing each other again. I'd prepared a low-key, soft-sell invitation, rehearsed it aloud like a bumbling clod and amended it five or six times, but I never make it to her vehicle. As she's leaving, with me beside her, she seems to sense my intentions, and she halts at the edge of the porch and informs me I don't need to go any farther, her tone firmly polite and imbued with a secondary message: Not a chance.

"Thanks anyway," she says. She's carrying her black satchel and wearing colorful tennis shoes.

"Oh, oh, okay," I stammer. "I appreciate all your kindness and help. I feel so much better." My tongue is dry and makes a clicking sound every time it touches the roof of my mouth.

"You're more than welcome. I'm confident you'll be perfectly normal by fall. You've been a great patient. I've enjoyed working with you." She smiles, glances at the barn and pecking chickens. "Good luck to you, Kevin Moore."

"I was thinking that maybe, after an appropriate interval, we might stay in touch," I say, but by the time I splutter the words,

146

she's already in the yard, her back turned, closer to the Range Rover than to me.

She stops and swings around to face me. "Patients always become attached to their doctors and nurses, especially if we're the only game in town."

"Well, there's Preacher Grimes," I reply. "And Homer, the mailman."

"Even worse, your rebound's so close to the glass that it'd be goaltending if I touched the ball."

"You a basketball fan?" I ask.

"I went to college in Michigan," she says with a grin.

"Well, I hope you'll keep me in mind. I imagine I'll be here for a while. Weeks and months."

"You'll be gone before you know it, living the high life again, winning important cases."

That night, around eleven, a thunderstorm wakes me, and my neck aches and my brain is a fleck or two defective, and I sit in the dark surrounded by the red and yellow pinpoints on the TV and computer and stereo and toaster, my chin fitted into the cradle of my hands, and I despair and gulp breaths, on the verge of tears because my mind is cloudy and slightly foreign to me, and I have no assurance that I'll improve, that I'll ever heal into my full, former self.

CHAPTER SIX

I return to SUBstitution on July 25, a
Monday, scheduled for five hours of work,
11:00 a.m. until 4:00 p.m. I arrive a few
minutes early, and Nelson comes tearing
from the shed and jumps on me — I don't
even correct him — and he's licking my
hands and pogoing on two legs and crying,
this sweet, insistent whine. I pet him, and
he sprawls onto his back and squirts pee on
himself, still a baby. I go inside and grab a
piece of turkey from the fridge and toss it
to him, and we do all the tricks, finishing
with roll-over. I hug him and repeat his
name and bump his nose with mine.

I'm still praising him and scratching his
neck when Blaine arrives. He greets me and
we flip through a three-part handshake,
regular clasp to thumbs intertwined to
hooked fingers briefly connected, and then
he wraps me up and slaps me on the back.

"Missed you, Lawyer Kevin," he says.

"Glad you didn't die."

"Good to see you, Blaine," I answer. "Sorry I put you in such an awful bind."

"Worst of it was having Luther's relaxed-fit-jorts-and-hair-tonic ass in here 'helpin'.' " Blaine laughs and mimics our boss's high-pitched squeak: " 'Them 'mater slices ain't free, boy. Two will do just fine.' Or 'Dig in that squirt bottle with a spoon and clean out the side mayo for them to-go orders. Dressings cost money.' " He rolls his eyes. "Even better, since you babysat him through his GED — and hell yeah, good for him — and he's now enrolled at community college, I was expected to tutor him — as in write the entire friggin' paper — for his Intro to Business Principles class."

"Hope you didn't overdo it. Anything above a marginal B would be suspicious."

"True that." Blaine shrugs. "But I'll give him a hat tip — dude's a millionaire and still willin' to be humbled by the Pythagorean theorem. Said he doesn't want to embarrass his grandkids."

"Speaking of college and class," I say, "and I'm sorry to hit you up first thing, but do you think you and your gizmo-savvy pals could help me with some Internet sleuthing?"

"Sure." We're at the kitchen entrance and

150

Blaine steps back into the parking lot, deftly flips open a silver metal lighter and fires a cigarette. "By the way, we've finally perfected our Indelible project." He exhales a jet of smoke and taps the Pall Mall with his index finger even though there's no ash yet. "Pretty damn choice, if I do say so myself."

I look at the ground for an instant. "Sorry. I know you told me, but what's that again?"

"You've had a lot goin' on. No offense felt on my part. It's our cyber trick that lets you post on somebody's Facebook page or website, and they can't erase or delete it. You need to blast a deserving asshole, he can't get rid of your little gift."

"Wow, yeah, I remember your mentioning that. Can you sell it, make money off the technology?"

"Nah. No bank to be earned, I'm afraid. Just the accomplishment. But me and my boy Big Money and my girlfriend will all be attractin' some buzz in certain circles."

"Well," I say, "I have some loose ends." I hesitate and arrange my thoughts. Talking is easier every day, more fluid and natural, but often I still have to plot and assemble and compose before I speak. "For starters, do you remember much about the man who came in here and zapped the surveillance DVD?"

Blaine slouches against the doorframe. "Not much. Chubby Draco Malfoy sans the Slytherin blazer."

"So, I was wondering if there's any possible way to get a line on the guy. Maybe there's some residue or imprint on the system that you could recover. Or a tool to fashion an Internet search. My friend Dan and I tried all kinds of name combinations and basic image searches, but big surprise, we came up empty."

"As for the disc and recoverin' the video images, that's not my area of expertise, but I'd guess it's impossible unless you're the FBI or the Dark Knight's trusty manservant. Anyhow, I think that the machine was flat switched off, so nothing was ever erased. As for the Net, where I *am* a genius, without a partial real name or an exemplar image to actually search, we're shit outta luck. Amoeba in a virtual worldwide ocean, I'm afraid."

"I thought so. Dan ran it past his IT people, and they hit a dead end too."

"Bummer." Blaine takes a drag from the cigarette. We're both watching the parking lot, in case a customer arrives for a morning sandwich.

"What we have for sure are two legitimate names: Melanie Culp and Eddie Flanagan.

Dan's people investigated them, and we didn't find much to help us. Flanagan's a probation officer. His wife's an elementary school teacher. His kid's a junior in high school. But he's dirty. He set me up. Culp's a nobody."

"I'll give it a shot," he promises. "But what's the big picture? What're you involved in? What am I tryin' to locate?"

I give him a bare-bones summary of my problems but include the proper names of the front companies: MAB and FirstRate.

"Damn, Kevin, that's a bitch." He tosses the Pall Mall onto the asphalt and twists it with the toe of his shoe. He bends down and collects the butt, then carefully drops it into his cupped palm. "I'll do my best, I will, though I'm not sure there's a findable pony underneath all the horseshit."

"Yeah," I say, and it's mostly a sigh. "Dan and I and his IT department have worn out the Internet, and you're right, even with all the information that's available, I'm not certain we can trace this to the crooks and prove I'm being railroaded. But I'd appreciate your poking around. Never know, and it beats doing nothing."

"I can create a digitized composite of Mr. Opportunity, and we'll go from there. Problem is, I don't remember all that much about what the dude looked like. I'll put together sort of a draft, then you can tweak it. I'll research the names and companies too, which is probably our best bet."

"Thanks." I glance at the highway, then the parking lot. Nelson bumps my leg. "Of course, the man we're searching for most likely isn't white-headed or heavyset. These people aren't amateurs. Caleb arrives with no warning and misdirects me with the flamboyant hair and red flower, and keeps fingering flashy cuff links that draw my eye. And the day they nail me at the probation office, it's late in the afternoon, and they obviously know I can't get my own test done until the next morning. Definitely not rookies, this bunch."

"Heavy-duty villainy, Lawyer Kevin. But if something can be found, I'll find it. I'll turn MAB and FirstRate inside out."

Phone calls to SUBstitution are almost never good news for Blaine and me. Usually, it's a large order from a factory or a business, and evidently they recruit the dumbest employee to handle the food run, because it's always a fiasco when the halfwit with the sloppy list arrives at the shop and we have to remake most of the sandwiches. Then we'll be pestered to ring up umpteen tickets separately so everybody can receive their nickels and pennies in change, this while our tip jar sits there empty save for the bait dollar we keep in it. I answer the phone at three, late in the afternoon for a big order, and the caller ID shows it's Ward Armstrong, and I'm pleased to see his number — I'm hoping he's been able to discover more information about FirstRate or MAB.

"So, Kevin, you're a lawyer, correct?" Ward asks, and I can tell he's unhappy.

"I went to law school," I answer. "Technically, right this instant, I'm not a lawyer. I don't have an active license."

He raises his voice. "And what do we always tell our clients? We tell them there are three people you don't lie to: your lawyer, your minister and your accountant."

"Okay," I say tentatively.

"You promised me you were clean. Both as my client and my friend."

"I am," I snap back at him. "I'm proud of that. Three hundred thirty-four days and counting."

"Cut the bullshit, Kevin. I just talked to Randy Clay. That name ring a bell?"

"Not really."

"He's the commonwealth's attorney for the city of Martinsville. Want to know why

155

he called me? He called because he's the prosecutor in your *new cases.*"

"Say what?"

"Clay will be handling your brand-spanking-new meth-with-intent-to-distribute case and the accompanying gun charge. The dope-and-gun indictment comes with a wonderful five-year mandatory minimum."

"So I'm actually getting charged with that pack-of-lies nonsense?"

"Indeed you are."

"Listen, Ward, I realize —"

"Enough already. Stop. Nobody believes this is a grand conspiracy. Let me practice my pitch for the judge. Kevin Moore was a junkie. He admits it. Then one day, like hundreds of other druggie probationers, he pisses hot and has meth packaged for sale and a pistol in his car. Kevin claims, however, he's the victim of a nefarious probation officer who's in fact a supersecret minion for some shadowy Dr. Evil enterprise. Yet remarkably — Clay shared this gem with me this morning — innocent Kevin's fingerprints are on the damn dope baggies found in his car. More inexplicable skulduggery from the probation officer, Your Honor. So now, Kevin, you have two new charges to go along with the probation violation. Worse, you've been lying to me. To everyone."

"Ward, okay, I understand this is hard to believe. But Blaine's right here. I can put him on to confirm the white-haired man is real. He'll confirm the disc was blank. The sheriff will tell you I begged for another drug test, and I was clean at the hospital after my stroke. I —"

"You were clean days after the dope had time to disappear from your system," Ward says sharply.

"Okay, fair enough. I don't blame you for being skeptical. I would be too." I watch three church vans turn into our lot. *Great.* Now I'll be rushed and harried with Ward. My ankle begins throbbing. Blaine looks at me, grimaces and puts on gloves. "But my ace in the hole is the DNA from the phony piss test. It isn't mine. It isn't."

"Sucker and eternal optimist that I am, I had Kelly ship a sample to the private lab in Greensboro. I paid for the analysis myself. To be incredibly cautious, and giving you the benefit of every possible doubt, I took the state out of the equation, except the Greensboro lab used the buccal-swab profile from your original possession case as a DNA comparison."

"My data in the state's DNA bank could

easily have been manipulated. This Caleb told me they can hack and change anything."

"The report isn't back yet, so I called to check. They're still doing the paperwork, but the piss isn't yours. They said so over the phone."

"Thank goodness."

"It's fake," Ward says. "Synthetic."

"Well, there you go. Hell, yeah. Flanagan planted it. Microwaved some pretend urine and tossed an old, dirty test stick down beside it. Now we have the proof — forensic fucking proof." At least thirty teenagers are swarming the parking lot. "I told you."

"Creative and sinister guy, this Flanagan," Ward says sarcastically.

"Hardly," I answer. "When Kelly happened by and then wound up with the cup, she sideswiped his plan. We'd *never* have seen that piss again otherwise. He would've simply claimed that I confessed, and that he'd flushed the urine, everything routine and standard. The piss, gloves and positive stick were props, for my benefit only, a behind-closed-doors reminder of his power over me. Window dressing. Obviously, that bogus urine was never supposed to be tested for anything."

"You're right: Flanagan *will* testify that

you admitted to being positive after Kelly left. He'll swear under oath that you owned up to the meth but said it was for personal use and asked him to give you another chance. Even apologized to him."

"This isn't too complicated, Ward. It's a pretty weak plan. How did synthetic urine test positive for meth? Makes no sense. Ultimately, it's my word against his."

"That's our problem," Ward says. "And since we're on the topic of your credibility, did you — within a week of my moving heaven and earth to convince a law-and-order, reefer-madness judge not to pop you with a felony coke conviction — go online and visit a site called Klean Stream, a damn stoner page that sells fake urine and flushing agents and hollow penises and traffics in how to beat drug tests? After I vouched for you and put my name on the line?"

"Do what?"

"Did I somehow start speaking Urdu and you can't understand me?"

The kids are knotted at the restaurant's door. "Okay, okay. Yeah, I did. I'm not going to lie. But I didn't buy anything." I press the heel of my hand against my forehead. "What miserable, rotten, shitty luck. They're already kicking my ass, and now I hand them this — a twenty-penny nail for my coffin."

"Well," he barks, "why in the wide, wide world of sports would you ever go to this site?"

I feel my neck color. The rush of stress and tension causes my face to burn. My lips tingle and begin to numb, even my tongue. "To see what my choices were if I screwed up and couldn't make it. There's a lot riding on my staying off drugs — my law license, my freedom — and I wanted to explore every option if I used again. Addiction recovery isn't always perfect and uneventful, Ward. And unless you're Nancy frigging Reagan, you ought to respect that. I wasn't anxious to ruin my life if I relapsed, so the day after Morris sentenced me, I planned for the worst and looked into contingencies. I think anyone would. But I stayed absolutely straight, clean as a whistle."

"So let's consider another possibility: You're surprised by a drug screen, right when you're feeling safe since you were tested just a couple weeks earlier, and you know you'll be positive, and the best you can do is throw away your real sample and refill the specimen cup with the Klean Stream fake while Flanagan's digging a gun and multiple meth baggies — *with your prints* — from *your car.* Then you demand that Kelly test for DNA so you can raise holy legal hell about the screen when the synthetic piss *you substituted* is discovered by the lab. *You* poured in the Klean Stream to make a hash out of things and gin up reasonable doubt."

"Never happened," I say.

"This ain't a winner, Counselor. The probationer with bags of meth in his car tested positive for meth. The probationer who browsed online for fake piss ended up with fake piss in his specimen cup. And of course —"

"Not my fake piss, not my dope, not my gun," I insist.

"Of course, let's not forget that there was absolutely no report of this heinous criminal fraud when you were supposedly solicited by an albino mystery man — only after you get jammed up does this half-baked fairy tale surface. Randy Clay will have a field day."

"Batter up," Blaine says. The first kid is bashful and difficult to hear, and his order is full of fits and starts and do-overs: I wanna change the bread to wheat and . . . oops, I meant Swiss cheese.

I trap the phone between my cheek and

shoulder and wiggle on gloves, but I remember I'm not supposed to twist my neck and risk aggravating my carotid tear, and my cheek suddenly feels deadened, as if it's not a part of me, and the phone slips free and hits the floor. The black plastic panel flies off, and the batteries pop loose and roll in different directions. *Fuck it.* I kick the phone out of my way, and Blaine and I race through thirty-eight sandwiches, and when we finish, my face is inflamed, my ankle's flimsy rubber and every single thought is buffering in my head, taking forever to clarify.

"Gadzooks, Lawyer Kevin," Blaine says, trying to make me laugh. "You're still the man. Might even make manager if you play your cards right."

A beanpole boy with whispers of a mustache comes to the counter carrying his sandwich on a tray. "Could you please wrap this up to go?" he asks me. "I'm gonna save half for later."

"I'll do it for you," Blaine volunteers. "Hand me your tray."

Sick and enervated as I am, and despite the short-circuits and crossed wires in my brain, the explanation comes to me the second Blaine reaches for the sandwich, before he yanks a section of clear sandwich

162

wrap from the dispenser behind the counter. "That's how," I mumble. "There's your prints. Caleb's to-go turkey-and-cheese."

"Say what?" he asks.

"Shit."

"Well, I think we got that bass-ackwards, didn't we?" Ward says. "I should be hanging up on you."

"Sorry, Ward. I apologize." My shift is finished, and I'm seated in the SUBstitution kitchen. Blaine and Izzy are running the shop. "I dropped the damn phone, and the batteries flew out. Then we had a platoon of kids come in."

"Apologies here too — I didn't mean to be a prick about everything." Ward's voice has changed. He's subdued. "There's just a mountain of evidence against you. My job as your lawyer — and your friend, for that matter — is to tell you the truth as best I can, and right now the truth is your defense isn't worth squat. We'll figure out something, I guess." He sighs. "You know what comes next?"

"Jail," I answer. "It's presumptive no-bond. Gun with dope, and I'm already on probation, so I'm screwed. I'll be stuck in jail until trial. Especially with Judge Morris, the three-hundred-year-old jurist. Any chance we can locate a judge who has progressed from a saddle to the horseless carriage?"

"I'm trying to work a deal with Clay. He's a fair guy and an excellent lawyer. We all understand you're not a criminal or a bad person. You've got a drug problem. Not the easiest disease to cure. But a meth-distribution charge is going to be a bear."

"I wasn't selling meth, Ward," I say by rote, with no spirit. "Before I wave the white flag and plead guilty, let me ask you something: How the hell do they have that kind of detail on my computer history? How do they know about Klean Stream?"

"The court order keeping the original case under advisement contains Judge Morris's direction that the commonwealth can search your person, possessions, home, vehicle, electronic devices and property without a warrant or any suspicion whatsoever. A complete waiver of your Fourth Amendment rights as a condition of probation. Judge Morris added it as a term of your second-chance plan. We didn't agree to it, but we didn't object either."

"Right," I say. "Flanagan used the blanket consent to search my car. But as I understand the law — according to *United States v. Knights* and a Virginia case called *Murry*

164

— even with that language in the order, there *still* has to be reasonable suspicion to search; and, more important, the commonwealth can't use this waiver to hunt up fresh crimes. Basically, an officer needs reasonable suspicion, and any search is limited to enforcing my probation. That's the law." I close my eyes for an instant, waiting for my thoughts to congeal. "Judge Morris can write draconian shit in his own blood and stamp it with a wax seal, but it's still not valid. It's not Constitutional."

"I'm relieved to hear that you're as shrewd as ever," Ward says.

"Well, right now I'm frazzled and hitting on about three cylinders, but the Supreme Court has ruled on this. Of course, Methuselah Morris is an arrogant old prick who thinks he can order whatever he wants so long as he's holding a gavel and covered in black polyester." I walk to the sink and pour myself a cup of water. I also wet a clean rag and hold it against the side of my face.

"It's a gray area, yeah. I'd already spotted the issue. But let's assume we can persuade the judge to exclude every mention of your Klean Stream adventure — then what, Kevin? That only really helps with your smallest problem, the probation violation and your under-advisement charge. Hell, you're still stuck with the gorillas, the distribution case and the gun-and-dope case."

"Tell me, Ward," I say, my voice firm, "exactly what reasonable suspicion, what factual basis, did Flanagan have to search my car? And how was that search tied to enforcing my probation?"

"A positive drug test, minutes before, would've given him a reason to believe that you possessed drugs."

"So even though he has me dead to rights on the dirty screen and probation violation, even though the commonwealth's case against me is already *made,* he can search my car? Why? Why would he even need to? Searching my car *after* I failed the drug test is just hunting up new trouble for me. Flanagan was improperly trying to discover additional crimes, which gives us a decent shot at getting the gun and distribution cases dismissed."

"Playing devil's advocate," Ward says, "the commonwealth will claim that once you failed the screen, you initially denied using meth, so this search was a reasonable procedure to buttress their test. Addicts are known to frequently stash drugs in their vehicles. The search was instantaneous and involved your *car.* We're not talking about your house or your bank box."

"At least it gives us a little opening. A chance. Of course, despite what Flanagan will say, he damn sure hadn't tested me before searching my car."

"Good luck convincing Morris that his own order's invalid. You'll cool your heels in jail for months while the case is heard on appeal, that's my prediction. Then maybe a fifty-fifty chance with the appellate courts."

"Who was cracking the whip on all this, Ward?" I ask. "Who green-lighted searching my Internet history on a frigging under-advisement possession case? I've *never* heard of that before. And who approved bringing the new chargers? Shit — *charges,* I mean." A drop of water trickles down my cheek, rides my neck and stops at my collar.

"According to Clay, Flanagan gave your info to Jane Klein, the prosecutor who was originally assigned to your possession case. Nothing unusual there. SOP. But northern Virginia prosecutors are typically far more aggressive than our people. She approved the computer search and prepared the new charges. She's five hours away and she's done her special-prosecutor time on this, and Clay doesn't have any conflict and Martinsville's his jurisdiction, so he's taking over."

I toss the wet rag into the sink. "Flanagan couldn't just sit on the planted gun and dope after the very public brouhaha with Kelly Napier at the probation office. Letting things slide would seem really strange and suspicious. He had to file a report with Jane Klein — or hell, maybe he planned to all along — and Caleb wins the door prize of my looking even more dishonest and junk-iefied."

"Whatever," Ward says. "At any rate, Clay's our man now. Actually, that's a positive for us. He's local and reasonable."

"I realize what an awful jam I've put us in. The Klean Stream visit was a stupid mistake — sorry. But I hope you can at least understand how difficult my situation was. How scary. I apologize for letting you down, though I swear to you I never *bought* anything. See what kind of bond you can work out for me. I'll start studying the car-search question."

"I'll do my best. You take care of yourself. Maybe NA or something like that would be a wise choice right now. Meth can kill you, Kevin. It's dire shit."

I say goodbye to Izzy and Blaine, fill Nelson's dish and feed him next to the shed. I sit with him while he eats. Normally a fast, dedicated gulper, this evening he keeps looking up at me and wagging his tail while he chews his kibble, in no hurry, perhaps concerned about his diminished human friend, or so I'd like to think.

Before work the next morning, I stop by Ron Weiss's office and volunteer for a drug test. My screen is negative for everything, completely clean.

"Sorry about your issues down in Martinsville," Ron says. "With Mr. Flanagan."

"Do you know anything about him?"

"Wouldn't know him from Adam's housecat. He's a Richmond honcho."

"Well, thanks for testing me," I say.

"I have to admit, I was shocked when I heard you failed a urine test down there and they found meth in your car. I've done this job long enough that ninety-nine-point-nine percent of the time I'm aware if my probationers are using. Mr. Armstrong called me, and I told him I'd kept really close tabs on you — back-to-back tests, Monday-morning tests, even that Saturday when I stopped by the restaurant. You've been working regular hours, you've paid off your court costs and you've never skipped an appointment. You've been a complete success with me."

"Thanks."

"Sure. Glad you're improving after your

stroke. Nothing's promised to us, is it, Kevin? We just never know what might be comin' our way next, good or bad."

I'm able to pull another short shift without too much difficulty. My face and eye tingle for several minutes at noon — aggravated by the heat from our daily oven charade — but otherwise I'm symptom-free. Blaine carries more than his fair share of the work and keeps reminding me to take a break if I feel tired or sick.

When I finish my five hours, I dawdle in the SUBstitution toilet, washing off the restaurant smells, combing my hair and brushing my teeth. As I'm clipping my nails, I notice the circle of pale, depressed skin left behind by my wedding ring. I've brought along a necktie and blue suit, and I put them on. Instead of raising my spirits, the lawyer clothes make me sad and wistful. "What a fucking dumbass," I tell my reflection. Some prankster has etched the outline of a dick and balls into the paint on the side of the stall, and from my angle, the trite graffiti appears to perch atop my shoulder.

I play with Nelson while I wait to meet Margo Jordan, my attorney in the malpractice case, who's driving from Norfolk to interview me. I crouch and rake his fur from his head to his hindquarters and treat him

170

to a Milk-Bone. I toss his tennis ball toward the woods beside the shed and he retrieves it, eager and amped, as if he could fetch forever.

"A man and his dog," I hear a female voice say.

"You must be Ms. Jordan," I reply. "You're early."

"Margo, please," she suggests. "What's the pup's name?"

"Nelson. We rescued him from the dumpster over there."

"Look at those blue eyes."

"He's a good boy," I brag. "I think he somehow understands that he received a second chance."

"Does he stay here or live with you?" she asks.

"Here for right now. I'm managing a farm for a friend, and we have chickens and guinea fowl, and they might be too tempting no matter how disciplined the dog. But I hope to have him in a proper home with me sooner rather than later. This is far from ideal."

We enter through the kitchen and sit in a booth by the window. She's neatly dressed in a dark pantsuit and carrying a well-made leather briefcase that's nicked and battered — an excellent sign, in my opinion. She's around fifty, slender, with shorter hair, and she seems confident and relaxed. When she smiles at my joke about our sitting at "the chef's table," she tilts her head back slightly, almost imperceptibly, as if she's on the verge of a full-blown belly laugh.

"Well, I have to confess, you're not what I expected," she tells me.

"What were you expecting?" I ask.

"A rheumy-eyed, skin-and-bones, chain-smoking catastrophe who's been beaten down by drug addiction and poor health. Sorry about your stroke, by the way. My daddy had a brain bleed, and it robbed any worthwhile quality of life from him."

"I'm glad I could disappoint you."

"So I've spoken with Ward. He's very concerned about you, more as a friend than a lawyer. I've also had chats with Mr. Flanagan, Jane Klein and Mr. Clay, the commonwealth's attorney. As you know from the suit papers, M. D. Jenkins is representing Miss Culp. I've had a couple of preliminary discussions with him. Or his associate, if I'm being accurate. Jenkins himself is in a three-week trial."

"He's the genuine item," I say. "I heard him lecture once at a trial lawyers' conference in Abingdon."

"I'm told he lives up to his billing, and as

you no doubt realize, Hunton and Williams has virtually limitless resources."

"I've always wondered," I say, "every time I see his name, what do the initials stand for?"

"I've heard Mad Dog and Mega-Dollar and, my favorite, Magic on Demand."

"You're no piker yourself. I read your bio online — not everybody makes law review at Washington and Lee and partner at McGuire, Woods."

"I suppose we'll soon see how effective I am," she replies. "According to Ward, our defense promises to be, uh, pretty unique and quite the Rube Goldberg contraption." Her tone is open and receptive. "How about I hear the tale from the source."

I'm very thorough and precise, start with the Sutphin girl and end by telling Margo that, only a few hours ago, I passed my drug test at the probation office.

"Did you ever have contact with this Miss Culp again after the visit last July?" she asks me.

"No, absolutely not." I'm emphatic. "She came in, I reviewed the option, told her it was legal and valid, and she left. That's it. Period. The entire lawsuit's humbug. She *never* told me to execute the option or to buy the land." I gesture with both hands, shrug and show her my palms. "I mean, seriously, Margo, think about it. Even drunk and high, I would've handled something so damn easy."

"I'd assume so," she says noncommittally.

"I'm a lawyer, so I understand how bizarre and improbable this all sounds, but before you scratch a five-million-dollar check, how about we at least pick some of the lower-hanging fruit?"

"You know the drill. Your insurer, Lawyers Comprehensive, is already unhappy they have to pay me to defend you under the terms of the policy. Five million bucks is a ton of cash when it's coming from their wallet. An experienced lawyer like M. D. Jenkins will —"

"Will become Make-a-Deal Jenkins and offer to discount the case by fifty or seventy-five thousand if you and your company agree to settle quickly and don't hassle him or his client. He'll give you an economic incentive to pay his client on what appears to be a dead-solid loser for our side. Fifty thousand is fifty thousand."

"Exactly," she says. "If we fight this, we'll lose the fifty-to-seventy-five-thousand discount M.D. will no doubt offer. Plus we'll spend several thousand on depositions, court reporters and my fees. For what? If my client can avoid forking over the absolute max, and the odds of winning seem non-existent, then Lawyers Comp will put this to bed."

"Believe me, I understand the math," I say quietly.

"I don't have much to persuade them otherwise. They're not inclined to throw good money after bad, won't be eager to sign up for a billion-to-one long shot." She gives me a look that's mostly compassionate, with a trace of resignation tacked on. "We start with lousy facts that we can't avoid. You admit you were drug-and-alcohol addicted when you had an office visit with Miss Culp, and her damages — on paper — are set in concrete. I wish you the best, but it appears you're now facing new charges and felony convictions, a huge complication for us. We're unable to produce hide nor hair of this mystery man. The corporate players seem like dime-a-dozen, regular old companies."

"Worse," I add, "I'm guessing that most judges will allow Jenkins to quiz me about drug use and my state of mind as I was speaking with Caleb Opportunity, and when I swear I was clean and coherent, I'll be impeached by my failed test from several days later and the bags of meth in my car."

"I'm afraid you're correct."

"Have you checked into the companies behind the fake sale?" I ask. "They're fronts and paper illusions."

"Sure. But many corporations are simply shells, for any number of reasons, some legit, some not. This MAB is a California company, and we've located several standard transactions they've been involved in. Completely ordinary swaps and sales. A strip-mall deal, for instance. FirstRate is totally owned by an LLC from the Caymans, the place where business information goes to die. I'm perfectly willing to suffer the sacrifice and fly there to investigate, but I don't see your insurer springing for any Caribbean research." She grins.

"That kind of ownership itself is a huge red flag," I complain.

"Not really. Not in 2016. These days, how many Fortune 500 companies *don't* have assets and operations tucked away offshore? My husband's landlord in Norfolk is some Chinese LLC, and he sends the rent check to a Florida post office box. Commerce is global."

"Then there's the impossible five-million-dollar increase in value over a few weeks, from $975,000 to six million. In Patrick County? That just stinks to high heaven."

"It's unusual, but a quick five-million spike in an area that's popping isn't unheard of, especially when investors and speculators are in the mix. Buyers are paying ten million for *five acres* in McLean, or several million for a Broad Street *lot* in Richmond's West End. Do the numbers: FirstRate purchased 173 acres and didn't even pay thirty-five thou an acre. Primland's right down the road, and they bought land for a song, and now it's worth twenty times what they initially invested, and some of their holdings have tax assessments well above thirty thousand an acre. I don't think attacking value is a promising strategy for us."

"How about we at least take a gander at Melanie Culp? Depose her? Get every scrap of data we can, then explore it and cross-reference it? She's obviously a big part of the con. Caleb called her his 'colleague.' She might slip or screw up. You can certainly convince Jenkins — without losing his discount — that you have to do a pro forma questioning before handing over millions. It'd be malpractice if you didn't. Maybe we send some routine interrogatories. I'd love to examine her closing documents for the land and check all the names and addresses and Social Security numbers, especially hers. If I have to, even as tight as money is for me, I'll pay for the deposition myself. I need to find a handhold in this. If not, I'm in line for multiple felonies and the penitentiary."

"Sitting here and listening to you, eyeballing you and weighing your story, I'm inclined to trust you, Kevin. You're very convincing. But in our world, as you know, it's not so much what the truth actually is, it's what a judge or jury will believe that then *becomes* the truth. Your situation has so many unique twists, and we have no hard evidence whatsoever. I'm not optimistic we could pull it off."

"Yep," I agree. "How ironic I'm now on the receiving end of that advice." An elderly man and his wife shamble by our booth, and I pause until they pass. "I've always warned clients that the criminal justice system doesn't calibrate well. It's like a seventies-model Snapper Comet mower — you have three basic blade settings and that's it. We can handle fistfights, killings, shootings, knife scrapes, larcenies, heterosexual divorces, boundary-line disputes and drug sales, the same old same old, but a well-done hustle as rare and layered as this will usually overwhelm a creaky contraption built by bewigged rustics who'd never heard of penicillin and would *ooh* and *aah* at a lightbulb."

She laughs and shakes her head. "True. Absolutely. And not encouraging for us. But it can't hurt to spend an hour or so with the plaintiff, and I figure I can convince Lawyers Comprehensive to underwrite that much. You realize this'll cut both ways — if I depose Melanie Culp, Jenkins will want to question you?"

"Yes," I tell her.

"I'll see what I can do," she says. "You stay out of trouble in the interim, okay?"

"I'll try my best."

"I'll interview your friend Blaine and take some photos of the security equipment."

"I appreciate your help," I say sincerely. "I'm grateful."

"I'm curious," she says. "What kind of name is SUBstitution? It makes no sense, not to me. It's as if the restaurant's advertising that it isn't bona fide, proud that you can come in for an inferior, shoddy imitation instead of a quality meal. Am I missing something?"

"Nope. But we make money, solid money, almost every day of the year. The owner, Luther, came up with the name before he passed his GED test. The old owners had a Subway franchise, and Luther incorporated part of the abandoned sign. Before you write him off, though, it seems relevant that he's a multimillionaire, whereas I'm taking out his trash and sweeping his floor."

I hear the door-alert sound. Margo's facing the entrance, and she blurts, "Heavens to Betsy, don't see that every day," and she conceals an astonished, derisive laugh with both hands spread over her mouth.

I turn and spot two men, both dressed in Confederate uniforms, both open-carrying real pistols, a 9-millimeter and a .22, and Blaine and I make eye contact, and he mouths the word *damn* and winks at us.

"The town is named after J. E. B. Stuart," I inform Margo.

"Who? Never heard of him."

"You and about everybody else in the normal world," I say. "He was a Civil War general, and imagine this, the local judge didn't think it was such a hot idea to have a portrait of a slave owner, in full Confederate military dress, hanging above the defense table at the courthouse where black citizens come for justice and fairness. So he removed the painting and suggested it be relocated to a museum. Patriots like these noblemen got extremely upset, and they're here to rally tonight. Waive the Confederate battle flag and protest against the lily-livers who want to 'erase our history.' "

180

She uncovers her mouth. Her eyes are full of twinkle and amusement. "Nothing says 'Take me seriously' like a grown man in a costume. Complete with brown Skechers."

We wait for Blaine to make and bag sandwiches for the faux soldiers, a colonel and a corporal, and the instant they're out the door, he hurries to the window and starts snapping phone photos of them and their truck.

He beelines to our table, grinning, waving his phone. "That's a perfect score, and you're my witness, Lawyer Kevin." He acknowledges Margo. "Hello, ma'am. Blaine Richardson, pleased to meet you. You're helpin' Kevin, right? He told me you might want to speak with me about the security DVD."

"I'm Margo Jordan. I'm his civil lawyer. And yes, if that's okay with you."

"What score, Blaine?" I ask. "I'll bite. Especially if Margo and I will have to be involved in the certification."

"The website's called WOCKS and GOAMERS," he says enthusiastically.

"That's a new one for me," Margo notes.

"Acronyms," Blaine explains. "Whining old Caucasian kooks. The *K* is kinda flexible. It can also stand for Klansman or, well, I won't say it in mixed company, but my pal

181

Big Money claims it's for, you know, a funny spellin' of, well, it'd end with *sucker.*"

Margo laughs and touches the corner of her eye. "Okay."

"A GOAMER's a grumpy old aggrieved man. The *M* can also be for mothereffer."

"Tell me about the scoring," she says, clearly enjoying herself.

"1860 is a perfect score. Here we had the small, junky truck with some visible rust and red mud stains on the tires, two Confederate flags flyin' proud from the bed, a bonus *Southern by birth, Rebel by the grace of God* window decal, the yellow tea-party license plate, real guns in plain view, beards, uniforms, a Bocephus *Country Boy Can Survive* bumper sticker, and I got the colonel to say 'heritage, not hate.' "

"I guess we'll have to take your word on the conversational aspect," Margo teases.

"Not hard to imagine he'd say it, though." Blaine is scrolling through pictures as he talks. "Man, this is unbeatable. Pure gold."

"M. D. Jenkins truly doesn't miss a thing," she says, turning her attention to me. "I wondered why he'd sued you in Patrick County instead of Roanoke. It seems safe to assume there might be a few more potential jurors here who don't like lawyers, especially lawyers who 'fool with that ol' dope,' as my

Uncle Edgar used to put it."

"Well, Margo, if you think about it, these might just be my people. Most of them are pretty deep into conspiracy theories, and we could hint that Caleb is connected to the New World Order cabal. They'd be eager to buy the planted-dope argument — the truth, as it turns out. I'm serious. If it comes to a trial — and I realize that's not likely — a Patrick County jury might be a fine fit for me. Sad and crazy, huh?"

When I return home, my divorce decree is waiting for me in the mailbox by the driveway. I'm no longer married to Ava, and I have nobody else to blame for the loss and failure. The clerk of court's raised seal is on the last page, as well as a blue-ink date and signature handwritten into the blanks of a stamped certification, all of it very plain and commonplace. I rub the seal between my thumb and index finger, feel its blisters and dips, and soon I'm so mad at myself that I punch the dash. I can't fault Ava, not in the least. I sit there with the engine idling, wasting gas, and I replay Jacob Shelor's rescuing me and my frantic ride down the mountain, and I recall the hospital and doctors and my medical struggles, and I think to myself,

Maybe this is some kind of cosmic object lesson. Maybe Preacher Grimes is right.

CHAPTER SEVEN

The deal Ward makes with the commonwealth's attorney allows me to turn myself in on August 1, a Monday. As expected, the magistrate denies me bond, and I'm processed into the Patrick County Jail, though thanks to Ward's cajoling and gentle arm twisting, I'm spared the humiliation of being housed with the general population. I'll stay here until Friday, when Judge Morris will hold my bond hearing in Martinsville. Randy Clay has agreed that I'll serve these four days in jail, then he'll recommend a fifty-thousand-dollar secured bond, together with an ankle monitor, daily contact with Ron Weiss, random drug screens, and my attendance at the weekly substance-abuse classes offered by the probation department.

I'm a stranger at the jail, don't know a soul, and that's how I'd like to keep it. Local, rural jails aren't ordinarily dangerous. Instead, they're filled with tedium, pettiness, card-game squabbles, pudding-cup disputes and a wholesale lack of imagination and ambition. Virtually every inmate has been here before, and most of them will be here again. And again. They stole Grandma's checkbook and will boohoo and wipe snot on their orange-jumpsuit sleeves when they testify about how sorry they are and how this will never happen a third time if they could just get into a *program.* Or, high on beer and pills, they've punched a pregnant "fiancée" — who's actually still married to her second husband — and she's arrived at court and refused to testify, so they're serving only a few days from a misdemeanor-assault plea agreement. On their bad days, they spit at the jailers; on their good days, they read the Bible and promise the volunteer preacher they'll straighten up and fly right and cling tight to Jesus.

You'd like to believe there's a core of goodness in them, a spark of essential humanity that kindness and attention and the correct training could uncover, but you'd be dead wrong — these people are too far gone, too counterfeit, too shiftless and ill-equipped, and stealing and drinking and cutting and cursing and doping and fathering fatherless babies is vulcanized into their crooked natures, immutable. And here I am, same as they are, a jailbird, breaking bread and sharing a communal shower with them.

The irony of an imprisoned criminal lawyer is stark and comical, a brutal reversal, but I simply numb myself and mark time until Friday. I'm bitterly unhappy, but after some practice, any new miseries surrender their full potency and have no incremental effect. I've lost the love of my life, almost stroked out, forfeited my livelihood and most of my money, embarrassed my profession and been reduced to running a bad sandwich shop. My immediate friends are a mongrel dog and a pot-dealing coworker half my age. Jail's not the worst of it.

I'm also still uninsured. On July 20, after ninety minutes of 1-800 quicksand, the Obamacare lady promised I was enrolled in a healthcare plan, but I never received my confirmation e-mail or a notification in my "marketplace account," and I might as well have mailed my premium payment to Mars, for all the response I've received. The first unpaid medical bill arrived the day I left the mountain to report here. From the hospital, it's over sixty thousand dollars, and that's just the start.

Except for meals and showers, I'm isolated in my own cell, thankfully alone, and I mostly sit cross-legged on my wafer of a mattress, my eyes closed, the sticky air shrouding me, heavy and scented by kitchen grease and the smell of seventy other men, many of them unhealthy and unbathed, and I think about everything I can except the present, make myself distracted and find solace because I don't have to claw and fret and scramble for the next few days, a respite of sorts. Only so much I can accomplish inside the bars and painted cinder block, and I convince myself that the inertia is a comfort instead of a burden.

On Thursday morning, however, following my shower, after I return my disposable razor to the jailer, I inquire about a pen and tablet, and an obliging officer named Chad brings me a legal pad and a black ballpoint. I make notes for my bond hearing, consider and rehearse what I should tell the judge, then brainstorm about the bigger picture, jot down possibilities that might snag Caleb Opportunity and set me free from the civil suit and criminal charges. I ponder and scribble for more than an hour, but nothing new or compelling appears on the several yellow pages. I'm stymied.

Outside the cell door, I hear two inmates rowing and cursing over a pack of missing peanut-butter Nabs. Seconds later, another prisoner's bitching because he hasn't been temporarily released to attend his daddy's funeral. "You can't leave until we see a court order tellin' us you can leave," an exasperated officer explains three times. "Not until a judge signs the papers."

I write *order* and *leave* on my pad, then print the name *Dave Worthy* and follow it with a colon. Dave was the best lawyer I've ever known, and until he died in 2012, I would occasionally ask him for advice if I was involved in a tough case. I'd been practicing about two years when I watched him dismantle a plaintiff's expert in a personal-injury trial, the best cross-examination I've ever seen. Later, I complimented him on how nimble and prepared he was, how he seemed able to turn on a dime no matter the answer from a combative, professional witness. Dave was a friendly man who rarely smiled and never wasted words. "A good lawyer can turn on a dime," he informed me, "but a great lawyer doesn't have to. He's anticipated the twists long before they arrive and is already traveling in the right direction."

Amen, I write after the colon. "Amen," I say loudly, and it sounds deep and stately when it echoes off the metal and cinder block.

Two solicitous bailiffs help Judge Tyler Morris climb the modest steps toward the bench in the Martinsville courtroom. He revels in the attention and trappings, isn't the least bit embarrassed by his frailty, and once he's situated on the top step, he's handed his cane and begins creeping toward the judge's catbird seat.

Morris is a wretched jurist, a lifer who can't let go of the gig and its influence. He doesn't have the energy or concern to keep abreast of the law, probably last read a statute twenty years ago and now simply wings it in his rulings, orders whatever strikes him as "fair" and becomes irate and punitive if a lawyer politely directs him to the correct law as it exists in this decade. He sees the world in the black-and-white shades of a 1960s small-town chamber of commerce president, and for defendants like me, that means any drug use is viewed as a corrupt weakness, contagious and leftist and anti-police and anti-American and exactly what's wrong with this dadgum country of ours.

I'm allowed to dress in a blazer, tie and gray slacks, and Ward's beside me at the defendant's table. I've sat at these tables thousands of times before, the last occasion in Roanoke — June 6, 2015 — where I won a malicious-wounding case for a brick mason who'd been in a bloody bar melee. Randy Clay is as good as his word. He introduces himself to Judge Morris and announces that the commonwealth and defendant have a joint recommendation on bond.

"The defendant will post a fifty-thousand-dollar secured bond," Clay says, "and he'll be required to have daily contact with a probation officer and attend an intensive drug-education program. He'll also be confined to his residence via a HEM anklet, at his expense, and subject to random drug screens."

"Is that correct?" Morris is bald, and his face pinches forward into a rounded beak. He favors one of those giant Galapagos tortoises.

"Good morning, Your Honor," Ward replies. "Yes, that's accurate. For the record, Mr. Moore has *already* completed the classes you ordered as part of his under-advisement Roanoke case. He finished those in March."

Morris locks his dull, beady, tortoise eyes on me. I'm hoping he's unaware of Virginia's current bond statute and doesn't realize there's a presumption against my being released from jail. He doesn't speak but makes a show of tracking back to Randy Clay. "How old are you, son?" he asks.

"Thirty-eight," Clay says. "I probably appear older because every year as a commonwealth's attorney ought to count as five."

Several people in the courtroom grin or chuckle, but not my prehistoric judge. "I've been doing this job for almost forty years," he crows, "and I often wonder what's happening to our profession. How do you think this will look to the public, Mr. Clay? I hold lawyers to a higher standard. As I should. What Mr. Moore has done reflects badly on our profession. He's smeared us all. I gave him one break — the lady prosecutor from northern Virginia pushed that foolishness on me — and I knew when I did it that a dope addict doesn't change his stripes. I said on the record it was a mistake. And now here we all sit again, with a new, wet-behind-the-ears prosecutor singing the same song, only this go-round, Mr. Kevin Moore has graduated to selling powerful narcotics and carrying a firearm. And you want me to turn him loose?"

I watch Clay take a quick sideways glance at Ward and shift his weight before he replies. "I agree, sir," he says, and his tone is meek, bordering on reverent. "I understand where you're coming from, and I often think I was born fifty years too late for our profession." He pauses. "Of course, unfortunately for the commonwealth, the notion of bond is entrenched in the Constitution."

I clench my hands into nervous fists and hold my breath for a moment — waiting to see if Morris has any idea about the bond presumption.

"There's a lot of things in the Constitution," he huffs, and Ward and Clay exchange a quick, subtle look.

"Which is why," Clay continues, "I've reluctantly agreed to a bond, but required *double* what we'd normally impose, plus house arrest with the monitoring cost paid by the defendant."

"I don't have to accept it," Morris snaps. "I'm certainly not bound by whatever you and Armstrong cooked up."

I notice the knot at the turn in Ward's jawline become full and pronounced, but his expression remains staid.

"Understood, sir," Clay responds. "And we'd gladly invite your guidance."

"Judge," Ward adds, "we're not even certain my client can make a twenty-five-thousand-dollar bond, much less double what many other similarly charged defendants would have to post."

"Then let's double that," Morris proclaims, visibly pleased with himself. "Bond's set at a hundred thousand, secured. Plus everything else you two lawyers agreed on." He bangs a wooden gavel.

I cup my mouth and lean to Ward's ear. "Never, ever, have I seen a judge use a gavel. Never."

"Me neither," Ward whispers. "What is it they say about men and sports cars? If you have enough of a dick, you don't need a Corvette? That rule translates pretty well to Morris and his hammer."

"Nice to meet you, Your Honor," Clay says as Morris begins a labored rise from his chair.

"Hope you learned something here today, son," Morris answers.

"Indeed. Several lessons." There's no trace of needle or irony in his reply.

"Judge," Ward says, "these cases are here on indictments, but we nevertheless have a pretty good idea of the facts and issues. We'd respectfully request the court set a few hours for a motions hearing. We have some serious concerns about the search and seizure in this matter. I've alerted Mr. Clay."

Morris stops shuffling toward the steps. He grips his cane near the crook, doesn't point it, but instead gives it a small shake in our direction. "Yeah, you're entitled to your hearing, but I wouldn't count on those chickens hatching anytime soon."

As I'm being shackled for my return trip to Stuart, I overhear Randy Clay tell Ward, with a perfect low-key delivery, that "it appears we have a pro-commonwealth judge."

"Your biggest problem," Ward answers, "is that he'll cheat so much for you he'll muck up your case and give me all grades of appeal issues." He glances at the empty judge's chair. "Thanks for the way you handled this," he says to Clay. "I told Kevin that you're a class act."

"We'll see if you still think so when I prosecute the stuffings out of Mr. Moore, and he ends up in the penitentiary. Bond is bond. Trial's a different creature altogether. He's run out of chances with the commonwealth, especially if you drag me and my office through a bunch of nonsensical hearings about the dope and pistol in his car. The probation officer had a court order allowing the search and a failed drug test moments before."

"Well, Randy," Ward says, his dander rising, "you have a *Judge Morris* court order.

We'll see how far that takes you once we leave the town of Bedrock."

I'm back at the homeplace Friday afternoon, but I'm not permitted to walk to the double oak or the pond because they're past the boundary of my electronic confinement, so I make several exercise trips between the porch and edge of the yard, enjoy the sun, the long views, the hummingbirds hovering and darting above a planter of red impatiens, and the spotless mountain air, which has gathered into a breeze strong enough to raise the undersides of the highest tree leaves. I'm allowed fifteen minutes of grace at eight every night to feed the horses and check the fences. I can drive straight to my drug classes on Tuesday and Thursday evenings, and I can travel directly to and from work. If Ron Weiss requests a drug screen, I have permission to meet him at his office. House arrest, we call it in the legal trade.

Because I deeded our property to Ava and now own no land with which to secure my bond, I had to pay a Caddy-driving slickster bondsman named George O. Wood seventy-five hundred bucks to serve as my surety. His card reads: 24/7 KNOCK ON WOOD FOR BAIL GOOD LUCK. That's money spent, money I'll never see again, a chunk of my savings gone, but I'm out of jail, and I have a Dave Worthy plan and high hopes, and I've convinced myself that if I can finally catch a tiny break, I'll jujitsu the commonwealth and maybe even be better off than I was before. I'm determined to be optimistic. Like I told Ava, there's a lot to be said for rebirths and spectacular second acts.

On the way to the barn for my fifteen-minute furlough, I kneel and let Tesla and his hens peck scratch grain from my palm. Always a gentleman, he waits for his flock to eat their fill before he dives in. He looks at me with a sideways head and a single ringed eye. "That's right, big man," I tell him. "We're done fretting."

My Lexis subscription is still valid, and I spend the evening studying the search-and-seizure issue in both United States Supreme Court cases and decisions from other states, then I begin drafting my trial brief. My audience isn't Judge Morris, but instead the appellate courts that will have to reverse his ruling. I do my daily Google search for the name "Melanie Culp," and nothing new appears. I e-mail Margo Jordan to check on the deposition in the civil case, and politely remind her we need to take a crack at questioning the mysterious Miss Culp under oath. Around midnight, I pour a glass of well water, carry it to the screened-in porch and fall asleep on the outdoor sofa amidst the sounds of boisterous frogs and trilling bugs and dogs occasionally barking at one another in the distance, give and take, canine pals chewing the fat across the mountain laurels.

Saturday morning is hot, even in Meadows of Dan, a still, sluggish, sullen seventy degrees at sunrise. My first task of the day is to phone Melvin.

"I have some news that's not the greatest," I inform him. "I feel obligated to tell you, since I'm living in your house."

"Okay," Melvin says. "But don't beat around the bush. I'm at the airport, in a hurry."

"Although they're baseless, I've been charged with two new felonies. A meth case and a firearms case."

"Damn," he replies. "Sounds serious. Serious as a crutch."

"I give you my solemn word that it's been almost a year since I touched drugs or alcohol. My promise. Nor was I selling meth while packing a gun. The short version is that I'm being manipulated in an insurance scam."

"You still have all your teeth?" Melvin asks.

"Yep," I reply.

"And my belongings are all accounted for? Nothing stolen?"

"Everything is still here, and I'm doing a conscientious job of caretaking."

Melvin speaks the instant I finish. "I'll send Barnie Hylton over to have a look around. Can't blame me for that, can you? Simply smart business."

"I understand. No problem. We'll both feel better about the situation."

"Anyone else staying there?"

"Only me."

"I hear through the Mountain Mafia grapevine that you own a dog. Is the dog there, Kevin? If my bloodline rooster gets hurt, I'll take it out of your hide."

"I rescued a puppy from the dumpster at work. His name is Nelson, and he stays down at SUBstitution. He sleeps in the utility shed. I realize how much you prize the birds. He's never set a paw on the place."

"By the way, my wife and I will need the house for the week of October twenty-fourth. Leaf season."

"Sure. I'll make arrangements." As part of

our deal, I agreed to relocate to an efficiency at the Blue Ridge Motel whenever Melvin and his wife visit; there's a guest cottage on the property, but he's exceptionally private and wouldn't want me underfoot.

"Keep me in the loop," he says, and he's gone, almost cutting off the last word when he disconnects.

Next, I phone the health-care outfit and attempt to pry Lilly Heath's cell number from the receptionist. She agrees only to relay a message and ask that Lilly contact me. "Company policy," she declares.

Finally, I ring Minivan Dan at his mansion in Atlanta.

"Do you know who Lil Wayne is, Kevin?" he asks after he hears my voice.

"A rapper. My former paralegal Keisha's a big fan. Also known as Tunechi. Impressed?"

"Right you are. And guess what he just bought?"

"Uh, weed and Jolly Ranchers for the sizzurp?"

"Nope. Three Mini Thunder custom pieces, works of art all, and he's planning to use one in his next video. The fuse is now lit for my sales explosion."

"Well," I rib him, "that must about triple last year's sales."

"Thanks for the market analysis. What's up?"

"Because you're my friend and you're sort of invested in the situation already, I wanted you to know that the commonwealth did in fact indict me on the new charges. I'm on house arrest, wearing the electronic jewelry, and headed to trial on distribution and firearms charges."

"Damn, that's harsh shit. Sorry. Any luck with your insurance?"

"Nothing. My first check's never been cashed, I received a form letter from the exchange asking for more info, and my original phone contact — the nice lady who finally told me I was covered — seems to have left the insurance biz for greener pastures. The random new voices at the call center aren't helpful in the least. I might as well be talking to Nelson."

"You know I'll lend a hand if you need anything. Money, a fishing buddy, legal help, a superior minivan. Whatever. I'm your boy."

"Thanks. I had to spend four nights in jail before I made bond, and the downtime helped me find a more rational take on where I am. My health's stabilizing, and I understand the legal system — it's my home field. I know where all the Easter eggs, trapdoors and bonus levels are. I can fix this. No need to mope and whine, or act like a defeatist. I've razzle-dazzled guilty people right out the courthouse door scot-free, and hell, I'm innocent."

"Let me know if I can help. Nancy sends her love."

Melvin's antiquated phone makes each call a mystery, a closed set of velvet curtains; you never know who it'll be on a Monday evening at nine-fifteen, and discovering Lilly on the other end of the connection when I pick up is a happy surprise.

"I hope you're continuing your recovery," she says.

"I am. Better every day. A big part of that's due to your skill and encouragement."

She laughs. "That's a little overstated, but I appreciate the compliment. Checking your blood pressure and taking your temperature weren't medical miracles. Speaking of which, did you ever schedule your MRI? You need to have your dissection evaluated at three months. We discussed that."

"I'm on it, ma'am," I promise her. "They can do it in Martinsville, and I've been working with Dr. Wallace's delphic assistant to have it scheduled. I'm not insured yet, so we've been hesitant to set a specific date.

I'm waiting to see if my policy ever *is* confirmed. I'm not even two months past the stroke, so I've got some time to play with."

"No matter what — insurance or cash money — you need to get that scan."

"I plan to," I tell her.

There's a brief silence, two or three dead seconds, while I consider how to steer the conversation away from my health and her nursing duties. "I was just checking," I tell her, "to see if my possibilities have improved now that you've been gone awhile."

She laughs some more, and it's very sweet and genuine. "Not long enough," she answers, but her tone's agreeable and light and far from final. "Is that why you wanted me to call?"

"Yeah," I say. "You must've assumed as much, no?"

"It crossed my mind."

"So how about a crumb? A little glimmer? Something to keep me from becoming despondent and giving up?"

"Meaning?" she asks.

"I'll take anything: a middle name, a favorite song, the best size Louis Vuitton purse, your birthday, whatever."

"Six," she says.

"Okay. Your lucky number?"

"Nope. It's one of the ten digits in my old phone number. Not the new number, not my current number, but my number when I lived in Ohio. The disconnected, invalid number."

"And so it begins," I say. "Thanks. Wonderful. I appreciate the tiny gift."

"You noticed I'm calling from the agency's office, didn't you?"

"There's no caller ID here," I tell her. "It's safe to use your personal phone."

"I wasn't sure, but I didn't want to risk it."

"It would be a lot simpler if I could contact you without going through your employer."

"Simpler for you, perhaps," she says. "But not for me."

"E-mail?" I ask. "Heck, Nigerian flimflammers and the power company have your e-address. Bill collectors. Sears and Roebuck."

"*Roebuck?* How old are you?"

"Born in 1973."

"Here you go," she says, her mood still playful. "It has a small *a* with a circle around it near the middle."

CHAPTER EIGHT

After my jail release, I enjoy drinking my early coffee on the front porch, sitting in a 1960s glider that Melvin had refurbished at a Galax machine shop. I occasionally plant my toes on the painted boards and rock slow, level swings back and forth, the metal joints greased and smooth. Thursday morning, while the sky is still being birthed from bursts and streaks of orange, purple and deep red, I hear a vehicle coming toward the house. I stand and walk to the last step, and I spot a white truck, a diesel from the sound of it, loaded with lumber, chain-link panels and a stack of cinder blocks. More improvements for the pasture, I assume, though the panels seem unusual.

The truck stops, and the driver and two other men, one young and fleshy, exit the cab. The driver's wearing sunglasses, even at 7:00 a.m., and his name, *Barry,* is stamped inside a white oval on his blue work shirt. He's neat and immaculate. The shirt is spick-and-span; the pants have a crease. He approaches me and takes off the glasses right before saying hello.

"You Kevin Moore?" he asks. He smooths a graying goatee as he speaks. He hangs the glasses on the neck of his shirt.

"Yes."

"I'm Barry Ellis," he says, "head of maintenance for Mr. Harrell over at Micrometrics. He sent me out here to build a dog pen."

"A dog pen? Melvin? You sure?"

"Positive." Ellis sets his hands on his hips. He seems cocky and high-strung. His voice becomes firmer. "There's never any room for doubt with Mr. Harrell. He was real definite. He wants it done by quittin' time tomorrow. I'm supposed to put it on the east side of the barn. Mr. Harrell drew it up and faxed me the design. It's a regular palace."

"I'm surprised," I tell Ellis.

"No shit," he answers. "Me too. I'm behind at the plant, but here I am workin' for the SPCA. To beat all, Mr. Harrell awarded me his nephew to help." He jabs a thumb sideways at the heavy kid. "Right, Jethro?"

"My name ain't Jethro," the kid mutters.

"You need anything from me?"

"Nope." He shades his eyes with the spiffy Oakleys again. "Mr. Harrell said to inform you that if so much as a feather went missing from one of his chickens, he'd *take it out of your hide.*"

"Then, for sure, you'll need to build a quality lot."

"Yeah. I'll do my absolute best, Kevin. Backhoe's on the way, concrete's due at three."

"I've known Melvin since we were boys," I say, "and he's as unpredictable as they come. He's really something else."

"That's why he's a multimillionaire and me and you are pinchin' our pennies."

I go inside and phone Melvin to thank him, but there's no answer. I call again before leaving for SUBstitution, and I'm sent to his message box. That night, I receive an e-mail from him: "OK. UR welcome. So bring the hound, at least I have some protection now. NO FCKUPS. MH."

The next morning, Friday, when Blaine arrives at the restaurant, he has his pal Big Money with him, and they enter the kitchen nearly shoulder to shoulder, both smiling and animated. They're so loose and giddy that I wonder if Blaine's been sampling his own product.

"News flash, Lawyer Kevin," Blaine says. "We located some treasure for you."

"What's up, Kevin?" Big Money asks.

"You are, looks like," I say.

"Whatever," he replies.

Blaine drops his backpack onto the counter. "We Sherlocked the *full* story on your bud Flanagan. You thought we'd forgotten about you, huh?"

"I never lost faith," I assure him.

"Flanagan has a sister, lady named April Logan," Big Money says. He's dressed in colorful shorts that cover his knees, keeps his hands in the front pockets.

"She's got a fat job at the Shadrich Foundation," Blaine says. "Over a million a year, with perks like a car and club dues. She's the number-two person, basically wears the top hat and runs the circus. Does all the local morning-show TV rounds. They're the South Carolina humanitarians with the Gulfstream painted like a ginormous dove."

Big Money grins. "Doin' tutorin' and 'traditional education' for at-risk kids and burning sixty-three percent of contributions on overhead."

"So that gig," Blaine says, "would go straight down the tubes there at a puritan charity if she was found guilty of a little

208

DUI ticket."

"And let me guess," I say. "No conviction."

"No conviction," Blaine confirms. "According to the police report and newspapers, she was passed out in a Myrtle Beach parkin' lot, literally unconscious on her steering wheel."

"So she can't even blow for the test," Big Money adds, "and the cops take her blood to see just how high she is."

"But . . . wait for it, Lawyer Kevin," Blaine says. "The state lab loses her sample. Kaboom. It vanishes."

Big Money is concentrating on his phone. "Her version's that she was distraught and emotional because she'd just visited a friend with cancer and had to pull over and was in a 'spiritual trance.' " He holds the phone in front of my face. "Here's the Zen warrior's mug shot. Nick Nolte and James Brown ain't got diddly on her."

I laugh. "Damn. She's blitzed."

"You think?" Blaine says. "But she spun this like nobody's business. Played offense. All kinds of people from Shadrich claim they'd *just seen her* and swear she was sober and normal. The foundation made noise about suing the cops for not respectin' her First Amendment right to express herself in

209

public. Never even went to court."

"Well, this explains a lot," I tell them. "My friend Dan's IT people researched Flanagan's wife and kids and parents and didn't find anything."

"He and the dove lady are technically half-related," Big Money notes. "Same mama, different daddies and last names, but they were raised as brother and sister. I can promise you won't find a single picture of them together online. Not a paragraph with both their names in it. Nothin' to connect them."

"She does e-mail him, though," Blaine says. "Sends him these cute nature pictures with encouraging messages through his easily hacked state account with the Atari-grade security protections that were lame in the nineties." He turns away, and he and his friend make a show of whistling tunelessly and peering into the parking lot.

"I don't need to hear any more of the particulars," I say.

"Not the end of the story," Big Money tells me. He and Blaine face me again. "I have to admit this white-haired-dude-set-me-up plot sounded entirely sketchy, so I was just helpin' Blaine for jollies and to see what we could beat or crack. But we found some evidence that makes you look less like a guilty methhead."

"Three months after the dove lady's sprung from her cage," Blaine says, "and the DUI is dismissed, Holy Baltic Avenue, Batman, the Shadrich Foundation, which is private and operates in secret, plunks down three million bucks to buy property in Beckley, West Virginia." He's now focused on his phone, swiping from screen to screen. "Take a look on Google Maps what that money'll buy you." He hands me the phone.

"The place is *beneath* ghetto." Big Money wags his index finger. "Even the toothless Kid Rock tweakers who ain't afraid to crap in a fast-food bag and bunk with roaches aren't crashin' here. Tax value's a little under forty grand."

"Perfect," I say. "A private purchase in a bigger-but-not-major city. I'm certain it was billed as Shadrich's new transition center or some such. Eradicating the blight. Marching to the heart of the problem and bringing services to the most needy."

"Never any public mention of them buying it," Blaine says. "They kept it completely under the radar."

I lick my lips, lower my gaze. "Tell me, please, gentlemen, that the seller was First-Rate or MAB." I'm staring at the scarred, scratched tile floor as I speak.

"Sorry, Lawyer Kevin," Blaine answers. "Seller was an LLC called S. Smith Holdings."

"Damn," I blurt and shake my head. "And let me guess, S. Smith is a black hole."

"It's conveniently located in George Town," Big Money says. "For those of you who aren't into travel and leisure, that would be your Cayman Islands. Offshore trickeration."

"This has to be connected," I say. "Has to be. It's how they operate. They rescue *her,* and she makes *them* several million. Spends other people's money to pay them off, with nobody the wiser. Then, as a little lagniappe, they circle back and have her lean on her brother. They still have leverage because of the Beckley purchase — let the donor list get wind of that monstrosity and watch the Shadrich coffers go empty. She convinces brother Flanagan that all he has to do is bluff a guy who's a damn druggie anyway. It'll never amount to a hill of beans — no harm in the long run. Kevin Moore will get the message, he'll play ball, the fake charges will never see the light of day and sister dove's soaring once again. She persuades him that all he's really doing is delivering a message. Nobody gets hurt."

"Of course arch villain Flanagan's hosed

212

now," Blaine remarks. "They've trapped him too. Can't admit he lied and tampered with evidence unless he wants to be on the Green Goblin side of the bars."

"Technically," Big Money notes, "he's not an arch villain. The peroxide dude is the arch villain. Flanagan's a henchman."

"Guys," I say, "this is great. *Amazing.* Thanks so much. It's the first crack. I'm convinced I can win this, and you geniuses have given me an unbelievable boost."

Blaine and Big Money glance at each other, then look at me. Blaine speaks first. "We enjoyed the ride. But you don't think that we'd leave you hangin', do you? Serve you a soda and chips and deny you the entrée?"

"Okay," I say.

"You tell him," Blaine says to Big Money.

"You can," Big Money replies.

"No, man, *you.*"

Big Money steps back and mock-bows. "Your honors, Blaine."

"Okay," Blaine answers. He tucks his shirt deeper into his khakis. "Money and I learned that a ton of clerk's offices all over the country allow online access to documents. You know, deeds and wills. Land stuff. Taxes. Marriages. Debts. Not all of 'em, but a bunch —"

"It would take forever and a day to go through every office in every state and check the records," Big Money interrupts. "And you have to set up accounts and passwords for every flippin' place."

"So we coded our own search program that works across all the different platforms and software. Put so you'd understand it, we went state to state and county to county knockin' on doors. If there's no door, no online records, our e-gumshoe kept moving. If we received an answer, we went inside."

"Once inside," Big Money says, "our sleuth rolls to the bar, orders a whiskey and flashes the bartender a hundred. Asks if he's ever heard of FirstRate or MAB."

"The secret sauce is speed, accuracy and adaptability," Blaine adds. "All this data's meant to be accessed, but the different states use different software. We created a universally recognized guest. A type-O crawler. Not to brag, but I'd bet most people who tried this would stall at each office — you'd get through the virtual door and never leave. And probably never find what you're lookin' for."

"But not us. A little glitchy to start with, and for a while, especially in Oregon and California, we were perceived as a virus and quarantined, but in the end, we cross-referenced every land sale you can find on-line."

I clear my throat. "My lawyer, Margo Jordan, told me she'd found some other transactions involving MAB. There're a real company, and they do some legit deals for window dressing. Same with FirstRate."

Blaine and Big Money are quiet for a moment. Blaine breaks the silence: "Did Margo also tell you that S. Smith Holdings and your friend FirstRate did a fishy land deal in Florida four years ago?"

"No, she didn't," I say. "Damn. Incredible."

Blaine takes a twelve-inch roll from a clear bag, holds the bread above his head and lets it fall to the floor. "Mic drop, mother-fuckers."

"Diamonds in my chain," Big Money declares. He snarls, hunches his shoulders and flashes gang signs with both hands. I'm certain they're completely meaningless and made up for the moment, and you can tell he's just having fun. "You heard me, got *diamonds* in my chain."

"Fanboy gangster nerds," I say. "Sorry. *Gangsta.*" I grin, and it segues into a chuckle. "What could be better? Can't thank you both enough. Wow."

"My pleasure," Blaine tells me. "And rest assured, I'm repping two-twenty-five benches at the gym. No Pokémon or math club on my résumé. Money just earned his brown belt. His girlfriend's Miss November on the JMU sorority fund-raising calendar." He smiles. He's good-natured, and there's still a trickle of boy in him. "So the *nerds* want to know: How's the shine on *your* action these days?"

In March, Luther was recovering from hernia surgery, and I had to travel to a country store just past the state line and meet his "source," an assistant manager from a North Carolina Lowes, and pay the jittery grocer cash for a cooler of out-of-date meat, food that, according to company rules, should've been donated to charity or thrown in the garbage. After Big Money leaves, Blaine and I stock the counter with the usual marginal meat, and I put all the date-stamped lids in a small trash bag, knot it twice and immediately take it to the dumpster. Luther wants the telltale evidence gone quickly. Yesterday was the sell-by deadline for the honey ham and smoked turkey, but they'll be safe to eat for another week.

We load the vegetables and squirt bottles,

and then I phone Margo. Her secretary promptly transfers me without any fuss or questions about why I'm calling. "Good morning," Margo says. "I got your e-mails, and your insurer has agreed for me to take Miss Culp's deposition. It wasn't a hard sell, in fact. I was planning to get in touch with you today. Given my schedule and Jenkins's schedule, we're looking at late September or early October."

"Excellent. Thanks for going to bat for me."

"Well, as we discussed, it makes sense to at least do the basics before writing a seven-figure draft."

"I have some more good news," I tell her. "I've discovered a link between Flanagan and my insurance fraud."

"That *is* good news," she answers. "Let's hear it."

"Flanagan has a sister named April Logan. She's a honcho at the Shadrich Foundation —"

"The gaudy dove plane," Margo interrupts. "For the cost of the paint job, you could buy textbooks for every school in Appalachia. Talk about scammers. But they have some righteous TV commercials."

"True," I say. "April catches a South Carolina DUI, guilty as sin, drooling drunk in a parking lot, and her blood test is, somehow, lost."

"There's some charity for you," Margo says.

"She walks free. Nothing happens to her, and she even claims she's been mistreated by the cops. Probably made money on her boozing via an all-caps fund-raising letter warning the donors that their Constitutional rights are under attack by the government."

"Yeah," Margo scoffs, "the cops are always unfairly targeting drunk drivers."

"A few months later, the Shadrich Foundation buys a three-million-dollar piece of property in Beckley, West Virginia. Think about it: big enough city that the purchase doesn't set tongues to wagging, far enough off the beaten path that the investigative reporters from *The Washington Post* won't bump into it. Sort of similar to Roanoke."

"Does this April lady have any connections to Beckley?" Margo asks.

"No, not that I'm aware of."

"So who's the seller?" she asks. "Be handy if it were MAB or FirstRate."

"Some obscure, bogus LLC named S. Smith Holdings. Could you be anymore generic? *S. Smith.* Tax value for this slum corner is less than forty thousand. Shadrich drops three million."

"I'm betting they buy a fair amount of land," Margo says. "Who knows? Maybe they have insider information. Maybe this area's about to be revitalized with shopping centers and magnet schools. They call it land speculation for a reason."

"Here's the payoff: Years earlier, S. Smith did a Florida deal with, guess who, our old friend FirstRate."

"Really? Now, that's interesting. *Damn.*"

"No kidding." I'm upbeat, my voice enthusiastic.

"So," she says, "let's walk through this. We wouldn't be able to leverage April, because she has no influence with her masters. Embarrassing her, deposing her, putting her on boil — none of that will yield much. She'll deny everything, and we can't contradict her. And if she was recruited the same as you were, she truly can't give us a name or a traceable person. But her brother might be a softer target."

"Trouble is," I answer, "he's no more likely to confess and tell us the truth than she is, and let's be honest, I'm the guy with his butt in a legal vise and a prior drug habit, so every time you ask Flanagan a question, it'll seem loony and far-fetched, the pitiful defense of another guilty criminal grabbing at straws."

"We also have to concede that the connection is pretty indirect and perfectly legal on paper. It doesn't — from a courtroom perspective — establish anything. We could, with a little creativity and a few keystrokes, probably tie Flanagan to Kevin Bacon. Or Jack Ruby. Or Sasquatch."

"Yeah," I admit, "but I wanted you to be aware of this. As much as anything, I hope it'll persuade you that I'm not cutting my defense from whole cloth. That I'm not a desperate liar. This is the first tiny crack in their wall. My first genuine opening."

Margo sighs. "What we need — the only thing that'll save us in your case — is a link between Melanie Culp and MAB or First-Rate. Or a connection between her and their principals, who seem next to impossible to discover, since there's so much corporate hide-and-seek."

"Exactly. But we're getting warmer."

"Well," Margo says, "warmer is relative. We were naked in a blizzard, and now we have a hat."

"It's a start," I reply.

"By the way, how'd you find all this? That's some serious in-depth searching."

"It's public record," I say. "I have a lot of free time — house arrest will do that for you — and plenty of motivation." A lawyerly answer, true on its face.

"If we could locate another wrinkle or a piece of hard evidence, I might call my friend Bo McKelway at the *Times-Dispatch* and see if he'll bird-dog this. Would you care if I gave him your version of events? It'd probably put an unpleasant spotlight on you and your past problems."

"My name in unflattering print is the least of my worries right now, Margo, especially if he's able to expose these people."

"You feeling okay?" she asks. "Still on the mend?"

"Yeah. Thanks. My ankle and leg occasionally plague me, but the limp is mostly cured, only affects me in the evening after eight hours on my feet. No complaints."

As I'm leaving for the day and preparing Nelson's dinner, his kibble topped with a slice of Lowes roast beef that is truly too close to spoiled for humans to chance, I notice a sound, a rustle and a faint, faint squeak coming from behind a cardboard box of napkins on a shelf to my left. I stop and listen. Cock my ear. I don't hear the sounds again. Nothing. I fetch the broom, hold it by the straw end and use the wooden handle to slide the box across the shelf. I expose a black tray, about a foot long, with a gray lump rising from its center. I move closer, squinting. "Sonofabitch," I blurt, startled.

A small mouse is stuck in a glue trap, the little animal both alive and disintegrating, its fur and skin missing on its mired side so that I can see its organs and coils of wan, milky guts. Its upward eye blinks. Its free pink foot spasms and jerks. I feel a profound pity that quickly gives way to anger. I take down the trap, and the adrenaline shock makes my hands shake and sears through the damaged path in my mouth and face.

"Blaine!" I shout.

He peeks around the corner. "Yeah?"

I show him the trap. "What do you know about this?"

He comes toward me. "Oh damn. Diabolical. That poor mouse."

"Did you put this on the shelf?"

"Hell no, Lawyer Kevin. I'm no villain. That shit's Luther's idea. When Izzy closed the other night, she told me Luther'd seen some droppings and set a regular trap, but it kept missin' the target, so he went full kryptonite. Man, I had no idea this is how they worked. You can buy this kind of torture in a store? I'm no mice fan, the little sneaks could land us in trouble with the health department, but this is heartless."

"Listen," I tell him. "Take this thing

222

outside, end its suffering and toss the whole mess in the dumpster." I rest the glue tray and perishing mouse on top of a broken microwave.

"Me?"

"You," I instruct him. "I'm your boss, and I can't do it. Probably couldn't have before my stroke, damn sure can't now."

"Roger that, Lord Mansfield," Blaine says quietly.

"Are there any more traps?" I ask.

"Don't think so," he answers, "but I'll talk to Izzy. We've really never had a problem with mice or rats. Don't know why Luther decided it was so urgent."

"Pitiable creature was just looking for a bite to eat, just piddling along, living its own minor life, and — with no warning — *bam,* it's stopped dead in its tracks. Never saw it coming. Sound familiar?"

"A double whammy for you," Blaine says sympathetically.

"It's none of my business, and I'm the last person to give you advice, but I thought you were headed for Virginia Tech this fall. I figured you'd be giving your notice at this shithole and moving on. Wasn't that the plan?"

"Academics are a minefield, Kevin. Tough. Holy fuckin' bait and switch, Batman. My

223

adviser at the community college screwed up — and I asked and asked and triple-checked when I enrolled — and one of my math credits won't transfer, plus I need another science credit, basic shit I could've done blindfolded if they'd bothered to tell me. My adviser swears that Tech is changin' the requirements midstream, that it's their error, but it really doesn't matter who dropped the ball. I can't enter as a junior unless I take the two classes."

"That's awful," I tell him, "and wrong. I'm so sorry."

"Yep." He's holding a spray bottle and a paper towel. "Here's the fanboy nerd's real world: number one in my high school class, crushed my boards, worked this Joe job since I was sixteen, won the scholarships, landed the grants, and I'm hung out to dry by a bunch of dimwitted pencil-pushers. Also, I need twenty-one K for tuition and room and board. If I live like a pauper at school, I'll need another six thousand for expenses on top of that. Twenty-seven thousand, Lawyer Kevin, that's my goal, and even with grants and scholarships and my mega-salary here, I'm around thirty-five hundred short. And, hey, my supposedly rich parents with their huge combined *five-figure* income and two other kids make *too damn much* for me to get any more help."

"What're you planning to do?"

"Work here with you, and enroll in January or maybe even start at Tech next summer. The advantage is it'll spread my bills out, but I'll basically lose a year, be behind my class. I'm pretty discouraged, in case you can't tell."

"Don't blame you."

"I thought about enrolling at Virginia Tech now, then makin' the classes up at PH in the summer, but of course, they don't teach the fuckin' courses I need in the summer at Patrick Henry."

"I'll give you two thousand," I volunteer. "You deserve it."

"I can't take it, Kevin. I appreciate the offer, but you're in the lawyerin' penalty box and as hard up as I am for dollars."

"I have money in the bank and very few expenses. It's the least I can do." I gesture at the mouse trap. "Consider it hazard pay."

That night, I use Melvin's computer to search for "S. Smith Holdings" on the Cayman Islands Department of Commerce and Investment's website. I'm not surprised to learn that the only information available is the name and type of the company, its date of registration, the address of its home office and its current status. I'm also not surprised to discover that S. Smith Holdings is listed as "defunct."

On a different page, I check the names "S. Smith Holdings Florida" and "S. Smith Holdings Carib," and both are shown as available for current corporate use. I download a PDF file that contains the blank paperwork for starting a business in the Caymans; it warns that the government recommends I hire a firm or solicitor to assist me. There's also a paragraph boasting that all business details are held in strict confidence: "Disclosure of information by government officials, professional agents, attorneys and accountants and their staffs is prohibited." Caleb Opportunity and Melanie Culp are world-class grifters and won't make many mistakes. *But let's see how you fuckers like this move,* I think to myself.

I choose "S. Smith Holdings Carib" for *my* new LLC and type the name into the form.

Chapter Nine

I can't breathe, can't suck enough oxygen from the air to satisfy my lungs, and I'm suffocating, dry-mouthed and panting, and my left arm is numb. I hear blood thumping and gushing inside my skull. The room starts to fill in around me, silhouettes and vague shapes, everything dark except the clock-radio numbers, which are an unmistakable, infernal red: 2:18. I'm having another stroke, alone in the middle of the night in the middle of nowhere, and for a moment, I surrender, quit, think *What the fuck?* and consider doing nothing, just closing my eyes and funereally folding my arms across my chest, come what may. Instead, I stumble to the phone, push-button 911, and incredibly, three volunteer rescue squad members are at the house ten minutes later, the siren and strobe lights spooking the horses so that they snort and spin and buck and tear off for the far corner of the pasture.

"I thought we'd done whipped this nonsense." It's Jacob Shelor. He's wearing jeans, tennis shoes and a white Meadows of Dan Rescue Squad shirt. "Least you ain't bleedin' this go-round. Don't you worry, Mr. Moore. We'll have you at the ER in a jiffy. You'll be okay."

"My arm was numb, and I can't breathe. My face is burning. It's happening again."

They load me into an ambulance, and I hear Tesla crow before they swing the doors shut, evidently bedeviled by the racket and unnatural lights. Shelor's driving, and the ride's choppy over the gravel drive. As we're turning onto the blacktop, a squad lady with a ponytail and a soft voice informs me that my blood pressure is elevated.

"How much?" I ask from underneath an oxygen mask.

"Well, one-ninety over ninety-nine."

"I can hear the blood whooshing, if that makes any sense."

"How's your arm doin'?" she asks, the words blending with the engine noise and road sounds.

"Better. But my face is burning, and it's like the pain runs into my last two fingers. I can talk okay, though. Now I can. Using the phone was hard. But it's not as bad as it was in June. Still can't breathe so well."

They transport me down the mountain via the sweeping curves on Squirrel Spur and — because the Stuart ER is busy with an auto accident — deliver me to the Mount Airy Hospital. An orderly takes over and busts me directly through the entrance and introduces a doctor, Dr. Kipreos, who immediately asks questions and has me squeeze his fingers and push against his hands, and together they roll me into the CT scan room, old hat for me by now. There's no brain bleed, Dr. Kipreos tells me several minutes later as the orderly wheels me to another room for an MRI. My breathing has stabilized, my mind has cleared somewhat. "Probably a TIA," someone behind me says in a hushed tone.

Following the MRI, I'm parked in a bay with green-curtain walls. A tech draws blood, a CNA asks about my comfort, and a nurse jiggers the bag on my IV pole and resets a machine. Dr. Kipreos pops through the curtains — I hear the metal curtain rings soft-scrape against their rod — and he walks to the top of the gurney and we go through the stroke protocol again, pushes and pulls and a penlight shined in my eyes.

"Another stroke?" I ask. "Mini-stroke, maybe? It doesn't seem as awful as last time."

"Well, good news on that front. Your scans are normal. There's no bleed, no clot and no new damage."

I shift my position, roll so I can see more of the doc. "Then . . . well . . . okay, so what just happened?"

"You had a panic attack." He's kind and gentle, delivers the diagnosis with the same professional compassion you'd expect if he were informing me that I have terminal liver cancer.

"A panic attack? You're sure? I mean, I *felt* it. My face hurt. My arm was numb. I didn't imagine this. I could hear blood roaring. It was hard to dial nine-one-one. It was physical. I couldn't catch my breath. I was smothering."

As best I can determine, the drunk man in the bay next to me was wounded in a knife fight. He moans, "Woouhhh, motherfuckuhs."

"Everything you felt was real and manifested physically. Difficulty breathing is a classic symptom. I'm still waiting on the lab work to rule out a couple of long-shot possibilities, but I'm fairly confident that the circulation in your arm got cut off as you slept, then you woke up and became alarmed. Very understandable. The rescue squad captain tells me you live by yourself,

230

and that has to be scary on the heels of a serious medical event like a stroke."

"You're positive?"

"When did sensation return to your arm? The EMT said you had no strength or grip deficits from the time they arrived on the scene."

"Well, it was okay pretty soon, but I couldn't breathe and my face hurt and the pain actually traced down my arm into my fingers."

"Stress — and you've probably experienced plenty of this lately — will cause the old injury pathways to flair again. Same if you become too tired."

"Woouhhh, motherfuckuhs," my drunk neighbor repeats.

"So I'm okay?"

"I think so. We'll hold you here in the hospital until the morning, but I feel this wasn't any type of TIA." He hesitates to read a pager. "Of course, as you just learned, panic attacks are very real and can be debilitating." He's still earnest and solicitous. "I can give you a prescription, and we can monitor this, or I can refer you to a specialist."

"All this effort, especially the rescue squad volunteers who were dragged out of bed — I feel like a moron. I've wasted everyone's time because I fell asleep on my own damn arm."

"I might panic too, if I were in your shoes." He clips the pager back onto his belt. "As for wasting time, here's a positive we can take away from your visit: I checked your records from Forsyth online. June thirtieth, the blockage in your carotid was at least seventy percent, maybe more. Tonight, August fifteenth, it's around forty. You're healing and healing well. That's great progress. Keep doing what you're doing."

"Say what?" I prop up on my elbows.

"The blockage, the pseudoaneurysm in your distal carotid, is resolving. The stenosis has reduced from seventy to forty. Also, there's no indication of any new clots." He pats my shoulder, once, a brief encouragement. "I can't help but notice that you don't seem to have many obvious effects from the June event. Speech, strength and cognition all seem normal. Good for you."

I close my eyes, speak with them squeezed shut. "What a relief. Thanks. Thank you so much, Doctor."

"My pleasure." He checks his watch. "Would you like us to alert the police, let them know that you're here?"

"Huh?"

He points at my ankle. "House arrest. I'm

assuming you didn't call to inform the cops you were leaving home."

"Oh, okay, oh," I sputter, embarrassed. "Thank you. The monitoring number's in my wallet. Sorry. I apologize."

"We've seen it before," Dr. Kipreos replies. "It's the ER. Best of luck to you, Mr. Moore."

Luther's local newspaper ads and the paragraph at the bottom of the store menus announce that SUBstitution is "a family restaurant which respects the Sabbath," so I'm free every Sunday, and after work on Saturday, August 20, I load a worried, suddenly skittish Nelson into my car's front seat. Blaine and Izzy hug and pet him and wish him safe travels. I'll have the entire day tomorrow and a slice of Monday morning to introduce him to his new home and, most important, to teach him about his new chicken, horse and guinea fowl companions. He might clobber Tesla and the hens, or terrorize a guinea, but the quarter horses could easily kill a forty-pound mutt with a single, lackadaisical warning kick. Nelson whines and scratches the glass as we pull away, trembling and forcing his spotted nose through a narrow window crack.

It's ninety degrees in Stuart, but it's at

least ten degrees cooler when we arrive in Meadows of Dan, and every now and again there's even a puny breeze. Nelson is wearing a blue harness, and I hook him to a retractable leash that will allow him to roam for sixteen feet. Because of my house arrest, I had to order the items online — I can't so much as drive the three miles from the restaurant to Walmart. The plan is to acclimate him right off the bat, to let him meet the roosters and hens and horses rather than penning him and have them vex him while he's trapped.

Keeping a tight grip on the harness, I take Nelson out of the car and set him on the ground. Tesla and three tan-and-white girls are enjoying the shade of a maple tree, where they've wallowed small craters in the dirt to keep cool. Tesla's son, Jeremiah, flies from the yard to the top fence board so he can get a better and safer view of the stranger. Tesla stands and cocks an eye toward Nelson; the chickens have never seen a dog. The guineas go from chattering to screaming and then flee. Nelson is squirming and panting and trying to put his paws on my chest.

Tesla beats his wings and crows. Boom. Nelson suddenly wheels and bolts, streaking toward the rooster. The pup's sharp turn is so sudden and quick and strong and instinctive that I lose my grip on the harness, and the leash casing, which was resting beside me, rattles across the gravel and is gone with the dog. "Shit, Nelson!" I yell, and he continues hellbent for the chickens. "Nelson!" I run after him, stand so quickly that my head swims.

Tesla's fast onto a tree limb, and his hens follow him lickety-split. He leaves behind an iridescent blackish-green feather that separates during his hasty flight and swirls and sways until it hits the grass. Nelson stops underneath the tree, barking and pacing agitated circles. Jeremiah and his hen have flown higher, to the apex of the barn roof, and he's clucking and screeching chicken warnings, and Tesla joins him, fullthroat, and Nelson — who's been on the planet around ten months — is hardwired to go bonkers, can't help but bark and yelp and leap at an attraction thirty feet above his reach.

"No! Bad dog."

I grab the plastic casing and shorten the leash and recapture Nelson. He's barking and pulling and corkscrewing, doesn't have any interest in being held. I finally wrestle him so that he's facing me and tell him *no* over and over, my voice less harsh with each repetition. "Come on," I urge him, and tug him away from the maple and the shrieking birds.

We walk to the top of the drive, and I make him sit and stay. He's jacked and spastic, and when he spots Jeremiah, he zips toward the barn until his leash ends and jerks him to a cartoonish halt. We spend fifteen minutes walking on the leash, pausing to sit and stay. Occasionally I return him to the base of the tree and scold him if he shows any interest in the birds. Once, he barks and lunges and crazy-jumps again, and I kneel and use both hands to keep him planted on the ground.

When curiosity draws the horses to the fence, they aren't impressed or concerned. The sorrel mare, Ruby, lowers her head and gazes at the dog over the bottom board, and Nelson has the good sense to keep his distance, briefly stretches his front legs forward and bows and hunkers down so they're eye to eye, probably five feet apart, and he barks without conviction and then trots back to me. "Smart boy," I encourage him. The horses amble off, grazing as they go.

I lead him to his dandy new home, walk in with him and give him a treat, and when I shut the gate and unleash him, I stay inside while he explores the pen, sniffing and darting and, twice, standing on his hind legs and pressing his paws against the chain-link. I squat and wait for him to finish his survey. Then we sit there, his muzzle on my thigh, his pink tongue lolling sideways through his black lips, and I scratch his neck and pet his head, ask him if he likes this different place.

I leave him and go to the house. I return five minutes later. I leave and come back again, waiting twenty minutes this time, and around dark, with the chickens roosting, I let him out minus his leash, and he rolls in the grass and frantically zigzags after a firefly, all four feet sailing off the ground when the bright bug veers higher into the sky and he does his fervent best to snatch it.

At ten o'clock, I put his familiar bed and blanket in the five-by-five insulated box that Melvin designed. The box mimics the barn: white board-and-batten with a green tin roof. I lock him in the pen and leave him water and a bowl of food, which he doesn't eat. He does well until midnight, but then he starts to whimper and howl and complain, so I drag a metal chaise longue to the side of his pen and sleep there next to him, covered by a counterpane, the sky slathered with stars, the pond frogs festive, a screech owl reigning from a high pine.

We wake up with the roosters, in the dim gray, and I'm damp and stiff from the dew, and I didn't sleep well, feel frazzled and woozy. Nelson licks my hand through the wire mesh, and I open the gate and let him out and he's happy to be freed. He still hasn't eaten much. The pen has its own storage bin, and I decide I'll give him some fresh food and water, but while I'm scooping his puppy kibble, there's a sound in the woods — could be a rabbit, could be a deer, could be a possum, could be a raccoon — and damn if he doesn't run headlong into the trees and bramble, wild and gone. "Shit." I jog after him as best I can with my bum ankle, make it about ten paces into the woods, catch a briar across my forearm and start flooding blood because of my medicine. "Shit," I repeat, and give up my hunt.

Nelson hasn't returned by sunrise, and I'm worried he's lost or hurt, and every few minutes I walk to the edge of the woods and shout his name, but I'm restricted by my ankle arrest and can't search for him. I'm sitting on the porch, still pressing a wet dish towel against my cut, my hand held above my head to thwart the bleeding, my shirt stained red, when a Jeep Cherokee barrels in, stirring up dust, and a man dressed in khakis, a natty striped shirt and tall black Muck Boots hops from the vehicle. "Morning, sir," he says.

"Hello."

"I'm Barnie. Barnie Hylton. You must be Kevin. Hope you gave the other son of a bitch double what you got." He grins and walks toward me. He has dark hair weeded with a few strands of gray and is clean shaven and energetic, moves and speaks as if he's running fifteen minutes late for his next appointment.

"Oh," I say. "Yeah. Nice to meet you. Melvin mentioned he might send you over to make sure I haven't stolen the silver or raided his gun safe." As I understand the story, Hylton was a young junior banker who quit his job because his hidebound bosses refused, decades ago, to give his chum Melvin Harrell a business loan. Hylton hocked his home and invested his own cash, and now, in his fifties, he's loaded, a gentleman farmer who raises horses and grows grapes for his private winery.

"Mind if I come in?"

"Help yourself." The house, like always, is spotless and organized. "I'll wait out here."

"What the hell happened to you, Boss? Your arm, I mean?"

239

"Blood thinner. My medication. I went looking for my dog and tangled with a briar."

"Lord. That stuff'll cause you to bleed like a stuck pig." We shake hands, and he strides into the house, disappears for less than a minute, then returns. "Hell, the place looks better than he left it."

"Thanks."

"You find your buddy?" Hylton asks.

"My buddy?"

"Your dog?" he says.

"Nope. And I'm worried sick over him." I nod at my ankle. "I can't really search for him."

"Yeah, Melvin told me you've had some ugly luck." Hylton glances at the empty pen. "When did he go missing? Maybe he's still in the neighborhood."

"First thing this morning, around six. He heard a noise in the woods and was gone before I could catch him. It's even worse because I just brought him here from Stuart yesterday. He's been living in a parking lot."

"City dog," Hylton jokes. "Which direction?"

I point. "Other side of the barn. He was bookin' it."

"I'll go take a look for you. I've got a dog

whistle in the glove compartment, and I'll give it a try. Didn't work worth a shit for my feists, but you never know."

"I'd be grateful. Thanks."

Hylton opens the passenger-side door, locates a holster and pistol and straps them to his belt, then bends deeper into the vehicle, evidently rooting around for the whistle. He stands straight, shuts the door and shows me a slender chrome tube, and the instant he turns for the woods, here comes Nelson, loping toward us, wet and muddy, a stick wound in his tail, panting and grinning, his morning perfect, full of new scents and cold creek water. Seeing him makes me as happy as I've been in weeks, so joyous that I forget about my bloody arm.

"Damn!" Hylton exclaims. "Now that's a quality whistle."

Later the same Sunday, in the evening, Nelson and I are relaxing on the porch, waiting for a thunderstorm that's starting to black-build in a western corner of the sky, and I hear another vehicle coming and figure it must be Floyd Grimes making his preacher rounds. "Thank you, Lord," I say when the white Range Rover eases into view. "Wow. *Much* better."

Lilly Heath parks parallel to the porch,

rolls down her window and leaves the engine running. She's close enough that I can hear music, the strings-and-flutes meditations she played for our yoga sessions. "Sorry to show up without calling," she says.

"No worries," I tell her. "Come anytime. You're always welcome. This is a lottery win for me."

"Do you have a moment? Can I ask you a legal question? Sorry to be a bother."

"I'll squeeze you in," I tell her. Well trained when it comes to cars and people, Nelson sits on his haunches and watches Lilly but doesn't leave the porch. "Are you planning to talk to me from the safety of your cranked SUV?"

She switches off the engine. "I didn't want to be presumptuous. I have a legal emergency. By all accounts, you used to be a great lawyer. It's Sunday, so my options are limited."

"I'm prohibited from practicing law. I can't give legal advice or I'll wind up deeper in trouble. But I might be able to offer some general, universal information about how the system functions. Porch chatter between friends on a pretty Sunday."

"I'd be more than willing to pay you," she says.

"Oh, no. Goodness, no. That'd make it

worse. And I'd never take money from you anyway. I don't recall you billing me for the stuffed animals and fresh fruit."

"Okay," she says, climbing from the vehicle as she speaks. She walks briskly toward the porch. "This is your dog, I'm guessing? Nelson? I thought he couldn't live here."

"My landlord made an exception." Nelson is thumping the porch boards with his tail, but he waits for Lilly to address him before he scurries to her.

"What a smart boy," she says. "Especially no older than he is."

"Well, he's had several months to work on saying hello to humans. It's the new temptations that've been a bugger. He just arrived last night, and we've had quite the transition."

"You have dogs before him?"

"Almost always. My dad raised rabbit beagles, so I grew up around them. Ava and I had Earl the Australian shepherd until he died a few months before we separated. Best dog ever, that fellow."

She takes a long breath. "So." She's standing on the top step, fidgeting. "So —"

"You want to have a seat?" I interrupt her, and point at an empty rocker across from the glider.

"Thanks, I'm okay. So last night, the *cops*

243

come beating on my front door like I'm a criminal, and they hand me these papers, and I'm being sued for a quarter-million dollars, and, of course, I'm flabbergasted, and they warn me — in total *Dragnet* mode — that unless I do something in three weeks, the other side wins automatically, or at least that's what I understood."

"Let's see what you got."

She dips into her purse, withdraws a folded paper chunk, then walks over and hands it to me, every movement anxious.

I recognize a complaint for car-accident damages in about three seconds. I flip to the last page to check the demand amount: two hundred and fifty thousand. "You sure you don't want a chair?"

She finally sits in the rocker. "It's bizarre, Kevin. Just *wrong*. A month ago, I barely tapped a man at the gas pumps in Galax. He started pulling off, then stopped suddenly, for no reason, and I nicked his bumper with the front of my car. He wasn't hurt. How could he be? And now the cops are banging on my door, and this bastard's demanding a king's ransom."

"Well, welcome to the land of my TV-advertising brethren." I chuckle. "You realize your insurance company will handle this, right?"

"I thought that's how it works, but I'm worried because it happened on private property, and we didn't call the police. And won't I still have to pay for a lawyer?"

"No problem at all. You're covered, your insurer will provide an attorney, and he or she will handle this from soup to nuts. The bozos who filed this are bottom-feeders, and it'll never see the inside of a courtroom. They hope that they can shake down the insurance company for some nuisance dollars."

"I'm not in any danger, then? I don't have any financial risk?"

"Zero. At worst, the company pays a grand or so to make this nonsense disappear. Call your agent ASAP and give him a copy of the papers, then go back to healing the sick and doing yoga and forget all about this."

"You're positive?" She leans forward.

I laugh. "I'm positive."

"Thanks so much. What a weight lifted."

"Of course," I tease her, "I *am* disbarred these days, and brain-damaged, so maybe I'm not as competent as I like to think."

"I'll make it a point to confirm your advice with my insurance agent tomorrow." She rocks backward, tilts her head toward the porch ceiling and lets out a long sigh. "Whew."

"Can I offer you some ice water or grocery-store sweet tea to celebrate? Perhaps a nice, neighborly chat could be my fee."

"Okay, I guess. Fair enough. Water would be fine."

I go inside, pour us both a glass, add crushed ice from the stainless-steel fridge and rejoin her on the porch.

"What should we talk about?" she asks.

"The weather's always an agreeable topic."

Over the next twenty minutes, we have the house-arrest version of a starter date — courting, my mom and dad called it — and I learn that her favorite movie is *Casablanca* and her favorite writer is Barbara Kingsolver. She's a fan of Bonnie Raitt, Alison Krauss and Amos Lee. I admit to her that I'm an art philistine, but I'm sold on her enthusiasm for the Dadaist Duchamp and her disdain for "talentless postmodern hucksters" after she entertains me with the story of Rauschenberg's bullshit Iris Clert telegram portrait. But that's as far and as deep as she's willing to go, and she puts a quick kibosh on any discussion of her past life, her divorce or her reasons for settling in Hillsville, Virginia. The electrical storm keeps its distance, and sweet Nelson rolls onto his side and dozes, occasionally twitching or lazily opening his eyes.

We're laughing and goofing on how we're both so old that every new person we meet reminds us of an ancient celebrity or a family member — as in Judy's new husband could pass for Rock Hudson, or the kid at the office looks just like Uncle Roy when he came home from the navy — and we're hitting it off and cruising smooth, and damn, I hear another car poking up the drive, and this time it is in fact Preacher Grimes. He's as buoyant as ever, and his arms are full of brown paper sacks.

"Howdy, Kevin," he says. "Brought you some squash, string beans and tomatoes, and a strawberry cake. Best cake in the county, as I see it. My wife, Regina, fixed it for you."

"Thanks," I say. "Appreciate it, as always. You don't have to keep bringing me food, though."

"My pleasure." He faces Lilly. "Hello, ma'am. I'm Floyd Grimes. I pastor the New Temple of the True Gospel and Harvest Church. I've been visitin' with Brother Kevin ever since he come home from his stroke."

I haven't known Lilly Heath very long, and certainly don't know her well, but I'm positive she doesn't care for the preacher, not one iota. "Good," she says curtly. Her expression is stern and blank, and her distaste is apparent enough that it registers with Grimes and causes him to fall silent for several seconds.

"Well, okay," he eventually says, "nice to meet you, ma'am. So I'll be seein' you next time, Kevin. Gotta haul a load of cabbage to the West Coast this week."

"Thanks again, Floyd," I say, and it sounds forced, a little too bright. "You and your wife are very generous."

"Don't forget you're always welcome for services. Send Melvin my best. Tell him we're still lookin' in on you. And I left you a few tracts with the vegetables."

"Okay," I answer, my voice normal now.

"Take care, ma'am," he says to Lilly.

"I will," she replies, still dour and standoffish.

"I'm flattered," I say to her as the preacher is driving away, dust contrails pluming behind his pickup's tires.

"And why would that be?" she asks tersely.

"Seems as if you're upset because our excellent date was interrupted."

"Hardly." She stands from the chair, and it rocks back and forth — empty — a couple times. "Your preacher friend's a hateful bigot," she snaps. "And you tolerate him, take his gifts and mollycoddle him."

"Damn, Lilly, I mean . . . the man stops by occasionally and tries to be a helpful neighbor and an encouragement. Our many differences don't make him a monster or me a collaborator. And how would you know anything about him? You were with him for all of three minutes."

"Let's review the list, Kevin," she says. "Let's tick off the self-serving, vile trash he pushes. And I know exactly who he is because his little propaganda fliers were all over the counter when I was here taking care of you. 'Adam and Eve, not Adam and Steve.' How clever. That especially compassionate rant included the Bible verse suggesting we ought to kill homosexuals. My sister's gay, and I'd love to keep her alive awhile —"

"No argument from me," I interrupt. "I agree with you."

Her hands are balled and pressed against her hips. She talks over my last few words. "Then there was the lesson about women keeping their heads covered, their mouths shut and asking their husbands to mansplain what's what. Floyd makes the rules to reward himself, and we girls get to bake biscuits and change diapers. We both understand who Floyd Grimes is, and behind the frosted cakes and slick smiles, he's a mean-spirited, selfish, incurious hick who worships at the firearms altar — lovely NRA sticker on his truck — and hates everyone and everything that's not exactly like he is. And while I haven't seen the position papers on divorce, our Muslim president, alcohol, and white women marrying black men, I think we can safely extrapolate."

"I take it you're not religious," I say, grinning.

She sits again, very abruptly. She locks her knees and juts toward me. "Quite the opposite. I was a surgical nurse for years, and the people who know best, our little demigods, the doctors who can stop and start a heart or rewire your brain or plug your bleeding gut, the geniuses who're up to their elbows in life and death every day and can decipher the complicated schematics and fine-print assembly instructions, almost all of them are believers — it might be Jesus or Allah or Shiva or Haile Selassie or Angel Moroni, but the real experts, they're convinced. And if the smartest mechanics on the planet assure me there's a factory in Detroit making cars, then I believe there's a factory in Detroit making cars." She bobs through several half-rocks, the ends of the chair's curved bands never touching the porch.

250

"Damn good endorsers to have for the product."

"The product's just fine. Religion doesn't have a Zeus problem. Religion's problem is that the hirelings always insist on becoming the masters. Truth is, holy men are — by and large — impediments. We'd all be better off without the *chosen.* At best, they're spiritual static; at worst, they're flimflammers. A year ago, I sat in Saint Mary's Cathedral in Kilkenny, Ireland, and simply being connected to such a sacred space, I *felt* a genuine power and bigger purpose. A grace and goodness. An absolute god. Then the priest with his fancy *vestments* and squeaky voice appeared and started his noontime spiel, and his infallible scripture and tedious droning ruined everything. He managed to make the majestic completely trivial. My favorite ER doc used to say that religion should be like birth control: After some basic instruction, you figure out what suits you best and then you practice it in private."

"Yeah," I say and sigh. "The devil's in the details."

"The devil *demands* the details, Kevin. My spirituality is intensely personal, an experience that's completely intimate and unique and my own, and if it's working for me, why should I feel compelled to brow-beat — or persecute — the rest of the world for not finding peace of mind the same way as I do? Most churches are about money, power, politics and self-congratulation, and the worst of them, the Floyd Grimes tem-ples, are smug clubs that allow you to feel righteous about despising or dismissing other people. No thanks, not my cup of tea."

"Yeah, do I ever wish I could become convinced there's a beneficent watchman with miracles and lightning bolts in his di-vine bag of tricks taking care of me and my favored clan. How great would that be? I've really put my mind to it, really tried to get a handle on the big picture — early on, I even gave Preacher Grimes a fair hearing — but I'm still at a loss. Same as I ever was, noncommittal and hopefully uncertain. You're lucky if you've found *something* you can depend on."

"And I have. There's *a* god, and I've felt him or her or it and seen the handiwork and incredible outcomes." She continues to fast-rock; I'm not sure how much she's been listening to my part of the conversation. "But it's *my* business," she says forcefully. "My life. My deeply personal and *private* affair. I mean, just because it's my prefer-ence, would I run around declaring —

spreading the gospel, as they say — that everyone who doesn't use a seven-inch purple vibrator and Acme strawberry lubricant for exactly three minutes is going to be punished? No I wouldn't. I'd be embarrassed to talk about it. And if I did, people would think I was crazy. It's nobody else's damn concern. So, what's the difference?"

"Well, uh, I've never thought about it in those terms." I glance at the sleeping dog. Sip my water. Cross my legs. "Could I at least — now — have your e-mail address?" I ask. "Since we're more acquainted than when you arrived."

"Huh?" she says. "What?" She realizes she's been on a tear, and her features click at once, change and become softer and suffused with her genial nature. "Sorry," she murmurs. She briefly frowns. "But holier-than-thou bullies like Grimes really stick in my craw."

CHAPTER TEN

September 1 is a Thursday, and I receive permission from my electronic jailer to drive to Roanoke and meet with Margo Jordan, who'll be there for a motions hearing in another case. I'm sure she'd visit with me in Stuart again, but the trip is an excuse to see some different scenery and enjoy a few hours away from my numbing routes and routines. Like every lawyer, I occasionally bitched about my clients or my profession's stupid aggravations, but walking through the county courthouse's front entrance and into the hubbub and people and seeing the familiar hallway and big docket sheets just stone-solid drains my heart. I so miss being an attorney.

Wally Miller has been the cop at the metal detector for at least twenty years, and the moment he spots me, he leaves his table and races around to wrap me in a bear hug, then pops me several times between the shoulders with an open hand. "Welcome home, Mr. Moore," he says. "Come on through." Six or seven people are waiting in front of me, but Wally grabs my elbow and leads me past the line and the metal detector.

"Thanks, Wally. It's great to see you." In hopes of hiding my ankle tracker, I'm wearing a dark suit that's a stitch too large and slightly long in the legs.

"We all miss you, sir. And we're rooting for you. Not the same around here with you gone."

"I appreciate it. I miss you guys as well. And all this. I'll be free and clear soon," I say decisively, "if everything goes according to plan."

Margo is waiting for me on the other side of the security station, and we shake hands and take the elevator to an empty conference room on the second floor. We sit across from each other, her briefcase on the table but unopened.

"Thanks for driving over here," she says. "You didn't have to."

"Believe me, it's my pleasure. I received a pass for a few hours, and I'm so happy about the trip here you'd think I'd won a limousine tour through the Grand Canyon."

"Glad I could at least accomplish something for you."

"You've been as helpful and professional as anybody could be. I'm not giving you much to work with."

"So we have the mysterious Melanie Culp's deposition set for September twenty-ninth in Richmond. At Jenkins's office."

"Perfect. Thanks. If it's okay with you, I've drafted some interrogatories and a motion for production of documents. You can throw them away if you want, or edit them. Whatever. I don't mean to tell you how to do your job. But I think we really need to focus on the fundamental stuff, facts she can't change or whitewash. Facts we can confirm. Her maiden name, date and place of birth, all names she's ever used, prior suits, prior settlements." I hand her a large yellow envelope.

"Sure, I agree. And I'm grateful for the help." She lays the envelope on top of her briefcase. "So. First we need to decide whether you're going to answer Jenkins's questions or take the Fifth. I spoke to Ward, and he's emphatic that, with your criminal cases pending, you should refuse to give any statements in our deposition. Pretty standard, pretty routine. Jenkins will put on a production, but I doubt he'll be shocked. I'll quiz Miss Culp and you can sit tight."

"Nope. I'm planning to give him a full

dep. Answer everything."

"Seriously?" she asks. Her eyebrows rise.

"Yes. Absolutely."

"You're the criminal-law expert, but it's pretty much a day-one law school rule, isn't it? Why take the risk, why give the prosecutor a stationary target for later on? One tiny slip, one mistake, one ambiguous statement that the state can exploit, and you're screwed. Or you get the classic 'Well, you didn't say that in your deposition' when you're grilled at your criminal trial."

"I can handle it. It's what I do, Margo. I've already told Sheriff Smith the story, anyway. I want to put down a marker, have it set in stone. Plus, I want Caleb to know that I'm broadcasting the truth, that I plan to keep alerting people about this scam."

"Well, it's your call. But you need to clear it with Ward. I don't want him cross with me because of your hardheadedness."

"I'll talk to him."

"Can you also arrange to be in Richmond the day before, so we can prepare?"

"I think so. Sure." I trace an aimless pattern on the table with my index finger. "Where are we with my insurer and Jenkins? Money-wise, I mean?" I'm staring down when I ask the question.

"I finally spoke to M.D. He's very charming. He understands we have to do the deposition. As we predicted, he's offering to save us — well, your insurer — seventy-five grand if we settle within two weeks of the dep. They'll accept less than the full suit amount in exchange for a quick payment."

"How do you see that going?" I ask.

"Honestly, Kevin, as much as I sympathize with you, unless this Culp lady completely comes unglued and confesses, I anticipate we'll be paying them off. If we can save five figures and the cost of a trial, we will. You understand, I hope."

"Of course."

"Jenkins — at his low-key, seersucker and galluses best — also made it clear that if we don't settle, he'll amend his complaint and sue for an additional three million in punitive damages. As you well know, your policy doesn't cover punitives. Those dollars come from your pocket. He's filed a production request for your bank records — a shot across our bow."

"I wondered when he'd get around to that threat. But he'll soon discover I have about fifty thousand to my name." I peer up from the table and make eye contact with Margo. "Who's calling the shots on your end? Certainly not some front-line adjuster?"

"Vice president of this division, their

malpractice section. They have several other lines — cars, houses, floods. Lady by the name of Anne Mullens is in charge. Believe me, they've investigated your version of events. Thoroughly. There're simply no dots to connect, other than the remote overlap you've already found."

"The Shadrich deal isn't completely remote. Though I'll concede it would be next to impossible to prove in court."

Margo's tone is very direct, very final. "No offense, and as we've discussed, this will come down to a swearing contest, your word versus hers, and since you were impaired at the time of the office visit, I'm betting most judges will allow Jenkins to submit evidence of your testing meth-positive soon after you allegedly were approached by an albino mystery man, a meeting you never reported until your criminal charges surfaced. Interestingly, the insurance company sees the empty restaurant video as more of a negative — like *you* erased it to provide yourself a trial prop."

"I understand. I do. Will you let me know if and when you decide to pull the trigger on payment? I plan to fight this until the last second. Give me a few days' notice before you surrender, okay?"

"Yeah. I'm required to, and I would anyway."

"Much appreciated."

As you leave Roanoke on Route 220, there's a filling station embellished with a small deli and coffee bar and several booths, and it's on my route back to Patrick County. I pull in, pump ten bucks' worth of gas for cover, then find a parking spot, survey the cars already there, get out again, adjust my tie, center my belt buckle and drag a plastic comb through my hair. I check my appearance in the side mirror. I'm nervous and the tension causes my face and eye to tingle, my ankle to throb.

Ava is sitting in a booth, a cup of coffee in front of her. I haven't seen her in months, and she's gorgeous, tan and fit and dressed for work, absolutely lovely. A beauty.

"Thanks so much for coming on a school day."

"I'm glad to." She stands and awkwardly hugs me, her shoulder touching mine, but that's the extent of it, an arm draped loosely around me, then quickly removed. "You said we wouldn't be long, and it's my planning period, so I just ghosted. My aide's covering for me if anything pops up."

I slide into the booth across from her. "I

don't have a lot of time," I tell her. "But, as I said, I do have a favor to ask." I borrowed Big Money's cell to call her, the best I could manage in case, for some reason, the cops are listening to my phone.

"Okay."

"In a few months, or maybe a few weeks, I might need an alibi."

"Oh, damn, Kevin." She grimaces and shakes her head. "I assumed you wanted back some of the money you gave me."

"No. The money's yours. That's behind us. My mistake, your cash. I'm not an Indian giver."

"Warning, Kevin: That's probably a micro-aggression." She grins. She's looking at me dead-on, almost staring, trying to size me up. She slightly rotates her head. She narrows her eyes. "A point of emphasis for us in this year's always-worthwhile, start-of-school superintendent's address. *Paddy wagon* is also a no-no."

I smile. She's always been wry and ironic but never mean, no easy feat. "Thanks for the tip," I say. I appreciate the humor, her trying to make us comfortable.

"Are you in more trouble?"

"I am. I'm facing a probation violation for my original charge and two new felonies: distribution of meth and possession of a gun while in possession of the dope. Serious cases. I'm also on the receiving end of a bogus five-million-dollar lawsuit from a former client. I'm on house arrest, which is why I have to hightail it down the road in a few minutes." I extend my leg and hold it rigid, let her see the ankle monitor.

"I always wondered about that. I was worried you might've made a lawyer mistake when you were high. I'm sorry." She pushes her cardboard cup away, toward the salt and pepper shakers and a boxy napkin dispenser. "I've heard bits and pieces. You've really hit bottom."

"Can't argue with you." I hesitate. "I won't waste your time explaining how I'm innocent or going into detail about what's happening to me. But remember, Ava, that I walked into court and admitted my guilt with the coke, and I gave you chapter and verse about my failings as your husband. I owned my guilt and my mistakes, didn't quibble, and I'm telling you this time that I'm innocent. For the record, I haven't used any drugs in over a year. I'm proud of that. Look at me. You know me better than anybody —"

"You do seem okay, especially if you had a stroke," she interrupts. "I was afraid you'd be greasy and frail and wearing a soiled shirt. Or using a cane and Velcro shoes."

"I was lucky in the sense that a passerby found me seconds after my head misfired and I collapsed."

"So it *was* more serious than you let on?"

"I'm fine," I say. "It could've been a whole lot worse."

"What is it that you want from me? Want me to do?"

"To begin with, I want you to assume some things that aren't accurate. Assume I really did use meth and was selling it while I was carrying a gun. Assume I'm guilty. But after all our time together, you also have to know that I understand the legal system and can twist and turn the dials like nobody's business. I was damned skilled at my job."

"You're talking with your hands and modulating your voice," she says. "Your closing-argument tricks. I know you too well. You can't glamour me." She grins with half her mouth, sad and wistful.

"Then you should be reassured because I still have all the tools."

"I'm not going to lie or put myself at risk."

"You won't have to. Listen, it's a one-off, and perfectly safe. You'd drive to Richmond and use a prepaid phone to make a call. Don't have to speak to anyone. Just hang up. That's it." I shrug.

"It can't be completely safe if it's dishonest and I'm giving you a false alibi." She sips her coffee, peers at me over the rounded paper rim. "And it seems to me that you're not doing such a brilliant job of twisting the dials and gaming the courts if you're here with an ankle bracelet and begging me for a cover story."

"Well, please give it some thought. Whatever goodwill I have left over from our years together, I'd like to cash it in. And it's still possible I won't need your help — I'm just trying to plan for every possibility."

"We'll see, I guess. But probably not."

"You look like a million bucks," I say. "So beautiful. For what it's worth, I miss you every day."

She's silent for several seconds. I hear a lady at the deli counter announce that order eighty-nine is ready. "I miss *us*. Ava and Kevin pre–July 2015. It makes me so blue sometimes. Angry too, but I'm trying to move past being mad. That doesn't help me or you." She stares down into her cup. "Are you seeing anyone yet, Kevin?"

"Dating's difficult when you can't leave your own front porch or the sandwich shop." I wait for her to look at me. She keeps her head bowed, but finally glances

264

up and we connect. "I did run across one nice lady, but go figure, she wants nothing to do with me. Can't say I blame her."

Driving home from Roanoke, I tune the radio to the local AM station and listen to the *Trading Post,* a regular treat when I lived here. The half-hour is a broadcast version of a flea market or a yard sale, with people buying and selling and swapping everything from baseball cards to baby clothes to car parts. It's still summer on the calendar, still plenty hot, but the announcer reads an offer to sell miscellaneous Christmas decorations, including a small white artificial tree, "everything like new," for forty dollars, and I think, *How pitiful, there's someone worse off than I am.* When the announcer unenthusiastically recites the number to call if you're interested in used Christmas bric-a-brac during beach season, I'm so surprised that I lift my foot from the gas pedal and briefly squeeze my eyes shut. "540-340-6687," repeats the radio voice. A number I'll never forget. Amber Archer.

Until April of 2015, I was an alcohol novice who *might* have a rum and Coke or a glass of sweet white wine at a wedding reception or birthday party, and I'd been hungover twice in my life, both times during college. But on a Friday, the tenth of April, shaking off a harsh winter and sitting outside at Smith Mountain Lake, listening to a bar band on a warm, pretty evening, at the urging of my friend and client Frank Emerson, I discovered Kentucky Mules, potent bourbon pleasures that barely taste of liquor.

Three drinks later — my arm around Ava, the band covering "Brown Eyed Girl," an exuberant moon silvering swaths of lake water — I found the unmatchable lift and bliss and devil-may-care contentment that the perfect amount of spirits can deliver, neither too much nor too little, the happy elevation where most everything is delightful and balanced, around .04 on a Breathalyzer test. I loved my wife twice as much and the band sounded marvelous, especially the bass lines, and my work worries for next week were sealed off, replaced by a tiny euphoria that I could actually feel in my limbs. This was my parents' Friday-evening habit, I realized, the gift of a martini or a stout highball.

I bought my own ABC bottles and mixers, and the next Wednesday, then Friday, I included a cocktail with dinner, and that was it, one, no more, nothing to it. In May, Donna the Buffalo came to town for a show, and Ava and I both drank too much and danced for an hour straight and had to take a cab home, and we laughed about it, old, stuffy married people freewheeling like college kids. Afterward, I kept a two-drink limit on Fridays and Saturdays, though I did try the bourbon by itself, a jigger and a half over ice, poured into a stainless-steel cup, sipped while we walked the dog.

On May 21, I was an instructor at a lawyers' seminar at the Greenbrier, just over the state line in West Virginia, teaching my peers about jury selection and voir dire. Cheryl Greer, who'd won a very winnable rape case for a Manhattan banker in 2009 and often popped up on Fox News as a legal expert, was the keynote speaker, and she threw a swank, invite-only reception in her suite that Thursday night, around sixty lawyers and spouses. She was fifty years old, but thanks to quality plastic surgery and veneered teeth, she looked a decade younger. I ordered a Kentucky Mule, and the uniformed bartender delivered it to me in a cold copper mug.

"I enjoyed your presentation," Cheryl told me when I was about midway through my second drink. "Smart advice."

"Pretty routine, truth be told," I demurred.

A few minutes into our conversation, she was flirting with me, and she invited me to dinner with her "gang," and ten of us wound up at a Bacchanalian table in the steak house. I downed two more bourbons — just the brown liquor with nothing to tame it — and she kept touching my shoulder or wrist when she talked to me, and sat so that her skirt was snagged high on her thigh and split almost to her hip. Drunk or sober, I wasn't about to have sex with her, so when everyone migrated back to her suite before a trip to the casino, for me it was simply buzzed, happy-go-lucky fun — there was nothing dark or adulterous or underhanded about my sticking around for the rest of the party.

"Do you like to gamble?" she asked. She vamped every syllable, and her eyebrows communicated that the question wasn't altogether about roulette and slot machines. She poured me another bourbon from the bar in her room.

I took hold of the drink, number five, and even with food tamping down the liquor, I was fairly high. "I enjoy playing cards, mostly blackjack. But I rarely win." I pretended the come-on hadn't registered, didn't send her anything in return.

She walked around from behind the bar

and handed me a cocktail napkin. "Can I offer you a little something before we try our luck?"

"Meaning?" I asked.

"A trip to the powder room?" she said, her voice rich and honeyed.

"I'm married," I answered. "My wife couldn't make the trip. I'd better avoid lovely ladies in close quarters."

She giggled, which seemed odd because she was such a composed, commanding woman. "Cocaine, Kevin," she whispered. She giggled again, and I noticed that her forehead didn't crease and her mouth corners stayed level. Her lipstick seemed half a shade too red.

Cocaine, Kevin. More than most, I understood how ruinous the drug could be. I'd represented wealthy housewives brought low by coke, Hunting Hills ladies facing felony charges after their twenty-one days at the ten-grand rehab, their put-out husbands fidgeting in the courtroom's gallery, anxious to return to the office. I'd been hired by a priest — a devout public servant — who was speedballing in the confessional, and I'd once helped a seventy-three-year-old grandmother — didn't charge her a penny — who embezzled money from the PTA to buy crack.

And, of course, I'd witnessed the *thousands* of garden-variety defendants, the addicts haunting the dockets every week, emaciated and raccoon-eyed, with crumbling teeth and mushy sores, their public defenders duly mentioning military service or high school athletic accomplishments or the five years as a supervisor with the electric company, and we all, every one of us — judges, cops, clerks and lawyers alike — wondered, *How the hell do you go from then to now?*

When Cheryl offered the dope, I was disarmed by the liquor, and I was of a mind that cocktails had been a quality find, a hedonistic and harmless addition to my life, and I'd never tried cocaine, and I'd resisted Cheryl's other temptation, so I'd earned a little leeway and domestic bonus points to burn. Besides, I was in high cotton, at the top of my game, teaching other lawyers, staying for free at a five-star hotel courtesy of the American Bar Association, and this lady was a celebrity of sorts, so why not, why not upgrade and let loose large and full-tilt, *just to see,* just to get a glimpse behind the velvet rope?

There really was an anteroom outside the huge bathroom, and the wallpaper was both frenetic and white-gloved at the same time, tastefully festive fifties-style. The fulsome lighting underscored Cheryl's age, and I *almost* said "No thanks" and declined the dope — I flashed on the horror movies where the witch or warlock dies at the end, and the beautiful body regresses frame by frame to a hideously decayed thousand-year-old corpse. Even half in the bag, I understood this was a warning, that a dead end was lurking underneath the stretched skin and siren's plastic smile, but I was intending to only dip in a toe, and I was as disciplined and determined as they come, so I'd enjoy the basic tour and a Hollywood night and be done with serious drugs for-ever.

"Here you go, sweetie," she said, and lifted a miniature spoon cradling a white bump. It was apparent she planned on holding the scoop below my nose rather than handing the coke to me. She pressed closer, her chest against mine, her leg angled so it was wholly exposed through the slit in her skirt.

"I've never used cocaine," I said. I snorted the powder, and it burned my nostril, and the fire traced into my sinus and encircled my eye and then began conquering my cheek, and within seconds, a dose of energy and clarity hit me, a surge so pronounced and vivid it was as if someone had switched out my batteries and I was suddenly boosted and retooled and sublimely fueled. "Holy shit," I blurted. "This stuff comes as billed."

Cheryl built another spoonful, dipped from a tiny, ornate box. "Can't fly with only one wing," she purred.

"I'd say I'm pretty much soaring." I laughed. "So listen," I told her, pointing with my index finger, "you're a fun, attractive lady, and I'm having a ball, but you have to understand, I love my wife, and that's an immutable, so you and I can be pals and buddies and paint the town, but we *can't* go any further. Period. I don't want to take your drugs under false pretenses." I smiled at her.

"Let me know if you change your mind," she replied. "Until then, we'll just enjoy the bedroom tension and double entendres."

In the days to come, I absolutely embraced cocaine. I was *that* guy. It pushed every button, filled in every blank, matched my list to a *T.* I also quickly learned that it would dial back the bourbon, mitigate my buzz and any sloppy decline, so I could max-drink, hit my peak, then pump the brakes with coke and start all over again, a high and happy failsafe. Permaphoria.

I felt majestic strolling down the elaborate stairs that spilled into the casino. Cheryl offered me her hand for the last two or three steps, and I guided her onto the gambling floor, the men all in jackets or suits, the women all smartly dressed. The cards ran in my favor, and soon I was betting black chips, a hundred a hand, and I kept winning. I relished the cards themselves. The clubs and diamonds impressed me as little works of art, especially the queens and kings, and everything — the people passing by the table, the ice in my highball glass, the red stone in a lady's necklace — was distinct and illuminated.

After an hour, Cheryl leaned in to whisper that we might need another trip to her powder room, her flat hand on my thigh as she spoke, her lips brushing my ear for the last few words, and the contact caused me to get hard, just like that, crazy, sitting there in public, at a blackjack table, and my dick was ready to go, as if I were twenty again.

I immediately missed Ava, wished she were with me, wished *we* could have sex, and I buttoned my jacket, left the table and called her from the bathroom. I explained it was under two hours from Roanoke to the resort, and I could be in bed with her by midnight, and she laughed and said it was sweet and endearing that I wanted her to sleep with me, but it sounded as if I'd be passed out well before midnight. Cheryl and I visited the powder room again, and we were the last two people in the casino when it closed at four in the morning. We ordered room service before dawn, and I fell asleep on her sofa, still in a suit and tie, no hanky-panky, not even a kiss on the cheek.

I lied to Ava for the first time later that Friday, told her I was staying all weekend because the seminars were interesting and worthwhile, and then Cheryl and I embarked on a booze-and-coke spree that lasted until she hit the road early on Sunday. We fly-fished for trout while we were high and admired the wild rainbows' red bands and matching gill plates. We went falconing while we were high. We visited the spa while we were high. We danced in a disco while we were high. We took a carriage ride while we were high. We dressed to the nines and nibbled appetizers under spectacular chandeliers in the main dining room while we were high. We played more cards while we were high. We took a shot at bowling while we were high, cracked *Big Lebowski* jokes the whole time. "It's a league game, Smokey," I said after a gutter ball, and we thought this was knee-slapping hilarious.

I realize my drugged gallivanting with another woman wasn't doing right by my marriage, but — as I swore to Ava when I confessed months later — on my mother's grave, I never came close to having sex with Cheryl. I hugged her goodbye on Sunday morning, thanked her for the romp, wished her the best and didn't so much as exchange phone numbers. I was enamored of the cocaine, smitten by how it took me aloft, as if I were a Rockefeller or Jay Gatsby floating through the Greenbrier's grand rooms and mahogany bars with their twenty-dollar drinks. She was intrigued by the challenge, by a man telling her no but elongating the refusal over three idyllic, chemically endless days.

By Saturday morning, for me, the vibe between us was akin to boy-and-girl cousins on the family's last big summer camping trip before the eighth grade, an only-so-far affection born of board games, inside jokes and adolescent Truth-or-Dare secrets. I told Ava just that, but she was having none of it: "What an asinine thing to say when you were wasting our money on an old nympho with a coke habit."

Driving away from the sprawling white hotel, waving at the security guard, returning to the mundane world, I felt shabby and guilty and shaky, sickly, and I blasted the air-conditioning and vowed to myself:

"Never again. Line drawn." A few miles from home, I tried to choke down a fast-food hamburger and couldn't take more than a bite, and leaving the restaurant I thought about — *imagined* — a smidgen of coke, a remedy that would no doubt cure me and iron out the rest of the day.

The last Saturday in May, I drove to Richmond and met a seedy high school friend nicknamed Wizard and bought a thousand dollars' worth of cocaine, enough, I rationalized, to dabble in on weekends for months and months. I used it the day I bought it — needed to test the quality. The following Tuesday, I snorted a little in our garage. Twice. Soon, the euphoria didn't always arrive on schedule, and a single blast didn't always deliver the goods, and the high never persisted like it had at the Greenbrier, but I began craving the shit. The morning of my forty-second birthday, June 28, I was in the basement bathroom with the door locked, and when I jerked my head up from an 8:00 a.m. countertop inhalation, I saw my reflection in the mirror, skin starting to sallow, eyes nested in dark smudge pits, hair a shaggy rat's nest — a corroded version of myself.

I was smart enough to realize I was screwed: the it-can-happen-that-quickly-to-

276

anybody addict, rattlesnaked. The day before, the dope had made my nose bleed. I sat on the floor, wearing only boxers, the tile cool against the undersides of my bare legs, and the birthday cocaine started to creep into my senses, and I closed my eyes and gave in to it, lay flat on my back on the tiny throw rug, a wretched snow angel.

I didn't dare appear in court or attempt anything complicated at my office, and I never failed to give a client my sober efforts. I set appointments only between ten and noon on Wednesdays and Thursdays, and on those days I didn't use. Other days, though, I'd often get wired after lunch, gild the high with a swig of bourbon and play pinball — Monster Bash and Twilight Zone — at a bowling alley over in Vinton. I rescheduled cases and depositions and motions hearings, and initially, owing to my reputation, everyone accepted the routine excuses at face value, no worries, but then Judge Carson noticed how disheveled I looked at an early-morning July 6 infant settlement hearing. I'd already completed the work weeks before and was showing up simply to collect a hefty check for my client, but the judge, an old friend, was concerned and invited me into his office and asked, "You okay, Kevin?"

"Overworked and underpaid," I said. In preparation for court, I'd gone three days without alcohol and coke, and my head felt like it was under siege by a swarm of hornets. I had to clasp my hands in my lap to keep them still and steady. "Slammed at the office and can't shake the flu. Or whatever it is that's going around. Thanks for asking, though. Do I look that bad?" I laughed and tried to play it off, but I sounded weird and furtive. I did a line in my car the moment I arrived back at my office parking lot.

By August 15, a lawyer who for nearly two decades was usually in one court or another every day hadn't seen a trial or meaningful legal appearance in six weeks. My staff realized that something was terribly wrong, and Ava couldn't have been sweeter to me, gently quizzing me about work problems, asking if she'd disappointed me or hurt my feelings, and then, as I became more erratic, pleading with me not to drink, even scheduling a weekend vacation — that I refused — so we could clean the slate and I could cure my Maker's Mark woes.

The Monday before I was arrested, she and my doc, Gary Simonds, appeared at my office, and we discussed Antabuse and twelve-step programs and the fact that alcoholism is a disease, same as any other sickness. "Seriously," I told them, "I don't have a drinking problem. I'm just going through a little melancholy patch, and everybody dwelling on it only makes it worse. I'm okay." Ava never knew I was hooked on coke, always figured it was booze, though the night before my collapse, she asked, "Is there something else, like pills or drugs? Or maybe you're having an affair and trying to push me away?"

On August 25, Wizard, for an extra hundred in "carrying charges," agreed to meet me at a Roanoke roadhouse called the Coffee Pot and deliver another grand's worth of dope. I spent the afternoon before our meeting sequestered in my office, perusing the Internet for the best rehabs, and decided — in true junkie fashion — that I'd suffer through another week of coke, just one more, and finally tell Ava, yeah, I'm drinking too much, and then fly to Minnesota and get clean and sober, wash my sins away in the river of twelve-step redemption.

I didn't want Ava to see a thousand bucks in cash withdrawn from our checking account, so before leaving the office, I took my key, unlocked the money drawer and grabbed twelve hundred dollars, mostly in large bills. I didn't realize the money was a retainer, trust-account funds I hadn't yet earned, a fee dropped off ten minutes before closing by a regular client, Christina Phelps. Mismanagement of trust funds is lawyer poison, simple and easy for the bar to detect, and always guaranteed to prompt a license revocation. No matter how high I was, I *never* would've pulled a trust-account fee and used it as my own. Never.

Keisha, my paralegal, had been unable to make it to the bank before five, and in a rush, she'd stuck the cash in the drawer for safekeeping, intending to deposit it in the proper account the next morning. Following my arrest, I promptly refunded the cash to Christina — with a tiny amount of interest — and she wrote a letter defending me to the bar, described how her new attorney had charged a higher fee and "just done what Attorney Kevin Moore had already told me I needed to do." Keisha cried and apologized and also wrote to the bar, but it was my fault for any number of reasons. I was the lawyer, the boss who was responsible for "office management and accounting protocols," as that portion of my suspension notice worded it.

Wizard was already at the Coffee Pot when I arrived, seated at a table with a pitcher of beer and an order of chicken fingers and fries. Two women were with him, an unexpected complication. I didn't want to be seen with a drug dealer, and I assumed their hanging around would slow down our deal. I wanted to pay him, get the coke and be gone.

Wizard — whose given name is Stanley — was wearing what we in the business call a probable-cause ensemble: a tight tan suit, cowboy boots and a blue linen shirt with the top three buttons undone. His hair was gathered into a ponytail, he was sporting a single diamond earring, and he'd ditched his high school glasses for contacts. Imagine the guest villain on a season-three episode of *Miami Vice* crossed with a 2008 J.Crew catalog.

"My man," he said as soon as he spotted me. Wizard is not attractive. He's skinny and potbellied, and his features — especially his nose — are a size too small for his face, as if God's installers received the wrong hardware packet but pushed through the job anyway.

"Wizard," I said with no enthusiasm.

"I told you we're *amigos,*" he crowed to the ladies. "For years. Ever since tenth grade."

"I read about you in the paper all the

time," one of the women said. "You're famous."

"Not really," I answered.

"Take a load off and have a beer with us."

"I'm fine, thanks."

Wizard pinched a fry, dabbed it into a spread of ketchup, bit it in half and talked while he was chewing. "These goddesses are Amber and Tracey," he said, nodding at each lady as he introduced her. His angle was apparent: He'd bragged to the women about his long friendship with a high-flying lawyer, and he hoped to ride my coattails and leverage this connection, plus, of course, some free dope, into sex with one or both of the girls, and this was dismal news for me, because it meant I was in line to pay extra dues and sell the ladies on Wizard Stanley.

Still, I took a fling at ending my business and escaping the Coffee Pot. "So, Wizard," I said, "how about I buy you a shot, you and me, at the bar? A gift from an old bud."

"Hell, just have 'em bring me a Corona over here," he said. "Let's put this party in high gear." He tapped the table in front of an empty chair. "It's early. Sit with your friend. And order some more of those purple shots for the goddesses — right, ladies?"

"Sure," Amber replied.

"Thank you very much, Kevin," Tracey said in a silly, ingénue's voice that didn't square with her pierced nose and snug cut-offs.

I ordered two shots, the beer for Wizard and a straight bourbon on ice for myself. I gunned half the liquor before the waitress finished serving the table, while she still had Wizard's cold bottle balanced on her tray.

"Have you ever lost an important case?" Amber asked, pushing back her hair on both sides. Her several bracelets rattled. Her T-shirt tightened and slid up past her navel when she raised her arms for the hair show. "I bet you win all the time," she cooed.

She was about twenty-five years old, a hothouse orchid, lovely and ephemeral, a perfectly gorgeous woman by any measure, thick blonde hair and a starlet's smile, but you quickly sensed she was a beauty on borrowed time, and soon enough she'd wilt, maybe lose a tooth or gain a scar, and by forty, there'd be liver damage and yellow skin and a handicapped parking placard. *Right now,* though, any sad ending was miles away, and she was a carpe diem gal, living pretty while it lasted, Purple-Hooter-Shooter Cinderella.

"I've lost more than I've won," I replied.

"It's the nature of the business." I was in an anxious, pissy mood, and the bourbon wasn't taking my edge off yet.

"How about you and I have a little pow-wow in my office?" Wizard said, jerking a thumb toward the toilet.

"Sure," I answered. "I need to use the restroom anyway."

"You girls please excuse us," he said. "Help yourselves to more drinks or food, on the Wizard. With much more to come."

"Man," he whined as soon as we were in the small john, "you need to, like, chill with my girls. Come on. I'm sure you get more pussy than you can shake a stick at. It won't kill you to pull some wingman duty for your old pal."

"Listen, Stanley. I have no interest in the girls. None. They're hitting on me, not the other way around. The sooner I leave, the better off you'll be. I just want my package. I'll pay you and vanish."

"Then I'll look like a loser. Like I'm a stupid drug dealer and that's my entire thing. Seriously."

"You'll need to make it worth my while. I didn't sign up for this."

"Sure," he said. "Okay, okay. I'll forget the extra hundred. Free delivery."

"And . . ." I stretched the word.

"What?"

"Reach into your pocket and give me a sample before I have to return to the table and do my best lawyer's closing argument for these women. Consider it a fee."

"And you'll party with us? But not snake the girls?"

"Twenty minutes," I said, "then I'm outta here, and the ladies are all yours."

"Perfect. Fair enough. Aren't they foxes, Kevin?"

"*Foxes?* Christ, Stanley."

He locked the entrance door, and we jammed into the single stall, the commode between us, and we each took a snort. I felt improved when I returned to the table, and noticed Amber's chair was much closer to mine. I sipped the bourbon. I made up a story about how Wizard, as a senior, had cleverly hoodwinked our English teacher into giving us both an A for our last semester and allowed us to skip the final exam. Amber laughed, and she swayed and brushed against my shoulder. They all ordered another round, and the coke was partnering nicely with the liquor and erasing my ill temper, so I told them I'd have one for the road.

"Cool," Amber said.

"What do you ladies do?" I asked. "Work-wise, I mean."

"We're dancers," Amber said. "That's how we know Wizard. From the club in Richmond."

"As in gentlemen's club?" I asked.

"Yep," Tracey replied. "As in."

"But I'm planning to start college," Amber added. "Get my associate's in medical technology. I'd like to be an X-ray tech. Or something in the medical field, so long as there's no blood." She pushed away her empty shot glass with her index finger. "Can't strip forever. Nobody wants to see sags and cellulite."

"Well, no worries about that," Wizard gushed. He was damn near drooling. "I can promise you these two knockouts are as sexy as can be. I'm a personal witness to how built Amber is. No hearsay, Kevin. You can't object." He grinned big at his own wit.

"So you live in Richmond?" I asked Amber.

"No, over in Red Hill, about fifteen minutes from here," she said. "Tracey has a place in Richmond, and I work mostly weekends and crash with her when I'm down there."

"Guess what their stage names are," Wizard interjected.

I shrug. "Aphrodite and Diamond?"

286

Tracey giggled. "I'm Lolita. Amber's Merlot."

"Thoughtful choices," I said. I tilted my glass so the ice avalanched against my front teeth, drained the balance of the liquor and set the glass on the table, done. "Well, ladies, treat Wizard well. He's a champ. Enjoy the evening, nice meeting you both, but I need to go home and see my wife."

"You're married?" Amber asked.

"Hence the wedding ring," I said.

"How long?" Tracey asked.

"Eighteen excellent years," I said. "Why don't you walk me out, Wizard?"

"Don't leave now," Amber told me. "You're being a stick in the mud." She looked at Wizard. "Make him stay. Just for a little while. It's not even dark. And I have a delicious buzz — a shame to waste all the money and party effort and have to sober up."

Wizard received the message loud and clear. "Come on, Kevin. The night's young. We can't disappoint our guests. Don't be rude."

Over the next two hours, Stanley wheedled and begged and plied me with free coke, and I decided at around seven-thirty that this was my curtain call, my last drug binge, my farewell banquet, and I even told Wizard

I'd pay him for the half-ounce but he could just keep it and sell it elsewhere. I called Ava to let her know that I was safe but wouldn't be home for a few hours, and she was simultaneously concerned and mad, and she kept saying, "Your speech is slurred," and implored me to tell her where I was so she could come and take care of me.

"I love you, Ava," I promised her. "I'm checking in to rehab tomorrow. Please, don't worry."

At eight o'clock, a small band, three scruffy kids, began moving in speakers and instruments, and this prompted a boastful, discursive Wizard filibuster about how he "went backstage at the Richmond Coliseum and hung out with Donald Fagen . . . you know, Steely Dan."

"Who?" Amber mouthed to me. She shrugged.

"I have the picture to prove it," Wizard proclaimed. He began scrolling through his phone for the photo, found it, held it at arm's length and toured it from person to person.

A few minutes before the band started, I felt a tap on my shoulder and looked up and saw Simon Roberts and his wife, Sandra, and I'd essentially been on a coke-and-alcohol tear for over three months, so I blurted, "Simon, what the fuck are you doing here?"

Simon's an accomplished attorney, and his wife's a sweetheart. In 2014, we'd worked together as cocounsel and settled a products-liability case, but sitting there wired and incomplete, it seemed like a decade ago. He grinned and didn't flinch at my coarse, startled greeting. "Grandkid," he replied, gesturing toward the tiny stage. "The tall one's ours."

"He's a very talented musician," Sandra added.

If I'd been sober and this had been an innocent beer with an old friend, I would've said, "This is my pal Stanley, from high school. We went to Northside together. These are *his* Richmond friends, Amber and Tracey. Look forward to hearing your grandson play." Instead, I moronically announced: "Merlot and Lolita, meet Roanoke's best lawyer and his awesome wife. And this is Wizard."

Sandra didn't bat an eye. "Well," she said, "please sprinkle some magic and good spells on the band, Wizard."

"Feel free to join us," Wizard offered.

Simon's in his late sixties. He was wearing his signature gold watch fob and a tailored suit. "Appreciate it, but we're planning to order dinner, so we'll find our own table."

"Those are such amazing earrings," Amber said as soon as they were out of earshot. "Ten thousand, easy. How do you know them? He a lawyer too?"

"Yeah," I answered. "Unfortunately," I mumbled so she couldn't hear.

"Before I forget," Amber said, "let me give you my cell number. You have a pen?"

"You can just tell me," I answered. "I have a remarkable memory."

"Really? Okay, it's 540-340-6687. Amber Archer."

"Thanks."

"So did you really listen?" she asked. "What's my number?"

Even under the influence of liquor and a Schedule II drug, I recited the number.

"Wow, amazing. Maybe we might see each other after tonight, if you ever wanted to call me."

"I'd never cheat on my wife," I declared, and meant it.

"If she was included, it wouldn't be cheating. The three of us together might be super-sexy."

I told Ava that my recollection of my last couple hours at the bar was spotty and unreliable, full of gaps. I explained that the aperture in my mind became smaller and smaller, narrowed until I was peering through a puckered dot, aware only of whatever was immediately in front of me and not much else. I made a wrong turn on a trip to the toilet, got lost and wound up in the kitchen. I remember paying the band twenty bucks to cover Billy Joe Shaver's "Live Forever," and I recall sending bourbon shots to Simon and Sandra. I discovered the next day that I'd entrusted my truck keys to the bartender.

I also remember agreeing to have a nightcap and more coke at Amber's trailer, and we decided that she'd drive since I could beat the DUI in court if she were stopped by the police, plus she drove fucked-up all the time, so she could handle it. The band was still playing when we left, but I have no idea what time it was.

Her trailer had a clattering air-conditioning unit drooping from a window, and the black trash bag in the kitchen wasn't inside any kind of can or container, was half full and just squatting on the floor. Her bedroom smelled of cigarettes and plug-in Febreze baby-powder air freshener.

I sat on the edge of her bed, and she stripped for me. The music was Nirvana, she said, and it was druggy and loud and fast but not too fast, Bluetoothed from her phone to a wireless speaker. By the end of the song, she was naked except for low-cut panties, and she rubbed a butterfly tattoo that was partially hidden by the underwear across my cheek. "We can't do this at the club," she said, and stepped out of the panties. "This is for you. Private." Eventually, she pulled a condom from her purse. "Sorry," she said. "But you don't have to wear it if you think we'll be okay."

I confessed all this to my wife, thought she was entitled to know the truth if we remained married — informed consent, we call it in the legal field — and I explained that I'd sinned against her because I wasn't aware I was married at that strange, impaired, addled point. I was taking in the world through a peephole, processing the here and now, my past and my conscience and my history eradicated, as if I were subhuman, a lizard strictly focused on an insect within tongue's reach. There was no periphery, no sense of self, no soul's storehouse, no angel's nudge or devil's exhortation.

"Believe me," I said to Ava more than once, "I realize how awful this sounds. How mad I'd be at you if the shoe were on the other foot. But you know, as much as I love you, and as much as I love our marriage, I'd never, ever, make the *conscious* choice to cheat on you."

"How the hell do you forget you're married?" she fumed. "How do you not account for *eighteen years,* Kevin? That's even worse — you *forgot* me? Glad our marriage means so much."

"How? Well, you allow cocaine and liquor to strangle your personality and decency. It's my fault. No excuses. None. There's no possible way I can justify or explain away adultery. No way to put a gloss on my being a cad and a failure. I can only hope you'll forgive me. The drugs erased most of *me.* I wasn't normal. It's the same as when they gave you fentanyl and Versed at the hospital; you have no recollection of inviting every nurse and doc to our nonexistent beach house. It's called *dope* for a reason."

"Well, apparently your dick was normal."

According to the police report, they raided Amber's mobile home at 2:04 a.m. The cops weren't there for me or Amber or Tracey or, in a certain sense, Wizard. They were there because Wizard's supplier, Calvin Jurgens, a biker from Pennsylvania, was under surveillance, and he'd made arrangements to meet Wizard in Roanoke at the Coffee Pot, do a $10,000 exchange, spend the night and keep driving south. Evidently, there were the usual drug-deal hiccups and delays, so Jurgens and his burly enforcer eventually ended up at the Red Hill trailer with a shit-load of dope, guns, scales and cash at around one-thirty.

I fell asleep naked in Amber's bed, on top of the sheets, and I woke to shouting and commotion in the den, but I was high, groggy, so I processed it simply as noise and didn't understand what was being said, didn't realize it was a police raid until two hotshots with guns pointed at me burst into the room, shouting, "State police. Don't fucking move. Show us your hands." I was alone, no sign of Amber, and still loopy and disconnected, and according to the report, I said, "Why're you here?" I also asked, "Where's my truck?"

It took a few moments, but the details started to click, and I understood the police were in the mobile home and this was dire. I could hear cursing from the den, and Tracey was screaming. Lawyering is ingrained in me, automatic, and I looked around the room for dope and paraphernalia. Evidence of a crime. There was residue on a mirror beside the bed, along with the classic rolled-up twenty-dollar bill, but I could wiggle away from those facts in court if need be: not my trailer, not my bedroom, it was dark when I went to sleep, and I had no idea the dope was there beside me. Good luck locating a fingerprint on the twenty-straw, and even if the lab ID'd my print on U.S. currency, what exactly does that prove?

But oh fuck, damn, damn, damn, fuck me, my pants were tossed on the floor within arm's reach, and there was a gram of coke in the front pocket, the last powder I'd taken from Wizard for my *final* narcotics binge, and my wallet was in the hip pocket, and the I-grabbed-my-cousin's-pants-to-go-to-the-store defense never works, especially when the trousers fit me perfectly and the Coffee Pot credit-card receipt with my name on it was also in the pocket.

A third cop, wearing a bulletproof vest with POLICE stenciled in yellow across the chest, strolled into the room and smartass said: "Let's go, lover boy. Get dressed."

"Where's my shirt?" I mumbled.

"We're not your butlers," the cop replied. "You probably want to take that rubber off before you go to jail. Might give some of the inmates the wrong idea." The other two policemen snickered.

Okay, I thought, *so maybe I'll know one of these guys, maybe they're local and I can catch a pass, a backdoor exit and a lips-*

sealed ride home. Like many attorneys, I'd always done free or discounted legal work for the police as a professional courtesy, advised them on driveway-easement disputes, represented them in custody and divorce cases or prepared their basic wills and medical directives. I'd been aggressive and thorough and a fierce advocate for my criminal defendants, but I'd never lied or cut corners, never sucker-punched an officer, and any anger or bruised feelings because a guilty, asshole defendant escaped punishment usually — with one or two exceptions — yielded to a quiet, wait-till-next-time respect. Ava occasionally remarked that the cops and I were like Ralph E. Wolf and Sam Sheepdog, going at it tooth and nail until we clocked off and ended the shift.

I didn't recognize any of the cops. They were all state police, sent from Richmond, not deputies from Roanoke or Salem or nearby, and when I zoned in on the silver nameplate closest to me and saw *A. Hunsicker,* I knew I wouldn't be receiving any special treatment, not from a stranger with a high-and-tight haircut, black combat boots and a name as bellicose and spring-loaded as they come. In fact, Officer Andrew Hunsicker tightened the cuffs a click past where they needed to be, so my wrists were red-ringed by the time I arrived at the police station.

The arrest was embarrassing. Humiliating. The worst of it, though, was my booking shot. Not only did I look like a guy who'd been wallowing in a long-term drug orgy, but I was still discombobulated when I dressed to leave with the cops. I didn't dare claim my incriminating trousers, and I couldn't find my shirt. So I was photographed wearing socks, strange sweatpants and a T-shirt, an XL neon-yellow V-neck from a Myrtle Beach gift shop, evidently Amber's makeshift nightgown. I GOT LOST AT THE GAY DOLPHIN was written across the shirt's front in block letters.

In 2014, I'd represented a man named Harold Lambert in a custody case, and he'd deservedly received custody of his young daughter. It wasn't a difficult or close call for the judge. The mother was a maternal disaster named Shelly Burton. Shelly's sister worked at the 911 center, heard about my arrest, and my photo, which was public record and fair game, ended up on Shelly's Facebook page with the caption: "This is the man who cost me my kid and said I was a bad mom." The picture was cropped so that only I GOT LOST was visible on the yellow shirt, though a later Facebook post showed the entire Gay Dolphin message, which was probably even more humbling, a respected attorney reduced to wearing an ill-fitting, tacky tourist shirt from a trinket emporium. At least I'm now at the point where I can chuckle about it.

CHAPTER ELEVEN

I release Nelson from his pen as soon as I arrive home from my Roanoke meetings with Ava and Margo Jordan, and we begin working on our pet tricks. I have him sit, stay, then fetch a tennis ball from ten feet away. This is familiar stuff — he knows it well, learned it as a pup at the restaurant. Next, we substitute my car keys for the ball, and after a few balks and false starts, he understands it's the same routine with a new, different object and grasps the lanyard on my keys and brings them to me. I reward him with a dog biscuit. Finally, I drop my wallet on the ground, and he learns to fetch it as well. "Smart boy," I praise him. Soon, I'll put all three down together, and I'll teach him to select the ball or the keys or the wallet according to my command.

There's a message from Ava's insurance company on the answering machine, and I call the 800 number, navigate the phone-tree labyrinth and punch in the extension for Louis Dillon, a "senior claims administrator."

Dillon is somewhere between surly and indifferent when he answers and asks for my full name, the last four digits of my Social Security number, the policy and group numbers and the claim date or dates.

"Okay," he says. "Yeah, I see you've been calling for a while, and so now your claim has reached my final level of review, and it looks like, after a careful and full inspection of your file, you aren't covered under your wife's policy past the June thirtieth cancellation date. We can't pay for any claims that come after the policy has ended."

"Louis," I say, and stop.

"Yes."

"Louis," I repeat.

"Yes," he says in the same bored, arrogant voice.

"Let's start like this."

"Like how?" he asks.

"Are you near a computer?"

"Of course. Why wouldn't I be?"

"So," I say, "here's what I want you to do. I want you to Google my name, 'Kevin Moore,' and the words 'courtroom' and 'Clooney.' As in George. Can you do that for me, Louis?"

"Why?"

"Because, Louis, I want you to understand who you're dealing with. I'll wait. Read the article."

"I can't," he says. "I'd have to exit this screen and leave your file, and the facts are the facts. I could Google 'Obi-Wan Kenobi' and it could be you, but you wouldn't be insured after the thirtieth. Sorry about that."

"When you find the piece and read it — which you'll do, sooner or later — you'll discover that I'm a lawyer —"

"Yeah, I already know. Your file history shows you've told every claims rep 'I'm a lawyer' every time you called. So we've been aware of your profession for nearly two months."

"Excellent. Then you'll understand I'm not blowing smoke when I tell you this: The policy was never legally canceled."

"Policy clearly states that it's canceled on the day we receive the notice. We received your wife's letter on June thirtieth. Open and shut, sir."

"My wife's paid bimonthly, the first and the sixteenth. In June, she told you to cancel on the sixteenth of July, and her paycheck was debited on July first for payment in advance through the sixteenth. You accepted that premium and still have the money. The

301

law, Louis, Section 38.2-3503 of the Code, states that the cancellation's effective when you get the letter *or* on the date stated in the letter. We chose the *or* option."

"I'm sure her refund is being processed."

"Also, by law, you have to give me written notice of the termination and her employer has to offer me the chance to extend coverage through COBRA. Never happened. None of that. You swindlers are so lazy and corrupt that you *still* haven't bothered to send a proper cancellation notice or my extension options. There's no effective cancellation. So here's what's going to happen. I'm going to sue for the money I'm owed, and for bad faith and punitive damages. And I'll win."

"I can't help who you sue. Anyway, it's not my money."

"Well, Louis, your money is your money, correct?"

"I don't understand." His tone shifts from the indifferent monotone.

"You have my records there, yes?"

"Yes."

"And you told me that you've reviewed them?"

"Part of my job," he replies.

"You know what happened to me?"

"You had a stroke. Very sorry it happened." He's polite only because he's aware our conversation is being recorded.

"So here's my take on this," I say calmly. "I know for a fact that your position in the company and your compensation and advancement are based on your management of claims — in other words, the less you pay policyholders, the better it personally is for you."

"Not true," he almost shouts. "Not true. Urban legend. Myth."

"You believe you can take advantage of my disability for your own benefit, maybe earn a raise or promotion or the bonus vacation to Cancún at my expense by denying a valid claim for reasons you know — or should know, based on your training — are utterly false. You're wronging me to benefit yourself. I'm going to sue you too, Louis. Individually. For several million. Let's see how that looks on your résumé."

"You can't . . . you can't do that."

"Really? Why not? I just told you why I can."

"Well, you can't," he replies.

"Better yet, my friend, it won't cost me a dime. My legal services are free, and I've got nothing but time. How much do you think it'll cost you to hire an attorney to defend this? Don't count on your company paying for your lawyer. They'll run away from you as fast as they can — the toad who manipulated the claim of a stroke victim to fatten his own wallet. They'll cut you free and pretend they've never heard of this kind of corporate disgrace."

"So, okay, Mr. Clooney —"

"Moore," I interrupt him. "Kevin Moore."

"Okay. Well, this is some new information for your file. I didn't know about not sending a notice. Our records show we did."

I laugh. "Bullshit."

"If you'll give me a few days to explore this a little further, maybe we can agree to a compromise."

"Explore away." I laugh again. "But don't explore too long."

"I'll have you an answer in a week. Okay?"

"Tell me your cell number," I instruct him.

"Huh?"

"I want your cell number, Louis. I don't intend to get dumped into the claims quagmire and have to reinvent the wheel every time I call and land with another rep. You're my boy. I want a direct line."

"We're not allowed to do that," he frets. "I promise I'll call you."

"Your company took my money and promised they'd pay my medical bills. Why in the world would I trust you?"

304

I hear him sigh. He hesitates. "540-831-8904."

Ward visits me at the sandwich shop the next day, September 2, a gloomy, misty Friday. A clotheshorse and a bit of a dandy, he's wearing a blue sharkskin suit, a pink shirt with monogrammed cuffs and a navy tie with stripes that match the shirt's pink hue.

"Casting call for *Guys and Dolls* at the high school?" I rib him. It's the middle of the afternoon, not much traffic in the restaurant, and I meet him at the entrance.

"No, but I understand they're remaking *Fast Times at Ridgemont High,* and the producers need a down-on-his-luck restaurant employee in khakis and a dorky polo shirt to play the Judge Reinhold role. Might be your ticket out of this disaster."

"Ouch," I say. We both laugh, and he follows me to a booth, the same spot where I sat with Caleb Opportunity.

"I read your e-mail and your brief on the car search," he says. "It's well done. I'll be pleased to steal it, sign it and claim it as my own."

The speaker is dumping fetid country music on us, a song about drinking on a pontoon boat. "Thanks," I say.

"Let's start with the administrative side of your situations. You have a Roanoke violation on your under-advisement cocaine charge, and two new felonies in the city of Martinsville. Your civil case is in Patrick County. You're certainly spreading the venue love. Because the new criminal cases can impact your under-advisement possession case, we were gifted with Judge Morris on the gun and meth charges even though they occurred in Martinsville. As best I can tell, he volunteered for the job once he got wind of your unhappy day with Flanagan, asked for the designation in the name of 'judicial economy.' "

"And, ironically, that worked to our advantage," I add. "Any competent judge would've locked my ass up until trial. We stumbled into that good fortune — hell, I was bitching because I was stuck with him hearing my bond request."

Ward leans closer to the table. "But we both understand he's not going to grant a suppression motion on the gun and meth or declare his own order invalid. I doubt he'll even read the excellent brief you've written. So, if I'm being honest and realistic, we're looking at your being found guilty, receiving five or six years, some of which is mandatory time, and he'll revoke your bond the day you're sentenced."

"Then I'll marinate in jail while I wait for my appeal to be heard. For months."

"Plus, as we discussed, I'd guess your appeal odds are fifty-fifty. It's very possible that the Supreme Court will allow the convictions to stand. Sorry, but it's my job to tell you the truth."

I stare into the parking lot for a moment, notice the rain gaining pace and dimpling several puddles. "Yeah, damn. I can't argue with you there; it's a close call. You're probably right, but a suppression motion is my only chance. I'm not going to win a swearing contest with a probation officer, especially with my fingerprints on the dope bags and Flanagan testifying that I claimed the meth and pistol. You got the Shadrich info, right — his sister and the West Virginia land deal?"

"I did," Ward says, "but I don't see him rolling into court and me Perry Masoning him with five minutes left in the show. We can prove he has a sister who was charged with a DUI — which was dismissed — in another state, and that her charity overpaid for land in West Virginia. Doesn't help us."

I twist my trunk and nod toward the counter. "And there are your dope wrappers. Caleb had me make him a nothing sandwich so he could get my prints. I touched the wrap, and then they used it for the dope."

"Let's try to concentrate on the less fantastical elements of our defense," Ward says dryly.

"I just wanted you to know how it happened. I've been clean for over a year."

"Point made," he answers. "I'm thinking that we ask Morris to recuse on the new charges. No reason the Martinsville judges can't hear your Martinsville cases, especially the motion to kick out the meth and pistol. They have no conflict. It'll piss Morris off —"

"But," I interject, "it can't get any worse than it is now. The guy's got an ax to grind with me."

"There might even be a Constitutional argument that you're entitled to a judge from the community where the offense occurred, not some vigilante who volunteered for the job because he wants to teach you a lesson. Morris is from Culpeper, four hours away."

"Who'd hear my case in Martinsville?"

"Judge Williams."

"What's his deal?" I ask.

"Nicknamed Hollywood," Ward answers.

"Why?"

308

"No one seems to know, though he kind of favors a pudgy Burt Reynolds. I don't think that's actually the reason; the name's a mystery. He's smart and fair, and that's all we can ask for. A quality judge. He'll study the cases and brief we give him. A thousand percent better than Morris."

"Nothing to lose," I agree. "File the motion."

Blaine walks to the table and brings Ward a large Coke and a cup of ice. "On the house," he says. "Take care of Lawyer Kevin."

"I'll do my best," Ward promises.

"Superior threads, sir," Blaine notes as he's leaving. "That's how an attorney oughta dress."

"I realize you'll probably disagree," I say to Ward, "but I want to have my criminal motion first, see if we can catch suppression lightning in a jar, then I'm going to answer questions and reveal this scam in the deposition. I'm not planning to take the Fifth."

"Why?" Ward asks.

"I want to know where I stand, whether I'll need a bunt single or home run in the civil case. If I lose the suppression motion on the gun and dope, I'm cooked unless I can grab a miracle with Melanie Culp. Makes sense to know where I am factually and legally before Margo and I finally have the chance to quiz her."

"Okay," Ward says. "But it makes no sense — none — to let a star litigator like M. D. Jenkins take a free shot at you if you don't have to, especially when a tiny slip or small misstep will make your already bad criminal case even worse. Hell, Kevin, if I'm being honest, just telling your crazy story under oath — as opposed to accepting responsibility — makes my job more difficult. You have to realize it'll appear that you're lying and trying to dodge your obvious guilt."

"I want the story and the true facts on record. Broadcast. Somewhere, somehow, for somebody, it might shed light on what the Caleb Opportunity gang is doing. Might help some other poor sucker. Throw a wrench in their machine. It's the only fight I can give them, and I plan to go down swinging."

"Bad idea," Ward says firmly. He punctuates the sentence by jabbing a straw into the ice cubes. "Really bad. Margo Jordan already told me about you wanting to testify in the civil case before we resolve the criminal charges." He stabs the ice again. "Did I mention it's a completely idiotic idea?"

"It's unorthodox," I agree, "but even if I screw up with Jenkins, so what? No judge or jury will believe I'm being railroaded in a sophisticated insurance scam if I go to a trial loaded with crime-lab evidence and an experienced and seemingly neutral probation officer against me. I understand that. You understand that. Truth is, if I don't win this suppression motion, you'll be putting on your begging rags, taking hat in hand and scraping for the best plea bargain we can get. The facts aren't my friend in the gun and meth cases. But I mean to put as many spotlights and big bright flags on these people as I can, no matter what. There's no need for me to testify in the suppression hearing, so let's win that and then we won't have to worry about all the rest."

"I'll see if I can schedule us a quick hearing," Ward says. He twists open the soft drink, and air fizzes from around the plastic top. "Seriously, Kevin? You're a lawyer, an excellent lawyer. You're not seriously planning to tell that story under oath?"

"We'll see," I answer.

"Also, some old business while I'm here: I received a call from Investigator Brooks in Roanoke. Evidently, Calvin Jurgens is claiming the dope found at Amber Archer's trailer the night you were arrested belonged to some yahoo named Wizard. They're interested in what you can tell them, and whether you'd be willing to testify. Sorry to revisit such a bad night."

"I'm not a snitch, and I'm not interested in shining up my junior deputy's badge, but you can tell them that Jurgens is the kingpin, Wizard's the stooge. If need be, and if I'm called as a witness, I'll testify truthfully."

"I'll pass that along," Ward says. "Oh, damn, one last thing. I almost forgot. You're still counsel of record in a Roanoke case called *Sowerby v. Perry.* It's back on the docket and active again. Dickie Cranwell sent me a substitution order for you to sign so he can take over and represent your client. I left it in the car. How about walking out with me and signing it?"

"I will," I say glumly. "Shit. Sorry, but sometimes this whole unfair mess just wears on me. I've been Jay Sowerby's lawyer forever. Now I can't help him, can't practice law."

The rain's become steady by the time I finish work, and my ride home is sheeted with fog. Often it's so thick that I have to slow the Ford to a crawl. I burn the low beams as I start climbing the mountain, but they're overwhelmed and ineffective, gobbled up

312

inches away from the car. A logging truck almost slams into me from behind. It takes fifteen minutes longer than usual to make the trip from SUBstitution to Melvin's.

Following some trial and error and several hours of training — not to mention a flogging blitz by the largest hen — I'm now able to leave Nelson free in the yard during the day, and he keeps his distance from the birds. He's waiting on the porch, wet and hyper, happy to see me. He's destroyed a sofa cushion, the polyester filling scattered across the yard, the pillow muddy, deflated and lopsided. I scold him and point at the cushion, but it's too late to do anything that will help solve the issue in the future. Knowing Melvin, I'm positive that the cushion cost a pretty penny, and I hope I can find a single replacement online and won't have to buy an entire new set thanks to Nelson's bored misbehavior.

I put out his bowl of food and eat a Luther's Special and chips I brought home from the shop. I hurry through the meal, then sit at the kitchen counter and hand-write a letter to Minivan Dan. Regular, old-school post leaves no traceable footprint or e-record. I don't worry about intercepts or wiretaps. It's the safest communication I can have with my best friend:

MVD: May need a huge favor. Understand if you can't help. Will determine for certain following my deposition. Can you be here in person September/October? Need you to drive and leave no travel record. Phone confirmation is Professor Abbott. Thanks and sorry. BURN THIS. Kevin

I use Melvin's computer to access my patient portal at Forsyth Hospital and request an urgent appointment with Dr. Wallace. In the rectangular REASON FOR VISIT box I type: "I'm still having difficulties with my left hand and ankle and left face discomfort. I have trouble using my left hand, grasping objects at work, bending over without dizziness." I call his office and leave the same information on his answering machine.

The next morning, Saturday, the rain has vanished and the day is a delight, even for me, with my burdens and hobbles and house arrest. The sky is scrubbed and bright and reborn, the first teeny-tiny fall bite is threaded through the mountain air, and an early yellow leaf is chinked into a tall poplar. Nelson and I practice his bang-dead-dog trick, and he licks my face and hands when I bend down to fill his breakfast bowl.

At SUBstitution, traffic is slow for a Saturday, a welcome relief, and at three-fifteen the store's empty, and I step outside and join Blaine, who's smoking a cigarette. A nervous kid with a full beard and a Floyd-Fest T-shirt just came in and bought a bottled water and spoke to Blaine in a hushed voice. The kid left, met Blaine at the kitchen door and, no doubt, purchased a bag of pot. Blaine is watching his customer drive away. The bearded lad shoots Blaine a thumbs-up through his car window, and Blaine says, "Use the power wisely, my friend."

"You being careful with your business?" I ask. "Applying the rules I gave you?"

"You bet," he answers.

"You can't do the viper gig forever," I remind him. "Sooner or later, it'll go sideways on you, especially here in a small town."

"I hear you." He sucks in a long draw from the Pall Mall, exhales it from both his nose and mouth.

"I have a favor to ask," I announce.

"Absolutely," Blaine replies. "Anything I can do. You've been nothin' but great to me. A mentor."

I smile. "Hardly a mentor, Blaine. You definitely don't want to follow my example."

"Well, you know what I mean."

"This is serious, and there's potential risk. It has to be in complete confidence. Kevin and Blaine only."

"I'm assumin' this is connected to your legal hassles?"

"Yes," I say.

"What do you need?" The Pall Mall is still young, and Blaine taps it against the wall to kill the fire. He checks the tip and drops it into his shirt pocket.

"Last of this month, I'll know where I stand. I have some strong legal tricks up my sleeve and two excellent lawyers in my corner. I'm not boasting, but I'm pretty comfortable in a courtroom. I'm optimistic about my chances in the long run. This is a one percent contingency."

"Roger that," Blaine says. "I've read tons of articles 'bout all the dragons you slayed. Hard to believe, you endin' up here."

"You also know better than anyone that I was minding my own business, paying my dues, humbling myself, working my forty hours and staying clean, and a stranger strolled through the door uninvited and began ruining my life. You saw Caleb in the flesh, you discovered the blank DVD, and you and Big Money solved the riddle of why Flanagan's nailing me. The point being that

I'm innocent and tangled up in a shitshow I didn't see coming and don't deserve."

"And I'm your witness."

"But it's always possible that I could lose. Nature of the beast. There're no guarantees in court. Never."

"Bummer," he says.

"If I lose my motion hearing, and we can't bust this Melanie Culp woman, I could be facing five or six years in the penitentiary. Perhaps more."

"Holy throw away the cell key," he says, but it's strained and falls flat. He's truly worried and upset by my prospects. He removes the cigarette from his pocket and relights it.

"Let's put it like this: If . . . *if* . . . my spells and legal magic don't work, if I'm wrong about what I can pull off, I won't be here making sandwiches come early October."

"Okay." The word is uncertain.

"You catch my drift?"

"Maybe," he says. He hits the cigarette.

I point at the ankle monitor. "If I decide to take a vacation, I might need some diversion and feints and an alibi for a while, so I can get a solid head start. A jump on the hounds."

"Skippin' bail," he says, and he's very animated. "On the lam. A fugitive."

"Yes."

"What can I do?"

"I need you to help me with three things. Obviously, you've already cracked Flanagan's e-mail. I need you to teach me how to do that."

"Easy peasy," he says enthusiastically. "Old news."

"His banking info would also be nice. Checking account."

Blaine takes another quick puff. He glances at the ground, then the highway. A noisy cargo truck accelerates by the parking lot. "As much mischief as I've created in the ether, and as much as I'm willin' to help, I've never stole or taken anything. Me and Money are white hats. Gray at our worst. We might prank some agency or stick it to some deservin' douche bag, but we have a code. Don't know about liftin' the dude's money, even though he kinda stole yours. That's an FBI crime too. Invincible as I am, I'm not sure I want to cross the G-man line and take on the *federales*."

"Don't worry. I'm not planning to steal a dime. You have my word. I simply want to watch what comes and goes. Just need the bank and account number."

"Cool. A major complication gone. Okay, we can make that happen. We're already

318

spear-phished into his home and office computers. I'll also see about remote access, in case you want to have even more fun."

"Meaning?" I ask.

"His computer will be my bitch, will recognize my keystrokes and follow my commands."

"Damn, Blaine, I wasn't aware you could do that."

"Not troublesome at all, since we already phished him to discover the contacts with his dove sister. We spoof her mindless, cheerful e-mails to him, have him click on a bogus link and run VNC in the background. He never has a clue."

"Also, I need you to show me how to add a fake page to a website."

"Like for the state or government?" he asks. "The court system?" He makes the cigarette into Groucho Marx's cigar and wiggles his eyebrows. "The *jail*?"

"Lawyers. It would be a diversion, a false trail. Covering my tracks."

"Okay. It's called hijacking, Lawyer Kevin. Simplest request yet. Like some website for a firm or their Facebook page?"

"Yes," I say. "A Virginia law firm's website."

"Can do. But let's hope we don't need the

emergency parachute. Life in Mexico or Uruguay probably isn't too glamorous." He grins. "Give me the name of the firm; I'll start prying loose admin credentials for their server, which is probably in-house."

"Listen, Blaine. I realize this computer hacking is a big lark and adventure for you, but this is serious. If this happens and I leave illegally and the cops can prove a connection between us, you could wind up in a world of hurt. You need to understand that. I'm reluctant to ask, but since I'd be the only person who ever could incriminate you, and I'd never give you up, you're relatively safe. Safe unless you leave your virtual fingerprints somewhere."

"I trust you," Blaine says. "And you deserve the help. You've helped me every chance you got."

"Has to be solo," I emphasize. "No Big Money. No one else."

He immediately objects. "Money and I are a team. There're things he does, and things I do."

"It can only be you. You said the basics are already in place, and the rest is simple. You won't need him."

"True." He thinks for a moment. "But you never know."

"It's for your protection and mine. And

his." I put my hands together in front of my chest, press my index fingers into a steeple. "Listen, let me emphasize again, Blaine, that this isn't a game. If I hit the road and the authorities can trace your help or involvement, then you'll be staring at criminal charges yourself. That's why I want you to tell me, to teach me, rather than doing the hacks yourself. We need a layer of separation between us." I lower my hands.

"Technically," he says in a flat, measured voice, "every time we sabotage a site for shits and giggles, or trespass on my English professor's porn-viewin' history, or snooker Zack Snyder's Mac into changing his password or e-mail address, we're breaking some law and chalkin' up multiple felonies. We're always *double* careful. Open Wi-Fi and a VPN proxy in Russia."

"Who's Zack Snyder?" I ask.

"The heretic who directed *Batman v. Superman.* Wish we could do more to punish him."

I laugh. "We'll go through this again, more than once, and rehearse the hell out of it — I'll coach you on how to deal with the cops if they should come around asking questions. Seventy-five percent of people talk themselves into a conviction. Don't be that dunce. When the cops tell you they 'know you did it,' or they 'have evidence to prove your guilt,' or 'Kevin will confess and take you down with him,' or 'It'll go so much better for you in court if you tell the truth,' or they'll 'put in a good word for you with the commonwealth's attorney,' the answer is always the same: 'I didn't do it. I have no idea what you're talking about.' If they're persistent or arrest you, you utter four words *and four words only:* 'I want a lawyer.' Is that clear?"

"Clear," he answers, his posture suddenly straight and his features uncharacteristically somber. He extinguishes the cigarette against the wall. It's almost to the filter now. "Pretty much the same rule you told me if Five-O asks me questions about my side job sellin' weed."

"Repeat the rule," I direct him.

"Never confess. Always deny. If it gets too tough, say 'I want a lawyer.' "

"Never confess," I repeat. "There might come a time, maybe deep into the case, after you've spoken to your attorney, when there's nothing else remaining and it makes tactical sense to plead guilty, but never, ever admit shit to the police."

"I promise," Blaine says, "that you've drilled the rule into me." He smiles.

"Charles Xavier and Kid Omega combined couldn't move me off the script."

"Charles Xavier and old Omega combined couldn't move me off the scrip."

CHAPTER TWELVE

Early on, my caretaking duties included organizing a closet full of Harrell family letters, mementos and photographs. I attached hundreds of items to archival paper in acid-free, PVC-free albums and used fireproof file cabinets to store the filled books. I discovered vacation postcards, World's Fair tickets, pictures of lean boys wearing military uniforms, black-and-white shots of rawboned men beside plows and Model Ts, and posed photos of mountain ladies gussied up in dresses sewn from mail-order patterns. Melvin's daddy was almost always shown mechanicing on an engine or a farm tractor. The task occupied nights and weekends for more than a month.

The most engrossing find was a twenty-page letter, a narrative, written by Melvin's uncle, Gardner Turman, and sent to a lady named Hava at the end of World War II. Not only did I carefully preserve each page of the letter in its own binder, but I also typed a verbatim copy — translated Gardner's scrawl, as I explained to Melvin — and clipped in my effort at the front.

Trapped at home on Sunday, restless and lonely, I throw Nelson's ball until even he seems exhausted, practice his various tricks, spend half an hour walking the yard's perimeter for exercise and, after lunch, dig out Gardner's letter to see if I can decipher a couple of words that I skipped over because they were too difficult to read. I take the binder to the porch and sit in the glider, start at the first page:

While a prisoner of war in Germany. We were fighting in a little country between Belgium and Germany. Which is called Luxembourg. On Dec. 16th about 5 am we were attacked by the Jerries. We were first shelled by mortars and 88's and then the infantry hit us. We made it fine all during the day until about 6:30 pm. Here come the Jerry tanks and half tracks. Flame throwers and everything else they had. We couldn't do much with them for we only had rifles and machine guns. We had already run out of mortar ammo that morning. Also no artillery either. So we

were forced to surrender. After we surrendered we were _____.

I stop and study writing that's illegible. I
read ahead and try to solve the missing
word from the context of what follows.
Nelson is beside me, and his ears perk up
and he barks and trots to the top of the
porch steps. A car's coming, faster than
usual. I hear music and voices before I can
see the vehicle. Hallelujah. I don't care if
it's an encyclopedia salesman or Officer
Pruitt bringing more bad news. The day's
been so tedious that I've considered calling
my electronic jailer for a pass to an AA
meeting, despite how badly the smoke,
black coffee, and tales of loss and drunken
misbehavior depress me. Any human whatsoever will be a gift.

A red Jeep drives into view. The roof
panels are removed, and a woman is standing in the passenger seat, popping out of
the top, singing, a bottle of champagne in
her hand. I don't recognize her or the Jeep
or the song.

"Did we win the sweepstakes, Nelson?"

The Jeep comes closer, and the roof lady
says in a loud, happy voice: "Hey, Kevin!
Ready for a swim?" The Jeep stops behind
my Ford. The woman ducks back inside,

opens her door and scoots out, has to make a small jump from the high seat onto the gravel. She brings the bottle with her. I can see it clearly now: prosecco. When she opens the door, I catch sight of the driver. It's Lilly Heath. Nelson continues to bark. Lilly turns down the music.

"Hello, Kevin," she says. "This a bad time or a good time?"

"A perfect time for you and your wing-woman," I tell her. "Welcome to the Sunday porch."

"This is my very best friend, Blu," Lilly informs me.

Blu and her bottle have already made it to Nelson, and he's wagging his tail and triple-time sniffing her.

"Stay," I tell him, raising my voice. He's excited, crouched, and on the verge of leaping against her. "Sit!"

Lilly switches off the motor.

Blu looks at me, pets the dog, then turns toward the Jeep. "Damn, Lilly, you must be a fool if you're culling this guy."

"Am I *culled*? I thought I was still in the game. Thought I still had a fighting chance. I have her e-mail, you know."

Lilly is walking toward us. "Blu began with Bloody Marys around ten. You need to factor that into whatever she tells you, but

327

truthfully, I'm in the market for a guy with far less baggage and travel possibilities that extend past his front lawn."

"I'm Blu," the lady says, and offers her hand. *"B-l-u,* no *e."* As my mom used to put it, Blu's as attractive as she can possibly be, doing the most she can with what she's been given. She's trim and fit and — by design, I'm sure — her tailored top shows off an impressive chest. Her haircut suits her age and face. Her nails are painted. She's an attractive lady, but not beautiful by birth — her features are too sharp and etched, and she's slightly short-waisted. "Great to meet you," she continues. "I'm not a bitch like Lilly when it comes to handsome men."

I'm already standing, and we shake hands. "Pleasure to meet you too. Have a seat. Make yourself comfortable." I address Lilly, who's at the foot of the steps. "What brings you to these parts?"

"Blu's spending the weekend with me, and we've been touring the area: breakfast at Tuggles Gap, coffee in Floyd, wine tasting and the jazz at Chateau Morrisette —"

"Way too sleepy for a warm, sunny Sunday," Blu declares. She shuts her eyes and mimics snoring.

"Then to the bar at Primland, some sightseeing on the parkway —"

"Enhanced by a joint at one of the over-looks," Blu interjects. "Amazing . . . the view, I mean."

"Am I the only person on the planet who's never smoked pot?" I ask. "And never will, given my sobriety needs?"

"Perfect," Blu exclaims. "A hot man who can always serve as designated driver and will never suffer from whiskey dick. In case you haven't picked up on it, I'm single."

I grin. "As pretty as you are, I can't imagine that'll last long."

"Well, *today* I'm single." She smiles right at me; it's nuanced and double-edged, a surprise. "By design. It's not as if I lack options," she adds. She's informing me that she's buzzed, and rowdy and a free spirit, but there's a limit: She's no slut, and despite the bawdy talk and riot-girl swagger and rule-breaking, she's not about to hop in the sack with me or anybody else willy-nilly. She's a *character*. "And ready to drink more prosecco and go for a swim in your awe-some pond."

"Which brings us here," Lilly remarks. "Is that okay? We're not intruding?"

"You're not intruding." I haven't shaved, but to kill time earlier, I showered, trimmed my nails, brushed my teeth twice and dressed in chinos and a comfortable, wrin-

329

kled blue linen shirt that was somehow ruined by a bleach streak at the cleaner's in Roanoke. I notice the pant leg is bunched on my ankle monitor. "Welcome. Glad you decided to visit."

"I'll grab the cooler," Blu says.

"Can you come with us to the pond?" Lilly asks. "Your court rules?"

"By my math," Blu notes, "the bad-boy criminality's a definite plus. Nobody wants to spend time with a milquetoast or Boy Scout."

"Thanks for the vote of confidence, Blu," I say.

"If it helps with your decision," Blu adds, "I didn't bring a bathing suit." She winks at me.

"Our girl Blu," Lilly sighs, shaking her head.

"Well, damn," I say. "Let me see what I can do." I start for the door.

"I don't have a swimsuit either," Lilly notes. "Do you have an old T-shirt or something? Not a white one."

" 'Not a white one,' " Blu mocks her. "A forty-year-old nurse who's handled more junk than Fred G. Sanford, and she acts like she's Queen Victoria. Can you swim, Kevin?"

"Yeah. Used to be a lifeguard. My college

summer job."

"Well, you'll have to be strong as an ox to rescue Lilly when her chastity belt sinks her to the bottom."

I crack up, and it feels wonderful to laugh. "Thanks for stopping by, ladies. You've saved my day." I laugh some more. "I know what you mean, Blu — wasn't so long ago that Sister Lilly was lecturing me about sex toys."

"And some towels," Lilly says, ignoring us both.

"Sorry I don't have much to offer in terms of snacks, but I do have a cantaloupe — still eating like my nurse advised me — and a few peaches, and I can put some Kraft cheese slices on saltines for you."

"Fabulous," Blu replies. "Why'd we pay the huge bucks at Primland for food when this kind of hospitality is available?"

"Can't help you with the alcohol or marijuana," I warn them. "Sorry."

"Don't worry," Lilly says wryly. "Blu has that covered."

"Okay. Give me a sec." I go inside and phone the jail and ask the officer on duty if he'll grant me an hour-and-a-half pass. I tell him the fence is down and Melvin's horses have escaped. "I'll be here on the property the entire time," I assure him.

"They're near the pond, but I'll have to catch them and get a halter on them. I've already tried shaking a bucket of sweet feed and calling them, but they aren't falling for that, especially since they can graze clover and roam as they please."

"Ninety minutes," the officer agrees. "And you realize we can track you and check where you've been?"

"I'll be right here in Meadows of Dan, on the farm. If they run, I might need to follow them into the woods. I'll also have to replace a fencepost, but you guys are welcome to watch me every second."

"Don't worry, Mr. Moore, we plan to. Call and report back at sixteen hundred hours," he instructs me.

"Four o'clock?"

"Yeah." He snorts.

"A question: Will water damage the ankle hardware?"

"Of course it will," the cop snarls. "You break it, you bought it, and it ain't cheap. Why would it be wet?"

"The horses are near *a pond,* and there's a creek in the woods I might have to cross if they take that route. Just asking, sir."

"It better stay completely dry," he emphasizes. "You people," he mutters.

I poke my head through the door, tell the

ladies that I'll catch up with them, return to the kitchen and load a serving platter with melon chunks, peeled peach slices, cheese and crackers, and an unopened pack of graham crackers. I collect three bath towels and a green Montana Flyfishing Connection T-shirt from the pile of clean laundry in the bedroom. Lilly and Blu have left for the pond when I return, and Nelson and I trail them to the dock. As promised, Blu's top, bra, shorts and panties are draped across a chair, and she's naked and already swimming.

"The pond has never looked so spectacular," I tell her. "A sight worth going to jail for, if I've wandered past my monitoring limit."

She's treading water, her breasts partially above the surface, her hair wet and slicked back. "I knew I liked you, Kevin."

I hand Lilly the T-shirt. She's poured herself a clear plastic glass of prosecco. "Thanks," she says. "I hope the alcohol doesn't upset you or tempt you. Last thing I want to do is spoil your recovery. If it's a problem, I can forget it."

"It doesn't bother me. I have no urge — none — to drink or drug. I associate it with loss and pain. For me, it's the same as inviting me to have a root canal."

"You're sure?" she asks.

"Positive."

"Okay. So please turn around so I can change. And don't cheat."

She walks away, stops, and I can sense her moving and undressing behind me, and before she's finished, I ask, "Ready? Can I look now?"

"No!"

When she returns and glides past me, her bra is gone and the shirt has the effect of a short dress — she reminds me of a '70s go-go dancer or a cabaret girl, carnal and erotic, and she's especially attractive since Blu has already gotten the ball rolling with her flirting and skinny-dipping. I start to compliment her but think better of it, don't want to come off as a pathetic ogler, so instead I offer to bring them floats and inner tubes from the pond's stone house.

"Thanks," she says. "That would be wonderful." She steps to the dock's edge, pinches her nose shut and jumps in feet-first.

The sun is strong, there're only scattered clouds, and the two ladies swim and splash and float. I open another bottle for them. I shed my shirt and flip-flops, roll my pant legs to my knees and relax in an Adirondack chair. Nelson paces the dock, crying and barking and whining, interested in the water but unsure of it, and I finally coax him off a gradual grass bank for his first swim, and he takes to the pond like a purebred duck dog, paddling happily around. Lilly invites me to tell the story of how I found him, and Blu, who's belly-down on a black tractor-trailer inner tube, her butt whiter than her thighs and low back, observes that the dog was rescued like "Moses or something."

"He was," I agree. "We were both lucky."

"And look at those eyes," she says. She sips from her plastic glass. "He's charmed."

Lilly and Blu navigate their tubes close to the dock, and we chat and cut up for half an hour, then they send me to bring the Jeep down to the pond so we can listen to music. They dress in their dry clothes while I'm gone, and we sit on the dock and talk, a mix CD playing through the vehicle's speakers. They take tokes from Blu's joint and fill their glasses with the last of the prosecco. Blu's a Raleigh girl, and we're discussing Southern childhoods and swapping stories about snapping beans and shelling peas with our aproned grandmas, and Lilly raises her hand above her head and interrupts.

"Okay," she says. "Enough. The pot's slammin' me. I have to drive. I need to start sobering up." Her speech is awkward, a click too much volume, the wrong syllables emphasized. "I shouldn't have had wine at the jazz thing, then mixed it with prosecco and pot."

"Wet-blanket us, why don't you?" Blu complains. "Debbie Freakin' Downer. You have no work tomorrow, no responsibilities, you're with your best friend and a handsome man who's eager to wait on you hand and foot, we're visiting this lovely place that looks like a commercial for *Garden & Gun,* and you're worried about *leaving*? Really? Enjoy it. Relax. Be in the moment for a change."

"Well, Blu Buddha, how the hell do you plan for us to make it to my house? It's easy to be the party girl and all Zen and celebrate the *now* when you've got me taking care of you."

"There's a guesthouse," I offer. I point up the hill. "Two double beds, private bath."

"No," Lilly declares. "Absolutely not."

"Yeah, you're right," Blu says. She's sarcastic, but not rude or spiteful. She grins. "We need to hurry back so we can crash on the sofa and pig out on ice cream and binge-watch *The Walking Dead*. Or *Friends*. Who wants to stay here in this dump?"

I laugh. "I have two steaks — frozen, sad

to say — that I'd be glad to grill and split three ways. I've got some fresh corn, and a salad I brought home from SUBstitution. And nobody's even tried the graham crackers. There's your dessert."

Blu adjusts her top. "You realize, Kevin — as great and life-changing as it would be for both of us — you and I can't be an item, can't hook up or have sex? It'd be too complicated, since you're interested in my best friend, and I'd be a booty-call second fiddle."

"Regrettable, but understood," I reply. "Definitely my loss." My tone lets on that I'm just playing along, flattering her, having fun with her shtick.

"There's a lock on the guesthouse door?" Blu asks.

"Yes," I assure her.

"Listen, Lilly," Blu says. "How about we just enjoy the pond vibes and delay deciding for an hour or two? I'm content here for the time being. Happy to be high and away from everything and everybody."

"And eating will sober you up," I suggest to Lilly.

"Okay, okay," she says. "Whatever. I can't drive now anyway. We'll wait an hour and eat."

I drive us up the hill to the house, call my

jailer and report in ten minutes before my deadline, pop the steaks in the microwave and start the gas grill. While the steaks are thawing, I stack twigs and sticks and a small log over a rolled-up section of *The Roanoke Times* in the fire pit and use a long lighter to flame the newspaper.

"Anything we can do to help?" Blu asks.

"Nope," I say. "Just enjoy the evening."

"And you really can't leave?" Blu asks. The fire pit is in the middle of its own brick patio. She settles into a chair beside the burning wood, facing the pond and the mountains. From her seat, you can also see a section of the pasture and, beyond that, the hayfield, which is stippled with Jacob Shelor's round bales.

"No, girl, he can't," Lilly says as she walks out of the house.

"I really can't," I admit.

"I'm not sobering up at all," Lilly complains. "I'm getting worse, I think. I'm a rookie compared to Blu."

"Well," Blu says, "the bad news — or maybe it's good news for you and our hangover prospects — is that we're down to wine coolers and the nub of our joint, and for certain nobody can drive to the store and replenish our stock."

"Sorry," I tell them.

"Well, a wine cooler won't kill me," Blu says. "High as I am already, I doubt it'll make much difference."

"I'm done with the booze," Lilly declares. She hiccups. "Damn it."

I grill the steaks, boil the corn and divide the salad onto three plates, and Blu pours a Bartles & Jaymes into a water glass. We eat outside, and the air soon becomes chilly, so we leave the wrought-iron table and sit close to the fire, and I fetch the ladies blankets and flannel shirts, and Blu finishes the pot. I open the waxy brown graham-cracker pack and we pass it around. After a while, we're all quiet, watching the western clouds color with bright tints as the sun surrenders to the mountains. There's still a stray croak or trill or bug cry, but the pond, woods and creeks are closing shop, readying for colder weather. No one speaks until the sun's nearly extinguished for the day.

Blu breaks the silence. "There you go," she says softly, nodding toward Lilly. "A party casualty."

Lilly's asleep, the blanket pulled completely to her chin, her head lolling to the left, her breathing audible, her mouth open, one sandal attached to her foot, the other beside her chaise longue.

"How long have you been friends?" I ask.

"Since 1998. Our husbands worked at the same hospital."

"Where was that?"

"Cleveland," she answers. "You don't by any chance have a cigarette, do you? I quit smokin' years ago, but sometimes it still seems like the right thing to do when I'm drinking." She sounds fairly composed despite how much alcohol and pot she's put away. There's only an occasional mild slur or sloppy word. Her balance and coordination seem normal.

"No," I reply. "I'm not a smoker. So your ex-husbands are docs?"

"My ex-husband, The Salamander, as I refer to him, is an administrator and a serial adulterer. Lilly's ex is a heart surgeon. Ironic, huh? A real medical star, and not bad lookin' either. So many of those guys are geeks and bookworms. The mansions and spa treatments come with a prize. Price, I mean."

I laugh. "You sound like me."

"You seem damn healthy to've had a stroke."

"Yeah," I agree. "I dodged a bullet. I still suffer with my ankle, and my face isn't a hundred percent, but they're better every day, and my mind's okay. I have some lapses and occasional brain burn, but that's improving too. The worst is the worry, the preoccupation, the fear that every tingle or minor ache is the start of another catastrophe. Solitary days like today are awful. Until you two arrived."

"And Lilly was your nurse?"

"Yeah." I leave my chair and put more wood on the fire. "How long was she married?"

"Fucked-up and buzzed as I am, you'll only lawyer so much private info from me. I'm still on my toes, Kevin Moore."

"I don't doubt it."

"Lilly's husband cashed her in three years ago. The medical wives call it the McInerney Rule — why, I'm not sure. The bald, paunchy, middle-aged, boring-as-hell doctor trades his original wife for number two, who's half his age plus five to six years. That's the math, the rule." Blu's demeanor changes. She's agitated. She flings her hands. "That's fair, huh? And the women all know it goin' in. It's part of the bargain. But poor Lilly didn't see it coming. She was a true believer."

"Well, I can't say much. My one-night stand with a younger woman cost me everything, including the best wife ever. She dumped *me,* and she had a reason to." I calculate the numbers in my head. "But, yeah, the McInerney Rule's probably accurate for my mistake, at least for the age part."

"So many of these women diet and train like Olympic athletes just to stay skinny. They have their husband's golfing pal from the cosmetic department hack up their breasts and yank their skin tight, but at the first sign of BPT disease, the rich doctor or hospital administrator moves on to this year's model." She takes a slug of her pink wine cooler. "Can you tell I'm not a fan of selfish male doctors who leave their devoted wives for younger women?"

"What's BPT disease?" I ask.

"Belly past tits," she explains. "Mid- to late forties, it can be a problem. Though it won't be for me." She laughs. "Not with this rack — my stomach will *never* catch the D-cup divas."

"Does Lilly have a boyfriend?"

"No boyfriend," Blu replies. "The divorce court gave her two million. She deserved more — put his broke dick through med school and residency workin' PICU third shift, paid his student loans for their first years, raised an amazing daughter alone, doted on his haughty ass and looked like a supermodel the whole time. One day, he waltzes in and proclaims that 'sixteen years is a successful run, and I'm ready to restructure.' What a turd. 'Restructure.' So Lilly doesn't need money, and she's not in the market for a man. Not yet."

"Why Hillsville?"

"Why not?" Blu replies. "She wanted a small town. Wanted to live by herself in the country. She has the cutest little house with a pool and thirty acres. Found it online. Nothing like this spread, of course." She finishes the wine cooler, sets the glass on the patio. "By the way, what's your landlord's story? The loaded prince who owns this place? Is he spoken for?"

"Happily married to the love of his life, a fantastic lady."

"All the good ones are taken."

"The daughter?" I ask. "Lilly's kid?"

"A freshman at Ohio State."

"Last question: How would you rate my prospects with Lilly?" I'm still loitering by the fire.

"Honestly, Kevin, not too great. She likes you enough to drop by when we're both drinking and pulling a party, wanted me to meet you, thinks you're attractive and interesting, but only a moron buys the gorgeous, classic Jag if the salesman tells you the transmission is on the fritz and the engine's burnin' a quart of oil every week.

Pretty car, large maintenance problems. Who needs the aggravation?"

"Fair enough," I say.

"I don't see my best friend as a prison wife, bakin' cakes with files and bribing the guards so she can give you a handjob through the bars. It'd be like marrying an invalid in the prime of your life. She's done enough nursing already."

"On a one-to-ten scale, what would be my number?"

"Two or three," Blu replies. "Unless you shake free of all the legal problems, return to lawyering and stay sober. But I doubt she's interested in doing the heavy lifting to help you make it there."

"It could be worse, I suppose. At least I'm on the scale."

"Since we're playing twenty questions, here's one for you: You cheated on your wife, right?"

"Once," I admit. "One time, with a stranger, and I hate it more than anything I've ever done. I'd give anything to reconcile with Ava."

"I've always assumed the pretty guys like you are a lousy bet, just because of the sheer numbers. Women hit on you a lot, you have a ton of options, and finally you decide, 'Hey, damn, I've turned down ninety-nine

344

hookups, so how bad is it to finally give in this one time? I'm still ninety-nine percent faithful.'"

"Not me," I say. "Not at all. I don't recall a lot of adultery opportunities, and I wasn't looking for any. When I cheated, I was so high that I didn't think. I didn't do any math. Didn't crunch the numbers. If you're fucked-up enough, most anything can happen."

"Who knows? Maybe your wife'll forgive you."

"And you?" I ask Blu. "What's your —"

Lilly pukes. She's clutching the chair's metal arm and twisted over so she's throwing up on the bricks. Some of the vomit splatters her sleeve and some lands on the chair's cushion. "I'm sick, Blu. Sorry." Her speech is slow and distorted. She retches again.

Blu immediately kneels next to her, holds her hair away from her face and helps prop her up. "It's okay, sweetie."

Lilly wipes at snot and spit and vomit with her wrist. She closes her eyes and collapses back into the chaise longue.

"Guesthouse it is," Blu states. "Wish you and I could visit longer, but I think I need to put Courtney Love Junior to bed."

"Noooo," Lilly moans. "Take me home."

"Give me a hand," Blu directs me. She's remarkably collected. "I'm fine," she declares, as if she's reading my mind. "Shouldn't be drivin', but otherwise I'm okay. Not my first happy hour, and the food sawed my buzz in half. But we do need to stop by the Jeep so I can take my Taser with me to our little house."

I hear them leaving early the next morning, before seven, Tesla crowing, Nelson barking in his pen, the guinea fowl fussing and chattering, upset by the strangers and unfamiliar comings and goings. I watch Blu walk to the porch door, a folded piece of paper in her hand, but she doesn't knock or try the knob, just leaves the note behind and strides to her Jeep. The note is a kind thank-you, and Lilly e-mails me later and apologizes, then she telephones Monday night, and we talk for ten minutes, and she repeats that she's sorry and embarrassed about how she acted.

"No worries," I assure her. "You were charming and a lady even when you were off your game. Come back anytime." I pause. "And thanks to Blu, I learned all about you and your past."

"She can be a blabbermouth."

"She told me that on a one-to-ten scale,

346

my chances of romantic success with you are a three, if I'm lucky."

"She's my best friend," Lilly replies. "She knows me better than anybody else. Maybe three-point-five, since you were so nice to us and took such good care of me."

CHAPTER THIRTEEN

On Tuesday, September 6, while Blaine and I are preparing to open the restaurant, he sidles close and nudges me with his elbow. We're standing behind the counter, near the showtime oven. Blaine is holding a silver tub of lettuce that's covered in plastic wrap.

"So far, so good on Operation J'onzz," he says confidentially, his free hand shielding his mouth even though we're alone and the door's locked.

"Jones?" I ask, and also keep my voice lower than normal.

"Spelled *J,* apostrophe, *o, n, z, z.* J'onn J'onzz is the Martian Manhunter. He was once a fugitive but shouldn't have been, a victim of some unfair bullshit, and he has the power of invisibility."

"Well, let's hope it's Operation Never Happens."

"We're green lights on everything except the hijack of the law firm's page. I don't have credentials there yet. I've just barely scouted around, but I haven't found any easy hacks or unlocked doors yet. I will, though. Their system is nothin' special."

"Thanks. Remember: Be careful. You can't leave a trail."

"Don't worry. This is an elementary school caper."

"Well, there're people who fail the fifth grade."

"True." He drops the lettuce container in its slot beside the pickles. "Not my business, but why would you want your probation officer's e-mail and bank info?"

"The less you know, the better. Just in case." I walk past him, heading to the fridge in the kitchen. "But probation officers can grant travel passes for up to thirty days," I say without looking back. "And I wonder if our pal Caleb might be giving shitheel Flanagan an early Christmas gift either before or right after my hearing."

At twelve-thirty, we have a long line and we're busy making sandwiches, and Blaine answers the phone and says to me, "Dude named Louis, about insurance." I tell Blaine to take a number, and I call Louis Dillon an hour later.

"So, Mr. Moore," Dillon says, his tone combining ire and tongue-bitten politeness, "another review of your file revealed that we *can* offer you coverage for your hospital stay. Thank you for giving us the additional information we needed to finish processing your claim. You'll owe the deductibles, of course, and your coverage will end on the July sixteenth date we discussed. The new EOB we're sending you will show that your total payment is $968.11. We'll also ask you to sign a full release."

"That's good news, Louis," I say.

"I would think so."

"And an excellent start," I add.

"Say what? Start?"

"After browbeating me while I was suffering from a stroke, after trying to buffalo me and cheat me out of my coverage, and after kicking me in the nuts for two months, now you want to offer me what I was entitled to anyway, with nothing included for the anguish and stress you've put me through? Correct? Pay me nothing for the hours I spent under your jackboot?"

"It was an innocent oversight on our part," he says hastily. "A clerical mistake. The company apologizes."

"That's nonsense. This was intentional and systematic. It's how you people conduct business. But assuming it's true, the *Hindenburg* was an innocent mistake and so was the *Titanic* — you think the surviving families simply received a ticket refund from the negligent shipping lines that killed their loved ones?"

"What else could you possibly want?" Dillon asks, his voice spiking. "I'm single and don't have a firstborn child yet."

"To this day, remarkably, you've never sent me a legally proper cancellation notice or offered me a COBRA extension. I had an emergency-room visit a few weeks ago. In Mount Airy, North Carolina. You and I both know that if I'm uninsured, I'll be lucky to escape with a bill for less than ten grand. With your negotiated rates, it'll cost you maybe two thousand at most. My portion, if I have insurance, would be around four hundred, maybe five hundred dollars. Great system we have, isn't it? Insurance companies and the government are charged about a fifth of what a poor sap like me is billed."

"Come on, Kevin, you admitted that you canceled in freaking July, that was the deal, and now you want us to pay for something weeks later?"

"You *still* haven't canceled in compliance with the statute, and no one's ever offered me my COBRA benefits. If I had COBRA coverage, I wouldn't be facing a huge bill

351

from Mount Airy."

"The employer is supposed to give you the COBRA notice. How's that our fault?"

"So listen," I say, "let's you and I be creative and put this to bed. You accept coverage for the Mount Airy ER bill, pay them the two grand or whatever it is they've negotiated with your company, but subtract a thousand from my legitimate claim. You save me a ton. Doesn't cost you but a grand more, and surely I'm due that much for the numerous illegalities I've endured. What difference does it make to your company where it spends the money? Forsyth Hospital or Mount Airy Hospital, it'll cost you the exact same plus a measly thousand bucks extra. That's less than the cost of a bespoke club tie for your CEO, who made seventeen million dollars last year. A gnat's eyelash in the scheme of things, and I go from paying ten thousand to owing Mount Airy around four hundred or so. I have a net gain of approximately eighty-six hundred."

He's quiet. He clears his throat. "Yeah, okay," he finally agrees. "But that's it, the end, no suits, no more claims, no more threats, and we agree that you're not covered after July sixteenth, 2016, except for the ER visit. And you don't come after me personally for any made-up damages."

"Absolutely. Deal. Send me a confirmation e-mail and the release."

"I will," he replies. He stops talking, but I can hear him typing, a string of hollow-plastic clicks. "Kevin? Mr. Moore?" he says when he comes back on the line.

"Yes?"

"It's just a severely screwed-up system." He sounds weary and sincere. "I'm sorry. Nothing personal. Just doing my job, following my rules. I truly hope you recover from your stroke. For what it's worth, I'm glad my company's paying your bills. I'm leaving for a different job October first. This isn't for me."

"No hard feelings. Best of luck with the new career."

That evening, I'm at home, sitting on the sofa, studying Gardner's pages again:

After we surrendered, we were_____
and the Jerries took every thing we had all
our cigarettes, matches, watches, cigarette
lighters, and even some of the boys shoes
and all our gloves. Well everything they
could use themselves.

"Searched," I say aloud, the very first time

I read through the paragraph. The writing is a cursive riddle, loops and squiggles, but *searched* has to be correct, especially since I'm now convinced that the first letter is an *s*. I open my typewritten copy on the computer and make the addition. The phone rings a few seconds after I finish and close the file. Minivan Dan is calling from Atlanta.

"How's your health, Kevin? Thought I'd check in with my friend to see if you're still alive."

"Good, Minivan. Better today because I finally persuaded the crooked insurance company to pay the money they owe, so as of a few hours ago, I'm only on the hook for around two grand, not six fucking figures. As a little bonus, and to kiss and make up, they're helping out with my Mount Airy ER bill."

"Damn right," Minivan says. "Fucking A. Great news. Still, it's a crying shame you have to go to war with them just to receive basic fair treatment. What the hell do you do if you're not a lawyer, or too sick or too handicapped to fight?"

"There's still no policy in place going forward, but at least this is behind me."

"How's the romance with your nurse, the lovely Lilly?"

"Stalled at best. She did stop by for a visit, and I have her e-mail, and her pal, Blu, filled me in on her story. It could be worse, I guess. How're things with you?"

"Aces. You should see Zoe on the soccer field. I realize it's too early to predict, but she's a natural. Amazing. Unstoppable. I think she might skip an age group next year. She's dominant. The roofing business is cruising, and the Lil Wayne buy and publicity led to eleven new orders."

"According to the news online, if he's not careful, Tunechi's next purchase will be a customized mini-hearse."

"An old-school find for you," Minivan says. "I was in the grocery store today and came across the little Millers, the pony-size bottles. I didn't know they still made them."

"I've never noticed," I reply.

"Made me think of that night with good ol' Francis Allen at Professor Abbott's house. What a hoot. Remember?"

"Yep, it was quite a party. No doubt."

"At any rate, just wanted to check on you. Make sure you're okay."

"Thanks, Dan. Thank you."

"Well, I'll let you get back to your thousand-piece puzzle or computer solitaire or FarmVille or whatever else criminals on house arrest do to pass the time."

On Wednesday morning, I'm Dr. Wallace's first patient, and I'm in the examination room at his Winston-Salem clinic by 8:15 a.m. He's accompanied by a timid, sloe-eyed nurse. He greets me and shakes my hand and solemnly pats my shoulder. The nurse offers a muted hello.

"Mount Airy," he says. "The imaging studies. We're *cliybang* Everest, Mr. Moore."

I look at the nurse for a translation, but she doesn't speak. She's studying my folder.

"Pardon?" I say.

"Mount Airy, the emergency department, your MRI. I was gratified to see your progress."

"Oh, right," I reply. "My MRI from Mount Airy." I'm rusty in terms of breaking the code. I heard him frequently enough when I was hospitalized that on my last day there, I was able to follow about three-quarters of his accented babble.

"Good news, Mr. Moore."

"Yeah, the ER doc told me I was healing, that the tear is much smaller."

"Yes," he says.

"But I still lack strength in my left hand and my ankle, and I still get dizzy if I have to bend or stoop. For instance, picking up a knife or bottle from a counter can cause my head to swim. Once, I almost fell." I'd considered creating an even bigger lie about falling but decided against it. "I drop things, and I'm occasionally dizzy — I guess that's the bottom line. My ankle is much better but still not perfect. My face is recovered."

"Sorry," he says.

"I think I've leveled off."

He peers at the nurse. "Next *shedduelled* MRI?"

She flips through my file. "He's scheduled for his MRI on December nineteenth," she replies.

"Your medicine?" he asks. "The Plavix?"

"Yes. Every day."

"I see," he says. He has me sit, and he takes me through the stroke protocol, has me push and pull and smile as wide as I can, stick out my tongue, swallow, and repeat a handful of words. I feign weakness when he tests my left arm.

"Okay," he says when he's finished. "Yes, your left side *funshon* isn't symmetrical."

"It's not end-of-the-world bad, I can work around it, but I was hoping you might be able to fix me. If I drop the soap in the shower, I have to crouch and use my right hand and then stand up inch by inch."

"An inconvenience," the doc remarks, but he utters it like he's offering an epiphany.

I notice the nurse writing in my file. I speak to her. "I'm grateful that I've recovered to this point. I've come a long ways, thanks to Dr. Wallace and all of you, but the weakness and dizziness are major complications."

"Therapy," the doc says. "*Pheesecal* therapy might be a benefit."

"Well, I had therapy right after I was released from the hospital, and I've continued to do the exercises, but if you think something additional will help, I'll give it a shot."

"Can't hurt," he answers.

"You're the doctor."

"Also," he adds, "I'm not sure about the lumen and occlusion from the ER data. I'd like to have our people on it. An *ooltrasun*."

"Sorry?"

"*Ul-tra-sun,*" he says deliberately. "We'll double-check the carotid with an *ooltrasun*. ER departments and three-in-the-morning radiology — never know."

"So you're recommending some more therapy and your own ultrasound as a precaution, to make certain the carotid is open and continuing to heal?"

"Correct," he says.

"Yes," the nurse confirms.

"Well, how about you schedule them both a couple weeks away? I'm still waiting for my insurance coverage to be verified."

"We will," the nurse promises me.

"Esellant," Dr. Wallace says.

"I understand how lucky I am," I tell him. "If I could beat this dizziness and be able to bend over and use my hand, I'd be normal again, but I'm not complaining." I emphasize the words *dizziness* and *hand.*

Rose Vipperman Adams owns Vesta Supply, the general store her daddy, Coy, opened in the 1950s, and when I arrive home after work on Thursday, around eight, her pickup is parked beside the barn, and she's hauling bags of sweet feed from the truck's bed to the tack room. It's chilly, and she's wearing a jean jacket and gloves. Before my stroke, I'd always offload the feed myself, but the docs have warned me that I shouldn't lift more than twenty pounds, and I'm embarrassed because I can't help her.

"Hey, Kevin," she greets me. "How're you feelin'? I brought you a pint of sourwood honey from the store. They say a dab a day's good for your brain." I've discovered that the mountain people, the locals, have generous natures — "free-hearted" is the Patrick

County expression. They're neighborly and normally eager to pitch in, traits born of necessity and decades of traded favors. You can't pull a stuck cow from a mudhole by yourself, tractors and equipment always break down at harvest time and a single farmer can't hustle up three hundred bales of hay before a fluke rain ruins it. Last month in Meadows of Dan, there was a patchwork-quilt raffle, a Vera Bradley bingo event, an apple-butter sale and a barbecue supper, all to raise money for an Agee family whose house was lost to a fire.

"Better every day. Appreciate the honey, and I'm sorry you have to carry those bags. My mother would roll over in her grave if she knew I was letting a lady carry feed sacks."

"It's what I do," she says. "I'm used to it. Soon as you're healthy, you can make it up to me." She's a smaller woman, maybe five-six, and she might weigh one-forty if you include her clothes and Red Wing boots, but she's able to toss a fifty-pound bag over her shoulder as if it were a pillow and then march it inside and lower it onto a pallet.

"Thanks again."

"You hearin' much from Melvin?" she asks. She scoops the last bag from the truck and flips it across her shoulder.

"Not a lot." I follow her toward the barn. The horses have gathered around the fence, and they jostle each other and kick and bite, excited by the food's arrival. Nelson joins us and barks at them, careful to stay on the safe side of the boards.

"Melvin's somethin' else. They broke the mold on him."

"No doubt," I agree.

She steps inside the tack room. " 'Course he's about the only rich man I know who people don't resent. Never, I mean never, have I heard a bad word on Melvin Harrell." She stops in front of the pallet and begins to stoop, and she takes a last step forward, and she stumbles and loses her balance, staggers backward and falls on her butt, the heavy feed sack across her shoulder and chest, pinning her.

"Oh, damn!" I exclaim. "Are you okay?" I reach down and grab the bag with both hands and drag it off.

"Now *I'm* embarrassed," she says, popping up. "Lord, how clumsy. I stepped on the durn pallet, the edge of the board. Kinda dangerous — it's hard to see with this light, and it throws you directly backwards."

"You okay?"

"Yeah. Yes. Only my pride's hurt." She

361

laughs. She rotates her arm, makes a full circle and rubs her shoulder.

"You sure?" I ask.

"I'm sure."

"I took the same tumble a while back," I tell her. "I should've warned you."

She windmills her arm again. "Well, it's my fault. I've stacked feed in here a bunch. Oughta be more careful."

"Oh, wait . . . Wow! That's it."

"Sorry?" she says, confused.

"The same thing happened to me, and when you suddenly fall with fifty pounds of dead weight on you, it wrenches your neck and shoulder. I instinctively grabbed the bag and made it even worse. Afterward, I was standing right where you are, trying to stretch the twinge and kink out of my neck. May or early June — has to be what happened to tear my carotid. *Has* to be."

"Is that somethin' to do with your stroke?"

"Yes. Absolutely." I clap my hands together and hold them in front of me. "I'm sorry you fell, but this is a burden lifted for me. My goodness. Thanks."

"Okay." She sounds uncertain. "I suppose." She removes a glove and kneads her neck.

"Lots of carotid dissections are spontaneous. No one can say why — they just happen. Bad luck. The rest come from obvious trauma, like a car accident or a fight or a hard blow. Or from having a fifty-pound sack whipsaw your neck as you fall over backward. Unless they can connect it to an obvious event, the docs and their X-rays and angiograms can't tell if your tear, your dissection, is from trauma or just spontaneous."

"So you're thinking this is what caused your problems, stumbling with the feed and hurtin' yourself?"

"It fits," I answer. "The timing's right, the kind of torque, everything. The physicians ask about auto wrecks and gym accidents, the red-letter, dramatic mishaps, so I never even thought about my spill in here. It happened, I was fine, maybe a little stiffness the next morning, and I moved on, forgot about it. But I'm betting it caused the tear, and then your body starts trying to heal it, and here come the clots and the stroke."

"Probably some satisfaction in understandin' what happened to you."

I clap my hands again, making a noise that's almost lost to the barn's open space and high tin roof. "Even better, Rose, now I won't spend every waking minute scared there's some hidden defect lurking in my body. If you're a dissection victim, you want to know that you're not simply wired wrong, that there's an *explanation* for your problem." I take a breath. I study her. The sixty-watt light isn't powerful enough to do any more than shade her clothes into dim blacks and grays, but the bulb does illuminate her face and sets apart a swirl of dust and barely there hay flecks behind her; and if angels exist, I think to myself, this is how they'd appear, haloed, strong and charged with happy revelations. I'm flummoxed, unsure of what else to say. "So, well, thanks for, uh . . . falling." I sort of laugh. I stick my hands in my pockets. "But you're not injured? I'm proof you have to be incredibly careful with something like this."

"Three kids, seventy head of cattle and twelve-hour shifts at the store — my husband always claims the Vipperman girls are so tough that we'll be roasting marshmallows in the Armageddon fires and takin' the devil's money in a gin rummy game. I'll be fine, but I 'preciate the concern."

On Friday, September 9, I'm allowed to deviate from my route to SUBstitution so I can interview Eugene Harris. A few minutes past eight-thirty, I meet him at his modest brick house, lightning rods on the roof, a birdbath in the yard. He's wearing a wool dress hat with a felt band and a curlicue feather, a maroon windbreaker, corduroy pants that have a thick line of repair thread across the front pocket, and scuffed black wing tips. He invites me inside and offers me a cup of coffee. We sit at the kitchen table, its top a yellow 1960s faded laminate encircled by a silver metal band. There are four chairs, one a ladder-back that doesn't match the others.

"Thanks for seeing me," I tell him. "And thanks for the coffee. Hope I'm not bothering you."

"No bother," he says. "You're curious 'bout the land I sold?" He doesn't remove the hat or the windbreaker.

"I am," I answer. "Your sale is at the root of an unfair lawsuit that's been filed against me."

He stirs a teaspoon of sugar into his coffee, the spoon scraping the cup's sides and bottom. "You're the fellow what's livin' in the old Harrell homeplace? Over at Melvin's?"

"Yes."

"I heared y'all was kin."

"Cousins," I say.

"And your first name's what?"

"Kevin. Kevin Moore."

"I also heared you was runnin' a hoochie-coochie joint over in Roanoke and got tangled up with the law."

"Pardon?" I look him straight in the eyes.

"I heared you was running a girlie joint over in Roanoke. Drugs and the whole nine yards."

I laugh. "Mr. Harris, I've never set foot in a strip club or girlie joint, much less owned one. I'm a lawyer by trade."

"I heared that too. Don't know which is worse." He grins. Sips his coffee.

"Well," I say and chuckle, "you probably have a point there." I take hold of my cup's handle but don't lift the coffee. "It sounds as if someone has taken pieces of several tall tales and newspaper accounts and Frankensteined them into a big lie. I had a drug and alcohol problem for a few months, but I've been right as rain for over a year. I work every day at a restaurant in Stuart and tend to Melvin's farm. I've never been convicted of *any* crime. I'll be returning to my law office soon."

"Glad to hear it. Ain't no good in drinkin' that I ever could see." He takes off the hat and lays it on the table. "Didn't make no sense to me that a smart man such as Melvin would have a lowlife stayin' at his property. You hear all sorts of rumors and gossip that ain't true." Harris is balding and appears older without the hat, in his late seventies, I'd guess.

I drink my coffee. "So do you mind discussing your sale? It would be very helpful to me."

"Nothing much to discuss. It pained me to sell it. Land was in my family for generations, but it got to be too expensive, and we ain't farmed it for years. I kept the main tract and sixty acres we still use for growin' cabbage. Sold everything on the other side of the parkway."

"Expensive?" I ask.

"Taxes. Used to be, we'd pay around five hundred a year. Lots of the land me and the wife sold isn't nothing but dirt holding the earth together. Then Primland started snappin' up everything they could get their paws on and payin' ten times value. Next the mills closed, the jobs left, and the board of supervisors still gotta pay the bills, so taxes doubled and tripled and then went up some more. In 2015, me and the wife was payin' thirty-eight hundred a year for land what was just a-sittin' there. Thirty-eight hundred, and we was livin' off my little piece of farmin' money and our Social Security and the wife's pension from the plant. My daughter went to Tech and teaches school in Winchester. My boy's a lineman with Pike. Both of 'em drawin' good checks, and they ain't a-comin' back here to chop cabbage and run cows. Neither is my grandbabies. So we let 'er go."

"I'm sorry, sir," I say.

"Well don't be, I'm a millionaire now." He says it ironically, without happiness or satisfaction. "And even before we come into the money, I didn't have no problem with Primland. They provide jobs and offer a fair wage. A local boy's in charge of the place. My wife worked thirty-two years at J. P. Stevens — them jobs is over, so I figure we're lucky to have a world-famous hotel and fancy golfin'."

"How was it that you met the buyer? Could you tell me the details?"

Harris shrugs. "Never met nobody but my real-estate man, Mr. Lineberry from down in Stuart. Charles Lineberry. He took care of it all. He told me to start at $975,000, but we woulda took tax value, around six hundred."

"Did you ever speak with anyone? Maybe a lady named Melanie Culp? Any of the buyers?"

"No sir, I did not. Mr. Lineberry called me after the property had been on the market for nearly three months and said we had us a buyer, this Culp lady, but first we was gonna do this whatchamacallit deal to tie it up with her for sixty days."

"An option," I remind him. "You gave her an option to purchase for $975,000."

"And I was paid a thousand no matter what, even if she crawfished on me."

"And you never heard any more from her?"

"Not a peep. But at least we could keep the down payment."

"But then," I say, "you actually sold it."

"Sure did. Mr. Lineberry said it was a cash deal, some outfit from California. He was assumin' they was lookin' to ride Primland's coattails and build another hotel. Kinda like the beach or Gatlinburg, where they have a bunch of different places."

"And you didn't have any contact with anyone there?"

"Like I done said, we only was in contact with our real-estate man. He had a lawyer write up a deed, we went to Lineberry's office, signed it, and he give us the check minus his cut. Total was $916,500. A number I won't never forget." He peers down at the table. He hooks a finger in the hat's brim and slides it around the yellow tabletop. "Crazy, ain't it?" he says, still fooling with his hat. "Man could work his whole, entire life and never see a check big as that.

Me and the wife signed our name and the real-estate man give us darn near a million bucks." He looks up. "And I still wish I hadn't needed to do it."

"Would you mind, Mr. Harris, if I spoke with Mr. Lineberry and reviewed the documents in your file?"

"Don't see why not. The deed's at the courthouse. It's no secret. I went and seen it one day when I was in Stuart."

"You'll probably have to call him or give him permission in writing."

"What exactly is it that you're a-huntin'?" he asks.

"I'm trying to discover who's really behind the deal — a name, a contact number, an e-mail address. Other than that, I'm not certain. Anything and everything, I suppose."

"You ain't claimin' me and the wife done somethin' wrong, are you?" He squints at me, taps the table with the teaspoon's handle.

"No sir. Absolutely not."

"I'll talk to Mr. Lineberry. See if he can help you."

"I'm grateful. Thanks again for the coffee. Don't spend the whole $916,500 in one place."

He laughs. "Good advice. Hope you ain't

plannin' on tryin' to lawyer-charge me for it."

As soon as I arrive at the restaurant, I phone Charles Lineberry at Blue Ridge Real Estate. Lineberry has already received permission from Eugene Harris to discuss the option and MAB sale with me.

"From what Mr. Harris told me about your meeting this morning," Lineberry says, "I think he summed up the transaction accurately."

"So did you ever actually talk to this Melanie Culp?" I ask.

"E-mail only, except one short phone contact. She called to see if I'd received the signed and notarized option. We were on the phone maybe two minutes. Nothing seemed odd or unusual."

"Do you have her number?" I ask.

"I think so. Yep, here you go: 786-783-9012. At least that's the number she used when she called me, the number that came up on my caller ID."

"Thanks. And her e-mail?"

"It's melculp99@hotmail.com."

"Appreciate it." I jot the e-mail address and phone number on a giveaway notepad from an HVAC company.

"And you never heard anything else from

371

her? The option just lapsed? She just forfeited the thousand dollars?"

"I contacted her ten days before the deadline and warned her that we needed to get moving. I e-mailed and left a phone message. She e-mailed me back and said we were all good, that she'd turned everything over to a lawyer in Roanoke — you, evidently — and that you were handling the closing and would take care of executing the option. I e-mailed her again when no closing was set and time was running out, and then she finally e-mailed me kind of mad and hateful because nothing had happened and the option date had come and gone. She still wanted to buy the land, but MAB had already jumped in and made a full-price cash offer. The rest is history."

"What can you tell me about MAB?"

"Again, all e-mail. The purchase money was wired into my escrow from a California bank. MAB has a valid federal tax ID, and they're a registered California corporation. That's all I needed to know."

"Sure," I say. "I'm not blaming you for anything. Who was your contact there?"

"Gent by the name of George Brown."

"Of course." I scribble Brown's name under the phone number and e-mail address.

"This has been a very popular deal," Lineberry offers. "The lawyer for Miss Culp, a Mr. Jenkins from Richmond, called and spoke with me about her end of things and asked for copies of the e-mails." He hesitates. "For what it's worth, he claims that you were negligent, due to personal issues, and forgot to exercise the option. I'm not saying you did or you didn't — I wouldn't have any idea. Just want to be transparent with everybody involved. I don't have a dog in this fight." He pauses again. "I guess you're aware that MAB flipped the land and made millions."

"Yes. I am. And I damn sure didn't fail to do my job."

"Well, I hope this can be settled to everyone's satisfaction."

"Fucking dead end," I mutter as I fit the phone back into its base. "Shit."

"What's a dead end, Lawyer Kevin?"

"Hey, Blaine, didn't hear you come in." Blaine's at the kitchen door, sliding off his backpack. "I was chasing down possible evidence in my case. No luck. In fact, you could argue that my legal situation is worse — and that's saying a lot — based on what I've discovered today."

"Well, I can tell you what's not a dead end: Operation J'onzz is fully primed. We can log on to Flanagan's bank info at BB and T in Richmond, we can still use and read his e-mail, and I'm now a king for the site of Aaron, Charles and McMillian in Arlington, the humongous law firm."

"That was fast. Thanks so much. Someday, I hope I can repay you."

"Number one, I enjoyed the task, and number two, you gave me cash for school. I'd estimate that I'm still in the red."

"And it was only you? No Big Money? No girlfriend? No pals?"

"Solo Blaine. Two people know — you and me."

"Perfect."

Blaine steps into the doorway and lights a cigarette. "We do have a hitch. If you want this to remain dark and be a thousand percent positive you're hidden, you can't sit here or at your house and flip the switch." He blows the smoke out into the parking lot.

"Meaning?"

"Meanin' that our comrades who provide the Russian VPN proxy can tell who you are." Blaine's tone is direct and stern, rare for him. "They know. They have your IP address. We assume they won't cooperate with the police or Uncle Sam and let any cats out of the bag, mainly because they're

374

probably up to no good themselves, but shit can change overnight these days. Like I explained, we also always use open Wi-Fi. Then all the Russians know is that the input into them came from a coffee shop or hotel lobby. Mo' better protection. We're also fans of The Onion Router."

"So if I do this from my den sofa, people here will lose my trail in Russia, but if my enemies can somehow access the Russian server or persuade them to cooperate, it'll trace to me."

"Exactly."

"How can I avoid that?" I ask.

"You need to be somewhere with open Wi-Fi — as in open to any Tom, Dick and Harry — when this goes down. And to be even more careful, I'd use a disposable laptop. Like a burner phone. If you want to, you could give me the dollars, and I'd buy somethin' suitable and load it so you only need a few keystrokes to bring the super-powers. When you're done, you yank the hard drive, pound it with a hammer, then burn it so you don't get Freddy Kruegered."

"Sorry?"

"Like double-tapping a zombie. You kill it twice. Make sure it can't come back to life on you. Take precautions. Beat it, then burn it."

"Okay," I say. "Makes sense. But you're right, my house arrest is a complication."

"Just give me the word if you need this to happen."

"I'll see about getting you some cash for the computer." I watch a car pull into the lot. "I understand it's not perfect, but do you think you could install this Russian cloaking device on my landlord's home computer? A desktop?"

"Sure. I will. I could do it in the morning. So long as you understand there's an infinitesimal chance it might not hide you. Probably will, but I prefer the extra protection whenever possible and so should you."

When I arrive home from SUBstitution, the screen in the storm door is ripped away on both sides of the decorative, wrought-iron *H,* and there's a trail of trash from the porch to the double oak. I shove the transmission into Park, pissed off because a thief has ransacked the house. Immediately, I'm concerned: Melvin and the cops will think that *I* — the junkie tenant — stole Melvin's possessions and staged the burglary.

But as soon as I spot a partially chewed card that reads FALL LEAVES BUT JESUS STAYS and find several blue church tracts, the scattered apples and yellow squash, the shredded brown grocery bag, and the gnawed tin foil with a sliver of lemon cake still left in a tight corner, I realize what's happened. Reverend Grimes has been by for a visit, and he left a bag of vegetables and a cake trapped between the storm door and the stout wooden entrance door, and the bait was too much for Nelson, who has clawed through the screen, retrieved the bag and its cake and had himself a humdinger of a party. He has a clear conscience about the larceny and property damage, wags his tail and barks to greet me like always.

"Thanks so much, Nelson," I say. I point at the door. I raise my voice almost to a yell. "Bad *dog*!"

He drops his ears and ducks his head. His tail goes still.

"Bad dog," I repeat, less insanely. He cowers, then rolls over on his back and shows his belly. "And you smell like shit. Awful." I glance at the steps and notice footprints, mine, the ridges and jagged patterns of my tennis shoes written in dog diarrhea on the gray porch boards. "Damn it." I take off my shoes, put them soles-up on the glider seat. "More for me to do." I still haven't found a cushion to cure Nelson's earlier vandalism, and now I'll need to hire a handyman or carpenter to repair the fucking door.

The phone rings while I'm still on the porch. Wearing only socks, I slapstick slip and flail as soon as my feet hit the polished wood floor, but I don't fall or hurt myself, and I grab the receiver and snap a terse hello.

"And warm greetings to you as well." It's Ward.

"Sorry. I just got home. The dog has shit all over the yard and torn out the screen in the door. Not just any door, mind you, but the damn heirloom door with the Harrell family's initial in the middle."

"It could be worse, my friend. Could be a destroyed leather sofa and a *den* full of turds. We've been treated to that delight by our huskie. The joys of dog ownership."

"So what's up?" I ask.

"Good news — or, at least, I think it is. I was in Danville all day for a trial, but Judge Williams's assistant called the office, and he's hearing your criminal cases."

"So no Dinosaur Morris?"

"Correct," Ward replies. "We have a real judge who doesn't think that your drug addiction makes you a communist and a subversive."

"This is good news."

"As you're well aware, it's the Supreme Court's decision to make, and the big issue for Chief Justice Lemons is money — he doesn't see any need to pay Morris a per diem and mileage for three or four trips to Martinsville when we have a judge already here. I made that argument in my filing. Of course, Morris is such an asshole that I figured he'd volunteer to come for free and provide the hanging rope as a bonus."

"Do we have a date?"

"September twenty-sixth, two-thirty, for the motions. I'll deliver a copy of our brief to the judge first thing in the morning."

"Thanks," I say. "We're long past the point when I should be paying you. You need to send me a bill."

"I'm not worried about it," Ward says. "You'd help me if I needed it, if our roles were reversed." He sighs. "Anyway, I'm not sure how much all this effort will move the needle. Quality judge or not, we're fighting an uphill battle."

CHAPTER FOURTEEN

On September 13, I finally receive my health insurance policy in the mail, and the dec page states that I'm covered effective September 1, 2016. It's not the policy I was promised and paid for, not the "silver" plan with a $2,500 deductible and low co-pays, but, even with a five-grand deductible and only seventy-five percent provider reimbursement, it's better than nothing, and that night Nelson and I have dinner on the porch to celebrate.

I grill two hamburger steaks, one for each of us, and if I count my blessings and don't fret about what's coming next, and if I'm *mindful* — Lilly Heath's yoga instruction — I have cause to be content: My insurance woes are behind me, my neck is healing, my face isn't numb or misshapen, my stroke came from a feed-sack accident, not a carotid time bomb, and I have money in the bank, a roof over my head, a full belly and a blue-eyed dumpster dog who's smart and loyal and dozing at my feet.

And if I cheat and spoil the moment, if I think ahead and game the worst-case scenarios, I have a Dave Worthy backdoor route that will short-circuit the legal system, juke me past a mandatory minimum prison sentence, turn guilt into gold and leave Randy Clay grabbing at a will-o'-the-wisp.

CHAPTER FIFTEEN

Early the following Friday, around 5:45 a.m., I write Dan another letter and tell him I'd be grateful if he could travel here on September 29, the date of the Culp deposition. I remind him that "time is of the essence," a legal term we learned in our first-year Contracts class. Dan's confirmation to me is "No Worries," a Lil Wayne title I chose from an Internet list of his most popular songs.

Later, at dawn, as I'm releasing Nelson from his pen, a pickup comes into view, an eighties model with faded blue paint and a toolbox spanning the front of the bed. Headlights burning, the truck stops beside the dog lot. The driver rolls down the window and removes a pipe from his mouth. "Mornin', sir," he says. He dangles the pipe outside the window, and I can smell the cherry-flavored drugstore tobacco smoke.

"Good morning," I reply. "How're you?"

"Blessed," he says. "You're Kevin Moore, I reckon?"

"Yes."

"I'm Arthur McPeak. Preacher Grimes is my brother-in-law. He tells me he made a little miscalculation and your door took some damage. I'm here to fix it."

"Oh, great. He didn't have to do that, but I can definitely use the help. I've been asking around but hadn't found anybody who could repair it yet."

"Well, I'm gonna take it off the hinges and carry it over to my shop, and I'll have it good as new and back here by tomorrow evenin'."

"Thank you, and thanks to Reverend Grimes."

"He feels right bad over it," McPeak says, a smile forming.

"I'm happy to pay you for the work."

McPeak lets the smile roll. "Oh, no. Me, I'd rather just save this in my pocket till the next time I'm in hot water with my wife. You don't owe me nothin'." He takes a pipe draw. "Fine-lookin' dog. Is he the one what tore up the door?"

"He is," I answer.

"Who can blame him?" McPeak asks.

I go inside and cook breakfast. I scramble an egg and fry bacon and slice a peeled apple into quarters, and while the skillet and yellow yolk still cause me to flash on the morning my brain clogged and sputtered and almost killed me, they're not the black beasts they were a month ago.

I finish my coffee at the computer. I open a file named WINNER and work on a second motion and brief, polish them and add a 2015 court of appeals citation now that I know who my motions judge will be. I print the brief, stand at the desk and read it aloud, and then I anticipate Judge Williams's questions and practice answering them. I plan to sit on this legal argument until the morning of my hearing and claim that I last-minute discovered the defense on September 25. The ambush will rankle Randy Clay, and no doubt Williams will be mildly annoyed and allow the commonwealth ample time to respond to my "new" filing, but there's an advantage to being the first lawyer to write on a blank slate and plant a notion in the judge's head, and that leg-up definitely trumps any courtroom scolding I'll catch.

Blaine and Big Money are already at SUB-stitution when I arrive at ten-fifteen, and Blaine almost has the counter stocked with meats and vegetables and ready for business.

"We have a legal question for you, Lawyer Kevin," Blaine announces.

"Free legal advice," I say. "It's worth exactly what you pay for it."

"I hear you." Big Money grins.

"So here's the thing," Blaine says. "All over the roads, everywhere, like there's one in Ararat and I've seen 'em in Lynchburg —"

"Other states too," Big Money interrupts.

"You see these signs warnin': SPEED LIMIT ENFORCED BY AIRCRAFT. That's total bullshit, right? How in the world could they do that? It's the same as puttin' a dummy in the parked cruiser, isn't it? A trick to keep you honest?"

"Good call, Blaine," I say. "It is indeed an empty state threat, as far as I know."

"Had to be," Big Money adds.

"Yeah," Blaine says. "We were just curious and thought we'd ask the expert."

"How is it that you're here on a Friday, Nate?" I ask, using his given name.

"Man, you'd have to be a true college loser to get stuck with Friday classes or anything before nine, no matter the day." He nods at Blaine. " 'Course, if you're a super-senior takin' remedial math at PH, your academic commitment's probably a grueling three hours a week."

"And my student-loan bill so far is a gruelin' nothing," Blaine replies. "I'm valedictorian of my class too — I'll score extra ribbons on my graduation robe, a fifty-buck savings bond and the hundred-dollar scholarship from Chick-fil-A. Livin' the dream, Money."

It's not even ten-thirty, but we hear a knock on the front doors, and we all turn and check to see who's beating the glass. The hours of operation are posted in bold black letters. We open at eleven.

"Crap," Blaine gripes. "I mean, just how important could your six-inch tuna be at ten-thirty in the mornin'?"

It's difficult to make out the customer, because she's in the midst of a bright fall sun's glare and her face is surrounded by cupped hands and pressed close to the glass. She knocks again, then moves away from the door.

"Well, at least she's pretty," Blaine remarks. "I'll give her the tragic news — it'll be a while before we can hook her up."

"Oh, shit," I blurt. "Wow. It's my wife." I'm so happy to see her that I chirp the words, ecstatic. "Damn. It's Ava." And I *know,* I can feel it in my gut, that her visit will be another notch toward my salvation, because you don't skip school and drive

ninety miles to deliver a bitter message —
those come by phone or e-mail or text or
old-fashioned "Dear John" letter, not face-
to-face.

"Is this good or bad, Lawyer Kevin?"
Blaine asks sincerely.

"Excellent," I say. "I've been on a roll
recently, and I'm thinking my streak is
about to get even better."

"Holy Catwoman." Blaine smiles. "Eartha
Kitt, the irresistible feline villainess, has appeared. Be careful."

"I was the villain," I say, "not my wife.
My ex-wife." I step from behind the counter
and wave. Ava sees me and raises her hand,
and I start for the door, almost jog. Behind
me, Big Money and Blaine nerd-argue
about Michelle Pfeiffer, Halle Berry and Julie Newmar, debating who was most faithful to the spirit of the character.

I twist the deadbolt until it clangs and pull
the door open. I hug Ava and she wraps me
up as well, and I tighten the embrace and
kiss the top of her head. She squirms so she
can fold her arms close into herself and,
same as she's always done, for years, rises
on her tiptoes for a second and rests her
check against my chest. We stay stuck
together until I slide my hand underneath
her shirttail and skin-to-skin touch her

along her low back and she says "Cut it out" and wiggles loose.

"Damn," I say when we separate. "The best surprise ever. Come in. It's like you're a VIP Gold Circle member — we can let you in half an hour before the general public so you can snag the prime seat."

She laughs. "Thanks. I won't take long. I know you're busy."

"No problem. We're basically finished setting up, and the mornings are slow."

She steps into the restaurant, and I introduce her to Blaine and Nate, and they're stiff and sweet and oddly bashful, like two six-year-olds in knickers and knee socks meeting their elementary school principal on the first day of classes. They're uncertain of what to do with their hands, and Blaine's eyes jitterbug from place to place, never resting on Ava for very long.

"Nice to meet you both," Ava says.

"You too, ma'am," Blaine replies.

"Same here," Big Money adds.

"Lawyer Kevin's been a great boss," Blaine volunteers. He slightly lifts his arms and hands and drops them against his sides. "Well, I gotta get goin'. Take as long as you need, Kevin. I'll handle the last little bit of prep."

"You should be proud of that," Ava says

388

as soon as we sit down.

"Of what?"

"It's obvious that they really like you. Look up to you."

"I'm not sure why they would," I reply. "They're great kids in general, and respectful of everyone, even disbarred lawyers."

"So," she says, "I don't want to drag this out." She full stops. Swallows. Rapid-taps an orange painted nail on the table. She's not looking at me when she speaks again. "I'll always love you, Kevin. You'll always have a place in my heart. You were a great husband, and we had an amazing marriage. Until we didn't. The reason I'm here, the reason I drove to Stuart, is . . . well, to tell you I'm selling the house and leaving Roanoke. I want a clean start. I don't need every building and every restaurant and every friend and every intersection and every square inch of my home constantly reiterating my loss and heartache."

"Leaving? What . . . what about —"

"I resigned my job at Cave Spring — I'd already given them a heads-up over the summer, so they were prepared — and I'm moving to Virginia Beach. I have a job at the school board office there starting in January. It's a grant program, only two years, but I'm ready for a break from the classroom and really excited about it."

A feeble "Oh" is all I can muster.

"This sounds strange — my friends will shoot me if they find out I'm asking — but I sort of want your blessing. At a minimum, I thought I should give you the news in person. I owe you that much. I also wanted to offer you half the money one last time and —"

"Money's not important," I interrupt. The words come out hoarse and weak, so I repeat them.

"I realize this isn't my fault — I didn't lie to my spouse and commit adultery and become a coke addict — but I don't want to feel like a coldhearted bitch who grabbed the cash, hit the road and left you in the lurch, and gave up on us when times were tough. I understand how hard you've tried to save our marriage. I honestly, truly wish I could put everything behind me. Sometimes I'm mad at myself because I can't. I didn't tell you, but I went to see a counselor. I even quizzed Linda Mathers about how she's able to be happy with Lionel after he cheated on her, how they seem so lovey-dovey. I wish it were different. For me, it's as if I'm now a pauper, and every day I have to sit at the foot of the hill and stare up at the beautiful castle I unfairly lost to the dastardly prince."

"You're in hopes I'll tell you that I don't want you to be my wife any longer . . . which isn't true." My tongue sticks to the roof of my mouth and causes dry clicks as I talk. A speck of hurt starts at the corner of my eye and begins to web across my cheek toward my jawbone. "I completely accept that I brought this on myself. My mistakes. My lies. My drugs. My night of infidelity. You have every right to leave. That's not in any way wronging me. So in that sense you *do* have my blessing. I don't blame you. Your pals are right: It's weird to be saying this to you — *the innocent spouse.* I want you to have a huge, happy life. I'm sorry beyond measure that I ruined us, and I totally understand why you can't trust me. I deserve my circumstances. You don't deserve what happened to you. We've both done everything we could after my screwup, both been as fair to each other as we can be, but I guess it wasn't meant to happen."

"Then there's this whole crazy stroke horror, and Dan tells me — don't be mad at him — that it was really scary for a while. Are you okay? If you need me to take care of you or drive you to the doctor or rehab, I want to help. Selfishly, it'd make me feel better about myself."

"I'm almost recovered. But thanks."

"I can't notice any difference. You might've lost a few pounds, but you look and sound normal."

I lick my cottoned lips. Touch my burning cheek with my thumb. "Is there a man involved in the move? A boyfriend?"

"No," she replies firmly. "Absolutely not. Once I leave Roanoke, I won't be seeing Brian anymore — at least that should make you happy."

"It does. He's a dick. And a fool. You deserve far better."

She reaches across the tabletop and holds my hands. "Good luck. And thanks. I wish . . . I wish . . ." Her voice evaporates, and she takes a hand away to dab at her eyes. "Sorry." She pulls the other hand away. "You'll be gone from here soon, healthy and practicing law again. I want the very best for you also. Goodbye, Kevin. At least we don't hate each other; that'd be unbearable. Eighteen years, right? We did better than most people. We truly did."

She walks to her car and drives off. Standing outside, I track her Mercedes until it begins a left turn that erases it from view. There're two picnic tables at the edge of the parking lot, and I sit at the table closest to the store. The tables and pavement are spotted with dead, mottled leaves, and I stay there — listening to a couple of crows caw and rattle, watching ants swarm a scrap of meat, swatting at a stray yellowjacket — until the first customer arrives a few minutes before eleven.

"Bummer, Lawyer Kevin," Blaine says quietly when we cross paths in the kitchen. "Sorry."

"Thanks. I need to treat it as a lesson learned. We're divorced and we've been apart for over a year, so it's not unexpected news. Just horribly sad news. Nothing gained by moping and sulking."

The day only becomes more abysmal. At three-thirty, Luther Foley arrives in his shiny, gas-guzzling 2016 black Suburban, stalks into the store and invites Blaine and me into the kitchen. There're no customers in the sandwich line, and we just finished and packed a to-go order for the girls' volleyball team at the high school.

"Listen," he says brusquely, speaking to Blaine, "did you do some racial shit to a colored boy named Malik? Refuse him service? Him and his white girlfriend, a Sutphin woman from the welfare apartments?"

"No!" Blaine replies, clearly dumbfounded by the allegation. "Are you crazy? Why would you ask me that?"

"This Destiny Sutphin girl called my office in Roanoke and made a complaint, and she's threatenin' to sic the state on me. Claims she and the colored guy come in and you refused 'em service because they was a mixed couple."

"Hell, no. That's an outright lie, Luther," Blaine says, so upset that his voice quavers. "The girl and her *African American* boyfriend were here back in June and stiffed us for a sandwich. She ordered, couldn't pay and tried to sell us a bunch of food stamps. Totally illegal. Lawyer Kevin busted her on it."

"Absolutely true," I confirm. I move shoulder to shoulder with Blaine. "We were professional and restrained. She ordered knowing full well they couldn't pay, then offered to trade us an EBT card for an amount greater than the sale. If you want the state and Feds up your butt, Luther, let those kind of shenanigans happen in here. It had nothing to do with color, other than the color green. She couldn't pay. Hell, Blaine's best friend is black."

Luther scowls. "Damn, even a country redneck like me knows that's the worst defense: 'Hey, I have colored friends.' "

"Well, Luther," I answer, "I doubt you

have *any* black friends, especially if you insist on using the term *colored.*"

"NAACP," Luther snap-replies. "What's the *C* stand for, Kevin?"

"It's going to stand for *closed,*" I say, "if you don't support your employees."

"She wasn't complaining about June," Luther continues. "She claims they visited on July twenty-second, when you was still sick and not workin', and Blaine mistreated them."

Blaine folds his arms across his chest. I can hear his breathing, heavy and quick. "I told them they still owed for the sandwich from their earlier visit. Soon as she started ordering, I alerted her that she'd need an extra nine dollars. You want me to simply forget it, Luther? You're grubbing every possible penny, those are our instructions, and you're mad because I made her pay for what she actually ordered and the store lost? Seriously? And yeah, she started whinin' about discrimination. Pitched a fit. Total bullshit, and who calls weeks later if something really happened? They're also both druggies, Luther, so I wouldn't be too worried about it."

Luther taps his head with his index finger. His hair is so plastered with Wildroot oil that you can see the comb rows. "Part of bein' a successful manager is handling situations and makin' smart choices. Usin' discretion. Thinkin'. Maybe, Blaine, you made this worse instead of better."

"Luther," I tell him, "you're lucky to have Blaine. And if you're looking for someone to blame for Miss Sutphin's conniption, you can blame me. I'm Blaine's boss, and when she screwed us in June, right then and there, I instructed him to charge her if she ever came in again. It's completely on me. My call, not his."

Blaine's eyes jerk sideways toward me. "Well, not —"

I cut him off before he can correct my untruth. "Simple as that, Luther. My decision. My order to Blaine. We can't let people cheat us. Can't set that precedent. You want to punish someone, punish me. Don't blame him for doing what I told him to do." I'm irritated now also. I draw a bead on Luther. Flip my hands apart. "Can I guess, Luther, that she didn't share those parts of the story?"

He shrugs. He hitches his pants. "No, not really. So she owed you money from another visit 'cause you made her food, she couldn't pay, and we wasted the sandwich?"

"Ding, ding, ding," Blaine says sarcastically.

"If you'd like, Luther, you can look in the ledger by the register, and you'll see we made an entry contemporaneous with the event."

"You did?" he asks. "No kiddin'?"

"Same as we do when people return a 'flat' soft drink or claim they didn't order mustard and we have to remake an entire sandwich."

"Well," Luther says, "there's advantages to havin' a smart lawyer on the payroll."

"Other than having him serve as your academic ghostwriter, you mean?" Blaine is still pissed and defiant.

"Blaine," Luther shoots back, "I ain't got the foggiest idea why you want to be such a smartass with me when I'm just investigatin' a workplace complaint at my restaurant. Doin' *my* job."

"Are we done?" I ask.

"I'm gonna have my secretary call the girl and see if a twenty-five-dollar gift certificate will make this vanish."

"Why would you give her anything?" Blaine demands. "She's in the wrong. You're throwing us under the bus."

Luther smiles. "Ask Kevin how much he charges me an hour for lawyer work, even when I'm in the right. If I can end this misunderstandin' and have her put something in writin' releasing me for the price of a couple subs, I damn well plan to do it. And you keep a polite tongue when they come in for the free food, you hear?"

"We will," I answer for Blaine, who's glowering at Luther. "You want us to see about a red carpet and a cocktail band for their dinner?"

"Another question," Luther says. "You hearin' any noise about a new restaurant opening in Stuart?"

"Nope," I reply. "But I don't hear much of anything. I'm either behind this counter or at home."

"No, me neither," Blaine says. "Why're you asking us?"

Luther jabs his thumb in the direction of the highway. "Who's the shrewdest bidness-man in this county?"

"Melvin Harrell?" I reply.

"He don't count," Luther answers. "He stays in Florida."

"Evidently, Destiny Sutphin," Blaine gripes. "Seems she's earning about twenty-five bucks for three minutes of bad acting and a phone call. That's five hundred an hour."

"Larry Hutchens," Luther declares. "He owns that old dry-cleaning building across the road. It's empty and I know he's been anxious to rent it. I've heard Burger King and Jimmy John's are possibilities. And them Chinese guys who run the restaurant in Eden have been pokin' around here, thinkin' about opening a place. My cousin, Lonnie, who lives in Critz, said he'd seen a truck at the cleaners and a man in and out. Activity."

"Yeah, I've noticed a white service truck there a few times," Blaine says.

"Me too," I say. "Doesn't mean much, though. Certainly doesn't mean a new restaurant's coming down the pike."

Luther's tone grows more pleasant. "Well, competition across the highway is the last thing we need — right, fellows?"

"We'll send up the Bat Signal if we discover any kinda plot, Luther," Blaine suggests.

"I'll tell you how clever ol' Hutchens is — this might be a rouge. It's possible he's running one of his regular workers in and out, kickin' up dust, drawin' attention and spreading rumors about tenants just so he can sucker me into buying the place. Keep your ears to the ground, okay? Maybe mosey over and ask whoever's there what's happenin' next time you see the truck. Or see anybody."

"Ruse," Blaine says. "The word is *ruse.*

Amazing that you and I will have the same college degree."

"Are we done?" I ask again.

"Yeah, sure. And, guys, hey, I'm sorry if I came in on y'all a little hot and bothered. Runnin' a public bidness ain't as easy as it used to be. I appreciate both of you, you especially, Kevin. Thanks for every damn thing you do. I'm behind you a hundred and ten percent."

"Perfect," I say when I get home that evening, open the car door, step into an unexpected chilly mist and catch a whiff of Nelson, who's been sprayed by a skunk and stinks so bad that I can smell him from thirty feet away. At least the screen door is repaired, thanks to Arthur McPeak, and I found an odd-lot cushion on eBay that matches the one Nelson destroyed. Seventy-nine bucks it cost me, but it's due to arrive soon via UPS.

Nelson halts before he makes it to me and rolls and wallows in the grass. He stands on all fours, shakes, then sits on his haunches and rakes his snout and eyes with a paw. I have a good idea how he must feel.

Monday, September 26, I'm scheduled to be in Martinsville for my motions hearing with Judge Williams, so I have some electronic-monitoring leeway, and I take advantage of the flexibility to meet Lilly for breakfast, our first time seeing each other since her sick night at the guesthouse. We've occasionally e-mailed and twice chatted on the phone, but she's been tepid and hard to pin down. Still, when I e-mailed her on Friday and inquired about a "five-star morning date at Mabry Mill," she agreed immediately, replied from her phone and included a smiling yellow emoji.

We're supposed to meet at 7:30 a.m., and I'm there ten minutes early. It's brisk enough that I'm wearing a fleece jacket. I wait for Lilly in the parking lot, and she arrives soon after I do.

"Hey, Kevin," she says as she's exiting the Range Rover, dressed in her nurse clothes and a stylish coat. "What happened to our swimming weather?"

"It's fall on the mountain," I reply, walking toward her. I take her hand and kiss her cheek, and she doesn't seem to mind.

The mill's restaurant and gift shop are WPA, often-patched-or-repaired-but-never-remodeled, federal-government rustic: pine paneling, exposed rafters, uneven board floors and a dining section that's on an enclosed porch. The porch borders a thick

401

patch of mountain laurel, and it's usually drafty in the fall — the sills and windows aren't airtight, and there's no ductwork in the dining area itself.

We're seated quickly, and the whole setting couldn't be better. We can smell coffee brewing and food on the grill. From our table, we can see a spread of coloring hardwoods, a high mosaic of reds, yellows and fire oranges tucked into a green backdrop. The waitress is full of *honey*s and *sweetie*s, and we're not cold or uncomfortable, and we take our jackets off and drape them over empty chairs. It's as if we're being served homemade biscuits and a textbook breakfast on a plush 1950s camping trip.

"This is great," Lilly remarks midway through her meal. "I've never been here before. Good choice."

"Thanks. My landlord, Melvin, introduced me to the place years ago."

We talk about her job and a patient who's made a nice recovery, and Blu's new Jeep, and the dismal candidates running for president, and her spotty Internet service, and I tell her a funny lawyer story, and I brag on Nelson, how he's mastered his new fetch trick and recognizes *ball, wallet* and *keys* and is learning to bring my shoes from the closet to the recliner. We drink more coffee and then just sit quiet for a while, content with the silence, past the point where we feel constrained to keep the conversation unbroken, a small milestone.

At the register, I buy her a postcard from a wire rack, a picture of the pond, split-rail fence and gristmill with its wooden waterwheel. "Making memories," I say. "What good is a romantic breakfast without a keepsake?"

"This treasure's going straight into my scrapbook." She grins at me.

"Let's aim for a fridge magnet next visit."

"Thanks for inviting me," she says once we're outside and walking toward her vehicle. "I've been feeling drab and cooped up. This was perfect. And thanks for paying. You didn't have to."

"Well, thank you for coming. I know a little bit about being cooped up."

"So how's that going?" she asks. "Your cases?"

"Well, I have an important hearing this afternoon, and a big deposition on September twenty-ninth. I guess we'll learn in a few days whether or not I can be a proper boyfriend anytime soon."

We're almost at her car door, and she stops and turns to face me. "I hope you get the chance. I have no idea if we'd have anything in common long-term, there's no way to know, but maybe I'd at least like to have the *possibility*. This mess, the drug charges and strange lawsuits, sneaking a breakfast with me, no sane person would ever want to buy into that. I hope it all disappears. Hope you win."

"I'll call in a few days, after the criminal charges are dismissed and the ankle bracelet's gone, and we'll celebrate. Then I'll just be a regular ol' broke dude stacking sandwiches. Date?"

"Date," she says, and I kiss her again, this time for real, and she pushes flush against me — thighs, stomach, breasts. She shifts away after a few seconds, but I'm so smitten and happy that I replay the kiss over and over, become sidetracked by the recollection six hours later when Ward and I are meeting in his office to prepare for court.

Chapter Sixteen

A train buff, Ward has an original, signed O. Winston Link photograph hung on his office wall, and even at one-thirty on a mediocre September day, and even in a room arranged to favor diplomas, awards, newspaper clippings and an antique Lady Justice statue, the black-and-white picture of a steaming locomotive above the Hawksbill Creek swimming hole — the train, water, bridge and people all storybook lit — is something to behold, commanding. I focus on the scene, and the framed water sets me to thinking about the Mabry Mill postcard, and that chutes me to Lilly Heath and our morning walk to her car. Again.

"Am I boring you, Kevin?" Ward asks.

"Huh?"

"I apologize if this is tedious for you. I might as well be talking to the door."

"Sorry," I say. "I was caught up in your train picture." I give him my full attention.

405

"And we've been over this a hundred times."

"I just want to make sure we're in total agreement and have covered every base. Lawyers can famously make for difficult clients. Lots of second-guessing." He maneuvers his chair closer to his desk. "By the way — and not that it changes anything — the sample Kelly Napier sent to the state lab also tested as synthetic urine. No surprise."

"We're agreed," I assure him. "But speaking of bases, I thought of another argument that I believe we should raise."

"Really?" He sounds skeptical. "And when did this revelation drop from the clouds and land in Meadows of Dan?"

"Lucky for me, last night."

"Last night, huh?"

I open my briefcase and hand him a typed motion and memo. "Here you go. Barrel number two."

Ward reads the papers. "Last night," he repeats when he finishes and flips the stapled pages back to the beginning. "Lucky indeed. Randy Clay will have a stroke . . . uh, shit, sorry . . . Clay will hit the roof if I submit this today with no notice. And you want me to tell him and Judge Williams that this defense suddenly came to you last night and that you miraculously pulled this kind of effort together in a few hours?"

"Well," I say and grin, "you can tell them I worked on it last night and printed it out this morning."

"It's a damn clever card to play, Kevin, but you have to —"

"I understand Clay'll bitch, and the judge will realize that the filing's an ambush, but I'm a fan of making my point strong and first, and putting the other side on defense."

"Of course, Judge Williams will allow the commonwealth time to respond. He won't be thrilled with this eleventh-hour surprise either."

"Sure," I agree, "but we'll have the stage to ourselves today, and Clay will be chasing us from the get-go."

"Not to mention the grief I'll catch," Ward complains, but his tone conveys that he'll accept the fallout, part of a quality attorney doing his job. "I have to deal with these folks long after your case is over."

"First, you can blame it on me. It's my fault. Hell, I want to argue the motion myself, and I plan to, if Judge Williams will let me. Second, as selfish as it sounds, I don't give a rat's ass. I'm more concerned about avoiding jail than I am about legal etiquette and Clay not sending you a Christmas card." I focus on the train photo again.

"What was Caleb Opportunity's taunt: You want to ride on the train or have it run over you? I don't give a damn how much this pisses off Randy Clay if it'll help me beat these bullshit charges. The system's been really fair and mannerly with me so far, right?"

"Yeah, yeah, yeah, yeah," Ward drones. "I'll fall on the sword. It's why I make the big bucks."

Judge David Williams does put me in mind of an older Burt Reynolds, if Reynolds were hale and healthy instead of a brittle, toupeed skeleton. Williams begins court on time, welcomes the lawyers and wishes me a good afternoon. I've practiced law since 1998, and you can size up most judges within the first few minutes. My early impression is consistent with what Ward has told me — Williams is intelligent, he knows his gig, and he'll be prepared.

"So," Williams says, "Mr. Moore is charged with methamphetamine distribution and also possession of a firearm while selling the meth. Mr. Armstrong, you've filed a motion to suppress the gun and drugs allegedly discovered in your client's vehicle when he visited his probation officer. Is that where we are?" His tone is studied and neutral.

"Yes sir," Ward answers.

I've listened to judges intone the particulars of motions and indictments on hundreds of occasions, but hearing *my name* attached to these flimflam cases makes me so angry and frustrated that — without thinking about it — I stomp the carpeted floor underneath the table. Ward hears the noise and frowns, but fortunately, the leather-against-rug thump stays close and doesn't carry to the bench.

"Correct," Randy Clay agrees. He waits for Williams to glance at the file and shakes his head at Ward, miffed because he's had to spend hours writing a reply brief, interviewing witnesses and preparing for this hearing, valuable time wasted to defend a legitimate search against fanciful, straw-grasping claims by a doper lawyer, a lawyer who should be taking his lumps and apologizing to the profession. "The motion is the result of Mr. Moore's incredible conspiracy fairy tale."

Ward fires right back: "There's nothing incredible about our position other than an incredible and obvious Constitutional violation by the commonwealth."

"It's your motion, Mr. Armstrong," Williams says. "How do you want to proceed?

I've read your brief."

"Judge, this is the commonwealth's little red wagon. There's no warrant. None. Therefore, it's their burden to demonstrate that the search is allowable, owing either to consent or some recognized exception. We've formally objected for the record. It's now Mr. Clay's responsibility to explain how the warrantless intrusion into my client's car was legal."

Williams removes his reading glasses and jiggles them against the court file. "Well, it's not quite so cut and dried, is it, Mr. Armstrong? We have a speedbump, don't we?"

"Judge," Clay responds, "it's more than a bump. It's a mountain the defendant can't climb. We have a valid court order, not objected to by the defendant when Judge Morris signed it, that allows the search. Better, even if we didn't, we have the defendant's consent, and on top of those two commonwealth winners, we have probable cause."

"Well," Williams says, returning the glasses to the bridge of his nose, "Mr. Armstrong, do you stipulate to the sentencing order that Judge Morris entered in the possession case? The case he took under advisement in Roanoke?"

Ward slides a step away from the counsel

table. "Yes, Judge, we do. I've spoken to Mr. Clay. We agree that an order was entered by Judge Morris. We agree that this court may consider it, and we agree that Mr. Clay has submitted an accurate copy with his brief. We do not agree, however, that it would give Mr. Flanagan, the probation officer, the right to search."

Williams holds a yellow legal sheet so we all can see it. He studies the paper. "Well, my work's already been done for me, hasn't it? United States Supreme Court in *Knights,* our own Supreme Court in *Murry*? Justice Kinser wrote *Murry;* she's as good a judge as ever put on a black robe. Virginia law is settled on this: If the defendant objects to the court-ordered language modifying his search-and-seizure protections when it's originally added, all the commonwealth has to prove is reasonable suspicion to search, not even probable cause. If there's no objection at the time the order is entered, or if it's part of a plea deal" — Williams pauses to arch his eyebrows at Ward — "then it's a valid waiver and the commonwealth can search his home, car, belongings and so forth whenever and whyever, no justification required. They can do it for no reason. On a whim. The *Anderson* case establishes that rule."

Clay barely waits for the judge to finish. "And there was no objection when Judge Morris entered the order last year. None. In fact, I checked with the special prosecutor, Jane Klein, and I also had a transcript prepared — more wasted time for my office and more wasted money for the taxpayers — and Mr. Moore's under-advisement status on the cocaine charge was part of an agreement and recommendation. Judge, Mr. Moore agreed to this, accepted the loss of the right as part of receiving a significant break, and now he suddenly wants to cherry-pick from the deal he made."

"Did you object, Mr. Armstrong?" Williams peers over the reading glasses at Ward. "Did you protest the provision in the Morris order granting a probation officer the right to search Mr. Moore's person, computer, home or vehicle?"

"We didn't affirmatively agree to it, and it wasn't a part of our initial understanding with the prosecutor." I feel sorry for Ward. The weak deflection is the best he can do for me.

Clay snorts. He looks skyward. He tosses his pen on the table, and it rolls until it stops against a black Virginia Code volume. "Come on, Ward."

Williams's demeanor doesn't change; he's

412

seen plenty of lawyer theater before. "Did you ever object to the language in the order?" he asks a second time. "Did you say, 'Hey, Judge Morris, please don't add that as part of the sentence'?"

Ward's smart enough not to try the judge's patience. "Sir, we did not."

"Thank you," Williams responds. "So either the commonwealth wins automatically based on the order, or Mr. Clay has to show, at most, some reasonable suspicion for the search."

"And we can prove reasonable suspicion," Clay asserts. "In spades. Mr. Moore was dirty for meth minutes before the search, then denied using. What better reason could we have to investigate his car, a location where — by law — he already has a lesser privacy interest? Once he claimed the test was wrong, the probation officer was entitled to take reasonable measures to verify the results."

"Is that accurate?" Williams inquires. "Did Mr. Moore fail a urine test, then challenge the results?"

"For some mysterious reason, Judge," Ward says sarcastically, "and despite five calls and two e-mails, I've never had the privilege of speaking with Mr. Flanagan. Mr. Clay and I both subpoenaed him. I'd suggest we take some evidence and hear from the horse's mouth what he claims happened."

"Judge," Clay says, "in Mr. Flanagan's defense, he faxed Mr. Armstrong his notes and report, and he returned his call."

"Yeah." Ward smirks. "He's really been busting his tail to get in touch with me. Called my office number, once, around nine at night."

"If he's here now," the judge says, "then let's swear him in and see what he can tell us."

The bailiff walks to a witness room, opens the door, announces the name "Flanagan," and the bald little crook appears, and as he makes his way to the front of the courtroom, he does a credible job of appearing calm and professional. He sits erect in the witness chair, looks directly at the judge and answers the oath with a firm "I do." He's wearing a blue suit and a tie with an American flag motif. He's gained a full beard since I last saw him.

"State your name and occupation, please," Clay instructs him.

"Edward F. Flanagan. I'm a regional supervisor for the Virginia Department of Corrections, specifically with the probation and parole section."

414

"How long have you been so employed?"

"I began as a probation officer in 1989. I served in that job for sixteen years. I then became chief of the Forty-fifth District. In 2009, I was promoted to my current job as a regional supervisor."

"In June of this year, did you have occasion to visit us here in Martinsville as part of your job responsibilities?"

"Yes," Flanagan replies. He seems comfortable. No doubt he's testified at hundreds of trials and is accustomed to being examined and cross-examined by attorneys.

"And did you meet with the defendant, Mr. Kevin Moore?"

"I did," Flanagan says.

I tilt closer to Ward so Flanagan can see me in his periphery. I glare at him, but he fixes his gaze on the judge, doesn't respond or engage with me.

"Did you drug-test Mr. Moore?" Clay asks.

"Yes."

With each question, Clay has migrated toward Flanagan so that he's now almost beside the witness stand. He buttons his suit jacket and adjusts a yellow-ribbon pin on his lapel. "What were the results of the test?"

Flanagan opens a file, shuffles a few

415

papers and slightly dips his head. He reads: "I tested Mr. Moore at four-twenty-eight p.m. using the strip and cup authorized by the state. He tested positive for methamphetamines."

I slam against my chair's padded back and cross my arms over my chest, continue to burn holes in Flanagan. "Lying sack of shit," I whisper to Ward.

"Any issues with the test procedure?" Clay asks.

"None," Flanagan responds. He covers his mouth and coughs. "Sorry," he volunteers. "Fightin' a cold."

Clay pivots and starts toward his table. "And did you confront Mr. Moore with the results?" he asks over his shoulder.

"Yes."

"And what, if anything, did he tell you about testing positive for meth?"

Flanagan looks in my direction. "He denied it. Well, at first he denied it. Officer Napier also heard him deny that he was dirty. But later, when we were alone, and I was standin' there with a gun and the drugs and it was obvious to anyone the jig was up, he admitted to everything and begged me to give him a second chance."

"What happened next, after the initial denial, I mean?" Clay asks. He unbuttons

416

his jacket and sits again, extends his legs and crosses his ankles.

Flanagan closes his file. "Well, I told him that the court order gave me permission to search his vehicle. I informed him I wanted to search. Probationers with serious addiction issues are known to stash drugs in their cars. Him bein' a lawyer and everything, I asked him if he minded — I wanted to be extra-cautious. He told me it was okay. Gave me permission."

Clay lets the answer soak in for several seconds. "So, let's see," he eventually says, "you had a court order allowing the search, you had consent, and you had a verifiable reason?"

Ward objects. "That's leading, and it's basically his closing argument."

"Sustained," Williams says.

I've already explained to Ward that I never gave Flanagan express consent. I was very precise and careful, only told him, "Your call." I write UNTRUE on my legal pad, touch Ward's arm, and he sees the word and nods at me.

"Your witness, Mr. Armstrong," Clay says.

"Good afternoon, Mr. Flanagan," Ward says. "I'm glad that we can finally speak."

"Good afternoon to you, sir." The dig doesn't ruffle Flanagan.

Ward allows Flanagan to sit there on display, both of us locked onto him, until he finally looks in our direction. "So how is it that you came to drive from Richmond to administer a test for my client? He was being supervised by Officer Weiss, correct?"

Flanagan's a difficult witness. He won't rush, won't guess, won't lose his temper and will slow Ward's tempo every chance he has. He damn well knows that Ron is my PO, but instead of answering, he reopens the file, flips through papers and, after stalling for at least a minute, replies, "Yes, Mr. Weiss."

"And why did you drive 175 miles to give Mr. Moore a routine drug test?"

Flanagan addresses Judge Williams, ignores Ward and me. "As a matter of policy, I often check behind our officers in high-profile or serious cases. Everyone's protected that way."

"So an under-advisement case for simple possession is 'high-profile'?"

"No," Flanagan answers, "not really. But Mr. Kevin Moore is. He's kinda famous as an attorney."

I'm surprised Flanagan is so on point, given how nervous and uneasy he was when he nailed me with the planted evidence and faked test.

"List for me, please, the names of other probationers you've double-checked. Probationers you've randomly selected and screened even though there were no violations or red flags."

"Hmmm," Flanagan hums. "Well . . ." He drums his fingers on the wooden railing beside him. He smooths his beard. He covers his mouth and coughs again.

Ward cuts his eyes in my direction. I notice Judge Williams calibrate his posture: He sits taller and bends forward.

"Other probationers?" Ward presses.

"Sorry," Flanagan answers. "I'm thinkin'."

"No hurry," Ward says.

"There've been a number. I can't recall them all. How about just the last several?"

Ward's wearing pinstripes, and his shoulders sag, the lines in his jacket wilting for an instant. The judge relaxes and writes on his pad. "Shit," I mutter, and Ward pops me under the table with his knee.

"Okay," Ward says, maintaining a false confidence in his voice. "Tell us."

"So, the same month I saw Mr. Moore, I did Bruno Lancaster, the city councilman from Danville. Right after Mr. Moore, I drove to Mechanicsville and met with Oscar Lanning, the former governor's grandson, and three days ago, I went and interviewed

419

Tyson Alford, the drug dealer whose mom is the famous actress. I could name others if I was at my computer. Oh, yeah, a Miss Bullins, the Halifax County teacher who embezzled from the band-boosters club. That's four. If you'd like, I could search my files and give you a bigger list."

"I'll look forward to receiving the other names," Ward replies.

Ward's dogged, and he's also skilled and meticulous, and he makes Flanagan testify to every detail, every fact in my trumped-up arrest, and he often drills down on an answer or picks apart a response, and he probes and prods and pulls out all the lawyer stops, but at the end of twenty minutes the liar Flanagan is unscathed and completely believable, and the judge has taken several obvious ganders at the wall clock, and I understand this motion is a loser.

"Judge," Ward says after asking his last question, "could I have a moment to speak with my client?"

"Okay," Williams replies. "Do I need to adjourn us?"

"No," Ward says. "We'll just step in the jury room and be right back."

"I didn't do any more than nick him, if that," Ward says as soon as the door shuts behind us. "Sorry." He perches on the rounded edge of the table. "I vote we cut our losses and try motion number two."

"You did all you could," I assure him. "I'm amazed at how composed the little fucker is. He was a meek bundle of nerves the day he framed me. Today he's Patrick Henry crossed with Walter Cronkite, and there's really nothing for us to grab on to, no provable inconsistency."

"Sometimes people rise to the occasion, Kevin. Plus — and no offense meant — you and I know that judges always default to believing probation officers, especially when the defendant's trying to sell such a . . . well, novel excuse. It probably wouldn't have mattered if Flanagan was less than perfect." There's a metal pitcher and a stack of small plastic cups in the center of the table. Ward lifts a cup from the stack but doesn't bother with the pitcher. He rolls the cup between his palms. He's done a quality job for me, but he doesn't believe Eddie Flanagan is dishonest, and he doesn't believe Caleb Opportunity exists.

"Yeah," I say.

"Well, we have it on the record for appeal, and we've had our shot at Flanagan, and we can always attempt to leverage the issue if we need to negotiate a plea deal."

"Fuck," I exclaim. "Damn it."

Ward lowers his voice. "I understand you want to testify at your deposition, and you know I'm totally opposed to such a moronic idea, but certainly we can agree *today* that there's nothing to be gained by your taking the stand. The Morris order is what it is, the law is what it is and not helpful to us, and there's no way on god's green earth this veteran judge will buy into your conspiracy plot and believe your boy Flanagan's an operative for mysterious fraudsters, especially with your prints decorating the dope baggies. If we keep beating this dead horse, you'll appear guiltier by the minute, and we also run the risk of souring the judge on our ace-in-the-hole motion."

"This is an absolute nightmare." I'm so livid that I can feel my neck and face flushing. Adrenaline is carving up my guts and causing my hands to tremble. "No matter what," I vow to Ward, "I'm damn sure going to birth this awful story into the world at my dep. Honestly, as we've discussed, I doubt we'll ever go to trial, not with the minimums on these charges and the commonwealth's truckload of fake evidence against me, so I'm planning to do all I can at the deposition to bring this shit to light. But, yeah, you're right, this motion is a lost cause. Let's move on to our secret weapon."

We return and I sit at the table, but Ward keeps standing. "We have no additional evidence on this motion, Judge, only final argument."

Ward and Clay give the judge brief summaries, and Williams overrules my motion. "The unchallenged Morris order allows the search," he concludes, "and, alternatively, if I'm wrong about that, there's still reasonable suspicion to search — we're talking about an immediate search of a nearby car following a disputed positive test for meth. Also, the defendant hasn't challenged Mr. Flanagan's statement that there was consent." He closes the file and flips open a black planning calendar. "Do I need to set a trial date?" he asks, his pencil poised above the calendar.

"Judge," Ward says, "before you do, there's another issue we need to raise."

"Another issue?" Williams asks. "Did I miss something? I only saw the one motion."

"We'd ask leave of court to file a second motion today," Ward replies.

Clay stands. "I object. Today *was* the day."

"And, Mr. Clay, we're filing it today." Ward walks across the room and hands him the papers. "May I approach?" he asks the judge.

"Yes," Williams answers. "I love surprise gifts."

Ward walks toward the bench and gives another set of the motion papers to a bailiff, who passes them to Williams.

"Judge," Clay protests, "this is an ambush, plain and simple. They had more than enough time to file this, and now they've come in here and dropped this thing last-minute, intending to disadvantage the commonwealth in every possible fashion. We object as strongly as we can, but even if you allow this filing, we'll need time to research any new issue and respond."

Judge Williams begins skimming the motion and memo. "So you're questioning his probation status?" he says, still reading through our defense.

"Great, here we go," Clay complains. "Nice, Ward. I'm truly surprised you'd pull this."

Williams snaps his head up and scowls at Clay. "Well, Mr. Clay, I'm not crazy about the timing myself. But it's not the end of the world, is it? Not the first late motion ever filed in my court, won't be the last. How about you calm down?"

"I apologize," Clay says. He seems sincere.

"It's just that I've tried my best to work with Mr. Armstrong and be fair to his client, and I don't feel it's been mutual. But I understand the court's message. I'm sorry. And Ward and I've always had a good relationship."

Williams switches his focus to Ward. "So why *is* this so late? We were set for today. Even if you didn't have this handy-dandy nine-page memo ready, you still could've filed your motion and put us on notice."

"Judge," Ward answers, "my client prepared the whole thing, from top to bottom. He finished typing it last night. This defense didn't occur to me. Mr. Moore discovered it, and I just received everything today. I apologize for any inconvenience. In fact, Mr. Moore wants to argue it."

"Won't be happening in my court," Williams replies. "You're counsel of record. You'll do the talking."

"I understand," Ward answers. "We're happy to highlight this for the court today, explain our position and authorities, and then allow Mr. Clay as long as he needs to respond."

"Very generous of you," Williams remarks. "Nothing like having your opponent's hands tied while you box the first round."

"Judge," Ward says, "we'll proceed whenever and however the court instructs us to proceed."

"Give me a minute," Williams says. He picks up my motion and memo. "Put us in recess," he instructs the bailiff, and he leaves the bench and disappears through a side door. I catch a glimpse of him unzipping his robe before the door shuts.

"Damn," I say to Ward. "That's odd. What's going on?"

"I have no idea," Ward answers. "Maybe he has a conference call in another case? Restroom? Beats me."

"I think I'll do the same," I say. "I'll take a quick leak."

"You working the race?" Ward asks the bailiff as I'm standing, and Clay joins the conversation and inquires how much NAS-CAR pays the cops to provide security at the Martinsville track, signaling that there'll be no score-settling or lingering grudges owing to the late filing, nothing personal. The episode will go in the book as a defense lawyer being a defense lawyer. However, we all understand — should we get to plea negotiations — that the commonwealth is still entitled to punish me for not immediately accepting responsibility. Pleading guilty after I've tried every legal escape, only to find the exit doors locked, isn't the same

426

as owning up to my failings and surrendering as a matter of conscience.

I slip down a side aisle, check the front of the room where Ward, Clay and Bailiff Lampkins are debating when Ryan Blaney will win his first race, and I stop, crack the witness room door and see Flanagan reading a magazine. He peers at me impassively, stone-faced. "Your day's coming," I promise him. "And tell your Shadrich sister we know about the West Virginia three million dollars." I hesitate for only a few seconds and leave the door ajar as I walk off. There're five or six other people in the gallery, and a single attorney on the front row. No one notices me, and I'm confident Flanagan won't complain to the judge or Clay, won't dare open such a dangerous can of worms.

I'm alone in the toilet, and I pee, wash my hands, dry them on a section of brown paper towel that unwinds from an automatic dispenser and straighten my tie in the mirror. I'm wearing my luckiest suit, a dark blue Hart Schaffner Marx that's never lost an important case. My shoes are shined, my socks are new, but the left pant cuff is snug against the ankle monitor, and the device is apparent underneath the fabric.

Judge Williams remains missing when I return. "He still gone?" I ask Ward.

"Yep."

Clay and the bailiff are swapping stories about a retired cop named Doug, and Ward is scrolling through e-mails on his phone. I study the dead-judge pictures along the far wall and reread my motion and shut my eyes and replay my morning with Lilly. The door to the bench dais finally opens, and the bailiff commands us to stand and calls court into session. Judge Williams has been absent for over twenty minutes.

"Sorry," he says, "I needed to locate a file and do some research."

"No problem," Ward responds, still on his feet. "I'm so far behind returning messages that the gap was helpful to me."

"I'm not as industrious as Mr. Armstrong," Clay offers good-naturedly. "Officer Lampkins and I spent the time discussing racing and telling Doug Prillaman tales."

"Judge," Ward says, "would you prefer we argue our motion today, or set it for later to give Mr. Clay time to prepare?"

Williams has built a neat stack of files on the bench. A new file, thick and not mine, is on top of the pile. "You can go ahead and argue it today."

"Judge," Clay interjects, "I'm assuming, then, that the commonwealth will be given time to respond and file our own brief."

Williams doesn't even look in Clay's direction, doesn't acknowledge the commonwealth's attorney. "Go ahead, Mr. Armstrong."

"Well, Judge," Ward replies as he walks to a lectern, "as I indicated earlier, I didn't write the memo or think of the defense, but I'll do my best to outline our position." He places my motion on the lectern, an old oak stand with a silver microphone bracketed to the wood.

Clay appears baffled. He's slightly slack-jawed, as if he's on the verge of speaking. His brow's wrinkled, and he's scratching his head with a full five fingers.

"Okay," Williams says. "I'm listening."

"If Your Honor please," Ward begins, "our position is very simple and very fatal to these charges. Basically, Judge Morris took the cocaine case under advisement and never found my client guilty —"

Williams interrupts. "Because you asked him to, correct? To keep a felony off your client's record? As Mr. Clay's already reminded us, Judge Morris gave you a break."

"Yes sir," Ward answers. "There's no disputing Mr. Moore received a break. We were very fortunate. But I'd respectfully ask Your Honor to consider *how* Judge Morris gave us this break. Judge Morris never found my client guilty, never even found 'evidence sufficient for a finding of guilt' and never took the case under advisement as is allowed under the statute. He merely heard the plea and continued the case for a year and then put my client on probation. Let me emphasize that again, because it's critical. My client was never found guilty, yet Judge Morris attempted to place him on probation. The law, Section 19.2-303, allows a defendant to be placed on probation only following a *conviction* —"

Williams finishes Ward's sentence. "And Mr. Moore has never been convicted of anything, hence he can't be ordered onto probation. His case was just continued, nothing else."

"Exactly," Ward answers. "The code is extremely clear. Only after a *conviction* or under the possession statute can a court put Mr. Moore on probation. Neither of those occurred in this situation. Consequently, the order is void, and the drug test was illegally obtained. Mr. Flanagan forced my client to take a test under a void order. The test has to be excluded. Once the test falls, then there's no reason to search, and the gun and drugs must also be excluded."

Clay is watching Ward intently, but now

he doesn't seem concerned or flustered. He stands. "May I ask a question?"

"Yes," Judge Williams replies.

"Is the file there on the bench with Your Honor the *Commonwealth v. Sloan* case?"

"It is," the judge says.

"Thank you," Clay remarks, and sits again.

Williams pushes up a billowy robe sleeve. He's wearing a blue dress shirt underneath. He focuses on me. "The motion and brief are excellent work. Highly creative. However, we've already had the cousin to this issue, and I just decided it about three weeks ago. I may be wrong, and I'm positive my decision in the *Sloan* case will be appealed, but in my opinion this kind of order is not void. It's only void*able,* and if the court has jurisdiction over the subject matter — which Judge Morris did — and has jurisdiction over the defendant — which he also did — his error becomes final and the law of the particular case unless it's appealed within thirty days or someone asks for a rehearing within twenty-one days to correct the mistake. Moreover, I don't think you can invite error, then sit on it like a get-out-of-jail-free card. Simply put, the order isn't void, and it's voidable only if someone asks to fix it within the proper timeframe, but no one did."

The judge is still making eye contact with me, and I realize, technically, I'm not allowed to comment, and that if I do, it needs to be quick and respectful, in keeping with the small professional courtesy Williams is perhaps offering me.

"Judge," I say as I rise, "I would suggest that the *Greer* case at sixty-three Virginia Appeals is controlling and supports our position: The order is void and all commonwealth action flowing from the void order is improper." I promptly sit.

Clay scrambles to his feet, anxious to bat down my position. "Judge, as you correctly held in the *Sloan* case, *Greer* is an outlier, and it dealt with a judge allowing a rogue jury to nullify a mandatory-minimum sentence over the commonwealth's *immediate* objection. It's a rare bird, and three other cases on the topic — *Hardy, Gautier* and *Smith* — hold that any error becomes binding on the specific parties affected, unless and until someone asks that it be corrected. The time for askin' is now long past. Judge Morris's order, right or wrong, is effective against this defendant because the defendant never timely asked for any changes or modifications. And, for the record, we're not conceding that Judge Morris did anything erroneous to begin with."

Williams shifts his attention to Ward. "It's obviously self-serving of me to evaluate my own work, but I think I decided *Sloan* correctly, and I'm going to hold to that reasoning. Your motion is denied. I'll be the first to admit that the guidance we receive from the appellate courts can be muddled and contradictory, and often my job is more art than science, close to reading bird entrails, and it's possible Mr. Moore's position might carry the day in Richmond. There's language in *Greer* that's arguably inconsistent with the other three rulings. Certainly it's something for the commonwealth to consider."

"Judge," Ward says, still poised and determined, "could we have time to review your *Sloan* decision and submit further argument and authority?"

"No," Williams replies. "I've read your brief, allowed you to present your argument and given you a fair listen. No need to delay the inevitable. I've already spent a bunch of time trying to solve this question in the other case, and I've decided. Sorry." He's not curt or a jackass about it. "It's an interesting issue, and the Supreme Court might disagree with me, but my ruling will be that the probation officer had authority to demand the test."

"Thank you for your consideration," Ward says. "We appreciate your allowing us to file the motion today."

We set November 28 for my trial, and Clay requests a jury. The clerk has me sign paperwork, and Judge Williams calls the next case on his docket. As we're leaving, I pass by Clay, and I reach to touch his biceps. "Sorry for the last-minute motion," I say.

"No worries," he answers. "I'd probably be filin' stuff to beat the band if I were in your shoes."

I force a smile. "Thanks."

"Seems I needed a judge brighter than Morris, but not quite as smart as this guy Williams," I remark to Ward once we've stepped into the jury room again. We both sit, Ward across from me and one chair offset.

"Yeah, damn," he says. "But I'm still not totally convinced he's correct. I'll read the cases and take a peek at this *Sloan* file. At worst, we have a bargaining chip to use if we have to plead." His ankle is resting on his knee, and he notices an untied shoe and catches a lace end with each hand. "Did you know about the other line of cases, the rulings that're against us?"

"I did. I had a lot of time to do research

434

and only the one motion to prepare, so yeah, I wasn't completely shocked. I mentioned the pro-commonwealth decisions in a footnote and thought I'd distinguished them. Maybe it's wishful thinking on my part, but I just don't see how he can rule against me."

"Well," Ward says, finishing a tight knot, "he damn sure did, and that leaves us in a tough place." He pops up and looks at me square. "And, yeah, I'm positive he's not in league with the invisible insurance villains and Caleb, the albino scoundrel."

"So . . ."

"So," Ward repeats.

"Go ahead and put on your zany costume, grab the hard-boiled egg and see if Clay's ready for some *Let's Make a Deal* action."

"Sorry," he says.

"Don't commit to anything yet," I caution him. "Not until we take a run at Melanie Culp. Just feel him out."

"I'll do everything I can," he promises.

"You've worked with him for years," I say. "What do you figure he'll offer?"

"He'll want a felony conviction, especially since you've already had the under-advisement chance. No one truly thinks you're any kind of drug dealer, and we've all seen plenty of people who're dragging along a drug monkey and buying their coke or meth or pills in bulk, so he'll most likely be flexible on the distribution charge. Also, there was no reason for you to be selling anything — you have a job, a house, a car and money in the bank, so the need to peddle dope to feed your habit doesn't make sense. You have no prior record, you're working your ass off in a menial job, you're attending rehab classes, you're pissing clean tests *recently,* and you've paid your court costs. A felony will cause you to lose years from your career and cost you hundreds of thousands of dollars — a huge punishment in itself and something that doesn't happen to most defendants. We can march in an army of former clients and lawyers and grand pooh-bahs to vouch for —"

"I hope so," I interrupt. "Bottom line?"

Ward doesn't hedge or dillydally. "I'd guess he'll offer to convict you on the original charge, reduce the distribution case to felony simple possession, amend the firearms charge to a misdemeanor — maybe disorderly conduct — so we can avoid a mandatory minimum, and want you to serve anywhere from six months to a year and a half, depending on how unhappy he is about the motions."

"Two felonies, a single misdemeanor and

a year or so to pull?"

"Probably," Ward answers, subdued. "Two years would be the unlikely worst."

"Not far from how I'd pegged it," I say. "Wait a couple days to let this cool down, and then see what you can do. Remind him we have legitimate appeal issues on the search."

"Our best bet is to persuade him this is basically just one long possession case, that you're a productive citizen who had a drug problem, and now it's behind you."

"Well, sell it like you're Billy Mays hawking OxiClean and my life depends on it. If we don't crack this Culp bitch, I'm screwed."

"Okay," Ward says. "Start working the phones. I'm sure you're friends with the influential lawyers in your part of the world, the Phil Andersons and Melissa Robinsons and John Jessees. Cops and other commonwealth's attorneys are always helpful — you know the drill. Have them call Clay and sing your praises. As many people as you can wrangle."

"If I have to plead, I don't want it to linger. I want to put this behind me ASAP and turn the page."

"I'll walk over to Clay's on Wednesday and pitch him in person. Hard to believe this is where we are. I hate it like hell for you."

I think about my handful of days in jail. I think about parasailing with Ava above a Puerto Rican beach, her feet and painted red toenails little-girl kicking at the sky, gleeful. Driving to Martinsville a few hours ago, I saw a trailer-park yard with a broken, sagging trampoline, its droopy black mat bellied against the ground, and that image rotates into my mind helter-skelter. "I realize it doesn't make any difference now, Ward, but I was clean on the day Flanagan tested me, and I truly have been framed. Besides my three-month coke-and-booze tear, I've been a faithful husband and an honest lawyer. All but ninety-some days of my time on this earth has been ordinary. Occasionally I've even been productive and helpful. I did the numbers last night. Over ninety-nine percent of my life goes into the plus column, but here I am, ruined and begging to keep my jail sentence as small as possible thanks to a .006 fraction. A blip."

"I'm rooting for you and Margo to find us a path out. I wish I could do more — guilty or not, you deserve a lot better than this."

"Everybody keeps telling me that, especially all the fine folks who're convinced I'm lying."

CHAPTER SEVENTEEN

That night, after I return to the mountain, phone my monitoring supervisor and feed Nelson, I begin creating my first Patrick County court order. I wear purple nitrile gloves from a box left behind by Lilly Heath and a shower cap I found in the bathroom closet, and I waste my initial effort because a sweat droplet drips off my nose and splatters on the paper as I'm eyeballing my draft for errors. I type another order, print it, inspect it and forge the three signatures with different color inks, two black, one blue. I scan a genuine letter from my files, then cut and paste the letterhead and fashion a piece of bogus stationery. Next, I take several stabs at producing a passable law-firm-grade, nine-by-twelve envelope, but none of my attempts are satisfactory. "How the mighty have fallen," I say to Nelson when I'm finished for the night and standing on the porch, breathing the crisp mountain air, a towel draped over my damp head.

Before going to bed, I e-mail Lilly: "No luck today, but there's still the deposition on Thursday. Fingers crossed."

I can't sleep, and I take a hot shower at 12:30 a.m., watch a BBC recording of Theresa May answering questions in the House of Commons, and finally open Gardner Turman's file and peruse his story. A few blanks still remain:

After we all were searched they started us out to marching back behind their lines. All along the road we would meet their trucks and tanks going to the front. I saw plenty of their trucks an half tracks with the Red Cross painted on them loaded down with guns and ammo headed for the Front. Also their medics were armed too. I don't think that is according to the Geneva Conference.

When we would take a Jerry prisoner that was about all he could talk about, the Geneva Conference. Which the Germans didn't live up to. I know our medics didn't carry guns at all although they should have.

All the time we were marching through snow an ice and the German guards were

_____ they would hollow out every little bit loose loose.

I rub my eyes and squint at the original pages. My best guess is "our harassers," but that sounds too poetic for Gardner, and the letters don't exactly fit. I read the paragraph again. Maybe it's a *b,* not an *h.* "All bastards" would make sense. I yawn and read past to the next line, and I keep trying possibilities until I fall asleep in the wooden chair, wake up to a dark den at three-sixteen in the morning, drag across the room and plunk onto the sofa, where I stay until Tesla welcomes a thin, gray coating of light around six.

I'm frazzled and jittery. I eat a banana and drink half a cup of black coffee, and I leave early for work. I stop at the SunTrust bank just up the street from the restaurant, and I withdraw nine thousand dollars in cash, wait there at the counter while a pleasant assistant manager counts it three times. She sails through the packs of hundreds and counts aloud as she riffles the bills. She tucks the wad of money into an envelope and wishes me a "happy day."

As I'm unlocking the rear entrance at SUBstitution, Blaine drives into the parking lot. I wait for him at the door, and he

441

hustles to meet me, grabs his backpack from the front seat but never shoulders it. He's wearing an unbuttoned flannel shirt over a yellow SUBstitution T-shirt.

"Man," he says as he's coming toward me, "it's like a to-be-continued cliffhanger. How'd you do with court? Me and my girlfriend were sending every good vibe and positive wish we could."

"I appreciate it, Blaine. Thanks." I point at my ankle. "I lost. Simple as that."

"Damn, Lawyer Kevin. I'm sorry. But there's still the interview — or whatever you officially call it — with the lady who scammed you, right?"

"It's called a deposition, Blaine. A dep. We're allowed to question her under oath to discover information and prepare for the actual trial. We'll do it at her lawyer's office."

"So you haven't emptied your utility belt yet?"

"Pretty close, I'm afraid." I slip the keys in my front pocket.

"That's *loco.* I saw the dude with my own eyes. The disc was blank. We found the land stunt with the Shadrich sister. The lawyer who was here, Margo, she knows I'll stick up for you?"

"She does," I say calmly. "And I'm in your

debt. Unfortunately, you didn't hear any of the conversation, and we can't find Caleb or attach a name. The disc was blank, but that doesn't prove much of anything, especially since you or I could've erased it. The land transaction is too remote and doesn't directly connect to Melanie Culp."

"Maybe this dep thing will turn out better. An innocent man oughta be found innocent."

I step away from the door and the security camera and motion for Blaine to follow me. "How much for the J'onzz computer? The burner?"

"Well, we need it to be reliable for at least a few weeks. But there's no need to splurge on bells and whistles and gigantic memory, especially since you're gonna double-tap it. I'd be comfortable with spendin' three hundred. If you want to cut it to the bone, maybe two and a quarter."

I remove the bank envelope from my hip pocket. "Here's four hundred." I hand him the cash. "Keep whatever's left for your trouble."

"No sir, no need for any tip," he says. "I'll bring you change."

"I'd be grateful if you'd also buy a Dell desktop and a printer." I give him a typewritten sheet. "Here're the details. If they don't make these same models, please get the closest match you can. From my research, we're looking at, ballpark, another thirteen hundred." I count out thirteen hundreds one by one and hand him those as well. "No paper trail, obviously."

"Holy gigabytes, that's a lot of money and a monster of a machine. The J'onzz plan doesn't require anything like that kinda firepower."

"Unfortunately, I'll have to destroy my landlord's computer and printer, and I plan to replace them before I leave. *If* I leave."

"Okay," Blaine replies, nodding in agreement. "For instance, if an individual had researched people, places and things, or escape routes, that history is just waitin' to get lifted by unfriendlies."

"True," I answer. "As I learned the hard way."

"I'll be in Harrisonburg tonight and in the mornin'. Money's frat's havin' a party. I'll take care of business then. Different stores for different computers, cash transactions."

"Perfect."

"Can I ask a question?" He sets his backpack on the ground. "Most of this I understand, but how does hijackin' this law firm's Web page hide your disappearance?"

I pause. I pocket the bank envelope. I glance at the maintenance shed. "It just does," I answer under my breath.

"I mean, I'm not tryin' to be a busybody, but the fun for me — other than helpin' a quality friend — is building the whole contraption and then watching it work. Scoping the lackey Flanagan's bank account to see if his bribe check has landed is a smart strategy, and havin' access to his e-mail could certainly pay off if you need that travel permit you mentioned or a pass to get a jump on the cops, but this law-firm play's a mystery."

"If we actually do this, I'll explain it then. Fair?"

"Cool. I hope we don't have to. It'll be pretty friggin' bleak here without you."

"You solved your college mess yet?" I ask.

"January is what I'm plannin'. This semester, I'm taking the math and science classes they fucked me over with. I checked directly with Tech's admissions office myself — I'm enrolled in the courses I need. Finally. Dollars are always an issue, but I should be okay. Thanks again for your help." He leans sideways and takes hold of a backpack strap. "Oh, while I'm thinkin' about it, would you write me a recommendation for when I move to Blacksburg? I'm gonna put in applications at different restaurants, maybe even a legit Subway. And I've closed down my weed business. Last of the Northern Lights is travelin' to Big Money's frat tonight, then I'm retired."

"I'd be pleased to write you a letter."

"Thanks. Maybe Luther will be runnin' this joint himself come January."

Chapter Eighteen

An important deposition in a civil case usually includes plenty of gamesmanship. On September 29, when Margo and I arrive at Hunton & Williams's Richmond office — their *tower,* as the physical address makes clear — we're greeted by an aloof receptionist and left to wait in the lobby for fifteen minutes, even though we're intentionally late ourselves. Naturally, we didn't alert M. D. Jenkins that we wouldn't be on time. A paralegal finally comes to retrieve us, hands us visitor badges and guides us into a massive conference room that features a view of the James River. The top-floor vista is costly and dazzling, and the room swallows us whole; it could comfortably hold a hundred people. I'm certain the firm has various smaller spaces, but using the major-league setting to ant us is part of Jenkins's program. Sharon, a freckled lady in her early twenties, brings us bottled water and

447

delivers a plate of fruit and pastries. "Would you care for coffee?" she asks.

"Do you have espresso?" I reply, hoping she'll report my peevish response to Jenkins.

"Uh, no. Sorry. Just regular." She's dressed in black tennis shoes, black pants and a neat white shirt.

"What kind?" Margo asks. "Who's the roaster?"

"I don't know," the girl answers. "I'll check for you."

"We'd appreciate it," I say. "Thank you."

The deposition then unfolds like a 1960s soul review. First, the court reporter enters and offers "Hellos" and "Good mornings" and unpacks her equipment and mics the table. Next, a young associate appears and apologizes for the delay. "Mr. Jenkins will be here shortly. One of our corporate clients was hit with a temporary injunction late yesterday, and Mr. Jenkins is on the phone with Judge Cavedo, trying to get that resolved." The associate's name is Mark. He has a tatty goatee and round glasses. He tugs and shapes the whiskers at his chin while he spins the exaggeration about Jenkins's absence. He leaves and a secretary arrives and arranges a fresh legal pad and three fancy pens on the table, ready for the maestro. The pens are dark blue. *Hunton &*

Williams is scripted on each of them in gold letters

Ten minutes later, the star of the show, M. D. Jenkins, strides through the door, goateed Mark and the secretary in tow. He's carrying two cups of coffee. "Good morning, Ms. Jordan. I'm so sorry to keep you waiting. I sent Sharon around the corner to Starbucks. Hope this helps make up for my wasting your time." He approaches Margo and serves her the coffee, places a napkin on the table and sets down a cup. "House Blend. The kids here tell me it's the best. Coffee's just coffee for an old philistine like me. I buy the big red tub of Folgers. Sharon can bring you cream and sugar if you'd like."

He circles behind us until he's on my left. "Mr. Moore, good morning and nice to meet you. Regret it's under these circumstances. Here's your double espresso." I take the cup, and we shake hands. The coffee production is Kabuki theater, but Jenkins gives the impression he's sincere and humble, an aw-shucks fellow in a three-grand suit who just happens to be the best litigator in Virginia, quite a lawyerly gift, and a gift that no doubt will endear him to a Patrick County jury.

"Thanks," I say. "I appreciate it. We were

late as well. How about you comp me one of those big-city pens as a souvenir, and we'll call it even?"

"Make that two pens," Margo quips.

Jenkins laughs. According to the Internet, he's sixty-three. His teeth are white and immaculate. His hair's a mixture of black and gray, close-cropped, a cut that requires a weekly trip to the barber. He's wearing suspenders and a bowtie that's definitely not a clip-on. "Fair enough. Probably the best deal I'll make all week." He settles in behind his legal pad, passes us each a pen, reaches into his coat pocket and digs out a yellow pencil with a sharpened tip and full pink eraser. He's across the table, cater-cornered to me. There're thirty chairs on each side of the polished mahogany showpiece and a single seat at each end. He jots something near the top of his pad, then addresses the secretary: "Would you please let Miss Culp know we're ready?"

The woman who enters is the same woman who came to my office and entrapped me, but her appearance is much different today. The July Melanie Culp was wearing a baseball cap, glasses, an oversize shirt, leggings and tennis shoes. Her hair was gathered into a ponytail, and she had mousy brown bangs curtaining her fore-

450

head. Her makeup was basic, and she seemed reserved and often spoke without making eye contact. The current Melanie Culp is dressed in a stylish, fitted pantsuit and modest heels, the glasses are gone, and her hair and makeup are flawless. She's confident enough to look directly at me as she's crossing the room. I rest my hands on the table and extend a single finger, my signal to Margo that we're seeing the correct con artist.

Jenkins stands and pulls a chair away from the table. "Melanie," he says, "have a seat, please. This is Ms. Jordan, and you've already met Mr. Moore. Soon as you're comfortable, the court reporter will swear you in, and we can get started."

Culp accepts the oath, swears she'll tell the truth, Jenkins and Margo agree to the rules for any objections and the use of this testimony at trial, and Margo organizes papers from her file in front of her. I'm anxious to the point of being sick — this is my last chance to avoid jail and a catastrophe — and I catch myself squeezing and twisting my new pen. I quietly drop it so that I won't look like a nervous hack or a doper with shifty hands. I'd be much more collected if I could question Culp, if I could practice law and defend myself. A ring burns around my left eye. The corner of my mouth tingles.

"Ma'am, my name is Margo Jordan, and I represent Kevin Moore. Good morning. If any of my questions aren't clear, please tell me, and I'll make sure you and I understand each other exactly. Your testimony is under oath and subject to perjury penalties, so it's critical that you listen to my questions and give me true and accurate answers. Okay?"

"Yes," Culp replies. "Thank you."

"Please tell me your full name and your date of birth."

Culp answers quickly and casually. "My name is Melanie Diane Culp. I was born on May twenty-third, 1966."

"Where, please?" Margo asks. "Where were you born?"

"Shreveport, Louisiana."

"Tell me your birth name and any and all names or nicknames you've ever used or assumed, whether by legal name change, personal preference or otherwise."

"I was born Denise Melanie Champoux. I took the name Denise Alston when I married my first husband. When I divorced, my name was changed to Melanie Diane Fredericks —"

"Why?" Margo challenges her. "That wasn't your name prior to the divorce."

"It was a bad marriage, and I was single again. I wanted no reminders of those years. I've always preferred the name Melanie instead of Denise, and my mom's maiden name was Diane Fredericks. I wanted to honor her and empower myself. So I chose Melanie Diane Fredericks." She unscrews the white cap from her bottled water but doesn't drink.

"Keep going, please," Margo instructs her. "I need every name."

"I became Melanie Culp when I married my second husband."

"When and where were you married?"

"Belarus," Culp answers. She pours her water into a glass but still doesn't drink.

"Where in Belarus?"

"Homyel."

Margo pauses for the rest of the answer. "When? The date?" she asks after several silent seconds.

"April seventeenth, 2005."

"Why'd you get married in Belarus?"

"My husband had family ties there. And Homyel is a very beautiful city."

"Are you still in that marriage?"

"I am not. My husband deserted me in 2008."

"His name please?" Margo asks.

"William Peter Culp."

"Are you divorced?"

"We are," Culp replies.

"As of?"

"August 2010. The papers were signed by a judge in Florida. I don't recall the exact date."

"Was that divorce contested?"

"It wasn't." Culp finally sips her water.

"Where is Mr. Culp now?" Margo asks.

"I have no idea. I've not laid eyes on him since he left me for no reason in 2008."

Margo glances at me, then at Jenkins. "How were you able to serve him for the divorce?"

"Serve him?" Culp bites her lip and turns toward Jenkins. "I don't understand."

"She means, Melanie," Jenkins patiently explains, "how you managed to give your absent ex-husband notice, to have the paperwork delivered to him so that the court could hear your case?"

"Oh, okay," she replies. "Sorry. I'm not a lawyer. We ran something in the newspaper. I remember because it cost extra to pay for the ad or whatever."

"But you elected not to change your name again? You felt sufficiently empowered with the old marital name after this divorce?"

"Right," Culp replies.

"So the current name on any state or

454

federal government documents is Melanie Diane Culp?"

"Correct."

"And you continue to use your former married name? Culp?"

"Yes."

"What's your Social Security number?" Margo asks.

"If it's agreeable," Jenkins interrupts, "how about we have her write it down for you so that it won't be accessible to anyone who might read this deposition?"

"Fine with me," Margo says.

Culp uses the firm pen to write numbers on a yellow legal sheet. She pushes the paper across the slick table until it's within Margo's reach.

"Thanks," Margo says. "To recap then, ma'am, you've used four different names in your life, and the name you now use, Melanie Culp, is the name on your Social Security account."

"I've never given it any thought, but yes, I suppose that's true."

"Melanie Diane Culp is a mostly fictitious name you chose years ago and is rather different from your birth name?" Margo's trying to bait her, to suggest something sinister by sharpening her voice and skewing her eyebrows and pretending that she's discovered an aha opening.

"In a sense," Culp answers simply.

"Have you ever been convicted of a felony or any crime involving lying, cheating or stealing?"

"No."

"To clarify," Margo says, "that question would include a conviction under any of your names, or any other name you haven't disclosed."

"Object to the question," Jenkins notes. "It assumes that she was untruthful in her prior responses. But you may answer the question, Melanie."

"I, myself, no matter the name, have never been convicted of any crime. None. Never."

"How was it that you came to discover this property in Meadows of Dan, Virginia?" Margo asks. "According to your interrogatory answers, you live in Florida."

"Primland. I visited the resort once."

"When?" Margo asks. "When did you visit?"

"The spring of 2014, April or May. Maybe early June."

"How long did you stay?"

Culp thins her lips. She turns toward Jenkins. "Why is this possibly important?"

"Go ahead, Melanie, you can answer her question. Take your time. I'll jump in if Ms.

Jordan asks anything she shouldn't. As I told you, bizarre as it sounds, Mr. Moore — and perhaps his very able attorney — is claiming that you're an imposter, that the option is a sham, and that you're part of some secret, national fraud operation. Ms. Jordan is entitled to explore why you were interested in the land and to confirm that you really were in this area. She's attempting to find a paper trail or some hard evidence that supports — or contradicts — your testimony." While I'm positive that he's already rehearsed Melanie Culp, his response gives her a reminder and a road map and puts her on guard.

"Appreciate your so thoroughly clarifying the question — and answer — for her," Margo says.

"Pleased I could help," Jenkins replies.

"So what was the question?" Culp asks.

"How long did you stay at Primland in the spring of 2014?"

"Long enough to look around and eat a meal. And it could've been 2013, now that I think about it."

"How'd you pay for the meal?"

"Cash would be my guess."

"Did you stay in the resort hotel?" Margo asks.

"I didn't."

Margo pauses. She writes on her pad. "So you drove from Florida, grabbed a sandwich and then drove home to Miami?"

"I left and followed the Blue Ridge Parkway north. Spent the night."

"Where?"

"At my sister's house."

"Where did she live then?" Margo presses.

"She lived in Lexington. Lexington, Virginia."

"Her name, please?"

"Julie Barton."

Margo pauses to drink her coffee. "Phone number?" she asks.

Culp sighs and looks at her lawyer again. "540-237-8876. I hope you're not planning to harass her about this."

"So there's no record of your being at Primland?" Margo says. "We have your word, and that's it."

"You have my word. Why would I make that up?"

"Well, why would you travel from Miami to eat a sandwich at Primland?"

"I didn't." Culp sounds exasperated. She shakes her head at Margo. "I drove from Miami to see my sister and stopped at fun places along the way."

"Then years later you decide to buy a

million-dollar property in Meadows of Dan?"

Jenkins has an unusual deposition style. He intently focuses on whoever is speaking, dramatically ping-ponging his gaze back and forth between his client and Margo. He actually perches on the edge of his seat and leans over the table, propped up on his elbows. "Correction," he interjects. "The option price was $975,000." He hesitates, lowers his elbows and sits erect. "In my world, twenty-five thousand dollars is a lot of money. Could we agree on that, Ms. Jordan?"

"I'll stipulate the exact purchase price is $975,000," Margo says curtly and pops him with a pissed-off glare. "We can agree on the nine-seventy-five number." She's irritated, I think, by the veiled reference to the proposed settlement discount, his first hint that this deposition needs to be quick and pro forma.

"Thank you for the stipulation," he replies, and hunkers down over the table again.

"Yes," Culp answers. "I signed an option to buy the land."

"How did you discover the land?"

"Online."

"Where online?" Margo inquires.

"Online," Culp repeats.

"The site, please?"

"Oh, goodness, I have no idea. It was months and months ago, and I looked at tons of land."

Culp's answer discourages me. My shoulders slump, and I instantly correct them. She's clever and well prepared. A genuine buyer probably wouldn't recall that kind of detail and would be miffed by having to answer Margo's picayune questions. A lesser hustler would tip her hand by offering specific websites and far too much information, and then Margo would ask: "You remember this months later, despite it being completely routine and ordinary at the time?"

"So you don't know where you discovered this tract of land?"

"Well, obviously it was on the realtor's page, Mr. . . . uh . . . I can't recall his name." She snaps her fingers and squeezes her eyes shut. "Mr. Lineberry."

I write *The Oscar goes to Melanie Culp* and slip the note to Margo, who doesn't change her expression and slides it underneath her file.

"And you offered the full list price?"

"I did."

"You didn't try to negotiate?" Margo asks.

"Well, it seems I got a heck of a bargain at

full price, since it sold for over five times more just weeks afterward. I didn't want to spook the sellers, Mr. Harris and his wife. And this MAB company was just *waiting* to pounce; they signed a full-price contract *two days* after my option lapsed. I called Mr. Lineberry, trying to save the deal, but MAB had swooped in. What's that tell you?"

Jenkins bounces his gaze to Margo early, before she speaks. He smiles. He scripted and planted the answer, and he's taking credit and enjoying the moment.

"Why this property, in this location?" Margo continues.

"Why not?" Culp answers, though she doesn't sound snide or evasive.

"Maybe you could offer a little more information about the particulars, why you selected this land miles and miles away from your home."

"I wanted out of the city, and it's rural. And beautiful. And the price was excellent."

"Were you planning to move there, to build a house there?"

"Eventually," she replies.

"So you weren't interested in reselling? You didn't buy this as an investment?"

"It would've been an investment if a company appeared a few weeks after the ink dried and offered me six million dollars.

461

Who wouldn't take that deal? You'd have to be crazy to say no."

"But your original plan was to live there, not to flip the land for a profit?"

"To some extent, but even then, my plan was to keep ten or twelve acres and build a home three or four years in the future. I didn't need the entire tract, and I was going to sell the majority of it to help pay for building my house. I knew the land was underpriced. I knew I had a bargain. But Mr. Moore let me down, and I wound up with nothing. I even called and reminded him of the deadline."

"I'll provide you with her phone bill showing a call to Mr. Moore's office number," Jenkins volunteers. "She called at five-eleven p.m. three days before the option lapsed."

"So, to be clear for the record," Margo continues, "this was not an investment."

"To be clear," Culp answers, a flash of anger in her tone, "if a company had offered me six million dollars soon after I purchased the property, I would've sold in a heartbeat. Common sense, right? And to be even more clear, I was planning to sell approximately 163 of the 173 acres no matter what."

"Where else did you search for land?" Margo asks.

"Asheville, Charlottesville, a little town called Floyd, other places here and there."

"Did you make contact with any other realtors or sellers?"

"No," Culp replies, now calm again. "Oh, wait. Yeah. I called a guy in Charlottesville about a farm there."

"Do you recall his name or the company's name?"

"Just that it was a farm near Charlottesville, with a pond and a horse barn. I don't remember his name."

Margo waits for Jenkins to focus on her. "Do you think, Mr. Jenkins, that I could still get some cream? The coffee's a tad strong."

"My pleasure," he replies. He taps in a text on his phone. "Done."

"Thanks." Holding the fancy pen like a pub dart, Margo aims it at Culp. "Is it fair for me to assume that you don't have a phone number for this unknown, mysterious realtor you contacted about such a *unique* listing — a farm in Charlottesville horse country with a barn and pond?"

"I'm almost positive that it was an eight hundred number."

"Of course it was," I say out loud, and Margo reminds me to keep quiet.

"The cash?" Margo asks. "Where were

you going to get the purchase price?"

"From my accounts, probably."

Sharon arrives with a small silver pitcher of cream and serves it to Margo. Margo thanks her, pours the cream and stirs the coffee with a spoon. She wipes the spoon dry with a paper napkin, takes longer than necessary and holds the spoon toward the window's light, checking for drips, before she lays it on the table.

Jenkins waits patiently for her to finish. "I have her financial records for you," he states. "The discovery deadline was tight, so as you and I agreed, I just had her bring everything along with her today. She had roughly two million in liquidity when she signed the option. Obviously that doesn't include her Florida home."

I hold my hand over my mouth and whisper to Margo: "Or the dirty, scammed millions she's hiding from us and the IRS."

"Why an option, then?" Margo asks. "Why not simply close and write a check?"

"Well, $975,000 is a lot of money and almost half my cash. I needed to see about selling my Florida house or maybe locating a lender for a partial finance."

"How did you accumulate your money? Not everyone has two million in the bank."

"I'm fifty years old, ma'am," Culp replies,

her tone matter-of-fact, "and I've worked every day of my life since I was sixteen."

"Yeah," Margo responds, "me too, but I sure don't have those kind of numbers to show for it. What's your secret?"

"I'm not sure I understand your point," Culp says. She drinks water.

"Tell me exactly where the money came from, please. How about I phrase it like that? Jobs, work history, investments, land deals, lottery winnings, inheritance, you tell me."

"Well, my first husband and I started an unsecured-salary-loan business years ago, and I've continued in that industry."

"Payday loans?" Margo spits the words derisively.

Culp bristles. "Short-term advances to working people with an emergency, people who're not up to snuff in the eyes of your white-shoe monopoly bankers."

"Whatever you want to call it," Jenkins interrupts, "here are her LLC's tax returns for the last three years. I've also included five years of her personal tax returns."

"What's the name of the LLC?" Margo asks.

"Melanie Culp LLC," she answers.

"Registered where?"

"Sarasota, Florida," Culp answers quickly.

"How many separate stores?"

"Three," Culp says, rapid fire.

"Employees?"

"Yes."

"How many?"

"Myself and my daughter and five others," Culp replies the second Margo finishes.

"You've never mentioned a daughter."

"You never asked," Culp says.

"Are you a member of any other LLCs in this or any other country?" Margo asks.

"No."

"You're certain?" Margo demands.

"I'm certain."

"Are you an officer, director or shareholder of any corporations or LLCs in this or any other country?"

"No," Culp repeats. "Just the one, for my loan business."

"Have you ever been so in the past ten years?"

"No."

"Have you ever, at any time and for any reason, had any prior contact with or dealings with MAB or FirstRate LLC?"

"I'd never even heard of them before I signed this option for my land in Patrick County. So no."

"Have you ever filed a lawsuit, using any name, prior to this one? Not including your divorces?"

"Yes, I have."

"Please tell me about the suits," Margo instructs her.

"Years ago, a pharmacist filled a prescription wrong, and it almost killed me."

"Where was that suit filed?" Margo asks.

"Here in Virginia," Culp answers.

"Which one of your four names did you use in that case?"

"Denise Alston, I think. Or possibly Melanie Alston."

"Where in Virginia did you file suit?" Margo asks.

"Let me stop you here if I could," Jenkins says. "As with many of these professional malpractice cases, this matter was settled and sealed, and Miss Culp was required to sign a confidentiality agreement. She's bound by contract not to discuss this matter — not her doing, but a settlement term imposed on her by the pharmacist and his insurer for *their* benefit. Miss Culp would be pleased to describe everything that happened, but she's not permitted to. I can provide you with the name of her counsel in that matter, but at this point, I'm instructing her not to answer, lest she violate the settlement agreement and risk having to refund her damage payment."

"Who was her lawyer?" Margo asks.

"Burt Chucker, from Waynesboro," Jenkins answers. "I have his contact info for you, and I told him you might be calling."

"Visiting your sister again?" Margo scoffs. "Is that why you were using a Virginia pharmacy?"

"Respectfully, I'm instructing her not to answer, Ms. Jordan. Feel free to contact Mr. Chucker, and if you want to see about unsealing the case and obtaining a court order that'll allow her to testify and still protect her settlement, have at it. But as for today, we're finished with the topic, which is completely tangential and unrelated anyway."

"Other lawsuits," Margo continues.

"That's it," she replies.

"How about your LLC — has it filed suits?"

Culp laughs. "Definitely. Hundreds. People don't always pay us back."

Margo sips her coffee, lets the room go quiet. Jenkins's head is stationary, waiting to bounce toward his client with the next question. Margo speaks while looking down and flipping pages on her legal pad. "How much was your share of the three million you people received from the Shadrich Foundation for the land in Beckley, West

Virginia?" She immediately locks onto Culp.

I'm studying Culp too, and she guppies. "Goldfishing," we trial lawyers also call it — the slight cheek-suck and lip-bunch, like a small orange fish drawing water through its gills as it opens and closes its mouth. Then she string blinks — one, two, three — and she's back to normal again. "Pardon?" she asks. She lifts her eyebrows.

"What was your share of the three million from the Beckley, West Virginia, sale?"

"I'm sorry. I don't own any land in West Virginia." She faces Jenkins. She shrugs. "I've never gotten any kind of 'share' from there."

"Let me try it this way, ma'am," Margo says. "Do you have any knowledge at all about a sale of property in Beckley, West Virginia, to the Shadrich Foundation from a company called S. Smith Holdings?"

"No," she replies. "I don't."

"Just a moment, please, Mr. Jenkins," Margo says. She leans closer to me. "Anything else?" she whispers. I write a question on her pad and show it to her.

"Miss Culp," Margo continues, "did you receive a monetary settlement in your second divorce? The divorce from Mr. Culp?"

"Yes," she answers.

"And what did you get?"

"A home and some cash."

I focus on Culp, taunting her with a giant smile.

"How much cash?" Margo asks.

"Well," she answers, "around two million."

"And how did that happen?" Margo presses. "Logistically and administratively?"

"Meaning?" Culp stalls.

"How did two million dollars change hands in a no-fault divorce where you can't even locate your husband?"

"Well, he had a lawyer, and they sent my lawyer the money and the paperwork for the house. My lawyer then gave it to me."

"Mr. Culp must have been quite wealthy," Margo says.

"He was." Culp crafts her answer to sound wistful, nostalgic. "He sure was."

"Thank you, ma'am," Margo says. "Those are all my questions."

Jenkins and Margo agree we don't need a break, and Jenkins announces that he's ready to take my deposition, and I can tell he's just going through the motions and doesn't expect me to testify in this case while my criminal charges are pending. He seems baffled when I raise my hand and the court reporter recites the oath. He asks Margo: "So your client isn't planning to assert his Fifth Amendment protection?"

"He isn't," Margo replies, "despite my advice to the contrary."

Jenkins begins with several straightforward questions, and I'm relieved that my nerves have settled. I feel much more comfortable because I'm finally able — even though I'm only a witness and a defendant — to at least somewhat control my own case. Like any experienced attorney would do in a discovery deposition, Jenkins eventually turns me loose to tell my story, doesn't interrupt or object as I describe the visit from Caleb, the blank disc, the planted test and dishonesty from Flanagan, and his ties to the Shadrich sister. I explain the West Virginia Shadrich sale and the S. Smith Holdings connection to FirstRate, and I mention how my fingerprints were obtained from SUBstitution's sandwich wrap. When I finish, Jenkins politely asks, "Are you through with your response?"

"Yes," I answer.

"Just a few more questions, Mr. Moore," he says. "You've already admitted this, but there's no doubt that a few days subsequent to this white-haired stranger appearing, you tested positive for methamphetamine. I completely understand you contend that the probation officer is lying and part of a conspiracy, but fraudulent or not, the commonwealth claims it has a positive drug test from the June encounter with Mr. Flanagan, does it not?"

"Yes, Mr. Flanagan planted a gun and drugs in my car and engineered a drug test with synthetic urine and has lied about my confessing, and the commonwealth is aware of this tainted evidence."

"Okay, thank you," Jenkins says. "And the only person who can corroborate — I'm using the term loosely — any part of your fantastical defense is your coworker, Mr. Blaine Richardson?"

"Well, your client could corroborate my defense if she weren't lying." I stare at Culp.

"Mark," Jenkins says to the younger lawyer, "would you have Arnie step in, please?"

Margo looks at me, then at Jenkins. Jenkins peers out the window at the James River, becomes inscrutable. The court reporter stops typing and shakes and flexes her fingers. I watch the door, and Mark returns with a man dressed in a tweed jacket and gray slacks, his starched white shirt unbuttoned at the collar.

"Mr. Moore, this is Arnie Wright," Jenkins informs me. "Have you seen him or met him before?"

"As best I can recall, I haven't," I answer.

472

Jenkins extracts a small, off-white folder from a pocket in his large accordion file. "Do you mind if Mr. Wright remains here for this section of the deposition?"

"No," I say instinctively. "Sorry," I catch myself. "Old habits die hard. Not my call to make."

"Fine with me," Margo adds. "If my client's happy, I'm happy."

"Mr. Moore," Jenkins says, "I'll offer you a series of photos and ask if you can identify them." He slides the folder to me.

"Okay."

I open the folder and immediately recognize the camera's vantage point, and then I notice a shot that shows the white service truck in the parking lot of Larry Hutchens's vacant building across the road from SUBstitution.

While I'm examining the pictures, Jenkins speaks to Margo: "Arnie is a private investigator, retired army. A Ranger. We've used him on several cases. Do you have a card, Arnie, for Ms. Jordan?"

Wright hands a business card to Mark, who passes it to Jenkins, who pushes it across the table to Margo.

"Correct me if I'm wrong, Mr. Moore," Jenkins says, his voice theatrically hushed, "but these surveillance photos demonstrate that your only witness — perhaps with your participation, sir — is running a fairly brisk drug trade out of the restaurant there in Stuart."

"Not true," I bluff. "The pictures don't prove anything." The bald lie sounds dumb and feeble.

"I'm no expert, but it sure looks to me like a bag of pot in a couple of the enlargements. And that's you standing with Mr. Richardson as your client drives away with the goods, flashing you a satisfied thumbs-up. I wonder if the local police and the store's owner are aware of this? I wonder how a Patrick County jury would evaluate this evidence when they hear you claim you're not a drug user or a drug dealer, just an innocent former lawyer who's being framed by a distinguished probation officer?"

"Is that a question, Mr. Jenkins?" Margo demands.

"I guess not," he replies. "My mistake. Sorry. But I do have one last *question.*" He ices his expression, a don't-fuck-with-me warning: "Did money ever exchange hands between you and Mr. Richardson? Did you ever give him a check for two thousand dollars? 'Fronting' is the street term, I think."

■ ■ ■ ■

"Wow, that went swimmingly," Margo says. We've left the conference room, and we're sitting on a spartan bench in the building's entrance lobby, between the security desk and the elevators. "You came off as a desperate kook and a loser selling pot with a kid half your age." Surprisingly, she seems more amused than angry or frustrated. "I warned you that M. D. Jenkins isn't some-one to overlook. He figures you'll take the Fifth, but he's still got his ducks in a row — have to admire his work ethic, if nothing else."

"I'm not selling pot. Jeez. But I received Jenkins's message loud and clear. I'd never, ever do anything to put Blaine at risk. He's a quality kid, headed to college on a scholar-ship. My hands are officially tied in terms of taking on Caleb and Melanie Culp or leveraging this case to beat my criminal charges. Blaine would get crucified."

"I'd say your hands, wrists, feet, ankles, calves, thighs, chest and forearms are of-ficially tied — you're damn close to being mummified."

"Interesting, though, what we've learned. I'd never thought of this before, but I suspect most of their bogus suits are sealed and have nondisclosure agreements — how clever. You can't find the cases to begin with, and if you do, then the scammers, our pals Caleb and Melanie and their partners, are legally prohibited from discussing the particulars. You think it's a coincidence that Culp hit the jackpot with a pharmacist, someone subject to a disciplinary board? That's straight from Caleb's playbook."

"But," Margo notes, "sealing settlements is par for the course. Every doc or lawyer or professional tries to bury the malpractice file and hide the screwup from the public and add a nondisclosure clause to protect his reputation and livelihood. Nothing unusual there."

"She's a money-laundering factory too. What better place to hide and store money than a couple of loan-shark businesses? And the Belarus wedding? Seriously? Come on. That never happened, and it smelled from the minute she said it. There's no William Peter Culp, and there was never a wedding, but who could ever prove differently? Good luck locating those Eastern European marriage records from 2005. The divorce was her Trojan horse, so she could have a court legitimize the several million being transferred to her."

"Maybe she's a romantic," Margo says. "Wanted a destination wedding in a castle or rustic inn."

"Did you catch her expression when you jumped her with the Shadrich deal? She nearly sucked her cheeks down her throat."

"She did seem bewildered and confused, almost as if she had no idea what I was talking about."

"You're certainly blithe," I say, "given the ass-kicking we just took."

"*Philosophical* might be a more accurate way to put it."

"After her performance, you think this is totally on the level? You're buying the staged five-eleven p.m. phone call where she hung around on voicemail for a few minutes to create a record? Don't worry about offending me or hurting my feelings; I'd be grateful to know what you make of her. The truth, warts and all."

"Truthfully, Kevin, you've always been sober, earnest and terrifically helpful in our dealings. You're likeable, and no one doubts you were an excellent attorney, but the clincher's the photo of you and your only witness selling pot. That's the sparkler on top of the admitted cocaine abuse, the failed Flanagan drug test, the meth in your car, the fingerprints on the dope bags and the

Internet search for masking agents. It's so terrible that it's almost comical. In short, we have zero chance of winning."

"The law's an unforgiving bitch, isn't it? Once you make a single mistake, everything else you do is viewed through a warped lens, and any new narrative begins with the assumption that you're simply up to more of the same old criminal bullshit. Guilty just like last time. But yeah, if I'm in your shoes, if I'm analyzing this objectively, I'd peg this case as a slam-dunk winner for Jenkins and Culp. I don't blame you for cutting your losses, not at all."

"I will say — and it's why I'm a little bemused — that there's something hinky in the mix. Culp's an odd character. Neither here nor there. She's definitely not some nervous novice in her first dep, yet she's trying way too hard to seem inexperienced. She occasionally *acted* like a babe in the woods when she obviously isn't — she pretends not to know what service of process is, but her LLC has filed hundreds of suits. Of course, my impressions and five bucks will buy us a specialty coffee from the chain shop around the corner." She smiles at me, but it's mirthless. "I'm afraid there's nothing I can do for you or my insurance company."

"I understand."

"Our defense is a farce," she states. "I'd need greasepaint for my closing argument."

"So what's next on your end?" I ask.

"I'll write my report and recommendation and send it to Lawyers Comprehensive and urge them to pay the money, so long as Jenkins will knock off fifty to a hundred thousand. It's the best we can hope for. And let's not forget that he's planning to add punitives if we don't settle — potentially thousands more, thousands you'd be personally liable for. The settlement takes that exposure off the table and protects you."

"But you agree with me that Culp's shady?" I ask.

"I'd agree she was strangely uneven in the deposition." Margo watches an elevator open. A man in a suit holds his arm across the vanished door's slot and waits for the other passengers to exit. "Of course, it could be that she was just overcoached by Jenkins."

"Would you do a favor for me?" I track the people walking by us and don't face Margo. "We both know this will absolutely destroy me, and Ward tells me I'll probably catch two years in jail. Will you give me to the end of next month to see if I can locate anything to contradict her statements today?

A last shot at saving my career? I'm not really asking for much. Go ahead and make your report to the company . . . are you still working with the same adjuster? Mullens, I think I recall."

"Yes," Margo replies.

"Give her your honest assessment, and tell Jenkins you'll have him a final offer in three or four weeks, but that an accountant needs to review her records and returns and you need to verify her names and history. Then, if everything's legit, you'll offer him the five million minus a hundred thousand."

"Obviously, we'll inspect her records and returns and run the names, but I don't anticipate finding a needle in the haystack. We've investigated her already. I'll have one of our tax guys take a trip through the IRS filings and see if he spots any red flags. That'll take maybe a week. What stone haven't we turned over by now? What do you hope to find? If you miraculously turn up an inconsistency or a misstatement, we're so deep in the hole that it won't matter unless it's the mother of all whoppers."

"Give me three or four weeks, please. Hell, what can it hurt? Maybe I'll bone up on Belarus. Maybe I'll poke around and see if she really has a sister who was living in Lexington. I *guarantee* she's lying about not owning other companies in the past — if they're dissolved or held offshore, I'm not sure how or where I can locate them, but I'm positive she's been in other corporations or LLCs. It's a big part of how they operate. Any loose thread might unravel this whole scam, and Lawyers Comp is *sitting* on the cash, not *waiting* for it — why would they care? Jenkins will hem and haw, but he's not about to pull the plug over a few weeks. It would mean the world to me, and it'll cost you nothing."

"Okay," she says. "I'm scheduled for a vacation soon anyhow. So you've got three weeks from today, then we'll pay this off. I can't fiddle-faddle around and lose six figures."

"One last request. I realize you have a duty to report back to Lawyers Comp and your contact there, and you'll have to give Jenkins the three-week schedule, but after that would you go dark on them?"

She cocks her head. "Excuse me?"

"Leave Jenkins behind the iron curtain after you give him the three-week news. The silence might worry his client a little, might make them sweat. Anxious people are more inclined to make mistakes."

"I wouldn't have any reason to talk to him after I give him the timeline."

"Then please don't," I urge her. "And as a precaution, would you also keep quiet with Lawyers Comp as well? Just put this totally on ice for three weeks."

"I have a professional obligation to respond to Lawyers Comp if they contact me. I understand why you might want to keep the plaintiff and her lawyer in suspense, but if your insurer contacts me, why in the world would I ignore them?"

We're seated at opposite ends of the bench. I shift my weight, bend closer to her. "I realize this will sound paranoid, but do you know a man named Tommy Deaton, a vice president with Lawyers Comp's parent company?"

"No," she answers. "It's a huge company. Should I?"

"Well, Deaton's near the top of their food chain."

"Okay?" she says.

"This could be nothing, Margo, nothing at all, but I'm at the Hail Mary stage now and spooked by every shadow and coincidence, so please look at this from my perspective."

"Okay," she answers again, the word sincere and concerned.

I'm about to lie to Margo. I wait for a deliveryman to hustle by us. "Deaton is an investor in a seven-figure land deal in Atlanta via an LLC. The deed to his company comes from a corporation that once did business with FirstRate in California." In truth, there is no connection to FirstRate; I'm creating a fiction to buy myself time.

"So what?" she asks, though she's not hostile. She seems sympathetic, like a mom reassuring a child about a beneath-the-bed troll.

"Think what an advantage it would be — if you were Caleb and his band of swindlers — to have an insider, someone to push your illegitimate claims through with the third-largest insurance company in the country."

"Let's assume you're correct and there's a sophisticated, invisible all-star fraud team, and that this Mr. Deaton's their mole and operative. How could it possibly affect this case? You and I both agree that Jenkins and Culp have a legal winner. You're not making sense."

I hold up my index finger and wag it sideways. "Here's exactly why it matters. If Culp and Caleb are tipped off that the three-week delay's just posturing and pro forma, that the money's coming anyhow, then they'll never feel any pressure, never fret, never blunder. I want them to sit in an information vacuum for three weeks and stew. Wring their hands. Maybe the waiting will unnerve them, and they'll screw up."

"You *are* seeing shadows, Kevin," she says gently. "Think for a moment how you're tumbling down rabbit holes. For instance, M. D. Jenkins — the gold standard for honest, ethical lawyering — does legal work for the governor. The governor and president are friendly. Therefore, the president is in cahoots with the albino fraud team."

"I admit we can Kevin Bacon this to death, but how could I have possibly made up a scam story — exploiting vulnerable professionals via e-mail hacks at state boards — that just happened to ring the bell with this Culp lady? How? What are the odds that the Florida woman with four names has filed a Virginia malpractice claim?"

"Today is Thursday," she says. She takes a phone from her purse to study the calendar. "It'll take a few days for us to unpack the financials and research the names, so my written report should go to them by e-mail next Friday, October seventh." She taps the screen twice. "After that, I'm on vacation until the seventeenth. It'll take me a while to catch up when I return, and I have a trial on the twentieth and twenty-first, so I won't be active in your case until around Monday, October twenty-fourth. So there you go, in the natural order of things, it's fair for you to assume I won't be talking to Jenkins or Lawyers Comp until then."

"Thanks so much. At least I still have a chance. You can't imagine how much I appreciate this. Thanks."

"You're welcome."

"And I have your word?" I ask.

"You do, but my promise comes with a huge string," she says. She drops the phone into her purse.

"Okay," I reply. "I don't have a lot of bargaining power, so you're bound to get what you want."

"I've had three names myself, Kevin: my maiden name, a different surname from a first marriage and my current name, Jordan, which began when I took my second husband's last name. My North Carolina brother filed a malpractice claim against an orthopedic surgeon here in Richmond — MCV attracts patients from all over the country. I think that you're bewildered and analyzing things to death. You're coming off a wicked substance-abuse sickness and you're split from your wife — hideous stressors. You've gone from the top of the mountain to doing jail time. I want you to commit to me that you'll make an appointment with a mental health professional."

Two young men in casual clothes walk by our bench, and the taller one playfully punches the other's shoulder, and I overhear a snippet about Jäger Bombs and last call. "Okay," I say, lying again. "I will. You might be right. And hell, it couldn't hurt. Fair enough."

CHAPTER NINETEEN

"Motherfucker, that's sixteen cents. Shit." The homeless man wearing a western shirt with snap buttons and a grimy, extra-large silver puffer jacket is indignant. "What am I supposed to do with sixteen cents?"

"You asked for spare change, and I gave you every coin in my pocket," I tell him. "Sorry."

He paces along with me awhile longer, cursing and complaining, then veers off before I arrive at Starbucks, a three-minute walk from Hunton & Williams's address. While I'm searching the line and tables for her, Ava taps me on the shoulder from behind. "Hey, Kevin," she says. I turn around and we hug, but it's forced and clumsy.

"Thanks so much for coming." I phoned her ten days ago, again from Big Money's cell, to arrange our meeting. "You want anything?" I ask. "Coffee? A snack?"

"Not really," she answers.

We sit at a two-top that hasn't been cleaned, still has a balled napkin, a stir-stick and a brown spill on my side.

"You look nice in your suit," she says.

"I miss using it." I check to see who is sitting near us and might hear our conversation. "How long was the drive from the beach?"

"Hour and forty-five minutes. Not too bad this time of day."

"How's it been so far? The coast in the fall ought to be great."

"Just what the doctor ordered," she answers. "I love the ocean. Definitely the right choice for me." A woman at the table beside us closes her laptop and scoops up a leather purse and starts for the exit. "I hope everything's okay for you too, but since we're here and you're fishing for a favor, I'm assuming your skies aren't totally blue."

"Correct," I tell her.

"On the phone, you mentioned our meeting in Roanoke. Is this going to be about my calling somebody for you?"

"Yep, unfortunately."

"So the deposition didn't help?" she asks.

"Nope."

"And you had some of your legal tricks up your sleeve. No luck?"

"The other lawyers had better tricks." I flicker a smile at her.

"Sorry," she says. "I truly am. You don't deserve to go to jail."

"No kidding."

"Who would I be calling?" she asks.

"A bank, BB and T here in Richmond," I reply. "You don't need to have an actual conversation. Simple as that."

"Why wouldn't you just take the medicine, Kevin, even if you feel like you're innocent? You can't have any kind of normal life worrying about every knock on the door or every cop you pass on the street. Do the jail time and —"

"Two years," I interrupt. "Two years is the number I'm hearing from my lawyer." I'm thinking that Clay will likely offer a year, maybe less, but I exaggerate because I want her to be concerned for me. "In theory, I could be locked up for decades. One charge alone carries forty years, and another comes with a mandatory five-year minimum."

"Well, me, I'd pull my jail sentence and clean the slate and try to pick up the pieces."

"I'm *not* you," I tell her. "I won't let these fuckers steal two years of my life. I'm going to dog them until I can prove I'm innocent. Basically, I'm just running out of time right now and need some breathing room to regroup. Sooner or later, I'll whip them and clear my name."

"What're your charges? You've never explained exactly what's happening to you. Two years for simple coke possession? Usually you attend some kind of rehab and your case is dismissed once you get a mimeographed diploma from the clinic."

"Do you want to know everything?"

"Of course," she replies, "if you expect me to help you."

For the second time today, I recite my story, begin with Caleb at SUBstitution and end with Margo Jordan urging me to see a shrink.

"No wonder things aren't working out for you," Ava declares when I finish. "Your excuses are plain crazy."

"The devil's greatest strength is convincing people that he doesn't exist," I say. "Caleb Opportunity targets a compromised Kevin Moore and then counts on people reacting the same as you just did."

"Well, this devil has the benefit of your adultery, your coke binge, your positive pee test, your fingerprints and your confession to a PO, now doesn't he?"

"If I were concocting lies to beat my charges, don't you think I'd come up with something a little less baroque? Look at me — do I appear to be a wasted junkie? After I was arrested, have I *ever* seemed high?"

A noisy group of college kids fills the empty table next to ours. Ava concentrates on me, doesn't acknowledge them. "I can say — and I'm an expert on the topic — that I'm certain you're clean today and that you were clean every time I've seen or talked to you since September 2015. I'm willing to bet you've been drug-free every second since your arrest. You learned your lesson."

"If you believe that, if you trust your own instincts as the person who knows me better than anyone else on the planet, then you necessarily believe my story. You believe I'm the victim of a faked drug screen."

She laughs. She peers at the ceiling and shakes her head and spreads her hands. "Kevin Moore, Esquire. I walked into your lawyer trap, didn't I?"

"It's not a trap, Ava. It's common sense and believing what you've seen with your own eyes. How many times did we talk or see each other? Almost daily. I was perfectly normal. I've been straight for over a year."

"So what do you want me to do?" she asks.

"I need you to call the BB and T number from a specific address — Knollwood Drive

— here in Richmond. Twice. Three times, if you could. I'll give you the cash, you buy a burner phone and make the calls, which will throw the cops off my trail. They'll think I was in Richmond. A diversion, like I told you. I want them wasting resources and hunting for me in the wrong place."

"Knollwood?" she says. "Sounds posh."

"It isn't," I assure her.

"I don't know why I'm bothering to ask, but you swear there's no risk to me?"

"How could there be?" I answer. "You drive down a street, stop long enough to hit the preprogrammed number on speed dial, never leave your car, use a phone that they'll ultimately trace to me thanks to clues I let them discover, and then you trash the phone and return to the beach for cocktails and oysters. You provide me cover and clearer sailing to my new location."

"Well, I —"

"Obviously this stays strictly between us."

"You mean I'm not supposed to brag to the gals at bridge club about how I'm committing felonies to help spring my ex?"

I grin. "Exactly."

"If I do this . . . I don't mean to sound hateful or bitchy . . . but if I do this for you, if I help you, then we're even-steven, okay? This is an *enormous* favor. If I help with your plan, we agree I'm entitled to a clear conscience about the money and our marriage, and . . . we're finished and done and on good terms. There won't be *another* phone call or rescue request. You promise you won't contact me a year from now and ask to crash on the sofa or borrow a hundred bucks or hide out in my basement because the cops are on your heels? And you *definitely* won't find an old, happy picture of us and mail it to me, or send me a sentimental birthday card, or have the florist bring me calla lilies on Valentine's Day? We're over and separated forever, friends who don't stay in touch."

"Yes," I answer. "We're even. Your helping me is more than I deserve. I'm the villain in the piece, not you."

According to the Postal Service's website, there are thirteen public collection boxes in South Boston, Virginia, and I sussed out several as I passed through the area on my way to Richmond. The least likely to be captured by any surveillance video is the box at 2500 Houghton Avenue. Traveling home, I stop at a strip mall, change clothes in the car, return to Route 360, stop again to duct tape my license plates when I'm less than a minute away from the box, drive to the 2500 address and park in the lot's most distant corner.

Wearing the full felon's panoply — Lilly's purple nurse gloves, a hat, sunglasses, a sweatshirt stuffed with a pillow, a jacket, a scarf and baggy sweatpants — I drop the first forged court order into the mail. The envelope will be opened and thrown in the trash, then the order will be time-stamped by a clerk, so there'll be no postmark to trace, but I'm not taking any chances. I'm building in double safeguards, same as Blaine. Of course, if all goes well, by the time anyone gets around to checking or trying to solve the order's history, none of this will matter.

Oddly, I don't feel anything when I break the law and cross a forever divide. I'm now a cheat and a charlatan, a finagler, an apostate who decided to turn the law books upside down, but there's no fear, no shame, no nerves, no anger, no rush of regret . . . nothing. My hands don't tremble, my lips don't tingle, my damaged eye doesn't ache. As I duck my head and scuttle back to my small car, I'm reminded of the night I almost died, how my brain was suffocating and there wasn't enough of me left to do much more than claw and hang on, bobbing in a vast blackness, the whole, big-ass world folding into itself until it finally fit inside my own skull, almost gone.

Dan is already at the homeplace when I arrive late Thursday evening, his plain white Dodge Grand Caravan pulled close to the porch. Nelson greets me with a ball, and I toss it toward the pond. He's completely airborne when he catches it on the second bounce, and behind him, the water's surface mirrors jigsawed crimsons and yellows from a semicircle of shedding hardwoods.

Dan's in the kitchen, cooking dinner for us. "Kevin," he says as soon as I'm through the door, "tell me that I'm making a victory feast. I'm on pins and needles. Tell me you stuck it to this bitch con woman in the dep today."

"Wish I could, my friend," I say softly. "But nothing's changed. I'm screwed."

"Shit. Man."

We eat baked chicken breasts, mashed potatoes and green beans at the kitchen table. Dan brought the food with him in a cooler, along with a chocolate pie from an Atlanta bakery. "The cupboard was pretty bare last time I was here," he chides me. We're drinking coffee and I'm picking at the pie when he finally asks why he's traveled six hours under the radar to Meadows of Dan.

"I need your help," I tell him.

"Duh, Kevin. Really? I thought you were just bored and wanted somebody to pal around with. That's why I left my cell phone in Atlanta, showed my face at the office this morning for alibi purposes and drove the plain vanilla wheels. Of course, that baby's next in line for full Mini Thunder customization. It'll soon be a rolling masterpiece."

"If you can, I'd appreciate your helping me vanish."

"Vanish? Vanish from where?"

"Wherever," I answer.

"You're not dumb enough to run, are you? That shit never works, not in this day and age. Sooner or later, you always wind up caught, and your situation is worse because you didn't take responsibility and caused the detective on your case to put in extra hours and miss his kid's piano recital."

"Not true. We have defendants on the Roanoke docket who've been gone since 2000. And if Whitey Bulger can disappear for years, then so can I."

"Why?" Dan asks. "It's not like you're facing the death penalty or something. You're going to lose a civil case, and your insurance company will pay the money. Zero cost to you. Who cares? I'm not a criminal lawyer, but how bad could the punishment be for your dope cases? You have a clean record and a great background. So you serve a few months in the clink, some of it at a 'treatment center' with tennis courts and an arts-and-crafts room. In my book, that hardly warrants becoming Edward Snowden."

"Everyone knows where Snowden is, Minivan. He's in Russia. That's not the plan." I use my fork to push a stray green bean toward the center of my plate. "I'm looking at a year or two in real jail, but you're missing the point. Would you let these fuckers chump you? Would you let them profit to the tune of five million dollars by hanging you out to dry? Would you let them steal your livelihood from you? If I'm convicted of a felony — a fucking felony — I'll be employed at SUBstitution for years to come, squirting mayo and pretending to bake fresh bread. I damn sure won't be licensed to practice law anytime soon."

"But how's growing a beard and living in the third world any better?"

"I'm not planning to just run and hide in the wilderness and survive on crickets and wild berries. I truly believe I can bust them, bring them down — I just need more time.

Hell, if I can't nail them in a year or so, if I've exhausted every possible clue and I'm out of ideas, I can always turn myself in and do the time then."

Dan takes the last bite of his pie, a shard of tan crust smeared with chocolate chess. He studies me. "You're my best friend. Hell, I still owe you a zillion favors from law school. But this doesn't quite add up for me. Doesn't sound like Kevin Moore. Is there something else? A hole card? Plan B?"

"I don't know why you're so puzzled," I reply. "This *is* plan B. It's a binary choice: Give up, go to jail, ruin my name, lose my law license and live on thirty grand a year when I'm released, or retreat and keep fighting. And the fight's on my home field — the justice system. I'll turn this around. I will. Also, it's an easier choice because nobody else is at risk — no wife, no kids."

"I suppose," he answers.

"Here's a question: Do you believe me? Do you believe I'm being made the patsy in a five-million-dollar scam?"

"Honestly," Dan says, "it's never really mattered to me, never had any impact on my decisions. From day one, I wanted to help you get back on your feet, so I've always played along. Guilty or not guilty, coke or no coke, I don't care — you're my friend and you needed someone to take care of you."

"So?" I say.

"You're telling me an improbable story. Probably wise to leave it at that."

I smile. "For what it's worth," I say ruefully, "I truly am being railroaded."

"I'll do whatever I can to help you, bearing in mind that I *do* have a wife and daughter." He stands and takes his dishes to the sink. "So what are my potential duties as your wingman and accomplice?"

"Pretty easy, even for a slacker like you. You mail some envelopes."

"And what exactly will be in the envelopes?"

"Forged court orders," I say.

"Fuck, Kevin. Damn."

"You'll need to take precautions so your flaming red hair doesn't feature on any post-office video. I'd suggest wearing gloves and dropping the envelopes in the large mail-collection box at Nicholson Roofing. No prints, and the postman dumps your items — along with thousands of other pieces of mail — into the giant pot at a main post office, and off they go. No possible way to connect you or me."

"I'm sure my hair will be plenty apparent in my mug shot if we get arrested," he says.

"I don't think you can wear a hat or wig down at the station for that particular photo session. Poor Phil Spector went bald overnight. What's in the orders?"

"Wouldn't it be better if you didn't actually know?"

"Better for whom?" he replies. "I'm not buying a pig in a poke, especially from a disbarred attorney."

"They're orders releasing me from my electronic monitoring. Think of them as 'head-start papers.' "

"The cops will figure out they're fakes soon enough. There has to be some kind of check-and-balance in place."

"But not before I'm in the wind, several days ahead of the hounds. Trust me, I understand how the system operates. I'll be fine. I can't just bolt with this ankle bracelet, and if I tamper with it, they'll be all over me in minutes."

"It's not you I'm worrying about," he says.

"I also need you to anonymously set up an answering service for an attorney named Lee Agnew and activate his Aaron, Charles and McMillian trust account. I've opened the account online, but there has to be at least one deposit for it to actually function. I have the cash here to give you, a thousand bucks, sealed and ready to mail. The deposit info is in the envelope. Same thing — simply mail it with the orders."

"Who is Lee Agnew?"

"My money man," I reply. The answer is, in the larger sense, true, but it's also intentionally misleading.

"Your *money man*?" Dan snorts. He's squirting blue dish soap onto his plate.

"He's a fictitious lawyer I'm about to create. I can't risk lugging all my cash with me, and even if I make it to my new home with my life savings sewn into my suitcase lining, I'll still be the king of conspicuous consumption when I start paying my bills with greenbacks. I intend to have a nice, untraceable nest egg waiting for me, transferred from a legit law firm — Aaron, Charles and McMillian — to a legit bank. I'll start with this modest, under-ten-thousand deposit and continue to fill it up."

"Can't the bank account be traced to the computer here?" Dan asks.

"This computer won't be around much longer. It also is on the dark end of a Russian proxy server."

"You've certainly given this some serious thought," he says. "And, boy howdy, listen to you: *Russian proxy server.*"

"You tend to be thorough when you're facing jail and a financial beat-down, and

501

you're reduced to your last fucking option."

"You're positive about this?" Dan asks. "This is dangerous and permanent. And, in my opinion, foolish."

"I'm positive," I say. "Worst result is I go to jail for a little longer on another day. In the meanwhile, I buy myself a shot at redemption."

"Okay. I hope I'm actually helping, not grave-digging," Dan says. "Where're you going?"

"Short-term, I'll be researching Belarus. They have no extradition with the U.S."

"I'm not improving," I lie to my physical therapist early Friday morning, September 30. "It's not your fault, you've been great, but this is my third treatment, and I'm the same, or maybe even declining — like I only have half a body sometimes. I constantly drop things at work, I can't bend over without getting dizzy, and my left leg's weak and unreliable."

"Sorry," he says. His name is Scott, and he has a gray ponytail. He's kind and patient and always sympathetic. "Strokes are unpredictable. You've made a fantastic recovery, and the brain can continue to heal for months after the trauma. I don't want you to give up and become discouraged. You

502

hang in there and focus on the positive."

"Yeah, I will. I'm just scared this is permanent." I spike my voice with fake fear, but I worry that I sound phony, so I quit the act and use my normal tone when I continue. "I've definitely hit a recovery wall. I really need to be able to count on my physical health, and right now I can't. Would you ask Dr. Wallace if he has any other treatment options?"

As I'm leaving the Patrick County Medical Arts building, Ward phones me, at nine sharp. "I have good news," he announces. "Twelve months misdemeanor time is Clay's offer for your active sentence. Gives you only six months to pull, but since it's a year on paper, the media and Facebookers won't go totally apeshit. It's also within your sentencing guidelines, if we run them without the mandatory-minimum case."

"That is good news," I say. I stop at my Ford but don't open the door. The wind kicks up and dances a candy wrapper across the asphalt. "Very fair. Thank you."

"I also have bad news," Ward adds. "Clay wants two felony convictions. The entire plea package would be a reduction of the distribution charge to simple possession and five years suspended. Also, a conviction on the under-advisement charge and another five years suspended. The gun-and-dope warrant is amended to a misdemeanor concealed weapon charge, and you'll do the twelve months and pay a twenty-five-hundred-dollar fine. Two felonies, ten years suspended, the fine, and six actual months in jail. There's still interest in your co-operating to convict Calvin Jurgens — that would be part of the agreement, though I understand it's not too likely his case will go to trial."

"How'd you sell Clay on such a reasonable sentence?" I ask.

Ward chuckles. "He's a reasonable guy, for a commonwealth's attorney. Also, I contacted some of your friends in Roanoke and asked them to lobby him. Did you ever call anybody?"

"Uh, no, I didn't," I reply sheepishly. "Never got around to it. Embarrassed, I guess."

"Well, I did. Word spread, and evidently Clay heard from over a hundred people in three or four days, everyone from Congress-man Griffith to the courthouse janitor. I think Phil Anderson spearheaded the effort. A ton of people went to bat for you — you should be proud of that."

"Yeah, I appreciate it," I mumble.

"It's the best we can hope for," Ward says.

"I realize the felonies will hamstring you in terms of your law license, but so would five years on a mandatory minimum. Clay understands the convictions will cost the hell out of you, and that sad fact, together with the potential appeal issues from our motions, gave me a little leverage. There's also the stroke factor. I didn't hesitate to remind him you've already suffered physically, and that the stress of these charges had to contribute to your illness."

"The pity defense," I say. "Playing the cripple card — poor, sickly Kevin. I've definitely hit the bottom of the legal barrel."

"Listen: You've paid those awful dues, so you might as well receive something back from the hardship. Why not?"

"Can I have a few days to consider it?" I ask. "I'm not complaining, since you've worked another miracle for me, but I need to think about it and tie off a few loose ends."

"Of course. It's an important decision."

"Like I told you," I remind him, "if I accept the deal, I don't want this to linger. I want to enter my pleas and turn myself in. My landlord, Melvin, will be here to visit soon, and that would be a perfect time for me to start serving my sentence. Oh —

could you see if Sheriff Smith will allow me to do my six months in Patrick County? For obvious reasons, I don't want to land in Salem or Roanoke, and my last . . . vacation in his jail was at least tolerable and the food was edible."

Once a week, I'm allowed thirty minutes for grocery shopping. That same day, after work, I buy coffee and canned biscuits at the supermarket, then stop by the liquor store next door and purchase a cheap half-gallon of vodka.

"A half-gallon today," the clerk kids me. She's about my age and always amiable when I see her in the store. "Must be a special occasion."

"Celebrating," I say.

"I know you've usually been buyin' the Aristocrat, but the Smirnoff's on sale, and it's a better product for only two dollars more."

"I appreciate your looking after me," I tell her, "but this will do just fine."

"Wanted you to know. I try to do right by my customers."

"Thanks much. Maybe next time I'll splurge on the good stuff."

Chapter Twenty

On Thursday, October 6, before I eat breakfast, I sit at the kitchen table and handwrite a checklist for the next two days, thirteen items on a sheet of white copy paper. Superstitious, I add a number fourteen: "Live happily in tropical paradise."

I leave for Stuart ten minutes early and stop at the Patrick County circuit court clerk's office. I use a public terminal to locate my civil case, open the file on the screen and start scrolling through the images, beginning with Melanie Culp's five-million-dollar complaint.

"There we go," I say under my breath after I've viewed several documents and found the forged substitution order.

Later, I TracFone Minivan Dan from SUBstitution, and we chat about nothing in particular, and I tell him that I was prompted to call because a lunch customer ordered *sauerkraut* on roast beef, the same bizarre combination Dan always fancied when we lived together in Charlottesville. The chance of my cell being tapped due to a state-level drug charge is almost zero, but we still use the code word, and I call from one of the three burners I bought while in Richmond.

"So, okay," he says. "Okay. Goodbye."

"Goodbye, my friend. Thanks for everything."

I visit SunTrust, withdraw the remainder of my cash and close my account. Including the thousand I gave Dan, I've removed a total of $51,274.23, every cent that I have to my name.

I've called Ward once before to let him know I was still considering the offer. I talk to him during a lull at the restaurant and tell him I definitely want to accept the plea deal. "I'll start the paperwork," he says somberly. "I hate the felonies, hate that you'll lose your law license even longer, but this is the right decision. A jury would eat you alive."

As soon as I'm home, I send Lilly an e-mail. Most likely, I won't see her for months — and possibly never again — and I try to fashion a note that explains my circumstances without giving away anything important. I also rewrite the goodbye twice, so that I don't come off as melodramatic or saccharine. Truth is, I barely know her.

Next, I search the Internet for "Belarus marriage records," the first Google inquiry on the brand-new replacement computer.

I cross off six items from my list.

I fill Nelson's water dish for the night, then sit on the cool ground outside his pen and rest against a metal post in the chain-link fence. The sweetest creature, he squats on his haunches and perks his ears and tries to decipher me with his blue eyes, stays put until I pat my thigh and he wags his tail and darts closer and wiggles his head into my lap. I pet him and scratch the underside of his neck, and I start crying, can't help myself, and I promise him — even though I'm hardly certain — that I'll make our escape work and he won't be discarded again. I wipe my eyes with my sleeve, dab at my nose. The sun is setting, almost played out, and Tesla crows from a barn rafter. He crows a second time, and I wait for the third, but he falls quiet, doesn't Judas me, and because I'm anxious and on edge, I try to convince myself that the squawkings of a pea-brained rooster are somehow supernatural, a blessing and encouragement, Jove's approval.

CHAPTER TWENTY-ONE

The following morning, I'm granted a travel pass to visit the hospital in Winston-Salem, where Dr. Wallace has ordered another MRI and an ultrasound to see if there is new carotid narrowing or some complication with the tear. He has the test results before ten, and we meet in his office on a high floor, and he tells me that my artery is continuing to heal and the blockage is now only twenty percent. "This is perfect," he informs me.

"So it's healing on its own, like a cut or pulled muscle?"

"Yes," he replies.

"Then why am I still having problems with my grip and strength and balance?" The untruth sounds believable when I voice it. "The therapy isn't helping."

"Following a stroke, there's damage. Now there's residual damage."

"Will it get better?" I ask.

He shrugs. He raises and lowers his hands. He raises his hands again, until they're level with his chin. He waits to speak. *"Pozzably,"* he says.

"Is there any medicine or procedure that'll help me? I can't even bend over in the shower to wash my legs. If I drop something, it's a complete production to retrieve it. My handicaps are making life tough." I'm very deliberate with the word *handicaps.*

"Maybe *bazzs,"* he suggests.

"Yeah," I sigh. "Maybe baths."

His assistant peeks up from taking notes and grimaces.

I leave the doctor's office and ride the elevator to the first floor and wander through the labyrinthine halls and passageways, get lost, retrace my steps, take a left turn and finally arrive at the food-court coffee shop, with its open Wi-Fi. Though Blaine assured me it won't matter, I'm once again wearing a precautionary ball cap and sunglasses when I enter the business. My ankle monitor will transmit that I'm exactly where I'm supposed to be, nothing unusual, a stroke victim visiting a hospital and his neurologist's office.

I sit in a corner facing the wall, remove the glasses, open my disposable laptop and access Flanagan's e-mail. There's a nasty glitch when I attempt to write a message from his account. I type the message — just as Blaine instructed me, same as I did on my practice run — but the keystrokes don't appear on the screen. It's as if my letters are being absorbed into the ether, lost. "Shit."

I suck a breath and rub my palms together. The tension provokes a burning band under my left eye, the first discomfort I've suffered in several days. My mouth is dry and my front teeth hang against my lip. Thoughts blender together in my brain. I close the page, return to the home screen, stand and stretch, blink my pained eye and start over. This time, the machine cooperates. I hit send, wait, then delete the message from Flanagan's Sent Items folder, lest he discover it and ruin my plan.

Hijacking the Aaron, Charles and McMillian site is a piece of cake. Blaine has primed and preloaded the computer, so the insertion is easy and smooth, and at 10:29 a.m., October 7, 2016, Lee Agnew joins 318 other attorneys as a member of the firm. I locate the site's search function, type in "Lee Agnew," and there he is, looking solemn and professional in his bio's headshot. A full partner, he attended law school at Columbia and has been employed there since 1998.

His e-mail is LAgnew@ACMlaw.com, and I use it to send my second message of the morning, this one to Anne Mullens.

I strike two more items from my list: *Flanagan e-mail* and *Agnew bio. Call Mullens, Hide money, Confirm Bahamas lawyer, Nelson food, Double-tap computer* and *Live happily in tropical paradise* remain. I'll practice my spiel over the weekend and be ready to talk to Anne Mullens from a fresh TracFone on Monday morning. If I can snow her — *if* — I'll leave my scheduled two-thirty drug test with Ron Weiss, walk a block and e-mail her again from the open Wi-Fi at Leon's Diner. Then, after work, I'll drive to the mountaintop and pack a suitcase and fill my dopp kit with toiletries. I plan to burn the list along with the hammered J'onzz computer and pulverized TracFones in the fire pit at Melvin's, then dumpster the remains at SUBstitution. Trash collection is scheduled for next Thursday. *Slick as a button so far,* I tell myself.

Chapter Twenty-Two

"What the hell," I blurt, waking up in the dark, juiced by an adrenaline hit. *Bang, bang, bang, bang, bang.* It's six days later, and I'm under siege by the police, sound asleep when a cop pounds on the home-place door in the middle of the night. Nelson's barking and leaping against his pen so violently that I can hear the chain-link rattling as I walk down the dim hall toward the entrance. I realize immediately the police are here to arrest me — the sheriff didn't send two cars and four officers at three in the morning to unlock my ankle hardware. They came on little cat feet, no lights or sirens, invisible until a detective beat on the door and began shouting: "Police! Open up!" Through a window, I notice a deputy crouched beside the azalea bushes at the rear of the house, waiting there in case I try to rabbit out the back.

I switch on the porch light, twist the deadbolt, open the door. Darrell Pruitt has returned, but he doesn't speak. A beefy man with a badge hanging from his neck crowds closer to me, steps forward so he can block the door if I should try to shut it.

"Kevin Moore," he announces, "I'm Lieutenant Rakes, from the Martinsville police, and we have felony warrants for your arrest."

"Arrest?" I ask. "For what?"

"Two counts of forgin' a public record. Court orders, to be specific."

"Court orders?" I repeat. "Are you sure? There's some mistake. Could you double-check this? It's *crazy.*" I stay calm and confident.

"Sir, I'm gonna take hold of you and cuff you. I'd 'preciate your cooperation." He pinches my shoulder with a thick hand. "Please turn around and place your arms behind you."

I do as I'm instructed. Recalling the Gay Dolphin tragedy, I ask if he'll allow me to put on my shoes, proper pants and a respectable shirt. "And my dog. I have to make arrangements for him. Please."

"Mr. Moore's never give me no trouble," Pruitt volunteers.

"Okay, what the hell," Rakes says. "Officer Pruitt and me'll go with you to find

515

some clothes 'fore I cuff you. No monkey biz, you hear? You're in custody and tryin' to escape'll be another charge."

"Thanks. I understand. I'm a lawyer."

"Don't know what to do 'bout the dog. We ain't takin' him with us."

"If you'd give me a few seconds to call my coworker, I think he'll stop by in the morning and take care of things for me."

"Okay," Rakes agrees. "But make it snappy."

Blaine's groggy when he answers his phone, but he's quickly alert and says "Oh fuck" after I tell him that I've been arrested at my house. His "How?" and "Why?" are panicked.

"The police are here with me now," I caution him, "but don't worry. I haven't done anything wrong, so this should be straightened out soon. I'd be grateful, though, if you could pick up Nelson."

"I'll be there in the morning. Early. I'm so sorry, Lawyer Kevin. Didn't see this comin'. But I'll take great care of Nelson."

The SUBstitution maintenance shed is stocked with five bags of Pedigree, treats, a new bed and two bowls, one for food, the other for water, but this isn't how Blaine expected his babysitting to begin. He's stunned because our foolproof Operation

516

J'onzz has become the Bay of Pigs and collapsed right from the get-go.

"Guess you're the boss for a while, my friend. You're in charge. Didn't mean to leave you such a mess." I hang up Melvin's phone, disconnecting before Blaine blunders and says more than he should.

Electronic monitoring is a bond condition for the Martinsville drug charges, so Minivan Dan mailed two of the forged orders lifting the restraint to the Martinsville clerk's office and the city jail. These new felony charges — forging public documents — were issued from there as well. Officer Rakes and another cop load me into a cruiser, and we set out from the homeplace for a trip that'll take more than an hour. As we weave down the mountain, the cop in the passenger seat recites my *Miranda* warnings and Rakes asks about the bogus orders, and I insist that I don't know anything about any forgeries, that this is a huge mistake and I'm innocent, and that I want to speak with my lawyer, Ward Armstrong. So there's no possible mistake, I repeat the request: "I want my lawyer."

At the Martinsville city jail, I'm searched, fingerprinted, photographed and issued a stained, threadbare jumpsuit. This is my third arrest in fewer than fifteen months, so the process is familiar. Sadly, my birthdate and Social Security number are already in the system. I shuffle into the general-population pod at 5:16 a.m.

The pod looks like a postapocalyptic movie set from the 1980s, metal and concrete and solid, painted walls, everything awash in heavy brown and yellow light. A pentagonal control center — thick plexiglass and riveted steel panels — broods in the center of the pod, and two guards lord over a fetid collection of criminals, triple the number that the space was built to hold. The ceiling is low. The air seems as if it's a molecule away from solidifying. My "bed" is a thin blue mat, and my "cell" is a strip of concrete floor a few scant inches away from a urinal with a permanent damp spot underneath.

My floormate is a chatterbox boy — nineteen or twenty — with stringy blond hair, buck teeth and a lazy eye. "What're you in for?" he asks, keeping his voice at a whisper because of the early hour.

"I'm not sure," I say. "Right now, I'm in for some sleep."

"They claim I was sellin' Oxies. Total entrapment, but my lawyer ain't doin' shit for me."

"Hope that changes for you." I roll over

so my back's to him — facing the urine slick is truly a better option.

"My name's Bobby. But people call me Junior."

I don't reply.

"What people don't realize is I got money hid for when I get out. Serious money. And women waitin' on me. I got more pussy lined up than you can count. My girlfriend's been writin' me, and she's gonna come and visit next Sunday. Then I got another lady on the side. If I could ever use the phone, I'm gonna sweet-talk her and start some action there. Only problem is my ex is takin' me to court for child support, and the Medicaid people is claimin' I owe for the baby bein' born. I'm gonna demand a DNA test. Wouldn't you?"

"No idea, Junior."

He asks another question, and I ignore him, and he then rambles on about buying his uncle's logging business. Later, during breakfast, he introduces me to his friend Luke, who's "writin' up a federal lawsuit for Constitutional stuff." The lawsuit is guaranteed to win us aggrieved inmates millions and ensure that harsh justice is delivered to Sheriff Percy Lane for his many misdeeds.

"Here it is," Luke says, and shows me a bundle of blue-lined notebook paper covered in pencil scrawl. "Money in the bank. I can add your name. All it takes is twenty dollars on my canteen account. To help with required legal expenses. Twenty bucks that'll make you millions. Junior's done paid."

"Sorry, I don't have twenty dollars," I inform him. "If my circumstances change, you'll be the first to know."

I meet Ward in the interview room after a lunch of pinto beans, an orange, and a white-bread cheese sandwich. I'm seated, but Ward stands, hands on his hips, boiling mad.

"What the hell, Kevin?" he demands. "Have you lost your feeble mind?"

"Well, no. Only minor brain damage from the stroke —"

He steps closer and interrupts me. "I put my name and reputation on the line, save your sorry ass a second time, arrange the deal of the decade, vouch for you — along with tons of other people — and this is the thanks I get?"

"Maybe, Ward, you can calm down and explain to me what's happening. All I know is that I was dragged out of my bed in the middle of the night because I'm supposed to be connected to some forged Martinsville court orders."

"Yeah," he almost shouts, growing more

irritated. "Forged court orders releasing you from the ankle monitoring that just happened to appear in both the Martinsville jail and clerk's office. Stop it. You can't bullshit a bullshitter."

"Have you seen them?" I ask.

"I have fax copies." He reaches into his inside jacket pocket, removes the copies and tosses them on the table. "Randy Clay is fit to be tied. And I don't blame him, no I don't. A lawyer doing this kind of wrong, trying to sabotage the system we've all sworn to honor, is absolutely unforgivable. I heard before I came over here that a third fake also arrived in the Patrick County clerk's office. Big surprise, since they were handling the monitoring for Martinsville — another favor I arranged so you could remain in Meadows of Dan."

I unfold the papers, study one order, then the other. "I didn't send them," I declare. "First time I've ever seen these," I lie.

"Then who the hell did?"

"What does it matter if the commonwealth can't prove I did it? Legally matter, I mean."

"I talked to Logan Rakes, who's in charge of the investigation. You want to tell me why you withdrew every penny in your account from the bank?"

"First, it doesn't prove anything. Second,

I was preparing to turn in to jail, and I planned to pay all my bills and invest the balance in a CD at another bank so I could at least make a little money while I was locked up. I don't really need a money-market checking account paying infinitesimal interest for the next six months, now do I?"

"Bullshit. Bullshit. Bullshit. Makes no sense."

"How did the orders end up here? In Martinsville?"

"How the hell do you think, Kevin?" Ward snarls. "The mail."

"From where? The postmark?"

"Of course, the clerk's office trashed their envelope, but the cops damn sure have theirs — an order sent directly to them rang every alarm imaginable — and it was mailed in Atlanta."

"My monitoring log will show I haven't been anywhere near Atlanta."

"So you gave the orders to a friend or mailed them to someone else, who in turn dropped them in a box there in Atlanta."

I'm wearing cuffs, and the chain hits the table as I scoot forward. *Thunk.* "Ask yourself, Ward, why in the world I'd do this, and do such a bad job? You've negotiated a sweetheart deal for me — six months, probably in the Patrick County Jail. I'd be serving my time in Mayberry with Otis and Andy and Aunt Bee. So why would I pull this kind of trouble down on myself? I damn sure know better than to send an order to a sheriff's department. Come on, *seriously*."

"You'd do it if you're desperate and only looking for a few hours' head start on the cops. You'd do it if you're Kevin Moore, and you believe there's nothing worse than losing your law license for years to come, so you plan to run. You'd do it if you're hooked on drugs or alcohol and not thinking clearly — the cops told me your garbage can was full of vodka bottles. They found a nearly empty half-gallon in the kitchen cabinet. And, as we both understand, jail — any jail — is *jail*, my friend. We've seen defendants skip town to avoid a weekend DUI sentence."

"They won't find my prints," I say, "because I've never touched any fake orders. So the commonwealth's entire case will be — on its very best day — that three forged orders appeared, one in an envelope from Atlanta. Mr. Moore wasn't in Atlanta, there's no DNA, no prints, and Mr. Moore has consistently denied any involvement. Mr. Moore is an attorney and would realize that Judge Morris wouldn't send a copy of his order to a jail, for gosh sakes. The charges will be dismissed as a matter of law, won't even make it past a motion to strike. Suspicious for sure, but there's no chance I'll be convicted. The commonwealth can't tie me to the orders beyond a reasonable doubt — you have to know that. It's Criminal Law 101."

"There's also the search for Belarus on your computer. The police went back with a search warrant. Didn't even have to do any forensics. That exotic vacation locale, which doesn't share extradition with our country, was in your recent history. Not to mention that most of your clothes and possessions were boxed up, and your suitcase was packed."

"Ward," I say, "I know you think I'm either lying, or a druggie and a drunk, or a crackpot, and I realize this will piss you off, but the reason I searched for Belarus is because of the deposition in the civil case. It's discussed on a court reporter's CD. That's a fact. Melanie Culp, the plaintiff, used a fake Belarus marriage to launder millions of dollars. The search is actually for Belarus *records,* not for Belarus houses or Belarus apartments. I'm at war with these assholes, Ward. At war. They did this. They're trying to put me away for years and discredit me because I'm fighting them and finally making some progress. As for the clothes, I have to move out when my land-lord comes to visit. He'll confirm that I'm telling you the truth."

"I'll meet with Clay once more — as I'm ethically required to do — and see if he'll still offer the original deal. After that, I'm done. You need to hire a new lawyer. I'd suggest Esther Mulberry or Jimmy McGarry. Maybe Joe Stone. Of course, you know the attorneys in Roanoke better than I do — assuming any of them will help you given how you've fucked everyone over and made us look like idiots. Have whomever you hire contact my office, and we'll do an order substituting counsel."

"Ward, I'm sorry, but I didn't screw you or anyone else."

"I should've quit you a long time ago." He fixes me with a look that's pure disgust. "This kinda shit makes all of us seem like crooks." He stalks off and slams the door so hard that it doesn't catch and bounces off the frame and comes to rest against the stop, wide open.

Esther Mulberry will tongue-in-cheek tell you that the only inheritance she received from her white furniture-dynasty daddy is her fancy last name and her stubby legs. "The rest is totally my mom — and thank my lucky stars for that." The child of Trey Mulberry and Tia Alcorn, a black supervisor at his family's chair factory, Esther was raised in Martinsville, graduated at the top of her class from Temple in 1989 and graded onto law review at Georgetown. Trey had an admirable heart, and when he — single and footloose at age twenty-five — discovered that Tia was pregnant, he happily married her and moved her and their dark-skinned baby into his mansion with the bowling alley and statuary garden.

The arrangement didn't sit well with anyone in 1967 Southside Virginia, especially the country club crowd, who'd built their segregated Shangri-La to avoid exactly this kind of *progress* and paid steep dues each month to keep the coloreds in the kitchen and out of the damn swimming pool. Poor Esther — defiantly named after Trey's grandmother — suffered a pendulum existence of wanton persecution and patronizing head pats until she left home for college at eighteen. By then, as Trey liked to say, she was tough as whitleather.

When the furniture industry went bust in Henry County and all the plants closed, when Tultex and DuPont and Bassett-

Walker and Mulberry Furniture were chained and padlocked and the bankruptcy buzzards picked the remains clean, when the Roman-numeral heirs weren't guaranteed a corner office or a trust fund, when the legacy ledgers went to red and Martinsville became a dust bowl, Esther Mulberry was long gone, working in the justice department for Bill Clinton, then George Bush, and after cashing out as a seven-figure partner at a powerhouse Washington firm, she — wealthy and well connected — relocated to Roanoke to be closer to her diabetic mom and penniless, alcoholic daddy, who died in 2014 but lived to see the local high school honor his daughter with the "distinguished graduate" award.

Esther meets me on October 18 at the jail's interview room. She's already seated when I'm escorted — shackled and unshaven — from the pod to see her.

"This is quite an unexpected reversal, isn't it, Kevin?" she says after the cop has left and we've made small talk for a few minutes. We know each other casually, and we worked together in 2013, represented codefendants charged with federal drug crimes. She's wearing a neck scarf and a gray dress. She's petite, maybe five-four, and every movement, every sentence, and every expression is badass serene, the demeanor you'd expect from someone who's been threatened by Mexican crime lords, white-collar price-fixers and seedy West Virginia coal bosses — and thrashed them all.

"No doubt," I answer.

She's quiet for a moment. "I've reviewed your court files and spoken with Mr. Armstrong. Tell me your version of events, please."

"How long do you have?" I ask.

"As long as we need," she answers, and truly means it.

We discuss my situation for forty minutes. She sits primly, doesn't take notes, and lingers on various pieces of my story, cross-examines me to see how well I'd fare at a trial. Her expression remains stoic and flat, never gives anything away. Occasionally, she asks a personal question: "Where did you finish law school?" "Are you and your wife on civil terms now?" "Did you enjoy being a lawyer?" "Why did you settle in Meadows of Dan, such an isolated place?"

I finish by assuring her that there is nothing — no DNA, no prints, no post-office video — to connect me to these forged court orders.

"What're your expectations?" she asks.

"Same as most defendants, I'd prefer to

be found not guilty. I'll concede that there's plenty of room for suspicion, lots of smoke, but there's no fire, Esther, and no chance I'll ever be convicted of these forgery charges, not unless Randy Clay's sitting on mystery evidence we're unaware of."

"Randy Clay is sitting on a five-year mandatory minimum in your gun case and forty years in the distribution case. Would you agree, based on these recent developments, that he's legally — and morally — entitled to withdraw his extremely fair offers on those charges?"

"I can certainly see why he's upset."

"So can I," she says. "I may very well win the battle for you on the forged-order cases — I won't have to do much more than sit there and make a motion to strike — but we risk losing the war and your catching five, six, seven years on the other charges."

"Correct. Have you taken Clay's temperature? How mad is he?"

She deflects the question. "Which do you value more? Your freedom or your law license?"

"My law license," I answer. "I don't have any way to support myself without it."

"Evidently, you have fifty-one thousand dollars and change, though I'm speculating it might not be domestic and easily accessible these days."

I smile. "Hard to live the rest of my life on fifty K."

"So what's the number, then? What's my bargaining range?"

I understand her question and her strategy. "Start with three," I say.

"Not enough," she replies.

"I'd take up to five or six. That's a long time to make sandwiches."

"I'll visit Mr. Clay as soon as I leave here." She stands. "I'll require a ten-thousand retainer. Any problems with the fee?"

"Well, as you mentioned, it might be a while before I can pay you in full. Unless the cops were unusually skilled with their search warrant, there should be seventy-five hundred of that fifty-one thousand hidden in my landlord's barn. A down payment."

"Well, let's keep our fingers crossed that the police didn't discover it — some observers might view it as road money, your transition cash for a sudden trip."

"I'm curious. I'm in no position to take any of my drug cases to trial, and if I did plead not guilty, I don't have much more than my raggedy word and a few co-incidences, but I was wondering what you make of the Caleb Opportunity piece of my puzzle. You're impossible to read. I'm

530

confident you'll go to the mat for me, but it's always helpful if your lawyer actually believes in your innocence. Ward has always been, uh . . . skeptical."

"You ever heard of Catalon Chemical?" she asks. "The Chinese company?"

"No," I answer.

"A brazen theft," she says. "The *governor* handed 1.4 million of taxpayer money to these characters so they'd locate a business in Appomattox. North Carolina had already discovered they weren't legitimate and basically warned Richmond not to trust them. The Catalon website was a cut-and-paste joke, and a few keystrokes and minor due diligence would've uncovered their cyber-ruses, fake addresses and many aliases. Yet you can go online and see the picture of beaming state and local officials giving away the giant check and cutting the ribbon with scissors the size of pruning shears. The scammers are right there in the photo — doesn't matter. Catalon took the money and vanished to China. Gone."

"Damn," I say.

"I'm open-minded about how much sub-terfuge there is in the world. I've seen captains of industry and major corporations get looted for millions, and we've all seen the almost-daily media reports about spectacular hacks and data breaches — those are just the tip of the iceberg, because most companies and branches of government aren't anxious to broadcast their failures. So, sure, Kevin, it's possible that devious people routinely intercept state-board e-mails and use them to their advantage. But like you said, I assume we're past the point of trying to sell a white-haired-mystery-man defense to a jury."

"Yeah," I agree. "There're all kinds of reasons for me to avoid a trial, but I'm happy to learn that you're at least willing to consider the slim possibility I'm not a liar or a lunatic. Just make the best deal you can for me."

"I will."

"Esther," I say as she's collecting her purse and briefcase, "I want this to go quickly. Before I caught these new charges, we'd tentatively discussed my pleading this week. The sword above my neck and the uncertainty and worry are additional punishments. Also, I want full credit for accepting guilt and not wasting the common-wealth's time and money. If Clay will package this, I'm willing to waive indictment on the new warrants and fast-track my cases as needed."

I return to the pod, where I use the public phone to call Melvin.

"Where in blue blazes are you, Kevin?" he immediately asks. "Sounds like you're at a party or a bar."

"Well, you're sort of correct," I say. "I'm *behind* bars."

"Christ, Kevin. Enough's enough. What is it this time?"

"A completely false forgery charge. I'm innocent." I'm aware that the conversation is being recorded. All jail calls are monitored.

"Yeah," Melvin snorts. "You and everybody else in there."

"The house is in perfect shape, clean and organized. You'll be pleased. Yard is mowed, fences are repaired. I've finished almost every word in the Gardner Turman story; the file's on the computer, the hard copy's in a fireproof cabinet. I'd already started moving and packing my stuff so I'd be out of your hair by the twenty-fourth, but I was arrested before I could finish. Sorry to ask, but maybe you could just store my clothes and my few knickknacks in the guesthouse for a while — I'd be glad to pay you for the space. There's chicken scratch in the barn, but the birds still have enough to eat in the yard and pasture. The horses are fine; they have plenty of grass, though they've become spoiled to a sweet-feed treat most days. My dog is gone. The doors should be locked, and your key's with a Patrick County cop named Darrell Pruitt. I won't be coming back anytime soon. I'm sorry, and I'm sorry for the trouble and confusion. Sorry to disappoint you. You've been a great friend to me, Melvin. I wish this were ending differently."

"I hope you can finally get straight and become Kevin Moore again. I do. But we understand each other: I've carried more than my fair share of the load, and the favor bank is empty."

"Yes. And thank you."

"Okay," Melvin answers, and, as usual, disconnects abruptly.

Next, I phone Blaine at the restaurant, but I keep the call brief. He's still spooked, still scared. He's never experienced any repercussions from his years of online tomfoolery, never seriously considered that a real brick-and-mortar jail might be lurking amongst the coding if an e-adventure falls apart.

"I'm in the Martinsville jail," I alert him.

"Nelson okay?"

"He's here with me. I'm takin' good care of him. Anything I can do to help you?"

"Just look after the dog. I'll be fine. Don't worry."

I hang up and join a scrum of prisoners watching a western on the communal TV. Out of nowhere, the man beside me asks if I know "a white dude named Hines. They call him Ace."

"Sorry, I don't," I reply.

"I was just wonderin'. You favor a man what used to run with him."

I nap on the floor, and my dinner includes a half-pint of off-brand whole milk. I haven't bent and separated a glued, waxy carton spout since elementary school, and the nostalgia distracts me for a moment, blotting out the bars and voices and smells.

At six-thirty, I'm shackled again, and I trudge and jangle to the interview room, a guard at my elbow. My orange jail slides are too large for my feet, and I lose a shoe and have to stop and backtrack and slip it on. The lighting in the room is poor. There's a crumpled silver-and-white gum wrapper on the floor. A couple of tiles — replacements — are brighter than the rest. Esther is standing in a corner, her belongings on the battered table. "I think we have a deal," she says.

I don't sit, either. "So what is it?"

She tells me the numbers.

We're both quiet, but she never breaks eye contact. "That's almost *too* generous," I say.

"Well, Kevin," she smiles, "it's why you hired me."

"Do you trust Clay?" I ask. "I don't know him. He has a solid name with the bar; I've never heard of him pulling anything dishonest."

"Not sure how much it matters — there's no opportunity for dishonesty once we sign a plea agreement. Everybody's locked in."

"What about the Feds?" I ask. "Maybe that's what's in the weeds. Maybe they're planning to charge me too."

"I've got a call in to the U.S. attorney's office in Roanoke. Anthony Giorno's a straight shooter. He'll tell me if they have any interest, but this seems far too small for them."

"The Feds are prone to grandstand, and they love to perp-walk white-collar defendants so they'll appear evenhanded."

She scowls. "When I was a Fed, I took a measure of satisfaction in convicting white-collar criminals because, one, they were guilty, and two, their crimes usually impacted thousands of innocent people, right down to the fixed-income retirees whose IRA accounts went to junk thanks to stock fraud, or the miners who contracted cancer after their greedy employer cut corners on safety and environmental regs."

"Sorry," I correct myself, "but we need to have them sign off as well. The orders were mailed, and there you go, that's a favorite tactic of theirs, and the moment I plead here, if we're not careful, Uncle Sam will tag me with three counts of mail fraud, and I'll catch more felonies and more time."

"I understand. Anthony will work with us. We occasionally shared western Virginia cases when I was in Washington, and he's a quality man. I'm not worried about federal charges. Not at all. This isn't even a blip on their radar."

"Are we missing anything?" I press her. "Maybe Clay plans to indict me for other charges. And the Patrick County prosecutor is on board? Stephanie Katt is her name. I hear she's very bright and a killer."

"I appreciate the backhanded compliment, but the offer isn't so incredible as to seem like a trap or tease to me. And yes, I've reached out to Mrs. Katt, and she's in agreement."

"We need to sew it up like nobody's business. Sorry to be paranoid, but we should include language about the deal covering crimes related to, or in any way connected with, any and all forged court orders —"

"I've done a plea agreement or two," she interrupts. "I understand the intricacies. This isn't my first trip to the opera." Her stolid expression doesn't change. She doesn't appear offended by my reminding her of legal basics. "Oh, wait. Okay. 'Any and all'? *Hmmm.* There were two matching release orders discovered in Martinsville, yet only one so far in Patrick County. Odd, now that I think about it. Perhaps there's another shoe to fall, and we need to account for a fourth fake release order?"

"Couldn't hurt," I answer, my head bowed, the words directed at the floor. "Things often come in pairs. Things can be delayed in the mail. Or temporarily mis-placed in the shuffle at a hectic office." I act guilty and chagrined, communicate that I definitely need immunity for another forged order.

"I'll handle it," she says simply, though she does pause until I look up at her. "And I'll provide you with the paperwork to re-view."

"I'd even mention envelopes and cover letters. In theory, they could also be the

538

basis of separate charges, especially with the Feds. And what about the whole *theft* family of crimes, identity theft and so on? Larceny by false pretenses, for instance — the commonwealth might argue that I'd receive something of value if I were released."

"Thank you for the guidance." She smiles; it's faint and ironic. "Nothing quite like a client with a law degree."

"I'm sorry to be a pain," I say. "You're a far better lawyer than I'll ever be, and as smart as they come. I just want to make certain this is totally finished and behind me and there're no surprises a month from now. It's a helluva lot different when you're on this side of the equation. Especially after everything I've experienced."

"I understand. I'd be very exacting and thorough if I were in your position."

"How about Patrick County and serving my sentence there? This place is a hellhole."

"I haven't gotten around to that yet," she replies. "The plea terms seemed more urgent."

"Well, I'd be grateful if you'd use your considerable skills on Sheriff Smith. You can tell him I'll pay my per diem in full, in advance, and I promise not to file any grievances or court writs or cause him the slightest heartburn. I'm the kind of inmate he wants."

"I'll use all the tools available to me to have you sent to Patrick County," she answers elliptically. "So we have a deal? You want me to confirm with Mr. Clay and put this on the docket for you to plead? We can do it on Friday, as was originally planned, with Judge Williams, assuming Judge Morris will agree to let another judge handle the old possession case."

I hear bits and pieces of a conversation as two cops pass by outside the door. At random, my mind pulls up an image of my dad in his last days, sitting on the edge of a bed, wheezing and hacking and coughing and straining to bring air into his lungs, his pallid legs dangling from a flimsy, tie-in-the-back hospital gown, his eyes red-rimmed and exhausted, ready to go. Then I flash on Smith Mountain Lake, where this horrific decline began, its fangs hidden at first, Ava and I hugged up to each other, jazzed by the alcohol, the swaggering spring moon full of promise, the band hitting high notes. I have an impulse to sink down to the tile and cross my legs and despair and sulk and not speak, but instead I shackle-walk to the closest chair, take a seat, plop my elbows on the table and drop my face into my hands.

"Yes. Okay. I accept the deal."

"You're positive?" she asks.

"Yes," I reply, still slumped, still staring at the table.

"I'll phone Mr. Clay tonight. He gave me his cell number." She hesitates. "If you'd like, I can remain here until you're able to compose yourself. Take as much time as you need."

"Thanks. I'm composed now. I appreciate your good work on my behalf. You need to get on the road — it's late and you have a long drive ahead of you."

CHAPTER TWENTY-THREE

On Friday, I don't even bother to request street clothes for my court appearance at four-fifteen, because what damn difference does it make, and who would collect the house key from the sheriff's department, drive to Melvin's, hunt through boxes and the closet, pick a suit, tie, shoes, socks, belt and shirt, then bring them to me in Martinsville? I do shower and shave and comb my hair, and a jailer issues me smaller slides, so I can actually lift my feet off the ground, and because of a call from Esther to the sheriff, I'm allowed to appear for my guilty pleas without cuffs or leg shackles.

Esther is waiting for me at the counsel table when a bailiff leads me into court from the holding cell. Judge Williams is already on the bench and watches me walk in. The gallery is empty. Two lawyers are discussing something near the exit doors, and they seem collegial and quitting-time jolly.

There's no press, but they'll learn about this soon enough, and my convictions will become below-the-fold news in the second section of *The Roanoke Times,* more embarrassment tossed onto the heap.

The judge acknowledges me and announces that the cases are styled *Commonwealth v. Kevin G. Moore,* then Randy Clay stands and details the plea agreement. "Judge, Mr. Moore, once a distinguished member of our profession, is here with a series of charges, and we're respectfully asking the court to approve an agreement I've reached with Ms. Mulberry. First, the defendant has a drug possession case that Judge Morris took under advisement over in Roanoke. We understand you've been in contact with Judge Morris, and he's agreed that you may hear his case as a part of this comprehensive plea deal so long as the under-advisement felony conviction is entered and there's some active jail time attached."

"Correct," Williams says. "And you have no objection as to venue, Ms. Mulberry? No objection to my presiding in all these cases? I only have the designation paperwork by fax from the Supreme Court."

Esther stands. "No objection. In fact, we're grateful to Your Honor; this combined sentencing event is very much to my client's benefit."

My client. I replay the phrase in my head. I'm the client, the felon, the loser on the wrong side of the law. I glance at Clay, at the bailiff, at Judge Williams. I keep my chin up, my posture proud.

"Mr. Moore will be found guilty of this Roanoke felony charge," Clay continues. He's wearing reading glasses and referring to notes. "He'll receive five years in jail, with one month active to serve. He also has the two charges that Your Honor is familiar with, charges that arose at the probation office here in Martinsville. The distribution of meth charge will be reduced to simple possession, and he'll receive another five years, with all the time suspended. The gun charge from here in Martinsville will be reduced to a misdemeanor of carrying a concealed weapon, and he'll serve the maximum of twelve months and pay a twenty-five-hundred-dollar fine —"

The judge interrupts. "I assume a reason for the commonwealth's flexibility is the possibility of Mr. Moore winning on appeal."

"Yes sir," Clay answers. "Also, before this he had no record, and I've received over a hundred calls, letters and e-mails supporting his good character. Factually, we believe he's an addict, not a seller."

"Go ahead," Judge Williams says.

"Finally, Judge — and this is sort of the worst conduct in the whole saga — Mr. Moore will plead guilty to three felonies of forging a public record. Fake court orders bearing Judge Morris's name were sent to our clerk's office and our jail. Also to Patrick County. These fake orders purported to release Mr. Moore from home electronic monitoring. He was on ankle monitoring because of his bond for the Martinsville cases, but since he lived in Patrick County, this was run through their jail."

Williams glares at me. He's livid. His neck colors. He rises out of his chair, pitches forward. He has a large head and a beard, and he's angled so all I can see is his enraged face. "Say *what*?"

"Three forged court orders were mailed, and they instructed the police to remove Mr. Moore from HEM."

"Good Lord," Williams bellows.

Esther leaves our table and walks to the lectern. "Judge, if I could be heard?"

"Sure," the judge replies. "Now would definitely be the time."

"While my client is pleading guilty as a tactical matter, we believe — and we think the court will share our opinion — that he'd never be convicted of these crimes. The commonwealth can prove that the orders were received from Atlanta. My client's monitoring records will confirm that he was nowhere near Atlanta on the day the orders were mailed. My client has emphatically denied any involvement. As a courtesy to me and Mr. Clay, the assistant chief at the state lab, a Mr. Thompson — who is my client's friend and former client — moved this evidence to the front of their line, and we learned this morning that my client's prints and DNA are *not* on the documents. Understandably, Mr. Clay wanted the forensic report before our tentative agreement became this final proposal to you, sir."

"Judge," Clay adds, "naturally, Mr. Thompson didn't perform the testing of the letters himself. He assigned the analysis to another technician."

Esther rushes to speak again, doesn't allow Clay to take over the narrative or spin the facts. "My client also removed money from his bank account in preparation for surrendering to jail on the first three charges, and he was packing his belongings at a rental house. Nothing odd about this conduct, which is very explainable. That's the extent of the state's case —"

"He was searching on his computer for *Belarus,*" Clay interjects. "A country that doesn't extradite to the United States."

"Who would have any interest in creating fake orders, *other* than Mr. Moore?" Williams asks.

Esther is steady and methodical. "Mr. Moore was doing research because that country was mentioned in a civil deposition he's involved in. I contacted the court reporter, and I have an audio file here today. I've listened to it myself."

"If you tell me it's mentioned, Ms. Mulberry," Williams replies, "I believe you. Unlike your client, your word has value."

"She played the deposition testimony for me, Judge," Clay confirms.

"To respond to the court's thoughtful question, Mr. Moore, an experienced attorney, would obviously know that sending a court order directly to a jail would attract attention and prompt immediate investigation. I won't bore the court with our theory of the case, but Mr. Moore is involved in high-stakes civil litigation, and we believe the forged orders were an effort by his opponents to compromise him. He'd no more think that he could pull off sending a fake order to *a jail* than you or I would, sir."

"We disagree there, Judge," Clay responds.

"I've never bought into Mr. Moore's grand conspiracy theory. It's silly and baseless. If you're desperate and impaired, and your trash can's full of empty liquor bottles, you don't think clearly, and you do desperate things in hopes of gaining a jump on the police when you hightail it to a far, faraway country."

Esther adjusts the lectern's mic, bends it lower. Her voice is amplified when she speaks. "These forgery cases would never make it past a motion to strike. Not a chance. In a certain sense, the common-wealth is receiving three felony convictions it can't prove beyond a reasonable doubt. And we all realize why my client is willing to plead guilty. Mr. Moore wants to put this behind him, and he clearly has significant exposure in the earlier cases, so this is a fair bargain for both sides."

"So what's his punishment for the three forge-public-documents cases?" Williams demands.

"His *jail sentence* will be an additional six months active." Esther hesitates. She gestures toward me. She's purposefully silent for a moment. "But his *punishment,* the real sanction, is an agreed-upon five-year law-license suspension, coupled with a complete prohibition from any work in the legal system for that same period." She steps sideways and looks down at me. "As attorneys," she adds, her voice now off the amplification system, "we know better than most people what pain this causes him. It's essentially a vocational death sentence. Five years from today, with a string of felony convictions on his record, my client will be eligible to petition the state bar for a license restoration. There's no guarantee the bar will grant his request, and if it does, he'll be a disgraced, tarred-and-feathered lawyer who's starting from scratch at almost fifty years of age."

"Is that the deal?" Williams asks Clay.

"Yes," Clay answers. "It's a global settlement too. Mrs. Katt has signed off on it for the Patrick County charge. There's been discussion of another possible order floating around Patrick County, and that's included in the deal. Ms. Mulberry informs me the Feds have also agreed not to bring any charges, but I'm not privy to their understanding. The federal concerns are handled in a separate document. I should mention, too, that Mr. Moore has agreed to cooperate as a witness in a case against a top-level drug dealer named Calvin Jurgens."

"And, Your Honor," Esther says, continuing to sell the judge, "I'd like the court to know that my client has suffered significantly over the last year. We readily admit he has a drug and alcohol problem — and we can honestly debate his degree of fault in those illnesses — but unrelated to this substance abuse, in June, Mr. Moore had a serious stroke. He still has symptoms and is lucky to be alive. While he'd never rely on his medical condition as an excuse, as his lawyer, I can't help but think that his brain injury played a role in his arriving before you here today. He's a fallen, infirm and broken man."

"So he'll have one year and seven months to serve?" Williams confirms.

"Yes sir," Clay replies. "That's exactly his sentencing guidelines' midpoint, so we feel it's fair, especially since he's prohibited from practicing law in any form or fashion for five years."

"Of course," Williams says, "the twelve months is misdemeanor time. So he'll actually pull around a year when all is said and done and he receives his various incarceration credits."

"Plus the twenty-five-hundred-dollar fine and the lengthy loss of his license and five felony convictions," Esther reminds the judge. "I'd calculate that the suspension, based on his past income, even if it lasts for only five years, will cost him over a million dollars. Certainly, Your Honor, that's a harsh penalty."

Williams finally relaxes into his chair. "Okay. I'll accept it. Reluctantly. Does he want to be arraigned?"

"He'll waive the reading of the charges," Esther says. "We appreciate Your Honor approving the plea agreement."

The bailiff brings me the paper to sign, waiving arraignment. Esther lends me a pen, and I start to sign my name. I write a slow, halting *K,* then drop the pen. I pick it back up, start again, stop. I brace my wrist with my free hand. "Sorry," I sigh. "Takes a little longer these days."

The bailiff is standing there waiting. He peers down at the floor. Clay's expression pity-softens. Judge Williams says, "No hurry," and it's apparent he feels bad for me. I finish my name — in shaky letters — and return the pen to Esther.

Judge Williams leads me through a standard guilty-plea litany, asks questions about my age, education and understanding of my six pleas. I stand tall and answer in a determined voice. I absolutely will not snivel or cry or quibble or make excuses or whine about the justice system's flaws or piss away the small dignity I have left. "Would you like to say anything before I pass sentence?" the judge inquires, after he's asked me the last question on the litany list, heard an evidence summary and declared me guilty.

"Only briefly," I reply. "I'm in debt to Mr. Clay for his professionalism and sense of fair play throughout this matter. Both my lawyers, Mr. Armstrong and Ms. Mulberry, have been excellent. I didn't possess a gun and drugs at the probation office, but it's to my advantage to plead guilty and accept this deal. I am, however, guilty of the original possession charge, and related to that crime, I've embarrassed myself and all of my brother and sister bar members. For The Substitution Order that I deeply apologize. Worse, I mistreated my wife, and there's no excuse — none — for that failure. I'm ready to serve my punishment, sir."

Williams monotone reads from the plea agreement, and it's done. I'm a convicted felon, and the next year of my life will be spent in jail. My law license is forfeited for five years. I'm past being mad, resigned by now, but the brutal unfairness does bite at me for a moment and cause me to sit dead still and consider how fucking random this is, how unlucky I've been. The bailiff is ready with the cuffs. A retired judge's oil-painted portrait hangs stern on the wall across from me.

Esther shakes my hand. "All best to you, Kevin." She cants her head. She knits her brow. "You okay? I've not had many defendants look so content on the way to jail. You're not . . . sick . . . or having another episode, are you?"

"I'm fine. I'm just relieved that everything fell into place. It's hard to explain. I played impossible cards as well as anyone could've. Legal wins come in all shapes and sizes, right? We've celebrated at my office, even shed tears, when a client in a capital case was sentenced to life. Life in the penitentiary without parole, but we won because he didn't receive a death sentence. The best possible result — given the circumstances — is always a defense victory."

She studies me. The bailiff is growing impatient. She finally unlocks her formal face, spreads a sphinx's smile. "I'm betting on an epilogue for Kevin Moore," she says, the words lively. "I'm not certain of when or where, and most of all — today, right here, right this instant — I'm not sure of *how,* Counselor, but" — she tiptoes slightly and leans toward me and covers her mouth so the bailiff can't hear — "somewhere there's a bamboozle, and Kevin Moore, a damned good attorney, represented himself quite well."

"Not sure I follow," I reply, "but thanks for everything." I stretch out my arms. Surrender. "Put 'em on," I tell the officer.

CHAPTER TWENTY-FOUR

It's still warm in November — we have a streak of six consecutive seventy-degree days — and because Sheriff Smith quickly promoted me to a trustee position at the Patrick County Jail, on November 12, a Saturday, I'm outside washing a police car with a soapy sponge and shooting the breeze with my guard, a burly farm boy named Elvin, when I spot Ward's red Mercedes sailing into the lot. It's a beautiful afternoon, sunny and bright. Ward parks, exits the car and starts walking toward me, grinning and shaking his head. He's wearing a paisley-print shirt, dark dress pants and tasseled loafers. "You son of a gun," he says as soon as I look at him. "Son of a *gun,*" he repeats as he comes closer.

I aim the hose nozzle at the asphalt and spray a warning shot near his feet. "Check it out, Elvin," I say, "it's my former attorney and former close friend Ward Armstrong, ready for Studio 54 throwback night at the Elks Lodge."

Elvin laughs. He's a happy sort, doesn't have a mean bone in his body.

Ward stops where he is. "Careful with the shoes, Kevin." He grins. "And hey, nothing carries more weight than fashion commentary from a man in a baggy orange onesie."

"You mind if I take a break, Elvin? Speak to my lawyer?"

"Okay by me," Elvin says. "You wanna use the interview room or stay here?"

"Here, please," I reply. Along with canteen snacks, Sunday visitation, writing paper, TV and sharpened pencils, fresh air and sunshine are jail luxuries.

Elvin's been sitting in a plastic cafeteria chair. He stands. "You can have my seat. I'll stay over yonder in the shade, so I can see you but I won't be able to hear none of your business."

"Thanks, Elvin," I say as he ambles away.

Ward shakes my hand, and we hug, and he slaps me on the back. "No!" he says as soon as we step apart. "No way. There's the damn cherry on top of the sundae. That's your dog, right? Has to be. What's his name?"

"Nelson," I answer. "He's my *service ani-*

mal. I'm a stroke victim and a disabled prisoner. I had a board-certified neurologist confirm that I require the dog for both routine life functions and my mental health. My medical records prove I've been struggling with bending, stooping and grasping. Even walking can occasionally be a chore. He's trained to assist me. You should've seen him collecting my keys and wallet when the sheriff tested him. Fetching my sneakers. I'm almost certain it was you who told me that I've paid the awful stroke dues, so I might as well take advantage of whatever benefits I can lay my handicapped hands on."

Nelson is lying belly-down on the heated pavement, dozing. I clap my hands and whistle. He pops to his feet and scampers to where we're standing, wagging his tail. He's wearing a red vest with SERVICE ANIMAL stenciled in white letters on each side. I instruct him to sit, and he immediately obeys. "Shake," I tell him, and he offers me a paw. I have Ward change places with me, and Nelson greets him with a cordial paw as well.

"I heard about how you couldn't even hold a pen at your sentencing hearing," Ward says. "Which struck me as strange since you seem recovered to me, and I've seen you sign your name without any problem."

"It comes and goes, Ward. Comes and goes." I wink at him. "The doc and my therapist are positive that I need the dog — they're expert witnesses to my handicaps. Today, thank goodness, I happen to be normal." I sly-smile and wink again. "Lucky for me — and what a coincidence! — Nelson just happened to have been in training prior to my convictions and is fully qualified for the job."

"Does the jail have to pay for his food? Seems your grand plan didn't miss any details, so are we taxpayers footing your kibble bill?"

"No, I agreed to pay for his meals. The crap they'd feed him here isn't fit for a dog."

Ward chuckles. "You want the chair?" he asks.

"No," I answer. "Help yourself. I've been doing a lot of sitting lately."

He straddles the chair, sits backward. "The shit hit the fan Thursday morning," he announces. "So far, I've been educated and quizzed by both the FBI and the state police. Oh, and Randy Clay. And Stephanie Katt."

"What shit? What fan?"

"I have news for you," he says.

"Okay."

"There were four bogus court orders, not three."

"Do tell," I say.

"Yeah, I'm sure you're shocked to your very core."

"Before we go any further," I say, "since you fired me, I need to rehire you if we're about to discuss my cases."

"Consider me rehired. I'm officially your lawyer again."

"Here you go." I reach into my pocket and hand him a Snickers candy bar. "Payment in jail currency. Our conversations are now privileged again, yes?"

"Yes," Ward agrees. "But they would've been anyway, as far as I'm concerned."

"So there's another order?" I ask, my tone flat, indifferent. I follow a brown deputy's car as it pulls into the lot and passes by us.

"Yeah. A substitution order. The order that receives the least scrutiny in our trade, Kevin. It's simply signed by the lawyers involved — no notarization, nothing certi-fied — and it's self-policing. One lawyer leaves the case and another is substituted in. It's administrative and routine. There's no reason for any mischief. The current lawyer departs and a new lawyer takes over, and they work it out among themselves and send in the paperwork. Judge skims it and signs it."

"Happens all the time," I agree. "Like the grim day at the restaurant when I had to stand in the rain and sign so that Dickie Cranwell could take over for me and represent my client Jay Sowerby. Or when you and Esther switched on my cases."

Ward tears off the top of the Snickers wrapper. "An order with forged attorney signatures was entered by the circuit court judge in Patrick County on October 5. M. D. Jenkins was removed as Melanie Culp's attorney, and a lawyer by the name of Lee Agnew was substituted as her new counsel. Cover letter was on Hunton and Williams stationery. They've confirmed it's not theirs. They use a pricier bond paper, but obviously, nobody was holding the watermark up to the light until recently."

"This Agnew cat must be phenomenal if Melanie Culp hired him to replace a star as talented as Magic on Demand Jenkins."

"He doesn't exist," Ward replies. "There is no Lee Agnew. Funny thing too: Lee's my middle name. My wife's maiden name is Agnew."

"So what? When I gave everybody a connection between First-Rate and the Shadrich scam and my situation, all I heard were

560

Kevin Bacon references and how we can tie anything to anything with enough keystrokes." I scratch my chin. "Maybe this is connected to Christie Brinkley. She's had to fork over a ton of divorce money to deadbeat spouses."

"Christie Brinkley?" Ward's chewing a bite of the chocolate bar, and he swallows after repeating the name.

"Yeah. Agnew was Nixon's Vice President, and Nixon and Liberace, who was called Lee by his friends, are both mentioned in 'We Didn't Start the Fire,' a famous Billy Joel song. Joel was married to Brinkley."

"That rolled off your tongue pretty damn fast, almost as if you'd been practicing it in advance."

"Like you, I have a quick mind. Also an excellent memory."

"The law firm addresses on the substitution order were incorrect, so the clerk mailed copies to the attorneys, but none of them — not Jenkins, not Margo Jordan and certainly not the nonexistent Mr. Agnew — received anything or had a clue that a new lawyer had taken over the case. The mailed copies wound up in postal limbo. By the time they bounce back, if they ever do, it won't make any difference."

"Holy cow."

"Interestingly, the order also directed the clerk to mail a copy to a lady by the name of Anne Mullens. Sound familiar? *Her* address was accurate."

"Of course," I answer. "She's the adjuster for my malpractice insurer, Lawyers Comprehensive."

"So, put on your best thinking cap and explain to me why anyone would go to the trouble to substitute a fictitious lawyer into your civil case."

"I'm winging it here," I reply, "but my guess is that someone wanted to take control of the case."

"Excellent guess, my man." Ward smirks. "Next, Anne Mullens receives an e-mail from Attorney Agnew. He wants to settle, and settle in a hurry. She has the order designating him as counsel of record, but she's traveled around the block a time or two, and she's no fool, so she calls Patrick County and confirms that the substitution order's been entered and is in the court file. She looks him up online, and there he is, a partner at Aaron, Charles and McMillian, a venerable, established Virginia firm. He phones her, and it's all perfectly normal. It's fairly rare for a lawyer to contact her directly, but he claims he can't get in touch with Margo Jordan. He knows the case from

A to Z, drops all the right names, can even guess the settlement number Margo Jordan has recommended after the deposition. He makes a joke about Mr. Moore's loony conspiracy defense and references his ongoing legal troubles."

"Mr. Moore was no doubt an easy target," I say dryly. "I'll bet they really yukked it up."

Ward peels the wrapper farther down the candy. "Lee Agnew explains that Melanie Culp is dating his cousin, that she's frustrated with all the delays and that she fired Jenkins because he was taking so long to settle an obvious, easy winner. He also informs Mullens that Culp's mom is very ill; Culp wants this over and finished so she can cash the check and move on with her life and concentrate on her waning mother. This is all fiction, of course."

"But great fiction if you're interested in a settlement," I note. I sit on the pavement beside my dog.

"You okay, Mr. Moore?" Elvin shouts from the other side of the lot.

I wave at him and holler, "Thanks. I'm fine." I glance at Ward. "Elvin's a good kid. His mom had a stroke, so he's very kind to me. Very sympathetic."

"What's the bait for Mullens?" Ward asks.

I peer up at him. I rub Nelson behind his ears. "Someone knew how fucking dishonest and greedy the insurance industry is. Let me state loud and clear that I didn't call her or forge the order, but if I had —"

"Slick, O.J. Nice."

"If I had, I'd understand she's highly motivated to save her company money because her livelihood, paycheck and yearly bonus are based on how much cash she keeps in the company's coffers. I'd cardealer her, give her the today-only price. She's already prepped and reviewed the case, she has Margo Jordan's memo and recommendation, the file is complete, 4.9 million's already been booked against reserves, so I'd offer her a double discount. I'd inform her that if we can settle today or tomorrow and make Melanie Culp happy, I'll knock off another hundred thousand and simply subtract the loss from my own fee."

"Remarkably, that's exactly what happened."

"You have chocolate on your cheek," I warn Ward. "Your left cheek."

He wipes it off with his index finger. "Mullens already knows how her excellent lawyer had evaluated the case, and it's the insurance company's decision to make, and she discusses it with her boss, and what a gift, this is a found hundred grand, a far better settlement than Margo suggested, so let's do the deal."

"This sounds as if it's about to have a bad ending for the insurance company."

"She phones Lee Agnew to confirm, reaches his secretary and is told he's unavailable, but he calls her back, on his cell, 'from the courthouse.' They agree to settle for 4.8 million, and he has his office e-mail her the info for the transfer to the Aaron, Charles and McMillian trust account."

"Uh-oh," I say. "Goodbye to those dollars. And, alas, since he called *her* both times they spoke, probably with a disposable phone anyway, probably at her company's main number, there's no phone info to track."

"Goodbye indeed," Ward remarks. "You want to speculate on the rest?"

"The account is titled as Aaron, Charles Civil Trust, or something that would look like the bona fide account but isn't."

"Correct," Ward replies. "The money hits, stays a few seconds and off it goes to Nassau, Bahamas, where it's removed by a so-called attorney there — no doubt for a fee — and then sent to who knows where. Gone. The paper trail ends. The 'secretary' for Lawyer Agnew is an old-fashioned answering service that was paid in cash, and Agnew's e-mail account, which the service used to report the call from Mullens, is routed through Russia and impossible to crack. A gobsmacked Anne Mullens also recalls that Lee Agnew had a thick Southern drawl and a cold."

"Almost as if someone were disguising his voice. Or using one of those voice apps you can download for free."

"Almost as if," Ward remarks.

"Any news on Eddie Flanagan?" I ask him.

"You're incredibly intuitive today. I feel like I'm talking to Max Maven."

"Not really. Seems like an obvious question, since he's a crucial player in all this."

"Thanks to a well-prepared but anonymous tip, the FBI discovered Flanagan had sent an e-mail to an address . . . hang on . . . l have the info on my phone, courtesy of the special agent who paid me a visit yesterday. Just a sec . . . okay, here's the e-mail Flanagan sent to MABinfo@hotmail.com: 'Been watering my lawn, and doing Moore than my part, but haven't seen any green yet.' *Moore* is spelled with two *O*s."

"Huh, same as my name," I observe. I make a finger pistol, point it at Ward and fire. "Pow. Like the little fucker was using code. And, you know, I'll bet *green* is his secret-squirrel word for money."

"You'd win that bet. Flanagan helpfully included a phone number in the e-mail for his friends at MAB to call — how convenient for the cops later on — and even though the number was attached to a TracFone, since the police *have the number,* they know this particular phone was used to call BB and T bank three times in a single day, and the Feds can ping the calls to within fifty feet of Flanagan's Richmond house on Knollwood Drive. Even worse for Flanagan, seventy-five thousand dollars landed at this very same BB and T bank, in his checking account. He e-transferred it within ten minutes and bought a CD."

"Let me see if I understand this, since I'm just learning it and there're so many moving parts. Flanagan sends an e-mail to what — on its face — appears to be the address for MAB, and it seems as if he's demanding crooked money, since he's using code —"

"Really dense, impenetrable code too," Ward says sardonically. "In an e-mail he sent to the general inbox, not anyone specifically."

"Flanagan's dumb as a post, and I'm sure he didn't anticipate the police reading it. And MAB is cunning and secretive, so that's probably the only way he could contact them. But I'm assuming the message was sent from Flanagan's account?"

"It was," Ward confirms. "How that clever trick was arranged is a mystery to me. The use of his own e-mail and the phone pinging have the FBI and state police convinced he's probably dirty."

"Then Slow Eddie calls his bank three times in a day — as if he's checking on a transfer — and voilà, seventy-five thousand dollars materializes in his account. He takes it out immediately and sticks it in a CD."

"Yep."

"I'd say he's in a world of hurt."

"He's been suspended from his state job, which he'll no doubt lose within a month or so. He's lawyered up, but according to Agent O'Brien from the FBI, he's making noises about having information to exchange with the Feds, which simply makes him seem *more* guilty. O'Brien will be by to see you later today, I'm guessing. He visited me to find out what I thought about your claim that Flanagan framed you. I told him that I believe you — least I could do under the circumstances."

"And suddenly it all fits differently, doesn't it, Ward? The scales fall from your eyes. The synthetic piss and positive test from a probationer who'd been clean for months — now we have a revised view of everything, don't we? How sublimely ironic that dipshit Eddie Flanagan will be squealing about conspiracies and mysterious forces aligning against him. Lovely. Perfect. I promised that asshole he'd pay a price. He's in an impossible vise. He can't come clean without implicating his sister, and if he doesn't tell the truth, he'll be arrested and prosecuted. He's about to have a nice, long taste of what I've been experiencing."

"As of a few hours ago, the prevailing wisdom in coptown is that the truth lies somewhere in the middle."

"Meaning?" I ask.

"We can agree, I think, that you're guilty of the original charge, the coke possession from Roanoke."

"I pled guilty," I reply. "I've never denied it. I accepted my punishment like a man and was playing by the rules, trying to rehabilitate myself and recover my career and repair my marriage."

"So far, the FBI and state police are inclined to believe — in retrospect — that there was misconduct on Flanagan's part. No matter how hard he tries, the sore-thumb e-mail and phone pings are impossible to explain away, especially since you've claimed from the drop that you're innocent and he planted evidence. You even left the probation office and went directly to a hospital and begged for another test. Who does that if he's drug-positive? Plus, ol' Eddie did in fact receive the money — from offshore, the Caymans — and electronically moved it from his account to a CD."

"It's classic that the cops will now be my pals and want me to testify against him."

"But," Ward continues, "what about Kevin Moore, who was feeling screwed by this rogue PO and the system he believed in? Agent O'Brien is thinking you might've decided to make the best of a rotten situation and somehow stole the money. Once it dawns on the police that they can't touch you for the theft, they'll realize you have the cash."

"Realizing and proving are two different animals."

"Stealing the money, well, money's swindled every day — in person, online, by mail, by telephone. The mechanics of your little production aren't so difficult, are they? Add a fake Web page for a lawyer — in a firm of over three hundred people — set up a bank account, then sweet-talk an easy, eager mark out of the check. The trick, the Kevin Moore signature, is to pull it off so that you skip away scot-free. The timing on this was intricate and tightrope. Ballsy. If you put this in motion and Mullens lags or won't agree to settle or is too slow with the wire transfer, then you're really screwed."

"There's not a shred of evidence to connect me to any Web page or any phone call or any money."

"Correct. Well done." He glances at Nelson. "Of course, it doesn't really matter, because you're bulletproof in terms of the swiped millions. Both Esther and I were at a loss to understand how the hell someone as accomplished as you would send forged court orders directly to a *jail.* Even high as a kite, you'd never make that mistake. I attributed it to the empty liquor bottles in your trash and, sorry to admit it, the fact that I believed you *were* a doper. You basically spotlighted your substance abuse for us by planting vodka bottles, and it became perfect misdirection. Everybody was more than willing to believe you were liquor-stupid enough to run, especially since you added the packed suitcase, cash withdrawals and Belarus search as window dressing — a nice touch."

"You stuck with me as long as any friend or reasonable lawyer ever would. Maybe longer. I'm grateful. From your perspective, I was a fuckup."

Ward finishes the Snickers bar. "So even if the state or Feds could prove you stole the 4.8 million, you're sitting on agreements that give you complete criminal immunity. I checked the files: You can't be prosecuted for crimes connected to *any and all* forged court orders received in Martinsville or Patrick County during the time period from September twenty-fifth until the date of your sentencing. 'Any and all' being the super-duper lawyer language. You and Esther even included immunity from state and federal theft charges in the plea agreements —"

"We were very thorough," I say. "Nothing unusual about that, not with multiple jurisdictions involved and so many potential charges to address. Esther built in a little cushion for me in the plea wording, and the prosecutors were satisfied so long as my immunity was limited to forged court orders that were received in the two specific jurisdictions during a narrow date range."

"True. It's a beautiful piece of work. The prosecutors — and Esther — thought they were dealing with the bogus electronic-monitoring orders, but you were far more interested in the routine substitution order buried in your civil file. You *intended* to get busted; that's why you served up the forged release orders on a silver platter. For six months extra in jail and three more felonies — and after one, what does it matter? — you hoodwinked everyone into accidentally letting you off the hook for the substitution order and the 4.8-million-dollar theft it made possible. You paid for three fake orders, but received four in the 'any and all' bargain. You can never be tried for stealing the money."

"I didn't forge any orders." I recite the lie with a straight face.

"You were going to jail no matter what, so why not risk a few months more and become a millionaire in the process? Why not gain a whole lot of something from a nothing situation?"

I swat at a gnat. "Theoretically, I'd be a multimillionaire, not just a millionaire."

"Can you imagine the conversation when Jenkins phoned Margo a week ago to finalize the seven-figure payday, and she thinks he's pulling her leg or clowning around and says, 'Hey, seriously, I received an e-mail from the adjuster telling me Culp had been paid and to close the file.' "

A cloud drifts off the sun, and I shade my eyes. "Margo's a good lady."

"It'll be wild cards and a free-for-all now. I wonder what Culp and Flanagan will do?

I doubt Jenkins will simply fold his tent and forgive the insurance company for sending his money to the wrong person."

I stand again and turn so the sun isn't blinding me. "This might help determine matters for Caleb and Melanie and Flanagan. Once the police do a little research, I'm predicting they'll discover the 4.8 million landed in — and was withdrawn from — a fairly new Bahamian dummy account called S. Smith Holdings Carib. It'll take them a while, there'll be some international pushing and shoving, and a for-show squabble, but in the end, the bank will release the S. Smith name on the account."

"Not sure I recall why that matters," Ward says.

"Shadrich and the dove sister paid S. Smith Holdings the West Virginia money," I remind him. "And remember, S. Smith has the verifiable Florida deal with First-Rate on the books. I'm also predicting the two S. Smith companies, the original S. Smith Holdings and the new S. Smith Holdings Carib, will have the exact same registered office in the Caymans. To close the circle, Flanagan's money was sent from there, from the Caymans, and he was e-mailing MAB. So maybe I didn't steal the money. Maybe Caleb and his FirstRate are the thieves — they have a connection with the suspicious offshore S. Smith name, not me. They could eliminate Jenkins's hefty lawyer's fee by diverting the cash to themselves. Or maybe Caleb double-crossed my dear Melanie Culp, snagged the whole check and cut her out. Certainly something to consider."

"Son of a gun," Ward says, but it's restrained this time. "Damn, Kevin, that's lethal. *You* created this second S. Smith company so you could use it to briefly land the money in Nassau and link everything and everyone together — a double bonus. This is some impressive, head-snapping, three-ring mojo. Wow. Melanie Culp will be on the receiving end of several pointed police questions, and she can't simply vanish without looking like a fraud." Ward stuffs the candy wrapper in his trouser pocket. "Think Lawyers Comp will come after you civilly?"

"They can come as big as they like — I don't have a penny to my name. My bank account's empty. Talk about a wasted effort. Why would they? And there's nothing to tie me to the money — not a thing — so how could they ever win in court?"

"My assumption is they'll keep this debacle close to the vest. If word gets out that they were fleeced, it won't be good for business. Either way, you're home free."

"I didn't ask for this," I say solemnly. "I would much rather be practicing law and living in Roanoke."

"Sure," Ward says. "I'm sure you would. As much as I bitch about my job, I'd miss the dickens out of it. It's a shame this happened to you. So there really was a Caleb Opportunity?"

"Yes, absolutely. More important, I didn't make any mistake with Melanie Culp. It was a straight friggin' scam. At my very worst, I was a competent attorney. I'm proud of that."

"You understand why I was skeptical?"

"I can't blame you." I take a peek at Elvin. Nelson is sitting on his haunches, alert for whatever comes next. I have his ball in my pocket. "The law's a dreadnought, Ward. To keep rolling, it has to be fueled by biases and assumptions, and it's often set loose on bent, slanted tracks. Once it catches momentum, there's no stopping it. And ninety-eight percent of the time, the court system delivers accurately. For good reason, nobody believes the criminal over the probation officer, and, innocence presumption or not, we inform our jurors that felons — even those with records a decade old — have marginal credibility. Why would've you believed me, especially after I stepped on my own dick with the Klean Stream search? I wouldn't have believed you either, my friend."

"If nothing else, I'm relieved to know you've put the drugs and booze behind you and that you're still as smart as ever. You zigged every time they zagged."

"The great Dave Worthy, the best attorney there ever was, used to say that exceptional lawyers never have to change course. They were headed in the right direction from the start."

"Anything I can do for you?" Ward asks. "Crossword books? Extra stamps?"

"No. I appreciate your stopping by, though."

"Thought I'd congratulate the master in person." His tone brightens. "This shit will become lawyer legend. Epic."

"Well, 'the master' is sitting in jail minus his wife and unfairly barred from practicing law. Hardly a storybook ending."

"Here's a little test," he says cheerfully. "For sport. How much are you making per day? To wash cars and play with your dog and read good books and sweep the floors?"

I know the answer by heart: "$12,876.71 per day if I pull a full year. Minus the cost of Nelson's food, of course. That also assumes — assumes, mind you — a twenty-five-thousand transaction fee in the Bahamas to withdraw the money, break the paper trail and redeposit it. Believe it or not, there're unsavory lawyers who do that. Not long ago, one of my drug clients in federal court was using a Nassau fellow to help him with those kinds of arrangements. So I've heard it can happen."

Ward laughs and slaps his knee. "Does that math include a seventy-five-thousand-dollar deduction for Cayman money that eventually found a home with Eddie Flanagan?"

"Yes," I answer. "And remember how you poked fun at me when I told you the scam was *only* for five million? I could just imagine you doing that Mike Myers riff with your pinkie. Here's another number for you: It comes out to $470,000 per year for the next ten years. That's net. No taxes, and it assumes no interest at all. A man could slide by on that, especially in Mexico or Jamaica or Belize."

"Remarkable that you'd have those figures at your fingertips."

"Same as you, I'm a quick thinker," I repeat. "I also have an excellent memory."

"Give me a call if you need anything," Ward says. "All and all, it could be worse."

"Sorry I ran you around in circles. Tell your sweet wife, the former Carrie Agnew, that I sent my regards from the Patrick County Jail."

CHAPTER TWENTY-FIVE

That night, the lights are turned off at ten, and I'm locked in my nine-by-five cell. My bed is a thin vinyl pad that rests on a metal frame. The frame is permanently bolted to the concrete floor. I've been issued a single blanket and sheet but no pillow. Because of my stroke and my past job as an attorney, I'm twice over a "vulnerable inmate," so I'm isolated, alone, by myself except for Nelson, and thanks to the legal system that failed me and robbed me, I'll be suffering this punishment for months to come. There are three bars in my door's small window, each maybe six inches apart, and the opening lets in occasional sounds, a phone ringing, a cough, the guards discussing their Thanksgiving plans. Stuck in the dark, I try not to dwell on my losses, and sometimes I recount advising clients how fortunate they were to receive only three months in jail and not several years, or a compromise settlement that cost them ten grand instead of the fifty they'd been sued for — legal wins, make no mistake about it.

My wife is gone, and she's never coming back.

There'll be no flash-forward to me relaxing on the white-sand beach, fat and sassy in a chaise longue, the waiter serving me and Lilly Heath our umbrella drinks and her laughing about how she wore a hat and sunglasses to collect the millions we lifted from the Goliath insurance company. The odds with her were long at best. She's a classy lady with much better prospects than a minimum-wage pokeyman, and though I had some gossamer hopes before my arrest, I realize, if I'm being honest with myself, that I'll never see her again. Even dumbass Junior has a couple of women to visit him on Sundays at the Martinsville jail, but I'll be doing my time without any chance of a girlfriend.

I'm wealthy, nearly five times a millionaire, but I'd rather be a ham-and-egg lawyer. I'll find a beach bungalow, grow a wanderer's beard and maybe take a crack at the bonefish, but I'd prefer to be in my hometown, trying misdemeanors in general district court and catching stocked hatchery trout from the Roanoke River. I understand how

Eugene Harris feels, sitting rich but still grieving over his lost land.

My stroke was unfair and inexplicable. I've learned to cope with my new brain and tender heart, and my carotid artery is almost healed. The clot was so sneaky that I'll fret over every sneeze or yawn or sore neck for the rest of my days — that's the worst of it, the eggshells. And despite what Greek poets and college theology professors would have us believe, brushing against ruin didn't make me wiser, deeper, stronger or more appreciative. So far as I can discover, almost dying didn't improve me.

I'm mad at myself, and like every idiotic fucking defendant who's ever spoken to the judge before sentencing, every few hours, I think: *If I could just travel back in time and not try cocaine at the Greenbrier . . .*

Still, I'm not to blame for many of my troubles: The justice system can be treacherous on this side of the fence if you're different and innocent, *too* blind and *too* set in its ways.

"But we came out as best we could, didn't we, Nelson? Especially you." He guns his tail when he hears his name but stays put, curled around my feet with his head and shoulders wedged between my shin and the painted cinder-block wall, living great for a dog, indoors with the humans. I kept my word to him.

I close my eyes. I picture Blaine — my only visitor until Ward arrived today — returning to work at SUBstitution, hauling the stepladder in from the shed, climbing the rungs and checking the glue-trap spot. I promised him I was okay, not to worry, and assured him that our plan had dominoed right down the line, flawless. Operation J'onzz had several layers and bucketloads of feints, and maybe I didn't allow him — or Ava or Minivan — the whole truth about what I was up to. But listen, for certain, *immediately,* he'd *better* take those infernal traps off the shelf and throw them in the dumpster.

Lying on my unforgiving bed, I imagine his face, his expression, when he looked behind a box of traps and found the fat yellow envelope with BLAINE RICHARDSON COLLEGE FUND printed on the front, opened it and counted the $40,074.23 in cash, honest cash, along with my withdrawal slips should anyone — someday, somehow — ever come asking. My note inside read: *Holy financial aid, Batman. Take this, keep your mouth shut and don't deposit it or spend it all at once. Your friend — Kevin.*

And I rejoice in this, in jumping him up

to the front of the line, past the bean counters, shiftless paper-pushers and Luther Foley. My joy's partly selfish, of course — I'm satisfied because I can still hold my own, can still deliver the impossible verdict when it's really needed, no matter the rain of fluke strokes and con man's snares, and what the hell, I might be a diminished, disbarred felon, but I do have millions waiting on me in a few months, enough for years of the high life until my renaissance, and just tonight, Elvin informed me that he's bringing an extra car to wash tomorrow afternoon, and the forecast is crackerjack, so I'll be in the sun and fresh air twice as long, for hours, as lucky as a convict can possibly get.

ACKNOWLEDGMENTS

Thanks to: Charles F. Wright, Smilin' Ed,
Julia Bard, Frank Beverly, Skip Burpeau,
Rob McFarland, Jack, Hollywood, Mrs. Ann
Belcher, Edd Martin, Eddie and Nancy Tur-
ner, Chris and Karen Corbett, The Baron
Aaron, Derek Bridgman, Genevieve Nier-
man, Nelson Stanley, Junior Taylor, Wood
Brothers Racing and my remarkable Heath
family.

I'm indebted to Sara Eagle and my pal
Gabrielle Brooks, a minor deity and an
alchemist of the first order.

As always, I'm grateful to my editor, Gary
Fisketjon. We've worked together for twenty
years now, and he's made every book and
every single page better.

A big tip of the hat to my agent, the smart,
patient and steadfast Sloan Harris.

My sweet Deana Clark has been the best
possible wife and remains "the hottest girl
in the joint," no matter where our travels

take us. This is her book.

Clay Gravely was the Martinsville, Virginia, commonwealth's attorney until his death on December 21, 2017, at age forty. He was my friend, and we spent a lot of time discussing fly rods, brown trout and what it feels like to be bad-off sick. Clay battled cancer and never bitched or moaned or complained about his miserable luck. I told him he was in the book by name, even read him a riff or two that had him speaking. He was a darn good commonwealth's attorney. In the best possible way, he was also a fierce smartass with a sharp tongue and the finest eye roll in the business. After his death, I worried that a larger audience might misconstrue my affection for him, so I cut several of the courtroom zingers and acerbic one-liners, changed the name, and made the character much more of a composite. That said, there's a lot of Clay Gravely — especially his sense of fairness and his generous view of the world — in the Randy Clay character, and I hope his family will still recognize flashes of the genuine article and think I did right by him.

ABOUT THE AUTHOR

Martin Clark is a retired Virginia circuit court judge, who served twenty-seven years on the bench. His novels have appeared on several best-seller lists and have been chosen as a *New York Times* Notable Book, a *Washington Post Book World* Best Book of the Year, a *Bookmarks Magazine* Best Book of the Year, a *Boston Globe* Best Book of the Year, a Book of the Month Club selection, a finalist for the Stephen Crane First Fiction Award and the winner of the Library of Virginia's People's Choice Award in 2009 and 2016. He received the Patrick County Outstanding Community Service Award in 2016 and the Virginia State Bar's Harry L. Carrico Professionalism Award in 2018. Martin's wife, Deana, is a photographer, and they live on a farm with dogs, cats, chickens, guinea fowl and three donkeys.